BROTHERS
IN THE
NIGHT

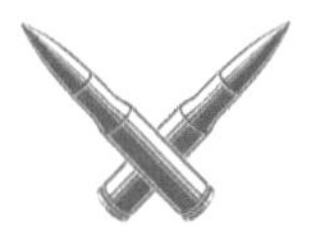

BROTHERS IN THE NIGHT

Inspired by the song, Brother in the Night,
by The Weeks

MICHAEL MULCAHY

This book is dedicated to:

Rose & Muck, for all else would be impossible…

&

The hungry and the fearful who persevere anyway…

PART
ONE

WELCOME HOME

CHAPTER
ONE

The house shook. The Elm's tree branches outside scratched against the windows like an animal clawing its way in. If not for the wind seeming to blow from all directions at once, Jude James was sure every part of it, down to the foundation, would be in West Texas or Arizona by now. Winter throwing its last haymakers at the rising Spring with those damn March winds.

At 34 years old, Jude's hair was still full and jet black, in contrast to his green eyes and red stubble. Jude's father was black Irish and his mother Mexican, and by appearances alone, he would have fit right in. But Jude was born a *coyote* – half Mexican, half Gringo – holding no place to belong even in the cultural melting pot of Taos, New Mexico. Not amongst the white pioneers like his father, the Mexican immigrants like his mother, the local *Chicanos* or the ingenious Pueblo people.

Jude watched his two sons, Wyatt, and Patrick, playing on the floor, their attention on the wooden fire trucks that zoomed and clunked on the Saltillo tile. With their momma's looks – blonde hair and blue eyes – and a full Gringo last name, they would not have to suffer that same unjustified plight. That didn't make it right, but Jude was grateful regardless. And so far, the boys had inherited her temperament, as well. If they were lucky – if Jude was lucky – they'd stay that way. And Jude was grateful for that too.

From across the den and into the kitchen, Jude saw Luisa watching him, gaze at their boys. She smiled, and he blinked slowly to her. She turned back to her bread making. She too was flawless, Jude thought. But how could someone so gracious and kind be so fiercely stubborn at the same time? No blurred lines, no grays. Not with Jude. Not with anyone. Her unyielding imposition the reason his ass was planted in this very chair each night now.

And then Jude wondered if that was really true?

Then his eyes turned to the spider web-like scar on his right hand. The bullet wound didn't provide an answer either.

Marveling at his family he almost forgot about the shot of warm whiskey floating in the glass in his palm. A tap at the door brought Jude back to reality. It was so light that Luisa did not hear it and Jude thought it was the wind. A second louder knock raised Jude from his chair. He put down the whiskey, checking his pistol was ready by the door. An old habit but one that would never die. Luisa ceased her work on the dough. Their eyes met.

Jude opened the door. A meager man of forty in overalls and an unkempt beard stood holding his hat.

"Ernie?" Jude asked, his voice scattering in the wind.

"Yes, sir. Sorry to bother you."

"Well come on in, before you let that draft blow out every fire in this house for the next ten years," Jude said, stepping aside and holding the door.

"Yes, sir," said Ernie, moving in. "Ma'am," he said, nodding to Luisa.

"Hello, Ernest," she said from across the kitchen.

"Sorry to bother y'all."

"It's no bother. You wanna a drink?" asked Jude.

"No, Sheriff, thank you. I best be on my way soon."

In a finger-snap moment, Jude and Luisa suddenly shared a very different look than earlier.

"Ernie, with all due respect, I've asked you on multiple occasions now not to call me *Sheriff* anymore."

Ernie coughed slightly and fidgeted with his feet, unable to make eye contact with Jude. "Sorry Sh…, Jude. Force of habit."

"That's all right. Now what can I do for you?"

"Well, there's some ruckus down at Sully's bar."

"Yea?"

"Yes sir. Two boys. Don't seem to be troublemakers, but causing some trouble, nonetheless. Mostly just drunk and having too much fun but they're fixing for a brawl or two."

Jude's eyes traveled back to Luisa, as she exhaled and went back to her baking duties. "Ernie," Jude said, his eyes back on the nervous mouse in front of him, "Being that we just established that I am no longer sheriff, I'm curious as to why you still feel this is my business?"

"Well, it ain't sheriff business."

"It sure sounds that way."

Ernie rubbed his dirty boot into the floor again and scratched the back of his neck. "It's your brother, Billy…"

"What about him?" Jude asked.

"No, he's uh one of the two fellas down at the bar raising hell."

Jude stood straight up.

Luisa put down the dough and walked over to the men.

"You sure?" Jude asked.

"Jesus, Jude, I know he ain't been around here for… what four years… but I know Billy when I see him. It's Billy all right."

Luisa tightly wrapped her arm around Jude's in the same moment he spoke. "Okay, let's step outside."

"Jude…" Luisa attempted.

"It's okay," Jude said, stepping out with Ernie.

The wind swung the door open as Jude held on tight before closing it outside.

Ernie clung to his hat and flinched from the dust and snow swirling around.

"How long has Billy been down there?" Jude asked.

"All night."

"How bad is he?"

"He been down there all night."

Jude nodded and exhaled. He gazed up at the sky, the orange-tinged clouds moving fast above as the stoic white moon stood undeterred. The air was biting and cold; little pebbles of snow started nipping at his face. The weather was not always comforting in Northern New Mexico, but it was rarely wretched and harsh. The spring winds of March along with the dust and mud and heavy snow was the exception. "I reckon I better head down there then," Jude said.

"Reckon so. You want me to join?" Ernie asked.

"No, I'll be fine. I appreciate you coming by, Ernie, I do."

Ernie nodded, placed his hat on his head and his hand on top of his hat and trudged back to his old green pickup truck. "Good luck."

Jude watched the truck putter off in the mud as the red taillights became smaller and smaller in the distance. He turned, looking off into the other direction, surveying the flickering lights of town. How often had he stood in this very place staring out at the horizon wondering if Billy was out there? Now, maybe he was one of those little stars of light fluttering over the dark horizon that now loomed before him.

CHAPTER TWO

Jude stepped out of his pickup. Even through the howling wind, he could hear music and fits of laughter, echoing off the adobe walls of the plaza storefronts. There were as many parked automobiles as horses tied to the posts on the street that circled the plaza. The snowflakes had become larger and flurried in front of the green low-hanging streetlights.

He strolled past the closed shops and toward the jubilant sounds. Snowflakes gathered on his stiff cowhide jacket, and the wide flat brim of his cowboy hat. He brushed the gathering weather off his tight Levi's as he walked. He turned the corner at the end of the plaza and down the cobblestone alley. The alley was black and obscured on all sides with stucco and adobe walls except a beacon of light shining at the end. The buzzing noise of the riotous gin mill became louder as Jude approached the heavy turquoise doors to the bar. A light posted up above illuminated a sign that read, *The Alley Cantina: Locals Welcomed, All Others Be Warned.*

Jude gripped the wood u-shaped handle of the door and paused. He closed his eyes tight and took a long deep breath. He had learned to temper expectations, seeing more flag-covered coffins come home than boys the last few years. He exhaled, the cold smoke of his breath burning off into the heat of the light and swung the door open.

When he entered Jude's eyes were immediately met with the thick rosy face of the bartender, Sully. Sully's attention turned back to the horde circled at the bar, as if directing Jude.

Jude slowly approached the raucous crowd, trying to peer through the drunks tethered together with locked limbs of laughter and arms over shoulders, hooting and hollering. They ebbed and flowed as one, like a water buoy on a stormy night.

A lowly fellow turned around, catching sight of Jude. He unhinged himself and stepped aside.

The swarm quieted like coyotes at dawn, each taking notice of Jude, as he steered between them.

Jude made his way to the epicenter.

Two men, one with an unfamiliar face and deep blood shot-eyes glared coldly at Jude, over the shoulder of the second man.

The second man, still with his back to Jude, continued to laugh in between his rambling story, unaware. And as Jude neared the second man, the saloon's caterwauling winnowed into a defining voice. His brother's voice.

"Billy," Jude gushed to himself.

Billy continued his blithesome yarn unaware his brother was behind him.

The first man, however, was rigidly aware of Jude's presence, boring his glassy stare into Jude. Another night, Jude would have noticed and already ignited, breaking the stranger's stare with knuckles and fists.

But like the raucous sound of the room reduced only to his brother's voice, so too was Jude's attention culled to his kin suddenly before him.

"Billy," Jude said again this time louder, placing his hand on Billy's shoulder.

Suddenly, Billy swung around, his fist already clinched.

Jude sprung back, both palms open in the air.

The first man vaulted towards Jude in the same moment Billy and Jude's eyes met.

Billy halted the first man's advance with a forearm to the chest.

Undeterred, the man tried to hurdle over Billy, punching wildly at Jude. "I know trouble when I see it," he yelled with another swing.

"Mister, you know dick," Jude said, shoving through Billy.

A messy fit of tussling erupted, some trying to hold Jude back, others pulling the man away.

Chairs fell, a beer bottle shattered, and indiscriminate vulgarity ensued.

Through the ruckus, the man managed to swat the top of Jude's head.

Jude detonated, bursting through Billy, landing his fist squarely on the man's jaw.

The man responded by lunging over Billy.

Billy took the opportunity of his position to wrap his arms around the man's waist, burying his head into his gut, driving him back until the man lost his footing, both men toppling to the floor.

Jude went to pounce in the same moment the man hopped to his feet.

Finally, Billy had enough room in between to hold out his arms and separate the two. "Sid, for fuck's sake, this my brother!" Billy yelled at Sid, before turning to Jude. "Jude, if you know what's best for you, stay the fuck back!"

Both men yielded but stood ready.

The crowd had fanned back as if a swath of rattlesnakes had slithered between them. Holding his hands on his knees and out of breath, Jude finally had a moment to survey his *hermanito*. He looked mostly the same. His blonde hair was longer, greased and slicked back around the sides of his head that was shaven close above his ears. Billy feral and uncouth, usually with hair to his shoulders, Jude didn't remember ever seeing the boy's scalp, but it was clearly no longer a boy that stood in front of him. There was a man now with a man's haircut. He still had his baby face and baby blues, though, even through red squinty eyes. And still sporting his favorite leather jacket, worn and faded brown, with a white tee peeking through at his neckline, tight Levi's, and black boots. His old attire.

"Fuck!" Billy yelled, out of breath, seemingly more perturbed by the cessation of good times than the perils of any brawl.

"Jesus Christ. You two *pendejos* haven't been in the same room for one minute and you're already stirring up shit!" Sully yelled standing between the two, his bear-hands grasping the bar tight. "Both of you, get the fuck out of here!"

"Sully," Billy pleaded, "Come on, we're done now."

"That's right, you're done," Sully said. "Fuck-o, you're out too," he said pointing his portly Irish finger at Sid.

Sid turned his wiry brown eyes to Billy for confirmation.

"Shit stick, he ain't the *jefe* around here, I am," Sully said. "And this is my business partner," he continued, pulling a double-barrel shotgun out from underneath the bar.

The crowd scattered.

Jude backed up in one direction and Sid in the other.

Billy stood still.

"Okay then," Sully said, pointing the shotgun somewhere in between the three men. "Jude, I love you, now get the fuck out. Billy, you're the biggest pain in the ass this town ever had, but we love you and we're happy you're back, thank you for your service now get the fuck out." Sully turned to Sid. "You, I don't know. Bring money and check your *juevos* at the door and you're welcome back, now get the fuck out."

The bar quieted like the curtain fall before an opera, the squeaky floorboards the men stepped across, the only sound.

Sully's eyes followed the men, their heads low like scolded school children until they were at the door. Jude swung the door open and stepped out first, holding the door for Billy and Sid. Billy made no eye contact with Jude as he passed. Sid nodded.

When the door shut, Jude extended his hand to Sid. "Jude James. I meant no disrespect in there."

"Sid Tollen. My apologies, I was swinging dick first."

Both men shook hands and nodded as Billy fidgeted between the two, fighting the cold and wet snow.

"Billy never told me he had a brother, or I might have slowed my wrangle," Sid said.

Jude had a stone-cold poker face, but he could feel his hurt eyes bending to Billy, who simply stared at his shuffling boots in the gathering snow.

"Maybe not, though," Sid continued, "We're all still walking around a little cocked."

"You in the service too?" Jude asked, his attention on Sid again.

"Yes sir. Overseas, with William here. Now making my way back to California."

"Your family there?"

"We'll see. They were before I left."

Jude could only nod.

A silence fell upon the men.

"Well," Sid finally uttered, "I'm gonna turn in for the night before I find more trouble to get in."

"You need a place to stay?" Jude asked. "We've got spare rooms with warm walls."

"I appreciate the offer, but William and I are sharing a room at the inn on the corner."

Jude's eyes once again bowled to Billy.

"Anyway..." Sid muttered, stepping around the two brothers, shuffling off down the dark alley.

Jude waited until Sid was gone.

Billy pulled out a cigarette and lit it with his Zippo before burying his hands back in his pocket.

Jude's eyes widened. "You smoke now, huh?"

Billy pulled one hand from his pocket only to briefly separate the butt from his lips, blowing out the smoke before another drag, ignoring his brother's question.

"William huh?" Jude asked with a grin.

"It's my name, ain't it?" Billy said, not sharing his brother's humor.

Jude felt an iciness more biting than the frigid air. "How long you been in town?"

"Just tonight," Billy said, smoke billowing from his lips.

Jude was suddenly flooded with the realization that his brother was home, alive and standing in front of him. "Jesus Christ, Billy, it's good to see you," he said, throwing his arms around his brother.

Billy's arms locked at his side and his head lowered.

Jude held onto the lumbering boulder, saying a prayer to the Good Lord, squeezing harder with every word until he was finished. Finally he let go and stepped back.

Billy rocked more incessantly and took a drag.

"I know it's late, but Luisa would love to see you. And the kids, shit you haven't even met Patty, that's my second son. I have two boys now," Jude said, a warm pride flashing over his face.

"Oh yeah?" Billy said, his face still turned toward the wet ground.

"You know our home is still your home, Billy. You don't need to stay at the inn, even tonight."

"No, uh, that's where I'm gonna stay."

Billy pulled one last long hit from his cigarette and tossed it. "Anyway..." he said, looking up at Jude for the first time.

"Okay, we'll I'll come find you tomorrow," Jude said, once again smiling.

Billy only blinked and began walking down the alley.

Jude watched the shadows cloak over him more with each departing step.

"Hey Billy," he yelled, his voice echoing down the alley. Through the obscurity, Jude could see Billy's head stop and turn around. "*Bienvenido a casa!*"

Billy's head nodded slightly before turning and disappearing into the shadows.

CHAPTER THREE

The plates clinked and rattled as loud as the Spanish that was shouted in the kitchen. Each booth was filled, mostly with *viejos* in flannels and western shirts reading the bad news of the day, while their *esposas* looked at a different subset of the same. Steam, from the heat of the kitchen inside and the frigid air still lingering outside, settled on the large windows overlooking the plaza.

Billy sat at the counter alone, just him and his hunched shoulders, eyes steeped somewhere in his black cup of coffee. Not trusting to move them anywhere else, fearing if he did, he'd see every person in the diner looking right at him.

Billy remembered the fresh private – shaking hands over his ears as all color fled his face, experiencing his first shelling, explosion, battle – yelling *This is surreal!* And all the boys who heard the man's last words respectfully laughing about it later. There was nothing in war that Billy thought was surreal. He'd seen enough violence back home, what humans were capable of. This was just on a larger scale.

And truth be told, he wasn't even sure he what the fuck the word meant, until now. Everything was the same. The same hard round spinning stool under his *nalgas*. The same grease and chile scented air watering the *ojos*. Staring down at the same coffee-stained linoleum countertop peeling up around the cracks like the *Sangre de Cristo* Mountains wedging up around the Rio Grande. But now, Billy felt like he was watching a movie about a guy sitting in a café while everyone else stared at him. Is that what the poor articulate dead private meant?

"You want me to top you off, dear?" Mary Lou asked.

Billy sat unstirred watching *the pictures* flick in front of him.

"Billy?" Mary Lou said again. Billy's eyes moved up to the plump motherly looking waitress in her mid-50s. "*Mas cafe?*"

"Oh, yeah, please. *Mil gracias*," he said with an absent smile. Mary Lou smiled back as she poured. "I uh forgot or never realized how good the coffee was here."

"You mean for a shit diner?" Mary Lou asked with a certain draw.

"No, no, I don't mean like that."

"I know sweetie, I'm just giving you a hard time, like I used to," she said. "Your daddy was that way. Always had a great sense of humor, but then he would take something I said so literally and fall off his stool apologizing. *Por que so serio?* I would ask and he would laugh. That never got old."

Billy snickered.

"It's the cinnamon and a pinch of red chile," Mary Lou said.

Billy looked up at her confused.

"In the coffee," she said, placing her index finger to her lips like it was some big secret, as she walked away.

Billy laughed again and pulled out a smoke.

"Been lookin' all over for you," a voice said.

Billy didn't even have a chance to light his smoke before turning to find Jude sitting on the stool next to him. Fawning over him like a Goddamn schoolgirl. Billy lit his smoke and pulled a drag. "Been sitting here," he exhaled.

The more Jude's eyes draped over him like a virgin puppy, the more Billy wanted to turn away. Maybe there were only two eyes after all, watching the man in the pictures, sitting at that diner, Billy thought.

Thankfully, Jude swung his stool toward the order line of the kitchen.

Both men looked straight ahead at steaming plates baking under the heat lights in front of them.

The food would come out of the oven blistering hot. Leaving you helplessly salivating while looking at the melted cheese plastered to the edges of the plate over scorched *frijoles* and crispy tortillas, all smothered in bubbling red and green chile. Sitting in front of you untouchable for ten fucking minutes so what was the point of the heat lamp? Ever since he was a little kid, Billy always wondered that.

"Where's your friend?" Jude asked.

"Who Sid?"

"You're an asshole, you ain't got no other friends, with no other friends." Jude said, hoping Billy would laugh.

He didn't.

"Kept moving this morning."

"I see. You order yet?"

"No, just coffee."

"*Bueno*, we can head home for breakfast," Jude said. "It's probably been a long time since you had a home-cooked meal."

Billy sniffled and took another drag.

"Or maybe it hasn't, I don't know," Jude said. "I guess I don't really know anything about the last..."

"...No, I'm just gonna have coffee..."

"Okay," Jude said. He turned over his coffee mug and Mary Lou was already filling it before he could even take off his hat. "*Gracias*, Mary Lou."

Mary Lou smiled, her eyes dancing between the two boys.

Billy's shoulders remained stooped, a barrier between his brother's glowing visage, and his head low. His eyes did catch Jude's attire, however. "You wearing a tie underneath your jacket?" Billy asked.

Jude looked down at his cowhide, and the tie peeking out from it. "*Sí.*"

Billy took a fuller look at his brother. "Where's your badge?"

Jude's eyes remained on his chest. "I don't wear a badge anymore."

"Jesus Christ, it finally happened huh?" Billy asked. Was it just like Pop said?"

"Did what happen?"

"That temper got the best of you, and you killed a man."

"What?"

"That's why they took your badge and gun."

"Jesus Christ, no," Jude said, shaking his head. "I'm still a civil servant, just not a sheriff anymore."

"What are you then? A fucking mailman?"

"A mailman? We don't even have… No, I'm not a mailman."

"Well then, what are you?"

"I traded in my badge and gun for a tie and a J.D."

Billy took a long drag of his smoke waiting for a real answer.

"A J.D. I'm an attorney now. Assistant District Attorney."

Billy sat back on his stool, taking a grander survey of his brother. "You're a Goddamn lawyer?"

"Assistant District Attorney. Yea."

Billy blinked hard. "*Un pinche abogado?*" he almost whispered.

"*Un pinche abogado,*" Jude smiled, watching the gears trying to turn in his little brother's head. "Instead of chasing bad guys down, now I'm in charge of lockin' em up."

Billy frowned and scratched his head with the same hand that held his smoke. "You loved being a sheriff. You were a fucking asshole, but you loved being a sheriff. And a marshal. You were good."

"Well, there are other things I love too. And those things became more important."

Billy tapped his finger on the counter and nodded slightly, as if he finally figured it all out.

"I guess some things have changed since you've been gone," Jude said.

"I guess so," said Billy.

"You got any plans now?"

"Yea, gonna see Adeline."

Jude smiled. "And some things never change."

Billy met Jude's eyes and grinned back.

"She write you when you were over there?" Jude asked.

"I don't know."

"You don't know?"

Billy snubbed out his cigarette and frowned. "Yea, I don't know."

"Well I ain't really seen her around with any one specific. If you're wondering."

"Oh, no?"

"No."

Billy nodded again.

"Anyway, Luisa made up your old room," Jude said. "Or you know, we got the *casita* out back if you want your privacy. I never rented it out or nothing, so it would be there when you came home."

"No, I think I'll find something else."

"That ain't my home, we're living in. *Es nuestra casa.*"

"Yea, I know. I'll find something else."

Jude slid off his stool and reached in his back pocket. "All right, well, you're coming over for dinner tonight. If you don't, I'm gonna have to lock Luisa up for your murder," he said, dropping some cash on the counter. "Mary Lou," Jude yelled, pointing to the money, "*Porfavor*, make the boy eat something."

Billy slinked back into the counter.

"Don't you worry, he ain't leaving without a full belly of chile," Mary Lou hollered back across the diner.

Jude stepped away to leave, patting Billy on the back.

"*De veras*, you really a lawyer now?" Billy asked, peering over his shoulder at Jude.

"*De veras*, I really am," Jude said smiling.

"So, what do I call you now, counselor or something?"

"You can call me *asshole* or your brother. I've been those a lot longer than anything else."

Billy laughed.

Jude gave him one more hard big brotherly slap on the back to remind him who was still the *real sheriff* of the family and walked out.

CHAPTER
FOUR

"Well, how did he look?" Luisa asked, holding a large heavy cast iron pan over the flame of the stove in one hand, while stirring the vegetables in the other. Motherly strength.

"How did he look?" Jude asked, placing a fork on the cloth napkin as he set the table.

"Yes."

"This morning or last night?"

"Either. Just in general."

"Well last night he looked generally drunk. And this morning he looked generally hung over."

Luisa dropped the large pan on the burner, the sound of metal on metal rang out in the kitchen. A casual observer would interpret this as a common incident in the culinary process. Jude knew better. He looked over at his wife, who was dressed like the president was coming to dinner. She wore a long flowing white dress and had her hair pulled up tightly while a few strays perfectly fell over her face. He loved her hair that way. And he loved that she cared this much about Billy being home. In the four plus years he was gone, Jude forgot that his wife also had a relationship with his brother. Jude wasn't the only person on the planet that missed the son of a bitch.

"Billy, you know looked like Billy," Jude said, yielding to wife's subtle warning. He paused for a moment, staring off, as a fork lingered in his hand over the napkin. "He looked the same but also different." Jude came to and set the fork.

Luisa returned to juggling the five pans cooking on the stove and peeked her head in the oven checking on the roast.

Jude took this as an indication his answer sufficed. He finished setting the table and then stopped again. "He seemed sad."

Luisa turned to Jude. "Sad?"

"Yea, sad. Maybe it was just maturity. I don't know. Billy was a boy when he left and now maybe he's a man." Jude looked down at his sons. Both had droopy smiles as they sat on the floor playing, delighted at the simple fact of being alive.

"Well, it's been a long time. People change in four years," Luisa said.

"Yea," Jude said and then laughed.

Louise smiled at him. "What?"

"Nah. Nothing."

"No. What?"

"He, uh. Billy couldn't believe I was a lawyer now. Or maybe he couldn't believe I wasn't a sheriff. Or both. I don't know."

"Why is that so hard to believe? You were always smart and you're still working for the law."

Jude adjusted a fork on the napkin and then moved a spoon and then moved it back. "I guess I always thought I was going to be a sheriff so it's natural for Billy to see it the same."

A slow tap at the door interrupted the conversation.

Luisa turned to Jude again and smiled excitedly. She brushed her hands on her apron before removing it. She looked as beautiful as the day Jude married her, he thought.

She walked over to him and looped her arm in his as they moved to the door together as if presenting themselves to a king. A breath of wintry air hit the two before the door was even half open. Billy stood on the other side, smoking a cigarette, his head to the ground. As he peered up, he was startled by the two presenters grinning at him.

"Oh, hey," Billy said, tossing his smoke. "Oh, I'll pick that up," he said, pointing to the butt.

Luisa tackled Billy in her arms, wrapping him tightly before he could even bend down. He stumbled back and his eyes widened, as they met Jude's. Jude raised his eyebrows and nodded in defeat as if saying, *What the hell do you want me to do?*

"Oh, don't worry about it. It's fine," Luisa said, nodding to the butt and unwrapping her arms. "C'mon inside," she said, leading Billy in by the hand.

Jude stepped aside and closed the door behind the two.

"I uh, brought these," Billy said, raising his other hand that held a whiskey bottle and flowers. "Jude," he said, handing his brother the bouquet. "And for you," he said, handing Luisa the bottle.

Jude and Luisa laughed, and Billy smiled bashfully at his own wit.

"Oh, it's good to see you," Luisa said, draping her arms around him once again, as the whiskey bottle dangled from her hand.

Billy bobbed slightly, seemingly shyer.

"Patty, Wyatt," this is your Uncle Billy, Luisa said.

The boys gazed up at Billy and drool dribbled down Wyatt's plump cheek. Billy stood idly above, as if looking at a stray dog that entered his yard.

Jude noticed and bent down, picking up one boy in each arm, raising them both to Billy. Billy cleared his throat and shot Jude a clumsy look. Jude rocked the boys faintly to keep their attention.

"Wow. You got real live human beings here," Billy said, staring at the two boys.

"We sure do," Jude said.

"Sometimes they act like animals," Luisa said smiling.

"Don't we all," said Billy, his eyes still on the boys.

"So where were you?" Luisa asked Billy over the heaping roast, garden of vegetables, large bowl of salad, tortillas and bottle of wine.

Despite Jude's relief, it had taken Luisa over a half an hour of prosaic dinner conversation before broaching the subject. He still secretly shuddered at the question, though it was an obvious one.

A log crackled on the fire of the orange lit room, and shadows from the fire swayed on the wall like reed grass in the wind. Billy cleared his throat and swallowed his food. He took a hit from his whiskey glass. He had politely declined the offer of red wine at the onset of the meal electing instead to open the bottle. "France. France mostly," he said. "And Germany for a while."

"Forgive me for asking. We just didn't hear from you after you were in boot camp," Luisa said. "Did they let you write while you were overseas?"

"Luisa," Jude zipped.

"No, no it's okay," Billy said. "I'm sorry I didn't write," his eyes careened between the two. "Straight to the point, like always," he said, grinning sheepishly at Luisa. "That's what I've always loved most about you."

"*Yo también,*" Jude said.

All three shared a tender laughter as the log fizzled once again.

"I guess I would be inclined to say the rapture was upon us, if I didn't hear her speak her mind."

"You better," Billy chimed in.

The brothers grinned devilishly at each other from across the table, as Luisa sat between the two at the head where she belonged.

"Hey, you two," she said wryly.

The boys continued their grin until a sobriety fell over Billy again. "No, uh once..." Billy sat back in his chair and his eyes went somewhere else. "Once I got over there. As soon as I got over there, it was pretty clear that most of us weren't coming home. I didn't wanna write and get y'alls' hopes up or nothing." His eyes remained fixed on the table. "Reckon, I'm still getting used to the fact that I'm alive."

Luisa's eyes filled with tears, she slid her hand across the table and squeezed Billy's tight. Jude's heart swelled and then he observed that Billy's hand remained limp to Luisa's embrace, unhitched and unaffected.

CHAPTER
FIVE

The barn always seemed like a church to Billy. Serene, holy and grandiose. It also served as his and Jude's playpen as children, sailing off the rafters into the yielding piles of hay, hiding and digging in the high mounds, and chasing chickens, as their old man's legs peeked out from whatever rust bucket, he was wrenching on *gratis* that day. Billy had seen a lot in the world, but never another barn that smelled like diesel oil, chicken poop and spicy alfalfa all at the same time.

He waited in darkness, feeling the thin hay under his boot and the dry earth. Even in complete blackness, he sensed the barn was different. He opened his eyes and then closed them with no difference. The obscurity made him feel small but safe like he was invisible. He heard Jude fumbling around for the lantern and the wind rocking the large door against the hinge.

Kerosene hit Billy's nostrils and suddenly the room lit up in orange and yellow. The small lamp guided Jude to the larger ones he lit with a long matchstick, each candle bringing more light and also more shadows.

Jude shook out the match and the thin smoke drifted off into the vast atmosphere. He walked over to an old wooden ice box and pulled out two bottles of beer, pointing one in Billy's direction.

"*Por qué no?*" Billy said.

Jude opened the bottles and coasted towards two wobbly and worn-looking rocking chairs that sat between two wired frame milk baskets.

"*Gracias,*" Billy said, as Jude handed him a beer. He raised the neck of the bottle to Jude and continued to stand.

Jude returned the gesture, raising his beer to Billy and hunkered down in a chair. He took a long slug, creased back a little further and put his feet up on the basket. He reached under the chair for his pipe that may or may not have been hidden along with a brown rolled up bag of tobacco. When he was done packing it, Jude exhaled, slid a little lower in his chair and took a pull from his beer and then lit the pipe, taking a hefty puff.

Billy's eyes danced around the rafters and beams until they made their way back to Jude, in comfort, relaxing. "So, is this the last frontier?" Billy asked.

"Meaning the last place where I'm still the boss."

Billy nodded.

"Luisa don't like the house smelling like smoke, so yea, this is where I come to get my mind right."

"She don't let you be a lawman no more. She don't let you smoke. She at least let you keep what's between your two legs?"

Billy didn't look at Jude when he asked this, but Jude studied Billy. "I'm still a lawman," Jude said after a moment.

Billy shot Jude a dubious look that said otherwise.

Jude exhaled agitatedly and cleared his throat. He took a heavy pull from his beer.

"That bullet wound through your hand have anything to do with you not being a sheriff anymore?"

"Well," Jude said, turning over his hand, "It represents my last gun-fight if that's what you mean."

"I'm not even sure you believe that," Billy said.

Jude felt his forehead heat up and his throat tighten, and in that moment, he sensed the urge to jump out of his seat, grab his smartass little brother by the cheeks of his know-it-all baby face and ask him who the hell he thought he was to call Jude a liar! And when Jude realized both the absurdity and truth in what just happened, all he could do was tip the bottle to his lips, swallowing his beer and his pride.

"Did I offend your soft sensibilities, *carnal*?" Billy asked, picking up on it.

Jude laughed slightly. "No, if you offended me, your head would be in the dirt already."

Billy smiled back at his big brother. Both realizing for the first time, that statement may no longer be true.

"You know," Jude said after a long silence, "I was always the one telling you how to live your life. Like I had some divine insight. Now it seems the boot is on the other foot. You find some truth or insight over there you wish to share?"

Billy lit a cigarette and took a long pull on his drag, seeming to study each crevice in the barn, or something else as he stood. "Nah, there was none of that." He continued to study the barn wall and Jude continued to study Billy. Billy blinked, came to, and sat down electing for a milk crate instead of a chair. His elbows bowed his weight on his knees and his shoulders slouched.

"Was it bad over there?" Jude asked.

Billy nodded slightly, more to himself. He picked a piece of tobacco off his tongue and spat. "Yea, it was bad."

Jude held silent. A mouse or rodent scratched and scampered somewhere in the hay.

"They fought like hell, you know," Billy continued. "I think people fight a lot harder when it's you in their backyard."

Jude took a hit from his beer. He swallowed slowly, maybe trying to swallow the words that swam around in his head and then he spoke. "When it was over, I would see the bus pull into the plaza, and I started seeing them blue uniforms from the window. I would come over every morning and just stand where people were getting off the bus thinking one of them blue uniforms was you. I did that for probably a year..."

"Like I said, I'm sorry that I didn't write. Let you know I was..."

"No, it's fine. I'm sure you had a lot going on. Just happy you're okay."

Billy rubbed his boot into the ground, staring at it, as he pulled a hit from his smoke. "I was injured towards the end. Shrapnel in my side. I was in the hospital for a while and then I got out. I held up in Paris. Me. Me and Sid."

"How was Paris?" Jude asked.

"To be honest, I spent most of my time there with a needle in my arm." Billy looked at his brother for the first time in the conversation.

Jude wasn't sure if it was in solidarity, guilt, or a combination of the two. He forced every cell in his body to not look sympathetic, or worse, worried.

"I met a girl over there," Bill said. "A Parisian. Reckon I just lost track of time with her."

Jude sat up in his chair and pulled his feet from the basket. He leaned in towards his brother, his shoulders slinking in similar fashion. "*Hermanito*, all you had to say was that you were chasing some French tail around Paris..." Jude said, with a wily grin trying to meet his brother in consonance.

"She died...Yea, she died," said Billy, nodding to himself again.

Jude slowly settled back in his seat not taking his eyes off Billy.

"She was sick too, like me. One night, we, uh, went to bed high. Fell asleep stoned in each other's arms and..." Billy's eyes gaped with tears, but none fell. "Woke up in the morning with her right next to me, still in my arms but she wasn't there anymore. She wasn't there..." Billy's eyes continued to widen; his fingers trembled.

"What was her name?" Jude asked.

Billy's face tightened, his lips pressed together, and his cheeks stiffened. "Marion," he said quietly. "Her name was Marion."

Jude leaned over, wrapping his hand tightly around Billy's shoulder.

"Anyway," Billy said stiffening up, shedding his brother's embrace, "I had to find her family. Let 'em know. After that, I got myself straight. Me and Sid. We decided to come home. Sid's family has an almond farm north of San Francisco. So, I'm gonna head there."

"I'm sorry, Billy."

Billy tried to brush it off. "It's okay. It is what it is."

"No, hey," Jude said, reaching over to his brother again. "*Lo siento, verdad.*"

"It's funny," Billy said, clearing his throat, wiping away a tear that finally escaped. "Of all the really horrible things I saw over there. All the horrible acts I was a part of..." Billy palmed the top of his neck and then the bottom of jaw with his hand... "That's what keeps me up at night. Marion." Billy's eyes looked as if the angel of her was now sitting directly in front of his face.

Jude let the afterglow linger until he finally asked. "So you're gonna be an almond farmer?"

Billy came to. "I guess. What the fuck do I know about almonds but yeah."

Both men laughed for a moment.

"You know it's something..." Billy continued. "Crazy how I'm feeling with Marion and what happened, and with all this...I still love Addy. Through it all, I still loved Addy. No one ever really tells you; you can love more than one person."

"Billy," said Jude rebuffing his embrace but looking him in the eye. "You could love every fucking person on this planet, but you'd still be chasing Adeline Simon. All the wars in the world, and the rapture of the human race ain't gonna change that."

Billy vented a fit of laughter that only pops out when confronted with something they know to be undeniably true. "Yeah..." he said, still laughing.

"Love, I guess it don't make sense because it ain't like anything else," said Jude. "I loved being a marshal and a sheriff but it's because of love that I ain't a lawman anymore."

"You're still a lawman."

Jude shot Billy the same condescending look that said, *Shut the fuck up.* "Anyway," he continued, his eyes now between his boots. "I've made peace with it, and peace with myself, I reckon, only because of love..." Jude's eyes made their way to Billy also greeting him with a sly grin... "And Luisa's iron fist..."

Both men chuckled another fit that only stems from unobjectionable truths.

Then, a silence then between the two boys again.

Both knew the half full beers would not warrant a departure yet for the evening.

Billy picked the paper label from the bottle with his fingernail, scratching at it like the undeterred rodent somewhere in the hay.

Jude palmed his cleanly shaven face and brushed his mustache with his index finger. "You know, Luisa and I met in a whore house?" Jude finally asked.

Billy stopped his scratching. "What?"

"Yep," Jude grinned almost boastfully.

"Was Luisa?... I mean I knew she was from New Orleans but..."

"...No." Jude said enjoying the mind muddling. "I was chasing a dirtbag from Albuquerque to New Orleans. I was dog tired when I arrived. I stumbled into some place that looked like a decent hotel and I was sitting there waiting at this reception desk in the lobby. I mean it was a hotel, and looked like one and all, it just happened to be a hotel filled with hookers. Anyway, I was waiting for the receptionist, I guess you would call it, and in walks Luisa looking as fine as a sunbeam on the Rio Grande. We get to talking. I was pitching woo, and she was polite enough to tolerate my advances, nothing more. That was probably going on for ten minutes before anyone came out. When this woman finally did, I found out right quick the true *modus operandi* of the establishment and excused myself. So I was just walking down the street minding my own business and Luisa comes up calling after me. She says, 'You're not looking for a lady?' I say, 'Perhaps, just not the enterprising kind.' She says, 'Well I ain't no harlot," and I say, 'I ain't no John. I'm Jude.' And the rest, as they say, is history."

"What a fucking trip. I had no idea."

"That's kind of the point. I don't think we can ever fathom or imagine what the Good Lord is capable of until it's right in front of our face. We can plan and assume but it's as good as a fart in the wind."

Billy laughed to himself and shook his head, still churning the story between his two ears. "So what was Luisa doing in the whore house?"

Jude sat back. "Just bringing a friend dinner," he said plainly. "*You* got a plan? I mean with Adeline."

"Her old man still alive?" Billy asked.

"Mean as ever."

"And her brother?"

"No bigger *culero* in the county."

"Guess it means, I got my work cut out for me."

"I'm sure there are plenty of beautiful women in California."

"I'm sure there are."

"You never did make it easy on yourself, did you, Billy.?"

"Are you asking me or telling me?"

"It ain't a question."

Both men smiled and finished their beer.

CHAPTER SIX

Billy lingered at the door like a fishing lure over water. The March winds had blown out the storm and then calmed. The sunshine gleamed overhead, warming Billy's forehead. He placed the bouquet of flowers under his arm, allowing him to bend over and slick his hair back properly with both hands. While facing the ground, he noticed a speck of mud that found its way on his just shined boots. He licked his thumb and leaned down further, wiping away the chiding blot. Gravity took hold of his hair, causing it to wither in the air. As he stood, it fell over his face. "Fuck." He bit his lip, exhaled, and cupped his hair with hands once more, making sure his ropey blond locks were properly fettered behind his ears. He straightened himself up, returned the flowers to his hand and then knocked on the door.

No one answered.

He peered across the dirt yard to the large barn where the Simon's parked their automobiles. The door was shut and locked. No help. He stepped back from the large white house and squinted to see in the window on the second floor. Every house in Taos was a one story adobe, modest and a color brown that blended with the earth from which it came. The Simon home looked as if a tornado had stripped it from the shores of Cape Cod and laid it down at the foothills of the Rockies. It was two stories, a bright colored white with blue trim and grandiose. This was completely intentional, Billy knew. A rebellious and scathing *fuck you* to the Northern New Mexico culture by the pompous prick, Edwin J. Simon, Adeline's father. Edwin came from money out east but made his real bonanza with gold and silver mines in the Land of Enchantment.

Mr. Simon had a funny way of showing his appreciation to the state that treated him so kindly. Forty years of being in Taos, and he still called the Chicanos *beaners* and *backward spics*, the Natives *heathens* and *dirt worshippers* and publicly lamented about how he missed the sophisticated and refined culture of the east coast. Billy always wanted to ask the son of a bitch, if he missed Yankee Land so much why didn't he just take his *pendejo* ass back there? Billy knew the answer though. If Edwin was as big an asshole out East as he was here, he probably got runned out, gunned out, or shunned out to never come back. The only reason Eddy boy was still alive in Taos and not hung from a tree, gutted like a fish, or dragged behind a pickup truck decades ago was because of Camilo Salazar.

Camilo was an old school Chicano and old school gangster. His great-great grandfather was the first butcher of the Taos Pueblo Indians and Camilo boasted proudly of the storied history. By the time Camilo and his six brothers were born, his family had ample land but no other form of real wealth. Their main enterprise was muscle and machismo. In a town of brazen gunfighters, manic outlaws, and virile cowboys, all of whom would have never allowed Eddy to blink twice at them, Camilo had managed to keep the loudmouth *puto* alive for three plus decades.

Billy placed his ear to the door but heard nothing, so he knocked again. The door swung openly almost immediately, catching Billy off guard.

Edwin's eyes hit Billy like a punch in the nose.

"Son a bitch," Edwin said. "I had hoped the Germans did me a favor, did all of us a favor..." Edwin surveyed Billy head to toe, "But apparently they have failed at that too."

"Sir," said Billy.

"*Sir?*" Don't get proper with me boy. Who you foolin'?"

"Ain't foolin' anyone. Clearly."

"You being smart with me? Even the military couldn't teach you manners, I see. Still rude as ever."

"Am I being proper, smart, or rude? Which one is it?" Billy asked.

Since being home, everything looked and felt surreal and delusive to Billy. The cockeyed leer Edwin was firing at him was the first normal sentiment he felt. It was oddly comforting.

"What do you want?" Edwin sneered.

Before Billy could answer, a second figure appeared, causing a familiar sentiment more potent and intense than anything the old man's nagging grimace could conjure. Billy's soul leapt from his boots, yanking his breath along with it.

"Billy!" Adeline yelled, breaking through her father's taut arm in the doorway. She sprang at Billy, cloaking her arms around him with such force that it almost cleared him out of those same boots.

Billy closed his eyes and wrapped his arms around her. Instantly, she felt the same. Smelled the same. And Billy was not standing at her doorstep, a weary dejected soldier, a man home from war, but a wild and disorderly boy, impassioned and tender, saying goodbye but promising to be back soon.

Neither said a word, simply holding the other.

When Billy opened his eyes, he found Edwin still staring back at him. He was a miserable old fuck. Any other time, Billy would stomp the teeth out of someone fronting him like this. But emotions that elicited those responses were not present in Billy's bones at the moment. How could anything else matter, when Adeline was at his side once again?

She pulled back to see her knight in shining armor, returned in the flesh. She saw his face was gazing behind her, and she remembered her father's presence. She turned around, while still holding Billy. "Daddy, please."

Edwin did not break his glare.

"Daddy," she again emphatically.

Edwin held one more long second. "Welcome home, boy," he finally said, before stepping into the shadows of the home.

Billy followed the sorrowful son of a bitch with his eyes, some of those emotions starting to stir until he felt the soft touch of Adeline's palm on his cheek.

"Hi," Billy said, finally seeing Adeline in all her glory.

She had those same floating eyes, emerald and deep green, and the purest white porcelain skin. Her wavy and wild auburn hair was longer, curling over her slender shoulders and down her chest.

"Hi," she said, grazing his face with her fingertips. "It's you."

"It's me," Billy said, his face flush.

"Oooohhh," she said, cooing.

"What?" he asked, smiling and turning his eyes down.

"You're bashful," she said gleefully, catching his eyes. "When did that happen?"

"I am not."

Before Billy could utter another lie, she hugged his face with both hands and kissed him deeply. Billy was caught frozen for a moment. Coming to, he let his mind sink into his heart, returning the embrace. Her lips pressed against his, and he was at peace, like softly falling through space, knowing you'll never hit the ground. He was one with her, and himself. His gentle dissent was suddenly interrupted by a hard fist to the chest.

"What the fuck, Billy? You're alive."

Billy stepped back muddled, seeing a different Adeline now.

"Yea, yea I am." He then understood the question, and suddenly he felt like the old Billy again. Or more so, the new Billy that felt like the old Billy until five seconds ago. Guilty. Confused. Disoriented. "Yea, I'm sorry," he muttered.

Adeline drew back, surveying him, seemingly torn within herself. As if, she could not resist or bear holding him. She threw her arms around his shoulders once again. "What the fuck, Billy?" she whispered in his ear. "I'm so glad you're alive."

Billy shut his eyes, willing tears not to come, holding her tight. He felt her heart thumping into his chest, her whole body expanding and then shrinking into his body with each deep breath.

"Can we uh... Can we take a walk?" he finally asked.

She let go, bringing her hand to his. "Yea."

They stepped away from the house and walked down the dirt road in rigid silence. The air was unmoving, and even the bright sun seemed to pause. The earth ceased to turn, and time stood still.

"Are you cold? Do you want my jacket? Billy eventually asked.

Adeline smiled. "I'm fine." She took in a deep breath and scanned his attire. "You still have that jacket."

He turned his neck, examining the fatigued leather raiment, once black, now ash. "Well yeah."

She ran her fingers over the jacket. "Did you have this with you? When you were over there?"

He nodded. "For the most part. Yea. I mean not when I was...but yea."

She continued to brush her hands over the stiff but amiable black leather. Adeline's hands returned to her side and her eyes to the cracked earth. "How are you?" she whispered.

It was a fair and relevant and simple question and it left Billy speechless. Billy had an Irish tongue and Latin blood that never left him short on words, but Adeline had a way of profoundly stifling him with seemingly little or no effort.

The two continued to walk.

"Have you seen your brother?" she asked after a while.

"Yea, last night. I was over for dinner."

"Those kids he and Luisa have are adorable."

"Yea." Billy smiled proudly for a moment and it warmed Adeline's heart.

"Patty is a little devil. Every time I see Jude, he's chasing that boy somewhere, trying to keep up," she said fondly.

"Oh yea?"

"Yea.."

Billy smiled again.

"Karma I guess. After what you and Jude put your parents through," she said.

"I don't wish that on anyone, even my own brother."

Both laughed.

"He's definitely got the Jude spirit," she said.

"I guess I didn't notice that last night. They seemed pretty calm, but I don't know."

"Why didn't you write me, Billy?" Adeline asked, another one of those throttling questions.

Billy turned to her and nodded. He had no words.

"I guess it's not my place. I don't know..."

"No, hey..." Billy stopped walking and turned to her. He then realized he was not able to look at her directly and speak at the same time.

He locked his hand in hers and began to walk again.

He prayed to God she would move with him. It was the first time he prayed, even for an instant, in over three years.

His prayer was answered, and she strolled by his side.

Off in the distance, a lone coyote howled. Maybe lost or confused in the light.

Both listened and then Billy spoke.

"When I first got over there, I wanted to write you every day. Tell you I was okay. And then... bad things started happening and I didn't know if I was going to be okay. I didn't want you to get some letter saying I was alive and by the time you got it, I wasn't. I didn't want to lie to you like that. It seemed like the worst thing I could do in the world."

Adeline stopped. Her eyes swelled with tears and her face hailed with light. "Do you still have your dress blues?" she asked, undressing him kindly with her eyes. "I never got to see you in them."

"Yea," he said timidly, his face flush.

Adeline footed back at Billy. "William Tyler James. You're bashful again."

Billy stuffed his hands in his pocket and kicked a rock with his boot. "I am not."

"Then you'll wear your dress blues for me?"

Billy laughed slightly. "Sure."

"Good. Tonight then," she said, turning and skipping back towards the house.

CHAPTER
SEVEN

"**F**uckin what!?" the muffled voice yelled from the other side of the door.

"Billy, it's me," Jude said in a hushed tone, as if to redress Billy's hollering and swearing with the other hotel guests.

"What do you want?"

"I want to not talk to you through this Goddamn door," Jude said, louder now. "Will you let me in?"

Billy cracked the door and stuck his head out, a burning cigarette hanging from his lips. "*Que pasa?*"

The smoke wafted directly into Jude's face.

Billy did not seem to care.

Jude fanned the smoke with his hands. "Can I come in?"

"I'm kind of busy."

Jude tilted his head a little low. "You got a girl in there?"

"No, I ain't got a girl in here. You always assumed if I was 'busy' it meant I was between the legs of some girl. That was your preferred act of leisure, not mine."

"Fair enough. So you gonna let me in or am I to just stand out here leisurely with my *verga* in my hand?"

Billy creeped the door open, allowing Jude inside, and then closed it immediately.

The straw-colored room was modest but cozy. A bed in the corner with a bed stand and lamp next to it, and a small wooden table with a chair positioned on each side.

Billy stood wearing an A-shirt, denim jeans and his boots. His dress blues hung neatly pressed on the closet door, over the mirror.

Jude walked over, observing the stripes. "You didn't tell me you were a sergeant."

"What's there to tell?"

Jude turned to Billy with pursed lips, impressed anyway, and then back to the uniform. "I don't know, making sergeant and serving your country might be considered admirable by some."

"It wasn't our country we were serving over there," Billy said, seemingly surveying a very different uniform through the cigarette smoke.

Jude only nodded, still taking in the grand outfit.

"She wants me to wear it tonight," Billy said after some silence.

"Who does?" Jude asked, turning back to Billy.

"Adeline. For some party or dinner or I don't know, whatever her dad is hosting."

"It's a fundraising event. More of a circling of the wagons."

Billy looked lost.

Jude noticed. "Edwin don't like the governor, so the old vultures are gonna get together and find a new one."

"That's this thing tonight?"

"*Simon.*"

"Then why did she invite me?"

"I came to an earth-shattering unfortunate truth a few years back."

"What's that?" Billy asked.

"All the books in the world. Experience under my toes. And love in my heart and I still don't know what goes on between a woman's two ears."

Billy squinted at the uniform and took a long drag of his cigarette. "Yea, I don't either." He snubbed out his cigarette. "That's who we were serving over there."

Jude now shot Billy a confused look.

"Those old fucking vultures."

Jude nodded and then spoke. "I learned another unfortunate truth. In this world, you either serve those vultures or God. I don't think there is anyone in between."

"You don't gotta go to this thing then? As the district attorney and all?"

"Fuck no. I'm the *assistant* district attorney. My job ain't to get elected. That's Phillip Patterson's job."

"That fat pig is still the District Attorney up here?"

"Sure is and will be until the day he dies."

"Then what the fuck are you doing?" Billy asked.

"Laying low. Biding my time."

"I didn't know *laying low* was in our genes."

"I didn't either. I call that one of them fortunate truths," Jude said. "Phil does all the leg work, sucking all the right tits, getting re-elected every four years. Last campaign, no one was even stupid enough to run against him."

"Then I don't see the *movida*," Billy said.

"Phil ain't got no sons. He does all the *lambe* work. I do all the real lawyer work, and when he dies, I'll be up next."

"So, you're just waiting around for some son of bitch to keel over? Don't seem like living to me."

"Like I said, laying low. My wife, my kids, that's my life now."

Billy scratched his face. Maybe because he didn't understand how this stranger got in his room or what the fuck he was saying.

Jude's eyes moved across the room. On one of the wood chairs, tucked under the table, he noticed a small bag of scag and a leather pouch.

Billy detected Jude's observation. "I ain't done it. I said I was clean and I am."

"Okay," Jude said.

"I..." Billy scratched his face again. "I got nervous. About going to this party tonight."

"Nervous about seeing Adeline?"

"Nah," Billy said matter-of-factly. "About dealing with her old man, and all that."

"I see."

"You know I left... I left for a lot of fucking reasons...but I left because I felt like I wasn't good enough. I was always walking around like I had something to prove and always felt like everyone had both eyes on me, you know? I thought, if I came back after being a soldier, no one could say jack shit to me. I realize now, I was probably an all-right kid with a good heart before I left and that should have been enough. And when I knocked on Addy's door today and that son of a bitch opened it, he looked at me like he always had. And I realized, everything I did, everything was all for nothing. And now Adeline is going to find out I ain't a good person anymore either..."

Jude walked over to Billy putting both hands on his shoulders. "Billy it was a full-time fucking job for me and pop keeping your ass out of the ringer, but we never had any doubt about you being an honorable and good person. Anyone that don't appreciate that, ain't worth the snot on the tip of your nose."

"Addy treated me right."

"Yes, she did. But I've come to understand another fortunate or unfortunate truth, depending on how you look at it."

"What's that?"

"I stopped fighting battles I wasn't ever gonna win."

"You mean give up?"

"Well, that's what I mean by fortunate or unfortunate. God's honest truth is you ain't ever gonna be right in Edwin's eyes, and this battle you been waging with him for years, with Addy in the middle, you ain't ever gonna win."

Billy shed Jude's arms and teetered in a small circle in the small room that suddenly felt even smaller. "This laying low talk and giving up talk, sounds like all you do now is bend over and take it." Billy's eyes narrowed on and Jude, dressing him down like a boot-camp drill sergeant.

Like bona fide brothers, Billy and Jude had come to fisticuffs growing up, but Jude never felt the scathing eyes now scorching from Billy.

"...And you know..." Billy continued, trotting in a circle again. "You want to act like you're some peaceful fucking Indian now, or some shit, but this ain't you. I know you, and this ain't you. You've even given up on yourself. You wanna talk about battles you ain't never gonna win, *carnal?* You're always gonna be you. A brawling hot tempered, holier than thou son of a bitch making the world right and fit with his pistol and his knuckles. You are you. Pretending to be anyone else is a battle YOU ain't gonna win."

"Maybe. But it don't take some peaceful fucking Indian to see Edwin ain't ever gonna let you and Addy be together in peace."

"Well, we'll see about that, won't we?"

Jude felt his heart pounding, sweat festering at his hairline, and his hands tighten. Maybe Billy was right after all, but he was going to give it his damnedest to prove otherwise. "Listen, I'm sorry. Clearly, you're a grown man now and it ain't my place to say or do nothing."

"No, Jude, I'm glad you came. My nerves were getting the best of me and I was pretty certain I was gonna do something stupid with that junk to try and get right. But I'm 100% right now. You can take that shit with you and if you'll excuse me, I got a party to attend."

Billy's eyes were wide and bloodshot, mainlined with ire.

Jude looked carefully at Billy, concerned and uneasy. "The old me wants to say be careful. I know how we both get when we're all stirred up like this..."

"The old you is gone, *carnal. Recuerdo?*"

CHAPTER
EIGHT

"It ain't like that."

"No?" Luisa asked but didn't really ask.

"No," Jude said, gulping down a shot of whiskey before pouring himself another.

"You sure about that?"

Jude swirled the tawny spirit around the bottom of the clear glass, his eyes following, making laps. "Yea, I'm sure," he said, hitting another. He poured himself one more and put the bottle back on the cocktail stand.

He moseyed over to his thinking chair and put up his feet. "I'm sure," he said again, feeling a flare from Luisa that was hotter than the bourbon in his belly.

Jude's eyes retreated to his glass.

Luisa turned back to the pile of yarn and knitting needles on the kitchen table in front of her.

The crackling of the dry *pinon* on the fire nipped at the conjugal silence.

Finally, Luisa spoke. "It's entirely your choice. It always has been."

"What choice is that?"

"The one you don't think you got."

Jude exhaled, sipping his drink now. Jude was an intelligent person. His J.D. certified he was probably more intelligent than most. That's why folks went to law school and hung silly pieces of paper on the wall in superfluous frames. So they can say, *Hey asshole, didn't you see that piece of paper dangling from the wall that says I'm smarter than you? Either shut the fuck up or open your eyes.*

Despite the over-priced toilet tissue, Luisa was the real brains in the relationship, and they both knew it. She sometimes talked down to Jude or over his head or asked him open-ended questions meant to elicit critical thought. His stuffy miserly professors in law school called that *The Socratic Method.* Apparently, Socrates had created the questioning, but Luisa perfected it. Hours after prodding, Jude would be involved in a separate and divergent task and the concept or answer would sail in like a crow and hit him over the head. This took an incredible amount of patience from Luisa. Some men could be wrangled, some beat over the end, but Jude, you had let Jude come to it on his own. She laid down the breadcrumbs, and given enough time, more often than not, Jude would follow them back home. And Luisa's brilliance was not made up of only intellect. Any filly saddling up with a James colt for the long ride had to be either profoundly foolish or notably brilliant to navigate the James sails of emotions. Luisa was the latter.

Louise realized this needed to be one of those gimmies. The gears in Jude's head were clearly filled with too much clutter and debris to turn on their own at the moment. The rye lubrication being ingested was certainly of no help either. "If you want to chase bad men to the far ends of the earth in the name of your justice, that is your choice. If you want to be a husband to me and a father to those boys, that's your choice as well."

"I know that," Jude said.

"Do you?"

Somewhere Socrates was grinning proudly.

Jude took a hit from his bourbon that said he wasn't so sure. "Billy always had a way of getting under people's skin. I used to defend him against the entire world, but truth be told, the son of a bitch could bury himself deeper under my skin than anyone else. I think he did it on purpose too."

"Probably. That's what family does."

Jude combed his thick black mustache with his curled index finger. His eyes found their way to Luisa's, there waiting, smiling back at him, kindly.

"Billy always did what he wanted," Luisa said. "And you always did what you thought was right. I would imagine that rapport could be exhausting and onerous."

Jude stood and walked slowly toward Luisa and the two boys playing at her feet beside the table. He laid down on his side, curling his long frame around his sons. Patrick looked over at him and giggled, his plump cheeks ripening up at Jude.

"You don't think this is where I want to be?" Jude asked, his entire face wide, making a funny face at his younger son. Wyatt caught wind of the goofiness, his face lighting up, joining the frivolous circle. All three boys exchanged comical gestures.

"I don't think it's that simple," Luisa answered, her focus squarely on weaving the thick needles between the narrow loops of yarn. "You're a damn fine lawman and that made you happy and gave you a purpose. You're a wonderful husband and a great father. I think that brings you a certain type of joy and a different type of fulfillment. Hence the choice,".

Jude exhaled long and heavy again, like wheezing air out of a tire.

"Oh the hard sad world according to Jude Tanner James," she mockingly lamented, putting down the needles, giving Jude her full attention. "You think you're the only one with choices staring you in the face every morning?" Jude looked up at her doe-eyed, as he often did after one of her revelations he finally grasped. "But I choose to be here with you," she continued.

Jude inhaled the savory smell of baking chicken and the sweet-smelling bayberry candles. He felt the comforting glint of the fire gently extend and warm the side of his face, as the other side was cool and barren.

Jude watched Wyatt and Patrick play with their little figurines. An apparent battle was erupting between the little toy men. Patrick smashed one figure on top of another and Wyatt knocked an unwitting casualty over with another that swooped in. Both boys giggled and hawed as the toy men fell.

CHAPTER
NINE

The uniform felt tighter than Billy remembered, almost smothering him. The wool fabric strangled him in his chest and clasped tightly around his arms like the nuns' boney grip when he misbehaved in school. He cleared his throat but still could not find air. Beads of sweat excavated from his pores despite the cold chill that ran up his spine.

"So do you think we'll make that mistake again?" the old man asked, his crafty smile evincing he was proud of this thoughtful question.

The expensive tux hung from the old man's skinny limbs like a scarecrow. He was feeble with age, but Billy could see his body was also impotent from never putting in one hard day of labor. Billy reasoned the old man was probably a banker or a politician or maybe he never did anything at all besides ask stupid questions that had no answer.

Billy's eyes swiftly scanned his surroundings, searching for an escape, or at the very least, someone else to pretend to like, but it was not in this space. The entire grand room was filled with the same stuffy guests and patrons, all donning the same fanciful costumes enmeshed with their redundantly fake charm. A chandelier hung from the high rafters, creating a sparkling light in a chamber of black souls. Butlers careened between the shadows, refilling champagne, and holding platters of fodder. Swine eating swine. Billy's eyes returned to the old man, who was still grinning ghoulishly. Billy realized the old man was not going to relent until his question was answered. "What mistake is that sir?" Billy asked, finding air and his voice.

"Sticking our nose where it doesn't belong of course," said the old man. His grin widened, clearly more impressed with himself.

"Oh I see. Yea, I think we'll make it again."

"And what makes you say that? Obviously, you witnessed first-hand the carnage and austere devastation from sticking our nose where it does not belong. I think our leaders and the American people certainly understand this now, no?"

Billy smiled at Adeline, who silently stood by his side, her arm wrapped in his. She looked stunning. More beautiful than Billy thought possible.

When he was laid up in the hospital, surrounded by sounds of grievous moans, and prayers of mercy to a god that was not present. Swarmed with odors of shit and urine and that sickly familiar deep stench of blood, Billy would close his eyes tight, and on the other side was always Adeline glowing there in front of him. As if she was in some dark cave, illuminated, not bright, but just there, with nothing else around her. In this image, she was dazzling and exquisite but always looked just the same, in a long, green dress and tan cowboy boots. Her auburn hair falling over her shoulders, dancing right above her freckled chest.

Billy thought that was the most beautiful she could ever look but tonight proved otherwise. Tonight, she wore a close-fitting white dress that spread across the floor like a canopy of tree branches upside down. Her hair was tied up, showcasing her soft neck that Billy so desperately yearned to kiss and suckle, and each curve through her gown drew his hand to it like a magnet.

Adeline smiled back at Billy, as her eyes pleaded with him to continue the placated dance.

"I'll take your silence as an affirmation," the old man continued.

"Excuse me?" Billy asked, plunging back to the world of ugly antiquated misers.

"You agree America has learned its lesson and will mind its own business going forward."

Billy squinted. The serene vision of Addy in the green dress disappeared like throwing sand into the wind. Instead, the face of every fat old white man that ever yelled at Billy, flooded to the forefront. "No, actually I don't agree," Billy said.

Adeline squeezed his arm as she continued to smile blankly.

"Why?" the old man blurted.

"Because our business depends on us not minding our own business. Look around. Right here in Taos, we are surrounded by a pueblo on three sides, directly in the middle of where we don't belong. Why? Because some white man decided to roll up on shore, some place he had no business being looking, to steal something that didn't belong to him in the first place. Then we decided to sail back across the ocean to kidnap some poor black chappies who were just minding their own business, I don't know, running around the jungle hunting lions or monkeys, happy as can be, until we dragged them here because we didn't want to personally work the land that we just stole from the other poor saps. And the rest, as they say, is history. No pun intended."

The old man twisted his crane-like neck, his beady black eyes staring sideways from the wrinkled slits in his head. "I never imagined to hear such foolish nonsensical dross from a soldier's mouth."

"You hang around a lot of soldiers do you?"

"William!" Adeline quipped, her voice squeaking through her pearly white teeth and counterfeit smile.

"If you'll excuse me," the old man murmured, nodding to Adeline, before turning his icy stare to Billy, who's face remained impassive and cold.

Billy's eyes followed the old man as he retreated into the thick sea of his fellow caitiffs.

"Why did you even come here tonight if you were going to act like that?" Adeline asked only when she was sure no one else was close enough to hear, speaking out of the side of her mouth like she was a secret spy.

Billy was not engaged in the charade however, and turned to her, like people do while having a proper conversation. "I came here tonight to see you and because you asked me to. I was answering his question honestly."

"Honesty has no place in this room with these people."

"Well, I ain't the only one speaking honestly now," Billy said, his eyes and smile falling all over Adeline, like a fresh blanket spreading on a mattress.

Adeline's fluttering eyes turned to Billy.

He looked handsome and kind, boyish and innocent, like when they first met, but also powerful in his uniform. She smiled and placed her hand on his stripes. "You know the game you have to play at these sorts of things."

"I don't want to play any games."

"That's not the world I live in."

"I know. That's why I want you to come to California with me."

Adeline's face suddenly grew serious. "What?"

Billy clasped his two hands on top of hers that bared on his chest. "I want you to come to California with me."

"What are you talking about?"

"I have a friend, who I was overseas with. He has an almond farm outside of San Francisco. I've seen pictures. It's beautiful there. Green and lush with rolling hills and sunshine. He told me you can smell the salt water from the back porch and the warm ocean breeze makes everything feel alive."

"What makes you think I would leave here? Billy, this is my life."

"What is? All this bullshit?"

"Yes."

"You don't want this."

"How the hell do you know what I want? I haven't seen or heard from you in four years and now you suddenly show up and have everything figured out for my life and what I want?"

Billy straightened. He gritted his teeth and chewed on his bottom lip. His eyes darted around the foreign place he suddenly found himself in. The uniform did not feel so tight anymore. It was no longer difficult to breathe. In fact, Billy was breathing hard now.

The festive sound of chitter chatter, the glasses clinking, the heavy soles and sharp heels shuffling on the hardwood floors amplified almost to a deafening level in his ears, worse than the ringing from any bombs exploding in the trenches.

Billy had been a stranger, an intruder in a distant land, where everything including the air seemed foreign and different. Billy was home now, less than a mile from the house he was born in, surrounded by people he knew his entire life, yet he was in a room filled with aliens, or worse, the only outlander in a room of denizens.

"I came back for you," he said.

"Well, you shouldn't have."

"You're still the same little girl afraid to leave daddy."

"And you're still the same selfish little boy..."

"Selfish? I joined up for us. I left for us so when I came back I could look your daddy right in the eye and say 'Sir, I'm a man now and I am requesting your daughter's hand in marriage.'"

"You want to be a man? In this family? That means doing things you don't like with people you don't like and pretending you love both. I don't think all the wars in the world could make you capable of that."

"You're right. I wasn't raised that way, and if I ever find myself on my knees again praying to the Good Lord, it will be in thanksgiving for that fact."

"You need to leave."

"I'm already gone."

Billy shook his head and twisted his body to the door.

He took three steps, his heart thumped twice and then he stopped and held his eyes closed tight. "This isn't what I imagined."

Adeline rested her hand on his shoulder. "It never is."

Billy turned back to Adeline. Her face was benevolent, but it did not say *stay*. Adeline had extended a kindness to Billy that no one else could fathom bestowing to a wild-eyed unrestrained hoodlum. They were lovers, and friends, and confidants but Adeline was also more. She understood Billy, more than anyone including himself. Jude and his father bailed him out of pickles but the first question out of their mouth was always *why*. Adeline never had to ask. Because she understood it did not mean she pardoned him. There were no free passes, and truth be told, that was probably the cardinal reason why Billy loved her so. Adeline didn't love him unconditionally and did not blindly support him. Adeline never seemed to *need* anything. She didn't need Billy. She didn't need her daddy's money. Perhaps having wealth that isn't going anywhere allows one the luxury of indifference. She was the only one that never tried to control Billy. And he was the only one that never tried to control her, perhaps until now. The great divide between the two was Adeline still recognized the obligation of being born a Simon and Billy did not.

"I don't want to stay here," Billy said.

"I don't blame you. California sounds nice."

Billy stepped in closer. In the trenches, before a bomb or grenade exploded there was always a moment where all the particles in the air became electric, as if lightning was fizzling all around, and everything became quiet. The same was happening now. "You know. When I came home, I half expected to find you taken up with Travis Russel or Jimmy Atwater, or I don't know, some other rich schmuck passing through on the way to make his claim in this world. When I found out you were still alone, it made me think you waited for me."

"I did, for the most part. And you know rich schmucks have never been my type."

Billy laughed and rubbed his dry hand and on his smooth clean-shaven face. He nodded and squinted, as if an echo chamber deep in his head, maybe his soul, yelled out something and it was getting closer and more clear. "What are we doing here?" he asked.

"Figuring things out, I reckon. Sounds like maybe you already have things figured out with California and all."

"What the fuck do I know about being an almond farmer?"

"Then why are you going?"

"I just didn't want to be here. I just wanted to be with you somewhere else."

"You know my father will never let me leave. He's nonsensical and insane and very sad. He never got over my mother dying and now that is my burden. And my brother is no help."

"Yea, I know."

"So you know what you want is not possible."

"I fucking love you."

"I love you too."

Tears flooded into Billy's eyes and shattered with red. His pale blues always turned bloodshot when he cried. Witnessing barbarity, brutality and evil somehow did not alter that.

He smiled with his lips pressed tightly. He leaned in, placed his palm behind Adeline's head, and kissed her.

The moment before the bomb dropped now passed and exploded and there was only black.

Billy felt Adeline's lips and nothing else.

No thoughts traveled through his head.

No plans, no emotions.

He was just there with Adeline.

When he finally opened his eyes, Adeline's were still closed. She was still surrounded in her black space of beauty and love.

He closed his for one moment again and tumbled back into that space.

Finally, both pulled away gently in the same moment, opening their eyes to one another. Both became conscious of where they stood and only Adeline seemed to care.

She straightened herself up and removed the hand she had placed on Billy's chest.

"Goodnight," Billy said warmly.

"You're leaving?"

"Yea," he said, just as kindly.

"Okay."

Unbeknownst to Billy the large room had become crowded in those few brief moments that were almost endless. As Billy turned to walk away, he suddenly realized the people all around him. His gaze shifted in one direction and then the other, but no one seemed to notice him or care.

He directed himself to the door when Adeline called out.

"Billy!"

He turned back around.

Adeline stood in the same sea of roisterers frolicking and clucking, just as unaffected as Billy, like a flock of birds parting around a large tree.

"What's next?" she asked.

Billy stared at the ground for a moment and then looked up at his paramour. "Figuring things out, I reckon."

Adeline smiled before plunging back into the brine.

CHAPTER

TEN

Billy leaned his shoulder into the wood beam of the porch, curling one leg behind the other as he stood. In one ear, he could hear the murmuring of the partygoers as one constant indiscernible sound winnowed through the hefty oak door. In his other, the howl of a coyote off in the distance. The howl did not pierce the silence of the night on the mesa. More like it was layered on top, in harmony, with the quiet wind and the moonless sky full of stars, and the divine smell of *piñon* burning.

The air was cold and dry and stung Billy's lungs, like the moment after you stopped running as hard as possible. Billy lit a cigarette, warming his breath with the rich heavy tobacco and there was a quiet in his head. As his shoulder canted against the treated post, he studied the sky. The indistinct forms of black trees littering the purple horizon, peeling up from the gray earth. In that moment, Billy thought of his mother. She had been dead for twenty years. He did not think of her often. He held few memories that were not filled with volatility and pain, so he chose not to think of her at all. He wondered if she ever felt peace in this life? If the voices were ever quiet? He often feared what she had would pass along to him someday, or already had. He always sensed both eyes on him from anyone that knew his mother but in this moment, he realized the two eyes he felt all along were his own.

"What did you say to her?" a voice interrupted.

Billy turned around.

Edwin stood, the door closed behind him, glaring back at Billy.

Billy leaned out from the post, both boots back on the ground. "Excuse me?'

Edwin stepped closer to Billy. "What did you say to my daughter?"

Billy took a long drag of his cigarette, sucking in the smoke as he spoke. "That's between me and Adeline. It don't concern you."

"I'm her father, of course it concerns me."

"Quite frankly, I don't give a good Goddamn who you are."

"Who the fuck do you think you are to speak to me like that?"

"I don't think I'm anybody"

"That's right. You're nobody."

Billy sniffled, cleared his throat, and then spit. "I'm leaving now," he said, turning away from the old man.

"You may show up at my party unannounced and uninvited but you ain't leaving until I damn well say you are," Edwin seethed, shoving Billy in the back with both hands.

Billy staggered forward, almost falling off the porch. "What the fuck?" he said more confused than anything.

Billy turned around to his aggressor and was immediately met with a fist to his jaw. It did not hurt so much as surprise him. He had been in more brawls than most in his young life, sometimes coming out the losing end, but he never allowed himself to be sucker-punched until now. He didn't think the miserable old fuck had it in him.

Billy held still jumbled and perplexed.

The old man swung again, sending his knuckles into Billy's ear. This time it did fucking hurt, sending an electric sting clear through to the other side of his head.

Billy stumbled for a moment before harnessing his momentum, clinching his fist in a long wide swing that did not stop until he felt his clenched hand collapse into the bridge of Edwin's nose.

Blood exploded from the old man's beak, tottering him backwards until he hit the door.

The old man pressed his fingers to his gushing nose. His eyes widened with anger and fear at the sight of his own blood on his hands. He started shaking like a dog shitting a peach pit and Billy knew the chicken shit had never been hit before and had his fill.

Billy also had enough.

He shook the feeling back into his fist and turned to mosey off the porch.

He heard Edwin take two steps on the hollow wood of the porch and that's when Billy felt the cold hard steel slide into his back.

CHAPTER ELEVEN

Jude dashed through the living room holding his pistol cocked and loaded. He recognized the *shit went South* bang at the door all too well having a schizophrenic mother and a drunk father.

As he neared the front door, he stepped to the side of it, out of harm's way. "Who's there?" he yelled.

"Jude, it's me!"

Jude didn't even have to ask who *me* was. He slid the long heavy deadbolt across the door frame, his finger steady on the trigger and the muzzle ready for someone in addition to Billy on the other side, coming up fast, after all, *me* always meant trouble.

Billy rumbled in before Jude could even open it, shutting it equally fast behind him.

Billy collapsed his back against the door and exhaled deeply.

He keeled over.

Out of breath and sweating.

Palming his knees with his hands.

Sucking air harder than a stuck pig.

Jude stepped back, trying to get a handle on how bad the disorder was going to be. His eyes widened, noticing the fresh stain on the wall Billy leaned against. "Billy, what the hell is going on?"

"It's bad," Billy said, between gasps, his head between his knees and his long blonde hair hanging upside down. "I gotta go. I need the truck."

Before Jude could respond, he heard the floor creak behind him.

"Billy?" Luisa asked from the hallway, the two children wrapped between her legs.

Jude darted around. "Luisa, you and the boys get in the bedroom and lock the door. Don't come out until I tell you."

"Jude, what..."

"Luisa please! Not another word," the tone in his voice was both stifling and pleading.

Their eyes met.

She wrapped her arms tightly around the children and stuffed them into the bedroom, closing the door behind her.

"Edwin Simon is dead," Billy said on cue, still keeled over, his head at his feet.

"What?"

Billy curled up to look Jude in the eye. "Goddamnitt, Jude, I was leaving."

Jude's eyes traveled to the swelling puddle dripping around Billy's torso.

"The old bastard stuck me with his knife," Billy said, catching Jude's eye.

Jude moved toward Billy. "Are you okay?"

"Ain't no noose around my neck yet but I gotta go."

Jude realized the necessity of slowing everything down. He had witnessed too many unforeseen unfortunate events turn to fucking nightmares thanks to adrenaline, nerves, and emotion. "Hold up. Just tell me what happened."

"I don't need that sheriff bullshit." Billy stood up, finally finding air in his lungs. "I need your truck, and if you got any money, I'd sure appreciate it."

"I'll give you both but you gotta tell me what the fuck is going on first."

Billy shook his head and gritted his teeth, knowing his brother wasn't going to relent. "I went to that party tonight with Adeline. I asked her to go to California with me and she said no, and then I said I had to think about some things. I was out the door, gathering my thoughts on the porch, minding my own fucking business and that son of a bitch comes out after me. I was just trying to leave..."

Jude's face broadened. "And?.."

"He sucker-punched me. I hit him back..." Billy's gaze teetered off, as if he was watching two strangers reenact the scene before his very eyes.

"Billy," Jude said calmly. "*Entonces?*"

"I was leaving, Jude. Goddamnit I was leaving. The miserable son of a bitch was never gonna see my face again until…"

"Until? ..."

Billy's bloodied hands answered Jude's question. "*Jodido* stuck me in the back. In the Goddamn back as I was walking away." He keeled over wincing in pain again. "And then we started tussling. He threw me into the window, or I threw him. I heard it break and I reckon that's what caused the crowd. At some point he lost the knife and I picked it up. He had a gun in his waistband, maybe he reached for it and that's when I stuck him. Next thing I knew, there was a crowd of fucking people all around me. I saw Darcy and that son of a bitch, Camilo, coming out with a 12 gauge. I pulled Edwin's pistol and fired in the air to clear everyone out and that's when I ran."

Jude blinked as hard as he grinded his mustache into his upper lip. "You sure he's dead?" Jude asked after a long moment.

"He was bleeding out like a damn geyser." Billy blinked, as if the curtains from the scene had now closed. "He's dead, Jude, he's dead."

Billy looked at Jude and Jude looked at Billy. *Nothin left to ask. Nothin left to say.*

Jude paced in a short circle replaying it all in his head. "Were there any witnesses?"

"Shit yeah. Half the fucking party by the end."

"Seeing Edwin stab you first?"

"Maybe. They saw me bleeding out of my back and him whole."

"Anyone see Edwin follow you out?"

"I mean I left, so I don' know what other fuckin people saw. I ain't got eyes in the back of my head."

"But there were witnesses that saw Edwin stick *you* with *his* knife first?"

"I don't know. The knife has his damn initials engraved in it. I saw it on the handle before I dropped the son of a bitch and took off."

Jude ceased his pacing and shifted to mash his mustache with his forefinger further. The gears in his head were now lubricated with the proper and necessary information and started turning faster and faster. "Well," Jude finally said, "I think you're gonna be all right."

"All right? What the fuck do you mean all right?"

"Billy, it was self-defense."

"That don't matter."

"If it was self-defense like you say, then the law allows..."

"The law ain't got nothing to do with this. Them rich sons of bitches are gonna string me up."

"That's not how it works."

"What country do you live in? That's exactly how it works."

"Listen, Billy. I know you probably saw a lot of things in the last few years that made the world seem upside down but there's still an order here in this land."

"Yea, and in case you don't know it, *carnal*, we're at the bottom of it."

"Billy, you gotta trust me on this."

"It ain't you that I don't trust."

"Phillip got fat off the good ole boys through and through but he's still an honorable man and a damn fine district attorney. It's up to him to press charges, and if it happened like..."

"What do you mean *if*? You don't fucking believe me?"

"I believe you, Billy. I just mean, that sometimes in these situations when the blood gets boiling people's recollection of the incident is not entirely...accurate."

"Well Goddamn, you are a chicken shit attorney now, aren't ya?"

Jude bolted at Billy. With one hand, he grabbed Billy by all the loose fabric of his uniform and slammed him up against the door. "Whatever high and mighty white fucking horse you rode in on, you better jump the fuck off," Jude hissed. "Now, I'm asking you these things because I'm trying to help you. Somewhere in my soul, I'm terrified you don't even want help, but I'll be damned if I ain't gonna try."

Billy's eyes broadened to the size of silver dollars, no different than when Billy's hand was literally caught in the cookie jar as a child. They told Jude everything he needed to know.

Jude relaxed his grip and stepped back. "Okay, first things first. I need you to think for a minute. If it didn't go down the way you say, you gotta run, and I'll help you. If it did go down the way you say, we got other options."

Billy glared back at Jude, no longer the little boy again, his ego returning.

Jude twisted his head slightly, and his eyes challenged Billy saying, *Don't fucking start again.*

Billy rubbed his face with all ten fingers. He only put on an aftershave two hours ago, but his face was already dry and cracked. He forgot how ravaging the thin desiccated air was in the high desert. He ran his fingers through his hair, the greasy pomade thick and soft like candle wax, and he paced. He palmed his hair behind his ears and sat on a wooden chair, his shoulders hunched over and his elbows on his knees.

He pursed his lips and nodded his head slightly with his eyes closed. His eyes opened and he sat straight up in his chair. "It went down like I said."

Jude looked at his brother. "Okay. We'll bring you in."

Billy stood and straightened his ruffled shirt.

Jude put his arm around his brother's shoulder.

Billy turned to Jude.

"Down to my bones, this feels like a mistake."

"You gotta trust me on this, *hermanito*." Jude said, snapping the chamber of his gun, ensuring all six rounds were loaded.

CHAPTER
TWELVE

"Now we can see who's faster, but I'll tell you right now, one will be on his back and the other will have a noose around his neck before the night is over!" Jude hollered across the otherwise still plaza, his cocksure voice echoing off the buildings.

He had almost forgotten how the whole world stood still when he was readying to kill a man.

The wind no longer whispered around his ear and brushed by his face.

The blowing *chamisa* no longer tickled his nose, and his thoughts absent of his wife and children. It would seem natural to have your brain swell with images of your adoring wife and treasured children, if you knew it might be your last moments in this world. To feel your heartbeat not to pump blood into your veins, but because it was flooded with love for those three beautiful creatures that made your life worth living. But Jude never had those experiences while facing down another man, and it was probably why he was still alive. He had killed two men in his life and shot a third, coming out unscathed twice. The third and last time leaving a bullet hole clear through his shooting hand. The first and last time someone drew faster than Jude. All that saved Jude was his immediate endurance and better aim. Aside from the Good Lord's blessing, Jude was sure it was because of his narrow focus. For one split second, time stood still for everything in the universe, except Jude. In that moment, Jude drew his gun, sending bulldozing bullets through the ether towards another soul, before that spirit could pull, before he could even blink. In those situations, if Jude thought of Luisa, or pondered what life would be like for Patrick and Wyatt without him, he'd be dead before the concept sunk between his ears.

"Goddamnit, Jude! Stand down!" yelled Landry, his voice as shaky as his hand around his holster.

"I don't know if taking His name in vain is a smart thing to do right now, Landry. You're gonna need all the help you can get if you don't step aside," Jude said.

Landry Hogart had served Jude well as his deputy sheriff for five years. He barely had hair on his upper lip when he came into the police station begging for a job at eighteen years old. Jude was the youngest sheriff at the time and Landry was his first real hire.

There were other more experienced and more qualified candidates waiting for the sheriff position when Wendell Dickerson finally kicked the bucket at the ripe old age of eighty-seven and handed the job to Jude. But Wendell and Cillian James, Jude's father, were close. More significantly, Father Alonzo had always taken a shine to Jude. He saw how caring Jude was to his ailing mother, Theresa, and sad drunk father, after her symptoms reared their ugly head kidnapping the lives of the James family. Billy was barely six, and Jude ten. Cillian had a causal relationship with the bottle before Theresa took ill at age thirty-three, but it seemed to be his only answer after. As she descended down the long spiraling staircase of hallucinations and madness, he followed his Mexican bride, drunk and heartbroken. Cillian was forty-five when she died, finding her in the bathtub with as much blood as water. He still had much of his own natural life ahead of him, and the gift of two young sons that Theresa left him before falling away, but for all intents and purposes, he died too that day, leaving Jude as an orphan and parent to Billy.

Father Alonzo saw the Holy Spirit in Jude, the way he attended to Billy early in his life and contained Billy later. In Father Alonzo's mind,

Jude would have been perfect for the seminary, despite his fiery temper, but there was no seminary in Taos, and Father Alonzo did not dare be an accomplice to ripping Billy's last living family away from him, even for such a divine purpose.

Father Alonzo realized the compassion and mercy Jude possessed could also serve the community and serve the Lord with a badge instead of the cloth. He was the one that recommended Jude apply to be a police officer, and Sheriff Wendell Dickerson, the devout Catholic he was, listened when Father Alonzo gave him the gentle nudge into hiring the scrappy young man on his deathbed. As the pearly gates began to appear before Wendell's very eyes, he held Father Alonzo's hand tight and announced to the world that Jude James, despite only having twenty-four years on the planet and six as a deputy, would be his successor. Technically, Sheriff Dickerson had no legal power to decide who would fill the soon-to-be vacant post, as that was the job of the mayor. But what mayor in his right mind could go against the wishes of the most highly regarded sheriff in the history of Taos, and the most powerful and holy man of the cloth?

So when Landry Hogart, barely eighteen himself, came shaking in the door like a shivering chihuahua, asking for a gun and badge, Jude, figured it was karma coming to collect. When Jude turned in his badge for a law license, Landry became the second youngest Sheriff of Taos County.

"I understand you got a job to do. And you gotta understand I gotta a duty to protect my brother," Jude yelled. "Now those aren't mutually exclusive but before I bring him in, I need assurances. Unfortunately for both of us, those assurances are above your pay grade."

Jude didn't like talking when he was about to shoot a man. He wasn't adept at multitasking. He also had no intention of shooting Landry unless he forced his hand, but he didn't want that hand being distracted either.

Landry stood halfway between the district attorney's office and Jude, which happened to be square in the middle of the plaza. The long green street lights above cast a yellow halo around Landry. Jude hoped to God it was not some kind of sick foreshadowing by the Maker. Then again, Jude stood in the dark shadows, in between the streetlights and the tall thick oak trees, and he hoped that was not a sign of things to come either.

Jude's position of where he stood was intentional, *Harder to shoot a man you can't see.* Poor Landry hung himself out like a target on a wall standing under that light. It was a lapse in decision making that would be learned with experience if he were lucky.

"Now I called Phillip. He's on his way," Jude shouted. He could see the fear overtaking Landry's eyes, and his skin, now pale and clammy, and it did not quell Jude's anxiety. Fear made people commit rash acts.

"Well, I'm glad you called the district attorney, your boss or whatever you call him. Y'all can hash that out all you want, but I need Billy, right fucking now, Landry yelled back.

"I already told you that's not gonna happen. You either accept that and live or we are both in for a world of hurt."

Through the dark alley, headlights suddenly beamed into the plaza, between the two men, as a pickup truck rumbled around the alley. The brakes squealed and the truck stuttered, stopping and shutting off, before it was out of gear, wedging itself directly between the two men.

"Well all right then!" Phillip hollered, before he was even out of his truck. He stepped out, closing the door methodically and slow. "Well all right then," he said again, turning his head in one direction and then the other, observing the standoff. "Why don't you two rabid oxen get it over with right now and stick each other until you both bleed out so I can focus on more pressing issues. We can have two funerals for the price of one. I am sure the two widows and four orphan children would appreciate the economic value in such an arrangement."

The few strands of hair left on the top of Phillip's head stood straight up and his western shirt was untucked from his wide waistband. Jude had never witnessed either before.

Phillip was probably safely tucked away in slumber not twenty minutes ago until that phone call, Jude thought.

The short stocky man with a salt and pepper beard, squinted out of his round wire framed glasses. "No? Fine. Here's what's going to happen then. Jude, you're gonna drop your holster right where you stand and then you're going to walk towards me. You're gonna keep walking all the way into my office and we're gonna have a chat. Landry, as God as my witness, you're gonna let Jude walk into my office unimpeded. You can stand outside the door if you like, freezing your *cojones* off, until Jude and I are finished, and I direct you as to what is going to happen next."

Phillip posted between the two.

Jude was impressed. He had not seen Phillip so impassioned or stalwart since his closing arguments during a five-count rape trial that happened to be forty eight hours before election day.

Jude kicked the proposal around in his head for a moment before answering. "For the most part, that sounds fine and reasonable to me," Jude shouted, but his voice calm. "But I ain't about to place my leather holster on the wet ground nor do I care for my pistol getting rusty with the snow, and dirty with the mud. I just cleaned the son of bitch."

Phillip's scrunchy head turned to Landry waiting for a response.

Even from the lengthy distance, Jude could see Landry blink hard and fast and nod slightly.

"I don't suppose I'd want my gun wet and muddy and either," Landry called out. "How about you remove your holster and hang it on that there tree?"

Like a tennis ball being hit back and forth over a net, Phillip's focus returned to Jude.

Jude coiled his head toward the tree while keeping both eyes on Landry and his hand around his pistol.

Jude studied the tree branch for a moment. "Yea, I reckon that will do..."

Phillip respired an exasperated but relieved breath sure to be heard in Colorado.

"...I have one condition." Jude continued.

Phillip inhaled again, the tension returning to his chest.

"...I'm not comfortable leaving my pistol hanging from a tree in the middle of the Goddamn plaza for an unspecified amount of time. Sheriff, if you would be so kind, once I am a safe distance from my firearm, would you please proceed to take the gun from the tree and hold it for safekeeping?"

The ball once again in Landry's court, Phillip shifted his head accordingly.

Landry's eyes opened and shut repeatedly and fast. "Yes sir. I can do that."

"Much obliged," Jude said, nodding his head in thanks.

Phillip knew better than to get too excited, and sure enough, Jude continued spurring the horse.

"I wanna make one thing clear though. I ain't gonna have my gun but that don't mean I will be coerced into giving up Billy until we talk this through, Phillip."

Phillip turned back to Landry before realizing his card was called. "Wait. Are you addressing me?" Phillip asked.

Jude paused for a moment.

Landry budged his head slightly to see around Phillip's shoulder, curious as well.

"I guess I'm addressing both of you," Jude said.

"Now, Jude," Phillip said, authority returning to his voice, "I made it clear on the telephone that there will be no special treatment from me, but there will be no coercion either."

"And Jude, my main focus will be getting your gun off that tree," said Landry. "I won't interfere with the business between you and Phillip unless Phillip tells me it's time to get it on."

"It's not time to get it on!" Phillip yelled, stretching out his arms in one direction at Jude and the other at Landry, like a crossing guard.

"Well, all right then," said Jude.

Phillip was going to hold off until his death bed to celebrate any further relief from this fuck pot of a situation.

CHAPTER
THIRTEEN

The headlights splashed across the crumbling adobe home like spilled paint, filling the dark windows with light.

Billy stepped out of the good *Padre's* home, squinting at the bright glow, shielding his eyes with one hand, holding a pistol in the other. Father Alonzo walked by his side, a rosary between his fingers that gripped a shotgun, seemingly unaffected by the trespassing glare of the headlights, or the steel in his hands.

Jude didn't even get out of the truck, pulling up next to the two men.

Father Alonzo stepped to the passenger door first and opened it. For a slight elderly man, he swung the rusty weighty door with ease.

Even in the dark, Jude could see the old man's owl like stare, discerning and composed.

"Jude," Father Alonzo said, slight contempt in his voice, as if Jude had done something wrong, not Billy. Fucking Billy always was Father Alonzo's favorite.

"*Padre,*" Jude said, tipping his hat.

"God's word is the only word that matters."

"*Sí, Padre.*"

"Remember that tonight."

"Yes, Father."

Father Alonzo stayed motionless, his carping eyes unwavering on Jude's soul.

Finally, as if he received some divine message that quelled his concern, Father Alonzo relented and turned to Billy, hugging him, and handing him the rosary. "*Via con Dios, Guillermo.*"

Guillermo.

Father Alonzo had always called Billy by his Mexican namesake and Jude was always secretly jealous of that. Jude could slip into speaking Spanish as fluently as the English that rolled off his tongue. This created a bond among both the Mexicans and Chicanos, but he did not hold their name or face, even with some of their blood in his veins. There was a solidarity in the brothers not belonging anywhere together, and by calling Billy *Guillermo*, Father Alonzo was implying there was also a place, or sentiment, held for Billy where Jude didn't belong. That left Jude completely alone in the world then. A big bad brazen lawman and gun fighter still yearning to belong somewhere. This made Jude angry at himself for the silliness of it and his Catholic guilt punished him for still being jealous of this little brother.

Billy stared down at the rosary, the beads spilling effortlessly from his open palm, the other still holding his pistol. "Thanks, Father," Billy said, stepping into the truck.

"How'd he seem?" Billy asked.

"Calm and steady but that's Phillip," Jude said, steering the lime green truck through the pitch-black night.

Up until that moment, Billy had been silent on the drive.

"I reckon after you see everything there is to see over forty years, it's hard to get your feathers ruffled," Jude continued. "Meaning one of the reasons Phillip was not riled tonight."

"It don't take forty years to become numb and dead inside. You see something terrible enough, it can happen in a matter of seconds."

Jude surveyed Billy from the corner of his eye. He didn't dare look at him straight, not out of fear of what Billy might do, but what Jude might see.

"Where's your gun?" Billy asked, matter-of-factly, his gaze lost in the night in front of him.

"Turned it over."

"What did you go and do that for?"

"It was one of the conditions," Jude said. Now, he was more than okay turning to Billy as he spoke. He had to make sure Billy had a full grasp on the situation and was not going to act like Billy acts when the situation involves four walls, rules, and Billy in the middle. "There are certain conditions here, Billy. We should discuss them."

"Like what?

"For one, before you step out of the vehicle, you're gonna have to relinquish that firearm to me," nodding to the gun Billy held in his lap.

"That's ain't gonna happen."

"You step out of the truck brandishing a weapon, they're bound to fire on you."

"That would be their last mistake."

Jude slammed on the brakes, sending the truck sideways on the sandy road and Billy's wounded body into the truck door. Jude was unbothered, gripping the steering wheel tight until the truck was at complete stop.

Dust enveloped the wagon like clouds during a volcanic eruption.

"Goddamnit, Jude. What the fuck?" Billy yelled.

Before the dirt could settle, Jude threw the truck in neutral, hinged the brake, and gave Billy his full attention. "Now you listen here. First thing I said when you agreed to us going about it this way, was you had to listen to me, and you had to trust me. So far, you ain't done neither."

"It ain't you I don't trust, *carnal*. I'm sorry, but I ain't about to just hand over my gun and throw myself at the mercy of these *jodidos*."

"That's exactly what you're gonna do if you want to do it this way. Now you still have the other choice. You wanna head to Mexico, you know where it is, nine hours straight south. I'll step out right now, give you the truck and every penny in my pocket and you'll be on the run for the rest of your natural life."

Billy stared straight ahead, musing the divergent fork in the road. He pressed his lips tight and gnawed his top lip with his bottom teeth. Finally he spoke, still staring down that fork. "What's your read on these sons of bitches?"

"I wouldn't lead you to the butchering block, Billy. Phillip is going to play us straight. They're going to have to investigate but the facts will show self-defense and that's what Phillip will let dictate his course of action. Nothing else."

"Man," Billy said, shaking his head with an icy stare. "I don't trust cops and I don't trust lawyers...No offense," turning to Jude.

"I call that a healthy taste of distrust, but I ain't either right now. *Soy hermano.*"

Billy turned back to the great divide. "He knows I stuck the brown-eye three times?"

"Yea."

"That ain't a problem?"

"Not an insurmountable one. Not with the witnesses and you being stabbed first."

Billy nodded, as if he were trying to coax himself into believing.

"I guess..." Jude trailed off.

"You wanna know if I meant to kill him. Stabbing him three times."

"I know it wasn't intentional."

"You don't know that," Billy said sharply.

Jude sat back now, resting his back against the soft corner of the worn seat, and the cold metallic frame of the truck.

"Not once did that sadistic prick treat me like a human being" Billy muttered, looking off into the past. "Not once did he extend a hint or gesture of respect or acknowledgment that we were more-or-less cut from the same flesh, maybe not the same cloth clearly, but the same flesh."

Jude held quiet.

He had witnessed confessions before and understood too well, they were not to be disturbed. Every moment, every word when the heart was pouring out, was precious and holy. Whether it be mass murders, petty thieves, or white collar chicken shit culprits, in those moments, God was speaking, and it was Jude's duty to listen.

"Edwin made nothing easy for Adeline," Billy continued. "I didn't expect him to ever come around with me. Never imagined he'd let me in with open arms. But he had no right to treat her the way he did. She didn't do nothing but love and care for the old fool. Maybe he should have treated me better solely because she loved me. Maybe out of respect for her,

Edwin should have respected me, respected us. I know as clear as a blue-bird day, that if Edwin just stepped aside, didn't even have to like me, just let me be, let us be, we'd be happy. We'd be married. Have a family of our own. I wouldn't have gone overseas. Wouldn't be who I am now...a killer."

"You ain't a killer, it's just the world we live in."

"Maybe it's the world that's stepping aside and letting us be what we naturally are. Not everyone is a killer, but make no mistake, *carnal*, *we* are."

Billy's stare shined directly into Jude's soul, as if he were the one coaxing a confession now.

Jude somehow felt the insinuation and didn't like it. It was a bridge he was not ready to cross.

"There will be a time when the credit of our good will and debit of our bad acts will be added up and codified," Jude said. "But it ain't tonight and it ain't by these sons of bitches. So, in the meantime, as your legal counsel, I advise you to refrain from calling Edwin a sadistic prick or a brown-eye, and refrain from calling yourself a killer. We got enough blood on our hands. We don't need our own."

Jude turned back to the road in front of him. He stepped on the clutch and shifted the truck in gear.

"When you killed those men, you were defending yourself?" Billy asked.

"Now ain't the time or place to talk about this."

"You knew if you didn't kill them, they would kill you right? That was the last thought in your head before you pulled."

"I just told you this ain't the time or the place for this discussion," Jude muttered.

"It's exactly the time, and I don't know of any place that's right for this conversation. Maybe a church. Should we turn back around to Father Alonzo's?"

"Why are you doing this, Billy?" Jude whispered, barely over the humming of the idling engine.

"Both of them men you killed; you'd been chasing them for a while?"

"Yea."

"Both sons of bitches committed some terrible acts or you wouldn't have been on their ass.

"Yea."

"Before you came upon them, did you spend time ruminating on the idea of a better world, without them in it?"

"I was doing my job."

"Which part was your job?"

Jude's eyes narrowed.

His jaw clenched tight.

Fingers gripped the steering wheel firmly.

"It ain't no secret, you got a fiery temper, Jude," Billy said. "I was the crazy and wild one, but you were always the one with the temper. You spent your whole life trying to control Ma, then Pop then me but the one person you could never control was you. You're a whole other person when that temper is coursing through your veins. That fire."

"Goddamn you, Billy, I'm only trying to help."

"You can't help me until I know."

"Know what?"

"When you're in that temper, do you know it? You feel yourself in it?"

Jude's eyes became glassy.

His face was dry and vacant but heavy like the stare of a wild coyote come upon in the desert.

"I wasn't angry when I killed those men," Jude whispered. "I didn't want to kill either of them. They left me no choice. There was no time to think. To be angry or have a temper. There was only survival."

"I know," Billy said, his shoulders suddenly slinking into his chest, his head low. "There's no choice, you know that deep in your soul, but you're still left wondering, right?"

"Right," Jude said softly, almost to himself.

"But you know, it wasn't malice, it wasn't murder."

"Yea."

"When you have that rabid dog of a temper overcome you, you don't know what you are thinking though, right? You could be reacting to something from that very moment, or something that had been stirring deep inside for a long fucking time. Maybe it didn't even have to do with the son of a bitch talking shit in front of you. Something else, eating away at you, slowly, like a Goddamn termite. Even if it was justified in some way, your response, you don't know if you were acting out of cause and reason or if the devil himself was really at work, and he happened to provide the circumstance and the alibi."

Jude turned to Billy. Color bled back into his face.

"You don't know if you killed Edwin in self-defense or not."

Billy's eyes reared to Jude's. They were wide, young, and scared, like they used to look when Billy woke Jude up after a bad dream. Jude suddenly felt incredibly sad for Billy, like Billy had been the one severely harmed. Molested. Violated.

The air was so cold and unforgiving that it stung Jude's flesh and made his skin tight.

He felt like there were needles in his lungs and he dared not breathe again.

He tried to speak without breath, but his words sank like a water-logged tree.

"I don't know..." Jude managed, the words he thought he found escaping him again. "This is bothering you. What you did is bothering you."

"Fuck him," Billy blurted out erratically, before wavering immediately, like light refracting through a prism. "Yea, yea it is."

"Father Alonzo always said guilt was God telling you, you did something wrong."

"I remember."

"I always thought guilt meant you're fucking good. I've never met a truly bad man that felt guilt. This may be something you will have to spend the rest of your life coming to terms with. But right now let's focus on making sure you have that opportunity," Jude said.

Billy straightened up.

He cleared his throat.

He studied the gun that lay on his lap.

"*Listamos*," he said, handing Jude the gun.

TRIAL BY FIRE

CHAPTER
FOURTEEN

At least *it was a jury of his peers*, Jude thought, scanning each face of the unlucky citizens. Jude knew every one, and every one knew Billy. Jude wasn't sure if that was a good thing or not.

There were eight gringos and four Chicanos in the box which would seem odd to most, given the proportional racial make-up of Taos County was 80% Hispanic. Jude hoped for at least six Chicano jurists, not because half the blood flowing through Billy was Mexican and every decaying bone in Edwin's body was white.

It went deeper than that.

Jude understood that a Chicano was more likely to think *fuck the disputable facts, the viejito came at him with a knife and got what he deserved.* There was a dignified and unspoken accord of responsibility and retribution in Latin culture. If Edwin didn't want to get stabbed three times in the gut, he probably should not have pulled a knife to begin with. Sure, this sentiment could also be shared by a gringo who grew up in the Latin culture, but it was more certain with a Chicano, because it was in his blood. So in that sense, it did not matter so much what blood was running through Billy's veins but the veins of those that held Billy's life in their hands.

If Jude understood this notion, then so did Phillip. It was why he so artfully whittled down the jury pool of almost all Hispanics to the four before them now. If Billy looked the least bit Chicano, there could have been an argument for racial bias on the part of the prosecution and would have meant the jury strikes were improper and not allowed. Jude still tried to make this point clear to Billy's official Counsel, Stanley Weiss, but it fell on his big white deaf ears.

This wasn't to say, Mr. Weiss was not an otherwise fine attorney. Jude had seen him in action. He was cunning, and sharp, a quiet rattlesnake never knowing what direction he was going to strike from until it was too late. But there were certain things not taught, even in a school as prestigious as The University of Chicago School of Law, and certain things not understood by a white man from New York City, even as smart as Stanley, even if he now resided in Albuquerque.

The room was stuffy and warm, and Jude could feel sweat gathering on his forehead. He had been in this same courtroom countless times but never noticed how old and musty it smelled. Perhaps he had never sat so still in it before, allowing the redolence and sense of the room to overcome him.

Phillip often joked that Jude was like a tethered bull in the courtroom. If he wasn't veering back and forth in front of the witness stand and the Bench, making everyone in the room nauseous with motion sickness, then he was fiddling and shaking in his chair like a wet dog waiting for his turn to bark again.

Now, Jude sat still.

His hands flat on the top of his legs above his knees. He studied the jury, each one of them with his eyes.

Old Mr. Yates had his long leathery hair parted neatly down the middle and tucked behind his ears. Through his thick brown eyebrows and beard that cradled up past his cheek bones, his ripened blue eyes caught Jude's. He held his eyes with Jude's for a moment before turning them back to Phillip, making his opening statement.

Jude wondered if Mr. Yates heard a word Phillip just said or understood it. Did it even matter? And was Jude an arrogant prick for even considering this idea? Jude's eyes moved to Mrs. Turnbeck sitting as stiff as a wide plank, her gray hair pulled just as tight into a bun. Her beady eyes leered out from the crow's feet. The old gal must have been eighty years old and still did not need or chose not to wear glasses. She looked brittle with her bony fingers and twig-like arms but as coarse and tough as an old rusty nail. Jude was sure, even in her now decrepit age, she could reach across the juror's box and slap him or Billy into next week, like she had done so many times before as principal of their elementary school. She was the only woman who was not a nun in the school, but her unflinching faith and wrath quelled any concern for her lack of the nun's habit. She was probably the meanest creature to ever pee between two knees. If anyone was going to send Billy' head to the guillotine, Jude figured it would be her.

But now, as Jude's eyes encountered hers, her face seemed to soften, her shoulders withered and her head turned slightly sideways, as if two say, *Oh Jude, what did you and Billy get yourselves into this time?"* The two held their confluence for a moment before she returned her attention to the good constable still blathering on. Jude swore the timeless ire that always owned her face returned with her focus on Phillip. Maybe she was on Billy's side after all?

Mrs. Turnbeck was brutal doling out punishment as the disciplinarian of the school, but it was never undeserved. She had a clear vision of right and wrong, and Billy and Jude never went before her because of some virtuous act they committed. Jude suddenly felt a kind of salvation in his heart. If Mrs. Turnbeck seemed to be on Billy's side, maybe there was hope.

The word *murder* boasted by Phillip snapped Jude back to reality, or more precisely, the present.

Jude's eyes deviated to Billy, sitting beside Mr. Weis at the defendant's table.

Jude begged Billy to wear his dress blues to trial each day, a not-so-subtle reminder of his service to our free and democratic State, but Billy refused.

"I'd rather they hang me in them," Billy had said.

It was an act of defiance, masochism, and an act of Billy just being Billy, but Jude heard a reverence in his voice that said, *I ain't using the stripes that way.*

Jude disagreed. There would be time for honor and humility after the verdict, but he respected Billy's decision, and was secretly proud.

Instead, Billy wore a brown suit.

Mr. Weis insisted he buy a new one for the trial, and have it tailored, but it never seemed to fit right on Billy, even after the third alteration. Billy was simply a man not made to wear a suit.

As if Billy felt his brother's pressing eyes upon him, he turned his head toward Jude.

They did not make eye contact, but their fraternal beings detected one another. *Don't worry little brother, I got your back,* Jude's eyes declared.

Billy's head turned back to Phillip as he rested his opening remarks.

Jude figured the trial would last a week.

Phillip's opening statement had already sucked up half the first day so maybe it would go on much longer.

Jude sat puckered and fastidious examining every word spoken and gesture made. There was no concept of time here for Jude, but he didn't know how long Billy could slog through. Billy had always been like a lit bottle rocket without its stick, flying in all directions at once. He could barely sit still long enough to take a shit. The dire circumstances the brothers found themselves in was filled with worrisome questions but one of the biggest for Jude was if Billy could simply sit still during this long monotonous process? Maybe the gravity of the situation burned away the prosaicness of the process for Billy. On a list of high hopes Jude held for this ordeal, that was near the top.

Just like that, the first day was over faster than a shooed-away fly.

The Judge's heavy gavel had not finished echoing throughout the courtroom before people started shuffling out. Luisa turned to Jude and exhaled while squeezing his fingers tight. Each time Jude turned to her, that first day, she seemed as attentive as a doe in a field of lions. There was no doubt of innocence for Billy on her face. Jude wished to God he felt the same. Luisa stood and Jude followed. Billy and his counsel did the same. Mr. Weis padded Billy kindly on the back as if saying, *One down, son.* As the crowded room scurried and tried not to fall over one another, scooting out of the narrow rows, Jude held up for Billy.

"I'll meet y'all outside," Billy said, noticing.

"We can wait," Jude said.

"I'm going to hit the head. I'll meet you out there."

"We can wait," Jude said again.

"Jesus Christ, you ain't gonna fucking hold it for me," Billy blurted. Immediately, Billy looked at Luisa remorsefully and then ashamed.

She seemed to hold less effect than either of the two boys. Billy embarrassed and Jude disjointed.

"We will see outside Billy," Luisa said kindly, looping her arm into Jude's, tugging him away lightly.

Billy nodded, buried his head, and then scampered off to the private bathroom.

Jude sighed and shook his head as the two stepped through the long splintered bench of the courtroom gallery.

Jude and Luisa dodged their way through the crowded courthouse hallway.

Adeline's brother, Darcy leaned off to the side of the building's pillar muttering to Camilo.

Darcy had received the short end of the Simon genes, looking nothing like Adeline. Adeline had wild raspberry hair. Darcy's was stringy, dirt-colored and looked like a head of wet noodles. Adeline's skin was as pure white as ivory. Darcy's looked like blanched potatoes, dull and colorless. Darcy dressed in all black as if he was attending a funeral, his slim frame in the suit made him look like a child playing dress-up.

Camilo was wearing his best all-white pearl-snap and his cleanest black Levi's and shiny matching boots. Jude was almost impressed.

A slim stranger with jet black hair, glassy eyes and a purple suit stood next to the two men.

All three men's scowl followed Jude as he passed and then Darcy spoke. "Your brother's a dead man!"

Jude stopped dead in his tracks.

Luisa winced harder than a squeezed fist. She desperately tugged at Jude's arm, a reminder, and a plea. When Jude's chest expanded, and she felt him pull away, she knew her plea had fallen on deaf ears.

"What did you say?" Jude seethed at Darcy, his eyes already as red as a hot coal.

The stranger stepped aside, looking almost curious.

"Move along, *pendejo*," Camilo muttered into Jude's face, his hot breath almost suffocating.

Darcy cowered behind Camilo's broad body.

Jude directed his attention squarely to Camilo, his stare as torrid as Camilo's breath. "In general, I got nothing against *putos*," he said. "It's only the undiscriminating kind that I find repulsive. The ones willing to put any piece of filthy ill-gotten flesh in their mouth and swallow for the right price."

Before Camilo could make his move, Jude had all ten fingers wrapped tightly in Camilo's black curly hair.

Jude yanked him across the width of the corridor in three swift steps, before smashing his face into the adjacent wall.

Camilo's legs held under after the first assault, prompting more brute force from Jude on rounds two and three.

Jude felt Camilo's legs buckle.

Camilo's body had not yet sunk to the floor before Jude was sailing back across the room landing his fist square into Darcy's jaw.

Jude wound back for another serving when his legs were suddenly kicked out from underneath him, his back was parallel in the air with the floor and his head slammed to the ground.

Before the pain hit, Jude opened his eyes to find the stranger standing above him, the heavy thick heel of his wingtips squarely on Jude's chest. His brown eyes, under his manicured almost purple eyebrows, and above his equally styled raven-colored pencil-thin mustache, staring calmly at Jude.

"That's enough, Mr. James," said the man coolly, displaying a pistol tucked in his waistband, under the lavender suit jacket. His southern accent as out of place as his attire.

Jude was breathing hard.

Darcy suddenly appeared over him, holding his jaw and his eyes watering, or crying. "You fucked up now, cock-sucker. You've been walking around swinging dick in these parts with your fast pull but your small time. Mr. Dahl here gunned down more men in his life, than you've even fancied."

"That's enough," Mr. Simon, said the man, equally dry and scolding. He spoke softly but with a royal sounding southern accent, like a grand-standing politician.

There was gasoline coursing through Jude's veins, a revving engine ready to be kicked into gear. He continued to lie on his back but ready to pounce when he suddenly became acutely aware of the crowd gathered around him.

The man must have sensed this too, as he removed his shoe from Jude's chest and stepped back, never shifting his cold eyes.

Jude scooted away and got himself to his feet, never breaking with the man. "Mr., I don't know who you are but before this is all over, there will be blood between you and I."

"I don't disagree with your assessment, Mr. James," said the man, as fluid as hot butter.

CHAPTER FIFTEEN

"You've got to be kidding me!" Stanley Weiss yelled, his gorilla-like hands gripping the table. Thick, unkempt hair rooted up to the second digits of his knuckles. Stanley was out of his chair, leaning over the small table at Jude, a vein pulsing from his forehead, and eyes as wide as a jam jar glaring at him through his wire-framed glasses.

Despite Stanley's stellar reputation, Jude was not sure Stanley was the proper constable for the family until now.

Jude knew Stanley had a sharp mind.

He was also aware Stanley was one of the guys that never won at anything until he went to law school, and then he never lost. This fed a constant fire in Stanley's belly that allowed him to be a piranha.

Jude was mindful that Stanley cared deeply about his reputation. It was why Stanley was extremely selective about what clients he represented, and why Jude had to practically beg him to represent Billy.

Despite all of this, Jude wasn't sure Stanley *really cared* about the well-being of Billy until now.

Jude sat quietly in his chair taking his lashes, his hands calmly on the table clasped together, his head low, like a guilty perp.

"We are not even on Day 2 of the trial, and you are assaulting the family of the alleged victim in the Goddamn courthouse?" Stanley yelled or asked.

Jude always found it funny when people said things that way. They would yell something at him that was a question but not really a question. It was more like they were still trying to wrap their mind around something that was abundantly clear.

Jude's eyes made their way to Billy, sitting in the corner, leaning back on the hind legs of the wooden chair. Maybe Billy was thinking the same thing because he grinned at Jude when their eyes met.

Jude didn't think Billy would be upset with him, and he seemed more amused and not surprised if anything. He sat there bringing the chair as far back as possible, before conceding the front legs to the floor again. He looked like he was enjoying the whipping Jude was taking. Truth be told, he probably was, the sick son of a bitch. It was Billy's neck in the noose, and Jude only tightened it with his temper, but as long as big brother was the one currently in the barrel, it was all fun and games.

Jude's eyes turned to Luisa sitting next to him. She sat hanging onto Stanley's every word, as if he was going to say something earth shattering. Perhaps she was just relishing someone else validating what she had been telling Jude for years. *No,* Jude thought, *that's not Luisa's style. She knows when she is right, and she don't need anyone else to confirm it.* There was a profound humility in that. Jude was almost surprised when Luisa said nothing about the outburst after returning home. Then again, her silence was more deafening and severe. Luisa also probably recognized that when Jude's blood tempered and his fist softened again, he realized the gravity of his actions and their possible consequences. He didn't need Luisa to rub salt in the wounds he carved out.

"What truly baffles me, Mr. James," Stanley continued, "Is that you are an attorney and officer of the court."

Yessir, but I'm also a James, Jude thought, as if he were compelled to answer Stanley, even if only in his own head.

"You would think you would act like one and not a thick-headed buffoon."

Jude recognized his actions were inappropriate, and he appreciated Stanley's obvious concern, but he was almost at that point of having his fill.

"Are you out of your fucking mind?" Stanley continued.

Oh Jesus, not that question. Jude always detested people asking him that. Perhaps because his mother was in fact out of her mind, and Jude' deepest darkest fear was that at any moment, the light switch would flip off in his head, and we would descend down the same long dark stairwell of insanity. Most people that asked Jude this question, or a similar one, had known Jude's family history. You would think they would recognize the sensitivity of such an inquiry but then again, Jude's actions that prompted such a query usually suggested *sensitivity* was not always coursing through Jude's mind either.

As if suddenly aware of Jude's feelings, Stanley un-gripped the table and declined back into his chair across from Jude. "Listen, Mr. James. I know you care greatly for your brother. That was abundantly clear the moment you walked into my office. But you have to understand, the deck is already stacked against us here. I may be a damn fine attorney and a Jew, but I am not Jesus Christ. I can't have the few cards we have left shuffled to the other side simply because you can't control your temper. You understand me?"

Jude raised his head, looking Stanley directly in the eye. "Yes sir."

"Good," Stanley said, almost sounding relieved that Jude possibly understood and that his task of scolding was over.

The pressure in the room seemed to dissipate with Stanley's temperament.

Stanley moved his attention to reviewing notes he had on a yellow legal pad.

Billy played with the toothpick that hung from his lips.

Jude reached for Luisa' hand under the table, and they held each other's tight.

There was a peace in the room until the knock at the door.

"Come in," Stanley said, his eyes still on his notes.

The door opened and Phillip stuck only his head through. "Morning, y'all," he said, his eyes making their way to each person.

"Phillip," Stanley said, putting down his pen, giving him his full attention. "Good morning."

"You all…um have a minute?" Phillip asked.

His timidity was worrisome to everyone in the room.

So were the bags under his eyes.

It didn't look like sleep found Phillip last night. Or the night before.

"Please come in," Stanley said, standing and motioning with his hand.

Luisa scooted closer to Jude, leaving Phillip some room at the head of the table.

Billy went back to rocking in his chair, twiddling with the toothpick on his tongue, both eyes on Phillip.

Phillip stepped inside, and then looked as if he was having second thoughts already. He almost moved outside the door again.

"Phillip, please come in," Stanley said again, noticing.

Phillip's troubled eyes moved to Luisa. "Um, Mrs. James, Luisa," he said with a nervous smile, "Would you mind givin' us a minute, please?"

"Yes, of course," Luisa said, standing.

"No," Billy said, still leaning back in his chair. "She can stay."

Luisa turned to Billy. "Billy, it's fine."

"Yes, it would be better…" Phillip said.

"No," Billy said again, the two front legs dropping to the ground. "She can stay. She is my sister. She can stay."

Luisa's eyes darted around the room for a moment. No one dared to say anything further, so she quietly sat.

Phillip exhaled deeply, his eyes making the rounds as well. "All right then," he finally said. His lips started moving but no words flowed.

Jude picked up on it. "Jesus Christ, Phillip, what is it?"

The lips continued to chatter until words finally followed. "This ain't exactly. Well, this is not where I would want to have this conversation, and in actuality, I don't want to have this conversation anywhere. However, there's people watching night and day everywhere else, so this is the only place that's safe."

"Phillip, what are you talking about?" Jude asked.

"That man, that whooped you yesterday…"

"…He didn't whoop…" Jude interjected.

"…Whatever…" Phillip said, uncaring to Jude's sensitive ego. "His name is Leslie Dahl."

"So?" Billy asked.

"He's a Goddamn Pinkerton," Phillip said.

Suddenly there was no air in the stale pale room.

Stanley cleared his throat.

Jude palmed his jaw with his hand.

Luisa desperately tried to read the face of each man.

Only Billy seemed unscathed by the news. He leaned back in his chair again and moved the toothpick to the other side of his mouth with his tongue.

"That night you came to me," Phillip said, sitting down now, cowering over the table, looking only at Jude, "I gave you my word and I intend to keep it, but that old son of a bitch was not in the ground two days when those cock suckers came knocking at my door."

"Darcy commissioned them," Jude stated matter-of-factly.

Phillip only nodded. "In so many words, they told me the facts dictated that Billy killed Edwin in cold blood and there would be witnesses to testify to that. I told them I didn't see it that way and showed 'em the door." Phillip's sheepish eyes peered up. "That's when they gave me this…"

Phillip slid a piece of paper over to Jude.

Jude picked it up and read it.

Billy studied the two men, still rocking in his chair, now with his arms crossed.

"I don't get it," Jude said. "Three addresses in three different states?"

"It's the addresses of where my daughters live," Phillip muttered.

Billy's chair planked back down on all fours.

Jude blinked hard.

Stanley stared at his notepad, not reading it.

"Billy," Phillip said, breaking the silence, "I had no intention of charging you with any crime. Not because of the relationship I have with your brother but because I did not believe you committed one. Had I believed otherwise, well…"

"I get it, Phillip," Billy said.

"That Goddamn, Yankee. That chicken shit, Dahl, he's gonna do everything in his power to make sure Billy goes away," Phillip said. His eyes did not move between Jude and Stanley, as if saying, *this is on you now, figure it out.* Phillip inhaled hard and deep again and then released. He pushed the chair out from the table and stood. "This is the last time we are going to be able to have this conversation."

Jude stood and nodded to Phillip as their eyes met, both seeming more sympathetic to the other.

Phillip turned, his head still low, and left the room.

Stanley's eyes raced from side to side, as if reading something very quickly on the notepad, but he wasn't.

The sharp 1000-watt light bulb that hung overhead hummed.

Somewhere down the hallway, a door slammed.

Finally, Stanley broke the toiling silence, still staring at his empty pad. "Mrs. James, would you please give us a minute?" Stanley stuck out his hand to Billy heading off the protest. "Please."

"Of course," Luisa said. Her eyes made their way to Jude, and she released his hand.

Immediately, Jude felt less comfortable. He was cocky and fearless, sometimes to his peril, but in the moments when he was most terrified – when Luisa told him he was gonna be a daddy – watching Billy board the bus to boot camp – Luisa had wrapped her fingers around his and a calmness filled his heart. It was not blind courage, just peace.

As soon as the door closed, with Luisa on the other side, Stanley peered up from his pad, venom in his eyes.

The snake was about to start rattling, Jude thought.

Stanley didn't even clear his throat before speaking.

He was puckered.

"Obviously, anything we say here, is protected by attorney-client privilege," Stanley said to Jude. "That is why I had you and I enter an attorney-client relationship, as well, Mr. James. I do not hold such a privilege with Mrs. James, which is the reason I asked her to leave."

"And here I thought it was just for two…what do you call them?... Retainers" Billy said.

"Billy, not now," said Jude.

"No Mr. James, it was not," Stanley said, curbing his head towards Billy, "It was to protect all of us. Mr. James can attest to that," he said, nodding to Jude.

"For the sake of my head not swimming, would you please just call me Billy and him *pendejo*," Billy said, "I can't keep up this 'Mr. James' dance any longer."

"Fine," Stanley said, exhaling, perturbed. "The three of us can speak freely, as we all enjoy the same attorney-client privilege."

"I understand," said Billy, "I was just jerking your chain."

"As your legal counsel, Billy," Stanley said, clearly not amused, "I see the following option. I can walk into the courtroom and make an announcement to Judge Terrance that I have reason to believe that Mr. Darcy Simon has hired Pinkertons to engage in witness tampering and bribery, threats to the jury, obstruction of justice and I'll even call Phillip to testify as to what he just told us here. I will then make a motion to have this trial removed to federal court where we will have federal protection of the law, with a federal judge, a federal prosecutor and a federal venue."

"What difference does all of that make?" Billy asked.

"It ensures you have a fair trial," Jude said.

"Bullshit it does," Billy said, almost laughing. "You think them sons of bitches can't get to a federal lawyer or judge? Shit, they're probably more corrupt. The higher they sit, the fatter the pig."

"Billy, it ain't…"

"…Jude, it's exactly like that. What you just don't seem to understand is we ain't never gonna win playing by the rules. You've had a rule for everything your whole life because you think it gives you control but it don't give you shit. You think they play by the rules? Fuck no. They write the rules and create the system to hold us in. Imprison us. Oppress. The sons of bitches I was fighting over-seas, all they was, was angry and fed up with the same. With the rules and the oppression. The tyranny. The system. I ain't saying ultimately what they did was right, fuck no it wasn't, but I understand. Stanley, I appreciate your counsel, but you can motion this, motion that, motion till you're blue in the face, but it won't matter when we're locked in the box, playing by their rules."

Stanley sat quiet. His lack of protest screamed louder than a yipping coyote in heat.

Jude stared at the table both blankly and centered. "Billy, I'm sorry I got you into this."

"The shit on my heel ain't from you. I stepped in it all on my own."

"That ain't entirely true. I was the one that convinced you to come in. Trust the system. Trust me."

"And it was my Goddamn fault that I let you convince me. It was my decision, even though I knew better…"

The front legs of the chair seesawed in the air, this time, not rocking. Billy simply let the chair free-fall back until it hit the wall, catching him. Had the wall not been there, Billy would have let it just slip away into eternity. "…I knew better…After all I saw…" Billy said, His eyes widened and reddened like he was just punched in the nose. He stared off at something that was not present in the room.

"Then you run," Stanley finally said.

"Yea," said Billy, dropping the chair again, narrowing his eyes.

"We do not know the extent of the Pinkertons' reach. You cannot give any indication that you are about to run, Billy," Stanley said. "No clearing out bank accounts or even buying a new suitcase at the Goddamn Five and Dime. You understand me?" Stanley said, authority, direction, in his voice.

Billy nodded.

"That ain't gonna be enough," Jude muttered softly, lowering his head.

"How's that?" Stanley asked, his eyes peering out from the top of his glasses.

"They won't stop with Billy. They'll chase him, yea. But they're gonna come after Luisa and the children…"

Stanley's head collapsed, if not attached to his neck, it probably would have hit the table. "He's right," Stanley muttered.

Billy removed the toothpick from his lips and rubbed it between his thumb and his index finger. "How many of these people are there?"

"The Pinkertons?" Jude asked.

Stanley only shook his head. Probably for many reasons.

"Yea. Can we kill em all?" Billy asked.

"I don't think so, Billy," said Jude.

"Then we cut off the head of the beast. If Darcy hired them, we kill him and it'll be over. I can go to jail or whatever, if need be, but it'll be over."

"Darcy ain't the only Simon…" Jude said, penitent head low but his eyes on Billy perhaps still soliciting.

"Adeline?" Billy asked.

Jude only answered with those eyes.

"I can't see her getting involved with these people," Billy said. "She ain't like that."

Jude exhaled as if saying, *Don't be so stupid! So naïve!*

"I can't, Jude," Billy said to Jude, but it wasn't Jude he was convincing.

"I think that might be worth considering before you two proceed," Stanley said, his voice quiet, but as commanding as Moses' from Mount Sinai.

"Something else, worth considering." Jude said. "You willing to take away her daddy and now her brother?"

"If they're coming after you and Luisa and the kids, there ain't even a question," Billy said, "I just hope to G…"

Billy stopped himself.

He gritted his teeth and looked away

"If there is anything decent and right in this world, she's not involved," Billy said instead. "If there ain't…" Billy's eyes moved to the ground, and his jaw slackened. "Then what the fuck is the point of anything?"

CHAPTER
SIXTEEN

He didn't know if she'd come.

A coin flip in the air had more certainty.

Billy had not seen Adeline since that night.

She had not been at the trial so far and was not on the witness list.

Perhaps this was Phillip secretly throwing Billy a bone, legally speaking.

Perhaps the opposite.

Then again, Adeline was not there when Billy knifed the swine, so why should she be called?

Billy could not find much to be grateful for of late, but if there was a greater Being, and he was equally cloudy on that question, he was beholden to Him for Adeline not being there when Billy killed her father. These questions of legal strategy were beyond him so he put them to rest. If Adeline was going to come, it wouldn't be under the guise of some judicial tactic.

Billy truly could not forecast if Adeline would meet him in his family's barn where he sat, hunched over on a bale of hay studying the top of his boots, and the fodder in between them. Billy had arranged for Father Alonzo to give Adeline's best friend a message, that she would in turn pass along to Adeline - to meet Billy in the barn. The last few weeks, the last five years really, had all seemed like a bad dream to Billy, but this arrangement seemed absurd, like something from a Shakespeare play. Billy always hated the uppity asshole. Couldn't understand five words the guy wrote, when he had to read that shit in high school English class. Mark Twain was more Billy's style. Honest, to the point, but with real emotion. Mark Twain made it all right for a man to feel. When Billy had first gone to war, he would read during the respite between the savagery. It reminded him that he was still human. Attached to the finger that pulled the trigger, the hand that held the bayonet, and the arm and shoulder that heaved the grenade, was a chest. Inside that chest was a heart, and somewhere deep in that heart, there was a soul. It would hide to allow Billy to survive insentient battles, but when he found a moment of peace he would read, to reacquaint, his body with his spirit. That's probably why many soldiers read the Bible, but that was not the spirit Billy was speaking to. He was parleying with the human condition, *his* human condition. He was unsure if he were going to make it out alive, but he was certain, if he did, he would need that soul to live out the rest of his life in reasonable peace.

The first night Billy decided to lie in his bunk, smoke a dry harsh cigarette and stare vacuously at the ceiling instead of reading, he knew he and his soul were no longer one. He was a little less human that night, and then the next and then the next.

Billy noticed most soldiers lost their minds first. If it wasn't their life, or an extremity, it tended to be their sanity.

Billy's remained intact somehow.

Headlong into bootcamp.

Through the two years of fighting.

The six months in the hospital healing from the shrapnel and the explosion.

The year floating through the heroin dream.

Getting clean.

And then burying his wife.

His dead wife. Billy began to think of her.

Billy was certain the ability for him to experience life again as human was not possible until the sunny spring day in Paris when he crossed paths with Marion. He and Sid had just scored. They were ambling down the cobblestone street, a warm breeze at their back, and sweet tar in their veins, when a gust yanked the beret from her head. Somehow even in his nod Billy sprang, swooping it from the sidewalk as it rolled. When he scuttled back to her, handing her his offering, he was immediately swept up in the ocean swell of her eyes.

He nodded.

She smiled coyly and they stood basking in front of one another until Billy spoke. "Mademoiselle, um may I buy you a café?" he asked.

"No," she said, her French accent as delicious as her apple red lips and eggshell skin. "But may I buy you? In gratitude…" holding up her hat.

Billy grinned, his soul conferring with his body, his heart once more. "*Oui.*"

That day never ended for the paramours.

Starting in the quaint café, dotting through small talk.

Continuing with a slow promenade of the city, bottle of wine in hand.

Persisting with the two watching the sun melt over the Seine river as it set, their legs dangling gaily off the bridge where they sat.

And when the opiates burned off and Billy found himself hungry, they dined, huddling close to one another in a tight plush red booth, fumbling with each other under the table in between nibbles of decadent food.

Afterwards, back in the hotel room, they got high together and made love.

They inhabited their sanctuary, their private haven, for almost a week, only departing for quick cigarette or heroin runs, and the occasional loaf of bread or bottle of wine.

Marion never asked Billy anything about the war, and he was grateful for that. She didn't seem to avoid such questions. She simply understood that the soldier and the war was not Billy now and hence irrelevant.

He told her about New Mexico and cowboys and shared stories of his Americana childhood.

She spoke to youthful memories growing up in the streets of Paris, the only child to a professor and a painter.

In Billy's mind, things were not moving quickly between him and Marion, they just *were*, as if he could not remember a time or place when they were *not*.

Two weeks after they met, they were married.

It was a small whimsical ceremony made up of Marion's closest friends, her parents, and Sid playing the best man. Her family was not religious, believing more in liberal intellectualism, fine wine, and a fine time, so there was no church. Instead, they found God in their hearts, sharing a love so pure, and the pure black tar.

The wide rickety door creaked and rocked lazily, almost closed, then almost opened fully again, hurling Billy from Paris back to Taos.

Billy's mind did not race as he waited in the cool damp barn, the smell of kerosene wafting in the air, which always smelled pleasant to him. Teachers, nuns, authority figures of all kinds groused and grumbled about Billy being wild, energetic, frenzy. Billy's father saw it another way. "When that boy wakes up in the morning he is just wound a little tighter than the rest of us," he would say, observing Billy buzzing at his feet. Because Billy had a frenetic spirit, they assumed he had a hysterical mind. Quite the opposite, however. When Billy centered on something-a car engine, an unruly bronco, putting a bullet between a combatant's eyes forty yards out while surrounded in chaos, his mind was focused and still. That rabid energy honed into precision.

Perhaps that was why his mind was a blank canvas waiting for Adeline. It was not whizzing back and forth, like a tennis ball, with questions.

Does she think I murdered her father?

Does she hate my fucking guts?

Is she at least partially responsible for the Pinkertons being involved?

Undoubtedly, those questions, more or less, had to be answered before the two brothers could proceed with their plan. Undoubtedly, Billy had to find a way to ask them without tipping his hand, in case she turned out to be a foe and not a friend. And undoubtedly, Billy had no plan or idea how to do so.

Perhaps this had nothing to do with Billy. How could any man ask his lover, whose father he had just killed, if she hired men to ensure his demise? All along while that lover schemed to kill her brother. Even that asshole Shakespeare couldn't write this.

The barn door squeaked louder and longer, and Billy turned to find Adeline.

He hopped up but suddenly found his feet in hard concrete.

Adeline pensively stared at him for a moment, as if sizing up the intention of a mountain lion you come across in the woods. After a long still moment, she turned and closed the barn door behind her. Not moving. Her back to Billy. Her palms pressed open on the door. Perhaps in deliberation. Perhaps her mind waiting for the canvas to be painted, as well.

As Billy stood watching and wondering, he could sense the feeling surge back into his legs, but now, he did not move for a different reason. He did not want to startle or force Adeline into anything. She had made the decision to at least come to the barn, that much was clear, but that also seemed to be the extent of her decision so far.

Adeline's shoulders raised around the back of her neck, as she pulled in a deep breath. Before Billy expected her to exhale, she turned around. Her eyes crashed into his. They looked both vacant and visceral.

Billy noticed how all ten fingers of her hands were spread broadly from one another, as if she was palming two invisible grapefruits.

She exhaled and cautiously walked towards him.

Suddenly, Billy's canvas was splashed with colors of guilt, regret, shame, and doubt. His head lowered, the closer she came to him. By the time she stood next to him, his eyes were parallel with the wood shavings in the dirt.

Adeline placed herself on the wide bale of hay that Billy stood in front of.

Billy lowered next to her. He steadied his shaky hands by palming his knees tight.

Neither said a word, the silence as heavy and thick as the grief and sorrow between them.

Billy could not breathe. He feared the sound of his breath would be deafening and only cause more pain in the world.

More pain to Adeline.

Finally, she spoke. "I don't blame you for what happened," gazing at the flakes of timber, straw, oil stains and tiny rocks on the ground. Looking at everything but Billy.

Billy's face tightened. He had to breathe now so he would not cry.

"I also feel like there is a part of me that hates you…or should hate you," she said.

Billy nodded and sucked down the tears and they did not fight to return. He realized he could probably manage Adeline holding adverse feelings toward him much easier than any forgiving magnanimous ones.

"Yea…" is all he could manage.

"How um…" Adeline's voice quivered into a trembling sigh until all the troublesome air in her lungs exited her body. Her shoulders raised with a deep breath and her words steadied again.…How are you doing?"

Suddenly those tears exploded once more in Billy. First in his gut and then blazing into his throat. "How am I ?…"

The tears choked him.

"How can ?..."

The tears strangled him.

Billy realized he could not speak.

Instead, he turned to Adeline. Through his tear soaked eyes he saw a bounteous and benevolent seraph staring back at him. Her mere existence next to him unfettered the grasp on his clinched throat.

"How can you ask me that question after what I did?" he asked, glistening tears running down his rosy cheeks.

Adeline respired, unsteady and slow and suddenly she was sobbing too.

She could not look at Billy but reached for his hand, her fingers clasping his hard and tight.

Billy grasped hers and he turned.

Both looked away, as they sat shoulder to shoulder gripping one another desperately to provide and receive some sort of comfort.

"I'm sorry," Billy muttered through his soft wails, "I'm sorry."

Each time he said it, Adeline clasped harder onto his hand.

Finally, Billy sniffled, swallowed hard and wiped the tears away with the back of his free hand. "That's really why I asked you to come…" he said.

Adeline finally placed her eyes on him.

In the black hole of sorrow, Billy suddenly felt a spark of softness and love. The two lovers catching a fleeting glance of one another through a dark foreign haze.

In that moment, Billy prayed he would never have to utter another word to Adeline.

Quiet moments passed, and Billy's prayer, his first prayer in decades, went unanswered. "I have to run," he said.

Adeline nodded prudently.

He waited for her response.

"You were um…you were married in France?" Adeline finally asked.

Billy looked at her confused for a moment. His mind finally caught up with the question. "Yes."

"I am sorry for what happened."

Billy's head rocked slowly back and forth, as if nodding, but perhaps not.

"Did you love her?"

Billy's head rocked a little harder and his lips opened. "I do. I did. I do…" Billy said, realizing his fluent words. Adeline could always turn the key to that impenetrable padlock.

"I'm glad it wasn't all bad for you over there," she said.

Billy's eyes widened and drifted somewhere else. "It wasn't all bad," he said, not to Adeline.

The barn door rocked, creaking in harmony with the howling wind, and shadows from the kerosene lamp fluttered like leaves on a tree.

Billy finally spoke again. "Something I realized, maybe over there, I don't know. You can be sure of something. Have no doubt whatsoever. Then you come to understand something else entirely. And you are once again certain. And then those two things collide and come in complete contradiction with one another. Challenging the very existence of both. But in the end, both can endure. Both can be real."

Adeline studied Billy's baby blues in a way she never had before. He was looking at her with tender, almost deifying eyes, as if they were once again fifteen-year old virgins but lovers still the same. Then she saw something more. A sad wisdom, perhaps.

"I think I follow," she said, kindly.

Billy nodded and looked away, as if there was nothing else to say. He blinked once more, and a final tear escaped.

"When you're out there," she continued, "Whatever happens, just know I forgive you."

Billy returned his eyes to her.

This time, the tears did not rifle in his gut.

Guilt did not compress his brain, and doubt did not drown out his soul.

He reached for her hand, and they held each other once more, in the same barn where two children of a pure and hallowed world unfolded into adults together, and where two wounded and tattered adults now parted, in a dark profane world, to go it alone.

CHAPTER
SEVENTEEN

"Well what did she say?" Jude asked.

Billy hugged his chest tight, and leered off, his eyes narrow, his lips almost pouty.

Jude knew the look too well. The *I ain't giving you a Goddamn inch* look Billy had since the first time his mother probably tried to shove her bosom in his mouth to feed him.

Jude's icy stare did not break. He had plenty of practice with his stubborn stare. The *I ain't moving a Goddamn inch* look he first used on perps, then defendants and hostile witnesses, and sometimes even a judge. Little did any of them unwitting dupes know Jude perfected the look before he hit puberty with his unruly little brother. The unstoppable force against the immovable object.

"See how you are?" Jude continued, his consummate stare as hot as a steam engine, looking at Billy across the table in the same little courthouse room.

Sensing the tension amassing and sizzling, like air particles turning electric before lightning hits, Stanley ceased his note scribbling and looked up between the two. "Billy, I understand the sensitive and personal nature of the conversation between you and Ms. Simon," Stanley said mutedly, unaffected by the brothers stare down. "Jude I understand…"

"…For fuck sake she didn't say nothing." Billy yelped, dropping his chair while standing in the same motion. He put up his hand at Stanley in a *stop* motion and winced, as if truly in pain. "Stanley, please, just shut the fuck up."

Stanley lowered his head and stared at the table.

Jude studied Billy, pleading with the universe for any read on his brother.

Billy now seemed to be in an endless orbit. He paced back and forth between the walls of the cramped room, running his hands through his hair as he circled.

After endless laps, he finally stopped as he stood in the corner, his back to Jude and Stanley.

He lowered his head and buried it in the corner of the coarse wall.

Stanley peered up at Jude, as if trying to comprehend Billy through Jude's appearance.

Jude did not stir, as still as a cat before pouncing.

The back of Billy's shoulders heaved up and then down, between the two cinder block corners, his head so low, it was almost impossible to see his neck.

"She didn't say nothing that leads me to believe she's involved," Billy finally said, his voice low and deadened, like it was buried in those cinder block walls. "Now you can either trust me or you don't but I ain't sayin' no more about it." Billy turned around and his voice shifted. "Jude, I know I got you involved in this now. I know Luisa and the kids are involved in this too…"

Jude fidgeted uncomfortably and cleared his throat.

"…If I thought there was any reason to believe that Adeline, or anyone else threatened our family, your family, I'd tell you and more," Billy said. "I know in the past I've been reckless in certain regards. I know you've probably always thought of me as a liability in some form or another…"

"Billy…" Jude said, standing and placing his hand on his brother's shoulder.

Billy stepped back and scowled, almost pouting. "No, let me finish. I think you always saw me as kind of selfish. Acting in such a way where it was clear that I held no regard for how my actions would impact others. You mostly. Shit, we didn't have no one else. And for the most part all that was probably true. I also know that my present actions of putting your ass back in the ringer just seems like the same old Billy all over again. Now, I ain't about to make some big speech about how I've changed or grown up or nothing. I'm just gonna say, when I saw you at home with your children, your wife, and I saw this beautiful life you now had. A life, I never thought a James boy was capable of having, well, there ain't nothing in the world I would let jeopardize that. Not even Adeline."

Stanley stared down at the table.

Jude nodded slowly and stoically, staring at the floor.

Then he looked up at Billy.

"All right then," Jude said.

CHAPTER
EIGHTEEN

The first day of the trial Jude sat directly behind Billy, in a sign of solidarity. Courtrooms were kind of like sporting events in that way. Everyone on Team Defendant sat behind the defendant's table and everyone on Team Nail His Ass to the Cross said behind the prosecutor's table. But sitting behind Billy only gave Jude a view of Billy's hind side, not allowing him to read his face, his eyes, the way he chewed on his lip.

On the second day, as both teams toddled down the center lane of the courtroom into their respective sides, Jude scooted in behind Phillip and the prosecutor's table. Luisa followed while shooting him a curious look, until they both sat, and her eyes found their way to Billy. She smiled to Jude in a way that only rooted intimate couples do.

Somehow it was suddenly the seventh day of the trial. It happened in both slow motion and at the speed of light at the same time. And by that seventh day, the novel chaos had burned off the jury. They no longer held the deer in the headlights look when they shuffled in each morning. The onlookers in the gallery chatted less and seemed less enthralled by the ordeal. Indeed, the circus shifted to a monotonous and tedious event until that morning.

Jude's clammy hand held Luisa's as they sat waiting for the small Chicano bailiff with a heavy *Norteno* accent and squeaky voice to stand and announce, *All rise!* as the judge entered.

Jude's face was flush, his eyes heavy and his gut empty. Since the trial began, he could barely eat, especially in the morning. By dinner time he would be faint, having to force down a meal simply to subsist.

His eyes found Father Alonzo who sat in the far corner of the room, rosary in his hand every moment since the trial started and nodded. Father Alonzo gazed back at Jude but was not sure if he returned the gesture. Perhaps the old padre was deep in prayer or perhaps the stouthearted son of a bitch was still blaming Jude for this mess.

The jury paraded in first, in an awkward line, one behind the other like a row of ducklings.

Stanley entered next from the side room where he and Billy met each morning. He walked past the jury and scooted into his chair at the defendant's table as Team Billy sat behind separated by a wooden railing rooted with thick posts.

Billy meandered in next. He always seemed to grow shy walking past the jury, Jude thought. Jude wondered if it was a clever ploy by Billy or an old habit? As a child, Billy would commit the most outlandish act and then plunge into a muted shyness. Another paradox of William Tyler James.

Billy caught sight of Jude and Luisa, in the same place they always sat, Luisa dressed to the nines and Jude looking like a tea kettle about to boil over.

As Billy ambled to his seat, he suddenly vaulted over the railing, toppling into the laps of the onlookers while swinging wildly.

Women screamed.

Men gasped.

Chairs fell on the ground, the hollow wood knocking against the wood floor as the swarm stumbled over one another desperately trying to escape Billy's wrath.

Billy managed himself on top of a man, pummeling him with his fist.

Jude leapt from his seat. Through the tumult, all he could see was Billy's tight fist raising in the air before hurling back into someone's face.

Jude shoved his way through the frantic crowd, but the bailiff got to Billy first. He made the mistake of grabbing him to stop. Before he could blink, Billy swung around, landing a hay-maker into the poor steward. He fell backwards over the defendant's table, and toppled to the ground, out cold.

Batons gripped, two sheriffs blasted through doors behind the Judge's bench, rushing to Billy. They did not make the same mistake, the pitbull sheriffs swinging as soon as they were in striking distance.

The first knock on the arm got Billy's attention, before he could turn, the second whack to the head sent him sideways.

The two sheriffs then pounced.

Jude could only see the sticks hoisted wildly in the air, ensuring proper torque, before plunging into the pile of ruckus that was most likely Billy's head and torso.

Jude clenched his fists readying for his plunge into the fray.

Before he could swing, he felt a round blunt force in his gut sending him backwards, stumbling onto his back.

He bent his neck up and found Phillip on top of him-out of breath, frazzled, his eyeglasses sideways across his face. "For God's sake stay down, Jude. Stay down. For your sake and Billy's," he uttered, his eyes pleading, his hands shaking, and his face red.

Jude relented, and from his back, he saw the two cops yank Billy up under his shoulders, his head dangling, barely anchored by his neck, bloody and unconscious.

The mob continued its hysterical retreat.

And Through the chaos…

The feet stepping on Jude.

The legs draping over his face.

With Phillip boorishly floundering on top of him, Jude saw Leslie Dahl.

Still in his seat, cold and almost indifferent if not for the slight grin and the wink he gave Jude when their eyes met.

CHAPTER
NINETEEN

"I represent murderers! And drunks! Thieves and fucking degenerates but I do not represent martyrs! You hear me?" Stanley yelled, shoving his finger into Billy's bruised chest.

It was hard to tell if Billy was wincing from the hard pointed object digging into his tender bole, or if he was trying to shield his eyes from Stanley's teardrop size spit spewing into his face between swear words.

The jail cell was cramped with the three men in it.

Jude hovered in the corner against the rough cinder block wall, arms crossed, his entire body stiff and tight probably to preserve space in the confined box and probably to calm his still fiery nerves.

Stanley bored over Billy, his tall stocky frame almost smothering Billy, as he sat on the jail cell bench still in handcuffs behind his back, defenseless to Stanley's onslaught, his face looking like raspberry jam from the beating and bruising.

"You want salvation well I ain't your Goddamn rabbi! You tell me right now if you're trying to hang yourself. Right fucking now you tell me!" Stanley continued. "Now I know, I've had some defendants who are actually looking for the guillotine. They spend top dollar to retain me and say all the right things about proving their innocence but in reality they're looking for a way out. The easiest way out where they don't have the God-damn guts to do it themselves. Is that you, son? Is that you?"

Billy languished helplessly on the cold metal pew as Stanley's assault continued.

"I asked you a Goddamn question and I've yet to hear a response," Stanley said.

"All right Stanley, that's enough," Jude said, unhinging himself from the corner.

Billy turned his head away from Stanley, as if surrendering entirely to the large bear clawing over him. "That ain't me," Billy muttered.

"What's that?" Stanley asked, still yelling.

"That ain't me. I ain't trying to hang myself," Billy said, his eyes against the wall, away from both Stanley and Jude.

Stanley eased back a bit. "Then you want to tell me what the fuck happened in there?"

Noticing he had more space now, Billy turned back towards the men, and hung his head low between his knees.

Jude patiently studied Billy. He could tell Stanley was about to begin Round Two, so he grabbed his shoulder, pleading in a sense.

Stanley backed off leaning against the same wall as Jude.

"*Que pajo*, Billy?" Jude finally asked.

Billy's drooping head shook sideways slowly between his sulking shoulders.

"Who is that son of a bitch you attacked?" Jude asked after another long silence. He and Stanley reduced to helplessly staring at the top of Billy's head, waiting for a response. Any sort of clarity.

"I don't know," Billy muttered.

Sensing Stanley was about to explode again, Jude grabbed the man by his hulking shoulders and pulled him back. "What do you mean, you don't know?" Jude asked. "Then why did you?.."

"…He…" Billy began to say before turning his head to the wall again. He took a deep breath and then continued. "I don't know who that guy was. I've never seen him before in my life but when I walked into the courtroom this morning and as I passed him, he was…" Billy stopped himself again, as if there was no oxygen left in the room.

"He was what, Billy?" Jude asked, hanging on to every word, every particle of air.

"…He was holding the patch of my brigade in his hand. Right in his palm. He made eye contact with me and then…" Billy sat up now, leaning his head and the top of his shoulders against the wall, with his handcuffed arms and hands under him, his shattered blue eyes directed at Jude and Stanley, bridled no more. "…The fucker spat on the patch. On the same patch worn by 27 of my brothers that died…that I witnessed die over there…"

"He spat on it? You sure it was the same patch?" Jude asked with confusion and disbelief.

"I'm sure," Billy said glaring up at Jude nastily.

"I have no doubt," said Stanley, dropping his head back at the ceiling, exasperated. "Congratulations, gentlemen. The Pinkertons have played you once more."

"They did this just to further harm Billy's character and credibility in the eyes of the jury?" Jude asked. "Is there anything these *culeros* won't do?"

"To answer your second question, I think the answer is no," Stanley said. "To answer your first, the short answer is yes and…" Stanley hunkered down next to Billy, his hands folded across his knees appearing like a doctor about to give a patient the worst possible news. Stanley's merciful eyes draping over Billy, only making him fidget.

"What?" Billy asked.

Stanley turned up to Jude. "I fear a more dire legal strategy at play here, gentlemen. I think this was done to allow Phillip to motion the court to revoke Billy's bail."

Jude cringed.

He bit down so hard on his forefinger, he drew blood.

"So what? Why do they care so much about me being out on bail?" Billy asked.

"They knew you were gonna run," Jude uttered, removing his bleeding appendage, pacing in the little space the cell allowed.

Stanley nodded dismally over and over, while staring at the concrete floor, as if the whole puzzle were coming together before his very eyes.

"Well how did they know that?" Billy asked, looking like a boy who was just told Santa Clause wasn't real.

Jude shot Billy a sinister glare. It was that same look Jude always held immediately before someone was about to lose blood or teeth or the proper bone structure in their nose.

Billy now understood the root of the menacing sneer. "No Jude, no way. It wasn't her," Billy implored.

Jude eyes narrowed, his teeth only grinded harder.

"I'm telling you," Billy said, pleading both to reality and to his brother for fear of what he might do.

"There was no one else Billy…" Jude said, defeated now. "No one else knew besides the three of us and her."

"I don't buy it," Billy said, his eyes whizzing back and forth in his head, as if he was trying to dissect every word, every moment he last shared with Adeline. "I don't buy it," he muttered, more conclusively.

"There ain't nothing to buy, Billy. Your ass has already been sold to the chopping block. I always believed Adeline was a nice girl but there's few things on this planet that are as clear as the Rio Grande or sure as lightning in July. It was always gonna be either you or Adeline's family. Never both. And she was never gonna choose you."

Billy now understood his position, his current circumstance.

There was conceivable no way out.

No angle to save him from the firing squad or the noose or however they decided to ensure his last breath was coming quick.

But in Billy's eyes, Jude saw a deep sadness, a heart-sickened teenage boy forlorn not because of his own impending doom, but the result of a deep penetrating betrayal, and love lost.

CHAPTER
TWENTY

Jude's arms hung outstretched on the table in front of him, his hands clasped together, almost like he was pleading or praying.

He was doing neither.

His eyes were fixated on his hands, now smooth and almost dainty, a lawyer's hands, no longer dry and perpetually cracked from exposure and real work.

Stanley angled his large frame between the two corners of the room.

There was usually a great deal of quiet idle time in these fulgent and cramped quarters, a vivid glimpse of what life will look like next for many poor souls.

Stanley, always wanting to make the most of his time, or rather, *his client's time*, usually spent these long moments reviewing notes, composing new ones, or prying through case law and precedent in search of a last-minute miracle. Today, he stood in the corner, his arms crossed tight, with no notes or case law, knowing the miracle was out of his hands. For a control freak, this distressed him greatly.

The door cracked open, Phillip's eyes teetering in first.

Stanley straightened and opened his hand to Phillip indicating for him to come in and sit across the table from Jude, who did not move or acquiesce to his presence.

Phillip closed the door behind him and took his proper seat. He didn't carry the worn and limber brown satchel he usually plunked up on the table and fumbled through before engaging in negotiation. From his face, you'd think Phillip was the one on trial for murder. Heavy purple bags hung under his weary eyes, his usually scrupulous silver hair now disheveled, as if he just escaped a tornado, and his wrinkles, usually appearing distinguished and flattering, sunk so low into his face, they now looked hoary and decrepit.

A silence fell upon the room.

No one moved, no one took a breath.

Phillip could do nothing but sit across from Jude, stripped and bare, waiting for Jude's call.

Jude's eyes ascended from the table to Phillip in concert with his voice. "You going to kill my brother, Phillip?"

Phillip shifted in his chair, and his eyes darted to Stanley, who provided no desperate support. "Excuse me?" Phillip asked, his eyes returning to Jude.

"You heard what I said." Before Phillip's eyes could escape Jude's fierce and severe scowl again, Jude continued. "Why do you keep looking at Stanley? He can't help you. He can't help you help us."

Resigned and defeated, Phillip's head drooped long and slow like a snow-logged tree branch. "No, Jude, I am not going to kill your brother."

"Good," said Stanley, clearly relieved by Phillip's answer and the fact that he was serviceable and relevant, again. "Then we need to talk about a plea deal," he said, taking a seat.

"What kind of plea deal?" Phillip asked, a mouse-like look, Jude rarely witnessed on the seasoned barrister.

"We know if this goes to verdict, Billy will be in a California collar before the next full moon," Jude said. "Running ain't an option now either after your timely motion…"

"…Jude that…"

"…It's okay, Phillip, ain't no hard feelings. We're passed that."

"Manslaughter, three-five," Stanley interjected, chomping at the bit.

"It's no longer a matter of saving Billy from prison," Jude said. "These bastards may still come after Billy but maybe he goes away for a little while and they'll leave him alone. Leave us alone."

"Also, the time is to be served at the Springer Penn," Stanley said.

"Father Alonzo's brother is the warden there," Jude said. "If the Pinkertons try and come after him in there, maybe he's more insulated."

Phillip blinked hard, his breath fast and raspy.

"I know this still don't guarantee your daughters', your family's, own safety, Phillip," Jude continued, "I know you have to consider them…"

"Those brown-eyed perverse sons of whores are gonna do whatever they please. At least if we go down, we go down upright, swinging," Phillip said.

Jude and Stanley breathed a collective exhale.

"Billy will sign the plea today. We can put it before the bench after the lunch recess," Stanley said.

Color and some vitality returned to Phillip's face. Maybe it was hope. "Off the record?" Phillip muttered, his eyes low and dancing between Jude and Stanley.

Stanley nodded.

"I've talked to Judge Mallik, to Terrance. He'd just assume be done with this as well. He don't want any part in harming Billy. For the sake of appearances, I think it would be best to offer the plea after closing arguments. Stanley, I know you can deliver one helluva an oration. Move the black off a cup of coffee. Without tipping our hand, I'll ensure mine is less than stirring so it looks like that's why we're making the deal."

"Good," Jude said, the vile and stingy scowl still not escaping his mug.

CHAPTER TWENTY-ONE

"It's my understanding the prosecution and defense have reached a plea deal?" Judge Mallik asked, his silver blue eyes hanging over the frame of his glasses, peering down between Stanley and Phillip.

Both men stood in unison.

"Yes, your Honor," Phillip said.

"That is correct, your Honor," said Stanley.

True to his word, Phillip's closing argument was lukewarm at best. True to his form, Stanley's speech was fiery and impassioned, but rational and judicious. If the court was not filled with kangaroos, Jude would have been confident in the verdict.

Judge Mallik lightly bit the top of his lip and turned his eyes back to the plea deal in front of him.

He cleared his throat and looked at Billy.

Cleared his throat again and returned his eyes to the page.

There was something different in them, just then, Jude noticed.

They looked timid and squeamish instead of bullish and robust.

And then Jude realized.

Oh fuck, they got to him too.

Jude's panicky eyes turned to Luisa.

She must have felt them.

She half turned to Jude, keeping one eye on the judge.

Her eyes widened and her grip on his hand grew tight.

She didn't know what was about to happen but the look on Jude's face screamed it wasn't going to be good. Her impassioned stare held on him for guidance or a further clue.

Jude took a long deep breath, sat straight up in the pew and readied himself.

Judge Mallick turned to the jury. "Mr. Stewart," he said to the foreman.

The jury foreman stood. "Yes, your Honor."

Stanley slightly pivoted to Jude.

He knows now too, Jude thought.

"It is my understanding you have also reached a verdict?" asked Judge Mallick.

The older gentleman who knew the brothers his entire life moved his woeful eyes to Billy and then Jude. "Yes, your honor," Mr. Stewart said.

Judge Mallick removed his glasses, tossing them almost carelessly on his bench.

"Considering we have entered almost entirely through trial. Considering the unique facts of this case, and the true question of whether this was murder, manslaughter, or self-defense. And considering the jury has reached a verdict on its own, I am not inclined to usurp the verdict that these twelve individuals have collectively reached together."

Billy swung around in his chair to Jude. The little brother finally catching on and turning to his older sibling to make sense of it all. Billy did not look scared or angry or even betrayed. More heart-breaking to Jude, Billy looked helpless. His eyes screamed out pleading for relief or clarity or aid.

Jude's face tightened, and he fought back the tears he felt coming. He had to be strong, for Billy.

"As such," the judge continued, "I am disinclined to accept the plea deal made between Mr. Weis and Mr. Patterson and I am inclined to allow the defendant to be judged by a jury of his peers, as both the United States

Constitution and the constitution of New Mexico not only allows but champions…”

“Your Honor!” Stanley yelled, his gorilla hands pressed hard against the table, leaning as close as possible to the judge from across the well, “I must object whole-heartedly…”

“The Court does not recognize your objection at this time, Mr. Weis. Sit down.”

“Your Honor, may we approach?..” Phillip muttered.

“No, you may not…” said Judge Mallik.

Phillip sheepishly looked at Stanley from across the aisle as if saying, *I tried.*

Stanley’s face broadened and grew flush, shooting Phillip a menacing look as if it was the poor bastard’s fault.

Stanley turned back to the judge. “Your Honor, I motion for Counsel to speak with you in your chambers.”

“Motion denied. Now sit down. The both of you.”

Judge Mallik turned back to the jury foreman, who stood more nervous and awkward than a cornered kitten in a doghouse.

“Mr. Stewart, has the jury reached a verdict?”

“Your Honor, I must vehemently dispute the Court’s rationale here and further argue how extraordinary, unusual, and unprecedented it is. As such, I insist…” Stanley said.

“You insist? You insist?” Judge Mallik growled.

The judge was gritty and tough but always even-keeled.

Jude had never seen him raise his voice, never mind holler. Those maggots must have borne down on the old judge to turn him so inside out. It was now the judge who was up in his seat, over the bench, vein pulsating through his forehead. “Counsel not another word or I will hold you in contempt!”

“No, your Honor, I hold you in contempt! I hold this entire charade in contempt! I hold each and every one of you cowards in contempt!” Stanley roared. “I hold everyone in this room that has allowed these cretins and foreigners to march into our town and command that we simply fall to our hands and knees in merciless obedience. I find it so regrettably shameful that the one true hero, the one protector of freedom and liberty in this room who sacrificed his mind and body to protect us from these very same forces, will be sacrificed to them because of your cowardice. Shame on you, your Honor! Shame on you!" Stanley seethed, spiking his finger at the judge, sweating, out of breath and literally foaming at the mouth like a rabid dog.

Billy stoically sat in his chair looking up at Stanley stunned and maybe impressed.

Jude scoured the courtroom in search of the Pinkertons, but they were gone.

Only Darcy remained, a haughty grin peeking from his *culero* lips, staring right at Jude.

"That's it! That's it! Bailiff, arrest Mr. Weis for contempt of court!" the judge yelled.

The bailiff rushed toward Stanley, grabbing him with both arms.

The slight Chicano was no match for Stanley's bare brute force, easily shedding the bailiff's clutch.

Phillip fell out of his chair in retreat.

For one brief moment his petrified eyes met Jude's.

Jude had seen Phillip sit across from murders and rapists unshackled without blinking.

Phillip observed executions and he once held the corpse of a slain baby in his shaking hands but in that moment, there was only chaotic horror on his face Jude had never seen. As if someone finally revealed up is down and down is up and the devil is the one true lord and savior.

A second bailiff stormed down the aisle tackling Stanley from behind.

"Mr. Weiss, you are out of order. You are out of order!" yelled the judge as the two bailiffs clumsily wrestled Stanley to the ground.

"No, you're out of order! Kiss my Semitic white ass, your Honor!" yelled Stanley, bending his head up from the ground, one bailiff yanking his arms behind him as the other held a heavy black boot on his head.

Phillip was right about one thing, Billy thought, *at least we went down swinging.*

CHAPTER TWENTY-TWO

"*Kiss my Semitic white ass?*" Billy said, donning an orange prison jumpsuit, shooting Stanley a smartass grin from across the shadowy jail cell.

Stanley removed his glasses and cleaned them with his rumpled untucked shirt.

The cops had taken his suit coat, shoes and belt and he looked more like he had just come from a three-day Tijuana bender, than a trial. What little hair he had left was frizzled up in all directions, and his face was still red.

"Not one of my finer moments," Stanley said, diligently trying to wipe away the smudge from his bent frames.

Billy pursed his lips and shook his head. "No. I was impressed. Didn't know you had it in you, counselor."

From his bent frames and smeared lens, Stanley shot him a condescending look.

Billy picked up on it. "No, um…I'm serious. Means a lot that you actually care."

"Of course I care," Stanley said, not content with his cleaning job, impotently fixing the glasses. "You're my client."

"All right, yeah I know the game. You can act all macho or nonchalant, but it was more than that."

Stanley relented. He tossed the glasses across the small cell, leaned against the steel bars behind him and looked at Billy. "My parents came from Russia. Their parents and their parents were farmers. Worked their hands to the bone everyday their entire life to save every nickel they could. My grandparents gave that money to my parents, and they started a grocery store in a town close to where the farm was. Most of what they sold came from the farm. It all came from their own grit and hard work. Then one day the Tsarist Autocracy rolls into town and takes everything from everyone," Stanley said, snapping his fingers. "Just like that. *Fuck you, we're taking it.* My parents escaped. They took the little money they had and got to New York. Again, they started a small grocery store, this time in Brighton Beach. I grew up first stocking the shelves, then running the cash register. Then one day, some fellow in an expensive suit and a fat face walks in and tells my parents that every week, they have to pay him. Again, *fuck you, we're taking it.* He says it's for protection. My father pulls a lead pipe out from under the counter and says, 'I treat everyone fairly and if anyone feels differently I have my protection right here.' The pig-faced motherfucker then pulls a pistol from his waistband and lays it on the counter, pointing the barrel directly at me. He says, 'How's that lead pipe look now?' I watched that same indolent lazy piece of horse-shit stroll down the street every week, his fat gut hanging over his pants, walking gingerly because his fat fucking pig feet don't fit in his expensive leather shoes, huffing and puffing out of shape from never working a real day in his life, shaking us all down. Once in while, someone would have enough and tell the magot fuck where he could stick it. They usually got one warning before their business or home was burned to the ground, didn't even matter if there were people inside, even children."

"The mob?" asked Billy.

Stanley hunkered down across from Billy. "Yea. Maybe. I don't know. Doesn't matter. You see, tyranny comes in all guises. Government and politicians, the tax man, the generals, the wealthy and elitists, even the Goddamn church. For years, even in my juvenile head, I plotted to kill that man, but deep inside I held the sad understanding that the fat fuck was irrelevant. I kill him, and the next day there is a new fat fuck, just as ugly with the same torrid breath, with his fat fucking fingers in the till. I kill him, and there's another and another. I would never have a big enough gun or magazine to eliminate every one of those thieves. And the way tyranny works, they control the system. I manage to put a bullet between the eyes of one of them, and I meet Old Sparky or spend the rest of my life in prison. I realized the real weapon to fight these parasites was within the system. I know it's not a perfect weapon or a perfect system, but it always at least gave us a fighting chance…until today. This trial, this lynching, these Pinkerton rat bastards…"

"I think it's you who miss the point," Billy said.

"How's that?"

"The Pinkertons are just soldiers taking orders, no different than me taking orders over there. They ain't the problem, not really, they're just grunts like the rest of us."

Stanley exhaled deeply, the air in his lungs trembling. He shook his head slightly and his face grew cherry-red again.

"Don't fucking do it," Billy said noticing the shift in Stanley's mug. "Don't fucking say it."

"I'm sorry, Billy. I'm truly sorry I could not help you here."

"What the fuck did I just say, Stanley? You know, the one good thing about them stringing my ass from the tree tomorrow is that I won't have to hear people tell me they're sorry anymore. Least I hope not."

Stanley sat up on the bench, raised his chin, and looked Billy directly in the eye from across the gloomy cell. "Son, whatever it is you did over there that you feel an enormous guilt about, it doesn't have anything to do with what they're going to do to you tomorrow. I hope to God you recognize that before that rooster crows."

"Maybe you're right but that ain't the end of your story either."

"How do you mean?"

"Your God don't believe in hell right?"

"'*My* God?' Have you read the Old Testament, my God, our God," Stanley said, pointing inanely at himself and Billy, "Is extremely vengeful."

"I misspoke. Your people don't believe in hell. After you die."

"Oh. Yes. That is correct."

"And yet you hold a tremendous amount of guilt over something. You still feel like you got some making up to do."

Stanley brought his long legs up on the bench, rested his forearms on his knees hunched over, and looked off.

"I heard your story about the Russian autocrats and the shake-down bums in Brighton and that's all probably well and true but there's something else you ain't right with," Billy said. "I do appreciate your hard work. I do appreciate you giving so much of a shit that they threw you in the same cell with a guy they convicted of cold-blooded murder but it ain't about me, or the tyranny of evil men or anything else. Whatever it is you're trying to make up for, it ain't on you, and I hope you realize that after some rooster crows someday or you're gonna be a miserable son of a bitch for the rest of your natural life and that's probably the greatest sin of all."

Stanley stared off somewhere between the cold steel bars, down the narrow dim hallway where the one orange light casted shadows on the old oak wall. Passed the door with the little gray window, and well beyond freedom on the other side.

CHAPTER
TWENTY-THREE

*J**esus Christ, the old Padre's truck needed new shocks.* Jude thought. *How could he constantly subject himself to banging around like this on the holes, and the washboard and the fucking arroyos?*

As Jude tried to sturdy himself from helplessly bouncing up and down in the pickup cab he suddenly felt an overwhelming guilt for allowing Father Alonzo's truck to digress into its current state. For years, every six months, like clockwork, Jude and Luisa would travel the crude and loutish road in Ranchos de Taos to pick up Father Alonzo's truck so Jude could service it. It wasn't like the good padre was churning out miles cruising for women or running *mota* from Mexico. Sometimes there was less than one hundred miles on the vehicle since the last time Jude wrenched on it, but that wasn't the point.

When did he stop and why? Jude honestly could not remember the last time he changed the oil on the truck. What the fuck was he doing that was suddenly so important instead?

And then he remembered.

Jude didn't know if other people could definitively identify the hardest most painful moment in their life. Perhaps a family member dying? A spurned lover? Jude probably could not pinpoint that moment in his own life…until tonight. Desperately holding Wyatt, and Patrick and Luisa so tight that he thought one of them would pop out of his arms and hit their head on the ceiling.

Jude had prayed before. He could not remember a time in his Catholic life when he did not. He said his Hail Marys and Our Fathers. He prayed for forgiveness and sometimes made requests to God. He remembered silly petitions, as a child, like sparing his ass from too many lashes with the leather belt when he did something wrong and heard the old man coming up the stairs. As a hormone filled teenager, he begged God that someday he would get to place his hands on Sally Brant's supple breasts. Of course, he prayed that his children would remain happy and healthy, and he and his wife would remain in love.

He never prayed about work or money. Didn't seem right plus, there would always be bad guys so he would always have work. He only prayed, when the time came, he was faster than the bad guys, and so far, the Good Lord had abided.

But with all the other countless pleas and prayers Jude made to God in his thirty-four years, he was quite sure he never truly *prayed for something* until tonight when he kissed his wife goodbye, took one long measured look at his beautiful perfect family, and begged the Good Lord to see them again.

If Jude's God were a bartering God, the moment he closed the door to his family, he realized there was almost nothing he wouldn't do to see them again. Almost. But it wasn't even a barter, or a choice and Jude was infinitely grateful Luisa understood that, as well.

Jude turned to Father Alonzo, hunched over the wheel, his owl eyes engrossed by the darkness in front of him, steering the allegiant chariot with a shotgun across his lap.

Was Father Alonzo praying right now? Jude asked himself. If so, what was he praying for? That they would be successful. That he would not have to kill a man? Suddenly, Jude found himself making the same request.

"*Padre?*" Jude asked, the words slipping out, almost unconscious.

Father Alonzo's deep and steady black eyes turned to Jude as the truck rumbled along.

"If you commit a heinous act, something truly terrible, but it's for the sake of a greater good, is it still a sin?" Jude asked.

Father Alonzo turned back to the road in front of him. "That is a reasonable and appropriate question, *mijo*, but it is not a question that will be of any help to us right now."

Jude exhaled deeply and snapped the cylinder from the six-shooter he held in his hand, ensuring once again that every chamber was loaded. "Amen."

The lime green pickup rattled to a stop in front of Jude's old sheriff's office. The streetlights on each side of the plaza set a blaze of white below them with darkness in between where the truck sat running.

Jude peered out towards one side of the street and then the other.

It was a quiet night, aside from the murmuring of a few drunks down the alley hooting from the Cantina. Jude drank, even heavily at times, but he hated drunks. The first one he ever hated, his own father. Tonight, however, he was grateful some tottering imbecile was clamoring on somewhere, so he didn't have to hear that deafening eerie silence that always fell upon him before it got real.

Jude shifted his focus to the thick brown door of the Sheriff's office and the dull yellow light that cracked out from the small window centered in the door. Jude always believed in an open-door policy, literally. Anyone could walk up to the Sheriff's door, dead of night or broad daylight, and find it open with a deputy waiting to serve. He prayed to God that Landry continued that policy. He still had a key to the door, assuming it did not change, but fumbling with that old lock would eliminate the element of surprise.

"You sure you want me to stay here?" Father Alonzo asked, holding the shotgun tight.

"Yes, I'm sure. You and the Holy Spirit just keep this old girl running and ready for when we come storming out," Jude said.

Father Alonzo's brown leather face below his short salt and pepper hair was stiff and motionless. He appeared more like a cold-blooded military assassin than a priest. "*Bueno.*"

"*Bueno*," Jude said, more to himself.

He took a long breath, and before he exhaled, he was out of the truck and across the street.

Before he could blink, he had swung the door open, and was pointing his large pistol inside the quaint and tidy sheriff's office.

The sheer force of Jude storming through the door startled Landry right out his chair, feet already on the desk, he was upside down on the floor before he knew it with Jude standing over him.

One pistol aimed squarely on Landry, Jude's eyes scanned the room as he pulled a second from his left holster.

"Jude?" Landry squealed from the ground.

"Don't fucking move, Landry. If you know what's good for you, don't fucking move," Jude said.

Landry curled up helplessly on his back toward Jude, his open hands shaking. "What in God's name are you doing?"

"If God had anything to do with this, we wouldn't be here right now. You alone?"

Landry nodded nervously.

Jude scanned the room again, while keeping one of his two compadres on Landry.

He noticed the coat rack in the corner had two coats on it. "Goddamn it, Landry, who else is here?"

Before Landry could answer, a toilet flushed and clanged.

Jude moved his eyes to the bathroom door between him and Landry. "You say one word, I swear I'll put a bullet in you. I'll only need one," Jude whispered.

Landry's head shook again indicating he probably just browned his pants and that he understood.

Jude bent his pistols so one remained steady on Landry and the other on the john's door.

The door opened and a portly white cop bumbled out still rubbing his hands from washing them.

He took two steps before even noticing Jude. "Holy shit!" he yelled, staggering back, before reaching for his side piece on his belt.

"Hank! You put your hands in the air! You put em up!" Jude said, aiming the second pistol square at Hank.

Hank's arms trembled and his hands floated at his sides, in no man's land. His rosy plum cheeks and green eyes gaped at Jude in bewilderment and shock.

"Hank, you listen to me and you listen good. There's no way you draw on me here. There are no options. You have three seconds to put your hands in the air or I put three bullets in you and a fourth in Landry before he can even draw his next breath."

The pupils of Hank's eyes moved to Landry for guidance.

"Why you looking at him, Hank?" Jude yelled. "He ain't the one with the gun pointed at ya."

Hank's fingers danced at his side, and his legs got shaky.

Jude knew what was next. "Goddamnit, Hank, don't make me do it… One.."

Hank's shoulders tightened up.

His lips quivered.

And those portly fingers inched closer to his gun.

"Fuck you, Hank. Don't make it do. Two! …"

The air got still. Even the dust did not move.

Jude turned his head ever so slightly, readying.

"Oh God!" Hank shrieked, throwing his arms in the air squealing, flinching as if he had already been shot.

"It's okay, Hank, it's okay," Jude said calmly, his tone shifting immediately. "You're still alive. We all are. Hank, you just hold up there for a second. Don't go anywhere, okay?"

Hank opened one eye slightly, peaking at Jude to see if he was serious.

"Landry, slowly, very slowly, I'd like you to stand up, but you keep both those fucking hands above you, you understand? They even try and move south, and I'll send a bullet straight to your chest," Jude voiced commanding but calm.

Landry nodded.

"All right then, we're all in this together," Jude said.

Landry's legs shook like a cold dog trying to cross a gushing river as he stood, keeping his arms in the air and his eyes glued on Jude.

"Good," said Jude, "Now very slowly, and I mean slower than a bug on a rug, Landry, I want you to reach down and unhinge your holster. Just let it drop to the ground. Hank, moving even crosses your mind and a bullet will meet you on the other side before you have time to finish that thought. You hear me?"

Hank nodded.

"Good," said Jude.

Landry slowly reached down and unhooked his holster belt.

The guns made a loud hollow thump when they hit the wood floor.

"All right. You did real good, Landry. Hank it's your turn now."

Hank's head bobbed and shivered indicating he understood.

As he gradually lowered his arms, Jude noticed Hank's index finger curling and then all five fingers on his firing hand.

"Hank! What did I tell you about thinking! Your hand reaches any closer for that butt and I'll paint the wall with your insides, you hear me?"

Hank's Irish eyes looked like granny smith apples, they were so round and wide.

The room went silent for Jude.

He no longer heard the hum of the swinging light bulb above.

The buzz of the small refrigerator that kept the constables' sipping beer cold, or the creaky floorboards below.

Jude zeroed in on each and every bead of sweat running down Hank's fleshy face and each moment his chest indented as he breathed in and arched when he breathed out. Everyone always took their longest breath before making their move, as if they somehow knew it would be their last.

"Hank, in two seconds it's gonna be too late. In three seconds you'll already be dead on the floor, and in four seconds, so will your partner and pal. In five seconds, your kids ain't gonna have a daddy no more and your wife will be a widow. Is that what you want?"

Hank's fingers relaxed and his arms quavered, shedding them into the air. "Oh Goddamn you, Jude," he whimpered. "I can't... I can't reach for my belt... I can't..."

"Okay, I understand," Jude said, inching closer to Hank while holding one cannon on him, the other on Landry. When Jude got to reaching distance, he stretched over to Hank and unhooked the holster.

"Oh God!" Hank screeched at the sound of the guns hitting the floor.

"It's okay," Jude said, backing away again, "You're a brave man, Hank Basby. Anyone in their right mind would squirm staring down a barrel.

Now both of you slowly walk over to that desk and take out your handcuffs…"

Billy and Stanley must have heard Jude's bellowing voice giving orders. Both men stood in the cell looking like chained dogs at the end of their leash.

"Jude, what the fuck is going on?" Billy asked as Jude fumbled with the cell keys.

"I'm getting you out," Jude blurted, his focus manically on finding the right key.

Billy looked over Jude's shoulder past the hallway to the office door.

"They're all right," Jude said, noticing.

He finally found the right key, sending it into the hole in the same moment he pulled the cell door open.

Billy popped out and Jude handed him the second pistol.

"It's ready if you need it," Jude said. "Stanley, I ain't gotta tell you that you didn't break no laws here."

"Yes, I'll be staying," said Stanley. "I'd ask what you got planned, Jude, but I don't want to know."

"Better if you don't," said Jude, tipping his hat. "I appreciate everything you did for us. You gave it your best. More than one way to skin a deer. We tried it your way, now the knife's in my hand. No shame in that."

Billy turned around to Stanley, looking him square in the eye. "You hear what my brother said?"

"I do," said Stanley exchanging the same steady eye. "Good luck out there."

Billy nodded and both men turned to run, before Billy bent back to Stanley. "What was it? If you don't mind, what was it?"

Jude head's nervously pivoted lost and confused. "Billy what the fuck?"

Billy stared unrelenting at Stanley while throwing Jude the finger. His entire snubbing gesture indicating, *I don't know about you, but I got all night, cabron.*

Stanley stepped back, inhaled deeply while his shoulders sank with his head. And then he raised both and looked Billy square in the eye. "When I was eighteen, I started pushing back against those clowns. My parents kept telling me to leave it alone, but I thought I was a tough guy, could teach them a lesson. My parents begged and begged but I wouldn't listen."

Stanley turned his head away.

He gathered himself and straightened again.

"Then one night, my younger sister was walking home. It wasn't late or anything, she was just coming home and three of those animals jumped her, dragged her into an alley and raped her. When they were finished, one of them filthy dago bastards whispered into my sister's ear. 'Consider this the last message we're gonna give your brother.'"

Billy stuttered back, sympathy and accord in his eyes, meeting Stanley's one last time. "I can tell you, that ain't on you, but it won't matter," Billy said.

Stanley pursed his lips and shook his head, *no*.

"Well, I'm gonna say it anyway, Stanley. In a world of dirty animals and rabid devils, there are few good men ambling among them. Trying to stay clean and unscathed. Stanley Weiss, you're one of them."

"As are you, son. As are you," Stanley said.

Jude curiously studied both of them before grabbing Billy by the shoulder.

Big brother leading the way, they flung open the jail door and swiftly sailed through the office. As Billy ambled by, he quickly glanced at the two cops chained to the wall with handkerchiefs stuffed in their mouths.

The brothers busted out the door, the cold air stinging on Billy's face reminding him he was still alive.

Billy noticed the old green pickup running, and the priest's tiny gray head hovering in the cab. "You got Father Alonzo to help bust me out? You're really going to hell," Billy said, slipping and sliding on the snow and ice as they crossed the street to the waiting padre.

"You ain't got no other friends, asshole," Jude called over his shoulder, "And we needed a getaway driver."

Suddenly, a state police car spun around the corner into the plaza, their headlights inadvertently centering on the two men like spotlights of a Broadway show.

Perhaps a man running down the street with a gun in his hand would only stir moderate curiosity from ordinary police, in a town of gunslingers, cowboys, Taos Pueblo and vigilantes.

However, a man bolting down the street in a prison jumpsuit and a piece would scream alarm even to the slowest wit deputy, never mind a statey.

Their sirens *blooped blooped* in the same moment their screeching tires skidded across the ice of the pavement.

The passenger door swung open, and the state police yelled, "Stop right there. Stop right there or I'll shoot!"

Anticipating the shots, Billy and Jude ducked their heads as they crossed into the plaza toward the truck.

Bang. Bang. Bang.

Three rounds rattled out.

The shots echoed around the plaza as if the boys were surrounded.

Billy peered over his shoulder just enough to see the police with his car door open, firing over it.

Zing. Zing.

Billy heard two bullets wiz by his head.

The two boys were almost to the truck. So close, Billy could see Father Alonzo's white clerical collar in the cab.

Zing.

Another bullet hissed past in the same moment Father Alonzo hopped out of the truck, swung the long-barreled shotgun over the hood of the truck, steadying it for a moment before *BOOM.*

Billy felt the heat of the blast sail by in the same moment he heard an explosion of glass behind him.

He shifted around to see the police window shattered, a leery officer hunkering behind.

He heard the shotgun cock again and turned around to see Father Alonzo, *BOOM*, firing another round.

TINK TINK TINK TINK TINK

The metal on metal sounded from the buckshot hitting the cop car.

Billy peeked around to see the second cop taking refuge behind the car.

"That's enough cover, Father!" Jude yelled, arriving at the truck first, then motioning for Billy to hop in. "We don't wanna create any angels tonight!"

Father Alonzo sent another cannon blast at the car for good measure and then jumped into the driver's seat and shut the door.

Billy dived into the dark cabin.

As Jude went to hop in, two bullets zipped past him and *PING PING*, into the cab.

He swung around firing before he could even blink.

And then he remembered who he was firing at.

Holding for a moment, almost praying his deadly aim was not so deadly.

Both shots whizzed by the officers and Jude took a breath before emptying the rest of the revolver around the cops' feet. Watching the lively souls dance.

CHAPTER TWENTY-FOUR

"What the fuck did you two *cabrons* do?" Billy yelled.

The truck rattled and shook, the men's bodies bouncing and banging into one another, helpless to the unsteady path before them.

"I think it's pretty clear what we did," Jude said, almost in a whisper.

"Fuck you both, you had no right! No fucking right!" Billy said, his scowl teetering between the two.

Jude leaned his right shoulder into the corner of the cab, elbow wedged on the thin window sill, hand gripped flat to the cab's ceiling, a futile attempt to hold still in the rickety speeding vessel. .

Father Alonzo leaned over the helm of the truck, perhaps in pain from the gut shot, perhaps to ensure the truck was as aerodynamic as possible in their getaway. He held his left hand on the top of the wheel, while cupping his right over his bleeding wound. The blood had soaked through the makeshift bandage Billy had fashioned with a shirt, a trick he learned in the war.

Even in the stark darkness, Billy could see sweat running down the side of the priest's face, and he knew it was only a matter of hours or he was really going to be in trouble.

Billy had never seen the priest perspire even when chopping dense pinon in the blistering sun or standing over sweltering tar as a roofer. Then again, he had never seen the priest operate a 20-gauge shotgun before either.

"You had no right!" Billy emphasized again.

"There was no way we were just gonna sit back and let those sons of bitches hang your ass," Jude said soberly.

"You should have asked me. You should of told me. I had three days rotting in that cell when you could have come to me and let me know what you were thinking. What you were planning."

"I know what you would have said, and I wouldn't put it past your stubborn ass to announce our plans to the world just to ensure we couldn't go through with it," Jude said.

"You're Goddamn right!.."

"…. Billy…" Father Alonzo scolded.

"Jude, you got more important priorities than your fucked up *hermanito*. You had your wife and kids, your family to consider."

"You are family, you ungrateful son of a bitch. And you ain't fucked up. No more than the rest of us…"

"And you," Billy said, turning to Father Alonzo, "You've lived your whole life as a holy and righteous man only to let me drag you down to hell with the rest of us sinners."

"We are all sinners," Father Alonzo muttered, not breaking his stare from the frosty windshield guarding the men from the black cold night surrounding them.

"Maybe, but you ain't killers! Not like me! Did Luisa even know what you were planning?"

"Of course she did. What kind of husband and father do you think I am?"

"And she just went along with this?"

"She went along with *us* protecting *our* family. Now you call into question any further me being a good husband or father and I'll put your fucking head through the windshield, you hear me?" Jude said.

"You sons of bitches," Billy seethed, his eyes turning red and teary. "I made peace with everything I did before you two came blasting in tonight. And now… I have all this new shit on me. Shit, I'll never be able to make it right. I've ruined your lives and the life of your wife and kids, Jude."

"Have I taught you nothing, Billy?" Father Alonzo asked dryly.

"Clearly not. You're talking to a Goddamn murderer."

"William, you take His name in vain one more time, and I will be the one that puts your head through the windshield," Father Alonzo said, before taking a deep breath and composing himself again. "Of all the gifts God has given us, even the most sacred sacrament he endowed to his only son, was the gift of free will. At any point while Jesus hung from the cross for those three agonizing days, he had the free will, the choice to end his own suffering. When the devil confronted Jesus in the desert, Jesus was also presented with a choice. A choice even God did not know the result of. I truly believe that God himself, our all-knowing Creator, does not force our hand, he allows us the free will to choose. Your brother, and his wife, chose to help you. With my own free will, I chose to help you. We understood there would be consequences, and with our own free will, we made our choice as well."

The tone in Father Alonzo's voice, his steady sermon in the wobbly cab speeding down the vague dirt road while bleeding from a bullet lodged somewhere in his intestines quieted Billy. Part of going to Catholic school required daily mass which Billy despised more than most. He would fidget, and then get slapped by the nuns. He would shuffle the pages of the missalette and then get slapped by the nuns. He would innocently stare up at the ceiling, directly where he believed God to be, and get slapped by the nuns.

Billy never registered a single word from any priest as they reverently floated on their raised pulpit, speaking gibberish in their silly gown, except when Father Alonzo said mass. He did not conduct mass often. He preferred the noble trades of carpentry and roofing, laboring elbow to elbow with the flock, even having a Budweiser or two sharing dirty jokes on a Friday afternoon as their weary legs dangled from the beams of the construction site. But when the nebulous chanting of the hymns and the gibberish of the Old and New Testament readings were finished and Father Alonzo shuffled to the podium and his lips started moving, Billy actually heard words. Words that formed sentences and sentences that shared feelings of sadness, doubt, pain, life. Even as a ten-year old boy, he understood it and tried to grasp it. Perhaps Father Alonzo spoke the language of the common man because he spent so much time with them. Or perhaps, Father Alonzo spoke the same language, had the same blisters on his hands from holding the hammer and struggled with the same plight, because he was a common man.

Billy never heard a single fucking order from the generals that barked. Never cared to comprehend a piece of intel from the mouth of the tactical commander holding the absurd tiny wand in his hand, slapping it at the equally ridiculous map behind him. But when his sergeant opened his mouth, Billy clung onto every syllable, even as exploding bombs shattered their eardrums, and bullets whizzed by their head. The sergeants, like Father Alonzo, was the common man and spoke the real gospel to Billy's heart, to his soul, and kept his ass alive and whole.

Billy held still for a moment before speaking. "So where are we headed? I assume you two crazy sons of bitches have a plan?"

"You and I are headed to Denver, then Chicago. If all goes well, that will be the end." Jude said.

"What the hell is in Chicago?" Billy asked.

"The Goddamn Pinkerton agency…" Jude said.

Father Alonzo turned his scathing eyes across the cab at Jude.

"Shit. Sorry, Father," Jude continued.

"I don't understand," Billy said.

"We are gonna try and make a deal with them. I tried to cut off the head of the beast. I scoped out Darcy's house for weeks, without telling you, but they had that place looked down tighter than a steel trap. We decided on Plan B."

"Which is?"

"Before we stopped by your office tonight, Father Alonzo and I paid a visit to Camilo. After some enhanced conversation, he gave up how much Darcy paid the Pinkertons for all of their hard work in this matter. We ain't gonna get to Darcy and I'm not sure if it would matter if we could. So instead we're gonna have a face-to-face with Allan J. Pinkerton III. All these whores care about is money so, we're gonna bring him a whole lot more than what Darcy paid them."

"How we gonna do that?"

Jude only answered with a sharp eye and a deep sigh.

"Luisa and the kids? Billy asked.

"They're safe, headed somewhere even the Pinkertons will never know to look," Jude said.

"And you?" Billy asked Father Alonzo.

"Me?" said Father Alonzo, "I'm gonna try and not die before the good nuns at the San Isidro monastery can dig this Goddamn slug out of my gut."

CHAPTER
TWENTY-FIVE

The three nuns stood stoic and seemingly unaffected by the presence of newly christened outlaws, each holding a dangling black rosary, their quiet magnified eyes drifting over the men through their soda-bottle sized glasses. They looked more like *abuelitas*, all Hispanic with ankle-length brown gowns and their long hair tied neatly in a bun, than the traditional nuns Billy and Jude were accustomed to with their imposing tunics, cowls, and hoods.

The *monastery* was as modest and humble as the nuns, an adobe casita with a barn. Only the large cross above the exterior of the front door and the small wooden sign reading *Protection of the Holy Virgin Mary Monastery* gave any indication it wasn't just an old mud hut

What the sign ought to read Billy thought, staring at the hanging placard, was *Protection of Three Dumb-Fucks Who Are In Way Over Their Head.*

They were barely forty miles over the Colorado border, surrounded in the same mountain range, standing over the same dirt, and under the same sky, and yet everything felt different for Billy. The mountains seemed sharper, less kind and rolling. The moon duller and less brilliant, and the stars didn't quite shine so bright. Even the air was less crisp and savory, perhaps from the lack of pinon scenting the atmosphere.

Billy had not reached the point of gratitude for his brother's heroic and straight-up ballsy act, but he did appreciate Jude's awareness to bring his favorite black leather boots and jacket. He recalled the first time he was forced to remove his boots that seemed more like an extension of his foot, strapping on the stiff and foreign *zapatos* the drill sergeant threw in his face. He remembered the soft leather sleeve of his jacket caress against his arm for the last time before sliding on the starchy and rough uniform. It was only in that moment Billy recognized the gravity of his decision.

Even after being arrested, even after being charged with murder, it was only when Billy's bail was revoked, and his boots and jacket poached from him by the prison guards, did the sobering reality of consequence reach him. Billy felt more comfortable now because of the jacket that hung from his shoulder and boots tied to his feet.

Billy's prison garb was now reduced almost to ash on top of the crackling fire. He watched the last of the orange fabric succumb to the flame, crinkling before being released as smoke to drift into the ether for eternity.

"Here," Jude said, tossing a heavy leather bag into Billy's gut, snapping him out of his gaze.

Billy's eyes drifted to the bag, half unzipped and filled with their family's collection of pistols and rifles, and boxes of bullets and ammunition.

Before Billy could respond, Jude hopped in the truck, steering it into the barn as Father Alonzo pulled an old maroon Chevy out.

Jude shut off the truck and exited the barn heaving one side of the door towards the middle while Father Alonzo shoved the other. When closed, the two men slid a large plank over the door, locking it in unison.

Since the jail break, it seemed the two men had a plan and Billy was just along for the ride. He sucked in a deep breath of remorse and contrition for being the catalyst of the journey these men were now on, and in that moment, the stinging in his lungs reacquainted him with the frigid early April air, the cloudless night providing no canopy of warmth. Billy noticed the nuns all wore sandals and he wondered how they were not cold? Perhaps they were just as unmoved by the frosty temperature as they were aiding and abetting criminals.

Suddenly, Father Alonzo's arms were wrapped around Billy, the old man hugging him as he awkwardly stood holding the bag of weapons. He let go of the bag, the metal clanging as it hit the dirt, and carefully embraced the padre, ensuring not to strike his wound.

As they held each other, and Billy felt his chin on the padre's shoulder, he realized how small the man was. He had always seemed so impressive and lofty before.

Father Alonzo stepped back and placed both hands on Billy's shoulders.

Billy looked down at his friend's blush souvenir, growing by the moment, through the wrap.

"Don't worry," Father Alonzo said, "It ain't the first time I've been shot."

"Maybe so, but that slug don't know that," Billy said.

"I'm in good hands. These sisters once dug a bullet out of Pancho Villa. Another, out of Teddy Roosevelt." Father Alonzo then paused, weighing the concern on Billy's face. "You are a good man, William. Your only real sin is you not recognizing that."

Billy's eyes fell to the dirt, not able to look at the priest.

Father Alonzo lightly padded Billy on the cheek. "*Orale, mijo,*" he said, causing Billy to look back up at him. "I almost killed a man tonight. And I will have to ask God for forgiveness. There are no excuses for sin, but I did not fire at him in vain. I did what I did to protect a righteous man. *Un hombre bien.* I don't know what God has planned for you and your brother next, but I know that you two will need each other to stay alive, to remain upright and honest. Whatever happens out there, God will forgive you. You will need to forgive yourself if you two have any chance to survive."

PART

THREE

THE RUGGED ROAD AHEAD

CHAPTER
TWENTY-SIX

"You ever been to Denver?" Billy asked, as the city lights began to sparkle in front of them on the horizon.

"Yea, a few times. You?

Billy nodded. "A couple. Addy and I would come up once in a while to get a taste of the big city."

"That's right. I remember that."

"Strange town," Billy said, glaring out the windshield, darkness in between the illumination of the headlights and the city in the distance.

"I don't disagree but what makes you say that?"

"I don't know. I could never put my finger on it exactly. Just seemed like I always got in fucking trouble there."

Jude turned to his brother with a dubious grin, as he drove. "Billy you got in fucking trouble everywhere."

Billy shook his head. "It's different in Denver. Everyone there seems like Good Ole Boys, like we grew up with in Taos, at least the *gavachos* you know?"

"Yea?" Jude asked and agreed.

"They dress the same, work the same, drink the same but they ain't humble like us. Act like their shit don't stink or their God's gift to this fucking world because they're from Colorado. Who gives a shit about Colorado?" Billy asked.

"Coloradans, it sounds like. I assume you brought this very important question up to a Coloradan or two, probably in a bar-like setting, and I'm sure they welcomed such a thoughtful and significant inquiry with open-arms."

"More like closed fists," Billy said.

The brothers grinned as they moved through the night.

"You think Addy gave me up?" Billy asked after a long moment.

"*No se*," said Jude. "And I guess it don't matter what I think."

"Guess it don't matter what I think either."

Billy stared out the passenger side window. There was only black, not even moving shadows or vague objects passing by the car speeding along the road, just flat broad obscure black.

A silence fell between the two until Billy muttered, "Just seems like there ain't nothing I can know as true anymore. Maybe we're all just as fucked up as the next. I sit in my head with these dark thoughts, confusing fucking feelings, and then eventually, more often than not, I pull myself out of it, just before it's too late. I'll put my boots on, go for a walk, have a smoke, and I'll see people promenading down the street holding hands, happy, their arms swaying like a child's play swing. I say, 'My God those people have never even had a word of the ideas that float into my head, them lucky sons of bitches.' I'll sit and have a cold beer at the bar and see two old-timers laughing, slapping one another on the back, and I say 'Them men been on this earth at least twice as long as me, seen more than I prolly ever will, and yet this world didn't drag them down. Here they are, not a fucked up thought between them, laughing at the ugliness of it instead.' And then I get envious, fucking jealous. Never wanted to be someone else, not even when we was kids going to school bare-foot and hungry while them well-to-do *cabrons* were throwing away half their lunch and running around in shiny boots and fancy clothes. Like they bought everything in the fuckin Sears catalogue. But there I would sit, contemplating walking over and punching one of them old timers in the face, just so maybe he can feel pain like I feel pain. But then I realize, it ain't the same. I walk out to the plaza, sit on a bench and my heart warms watching youngsters running around, laughing, playing, chasing one another with drool hanging from their face, grinning ear to ear and I think the world is a beautiful place, and I'm what's ugly in it. Even the war-there's always been war, there's always gonna be war but humanity ain't defined by it. But after it was over and I've come home, nothing makes sense no more and I've come to a very disturbing realization…"

Jude chewed on the left side of his lip, steering his eyes as straight ahead as the wheel, fearful if he turned them to Billy, he would see a man, his brother, broken and dejected, and he would break down and cry. Wail because his brother was in so much pain, and bellow because there was nothing Jude could do to help him. He could break him out of jail, unshackle the cold and heavy chains around his wrists, but he held no gun or key that could unshackle what weighed so heavy on Billy's imprisoned mind.

"What realization?" Jude finally forced himself to ask.

"Everyone is just as fucked up as I am. They may walk down the street smiling. They may be able to gaze into the eyes of their lover, wooing and gentle and kind, but they have that darkness in their minds too, they just maybe hide it better than me. It's a wonder humanity has survived this long…"

The German doctor that treated their mother when she got really bad warned their father, the illness could be hereditary. Jude remembered hearing that, eavesdropping down the long echoing and stale hallway of the asylum. For a while after, any time he felt sad, he wondered if it was Pandora's box opening in his head, the beginning of the madness, the end of his sanity. Never mind that most boys felt similar with news of playing second baseman when he wanted to be a pitcher, or Mary Beth holding hands with Stevie Dwyer on the walk home instead of Jude James.

Eventually, Jude came to understand, just because he had emotions it didn't mean he was emotionally disturbed, or mentally ill. But for a time, Billy's behavior seemed different, once again prompting concern. Father Alonzo's utter devotion to Billy and his unwavering insistence once again spelled Jude's worst fear, helping him realize Billy was wild, not crazy. Wild, Jude could handle, and he prayed everyday thanking the Good Lord that Billy was unrestrained and unruly, but not mentally ill.

This dread and apprehension did not rear its ugly head again until Billy returned from the war. Jude now saw something in Billy's eyes that he swore he remembered seeing in his mother's when she began to take that first turn for the worst. Luisa had insisted Billy was simply adjusting, and it was normal, and for a time, a few days at least, Jude believed that too. The death of Edwin or Billy whacking the guy in the courtroom didn't cause Jude trepidation again. Instead, it was the light that no longer seemed to shine in Billy's eyes. His wide beautiful, unbridled eyes.

What Billy was saying now only confirmed these deep-seated fears once again.

But then another thought entered Jude's head.

Perhaps Billy was correct. Everything that happened in the last few months, certainly seemed to confirm Billy's assessment. Nothing was square; everything upside down. Jude and Billy were now outlaws, being hunted by law enforcement and crooks alike. Earlier in the night, he witnessed the holiest man he had ever known, a priest for God's sake, fire a cannon at an innocent policeman. Meanwhile, Jude's wife and children were now on their way to living in a brothel in New Orleans, the only place in the country Jude knew they would be definitively safe. Either Billy was in fact infected with severe disease, but through that disease, it allowed him a sort of clarity not otherwise possible. Or it was not Billy that was sick, but the world.

Billy turned around and looked at the open bag of guns in the backseat, as if they were a third passenger left out of the conversation until now. "But the hell with humanity," Billy said, his eyes hanging on their third amigo, "How are we going to survive? You really think those *culeros* are just gonna let us buy our way out of this?"

"Well other *culeros* bought our ass into this didn't they?"

Billy nodded and palmed his face. "We gonna be bank robbers now too?"

"You know any other way to scrounge up two-hundred thousand dollars?" Jude asked.

"That's what Darcy paid to put my ass in the ringer?" Billy whistled. "I'm kind of impressed I had such an effect on the brown eye." Billy's eyes widened and gripped his face tighter. He was impressed.

"I'm kind of impressed no one has put that kind of price on your head sooner," Jude said grinning, finally able to look at his little brother.

"You don't know that. There might be some fucking krauts that got a higher ticket on my *nalgas*."

"I thought you liked French women."

Billy smiled and then his face stiffened, wilted and he exhaled.

Jude didn't regret what he said until it was too late.

"In all seriousness, I don't want to hurt no one else," Billy said. "With these robbing banks or whatever. No one innocent anyway."

"I don't either," said Jude.

"Jude James always with his damn plan for everything. You telling me now you got a plan for how we gonna rob banks *and* not hurt anybody?"

"*Simon.*"

"All right then. *Bueno.*" After a long moment, Billy spoke again. "Luisa and the kids? They're with that woman you told me about in the barn. The hooker in New Orleans where you met Luisa aren't they?"

"She's a 'Madame' now," Jude said, turning to Billy with a sly grin. "How did you know?"

"Because that's what I would have done. And it may sound crazy but you and I think alike. We just don't *act* alike."

"No words spoken more true, *hermanito*, but it wasn't my idea. In fact, it was hers, and I was hellbent against it. My wife and two young children holding up in a Goddamn brothel in New Orleans…"

"But…"

"…But hellbent ain't got nothing on *Luisa-bent.* Anyway, Luisa and the Madame always stayed in touch, and once I got over my own insecurities on the matter, and not like I had a choice, I realized it was a good idea. So I snuck em out of the house two nights ago. Made sure we weren't followed and sent them to New Orleans until I send word from them when I know it's safe."

"Luisa and the kids hiding away with her best friend, the hooker, excuse me, 'Madame' in New Orleans. The world truly is upside down," said Billy.

"The world is what the world is," said Jude.

Billy nodded. "Say we walk right into the Pinkerton Agency in Chicago with a big fat fucking bag of money that we somehow put together from robbing banks while not harming anyone after we somehow manage to get cross country with no money and every law man in five counties hunting us down, and they want to make a deal. They're just over the moon that we made it so fucking easy for them not even having to hunt us and to boot, we just brought them a free fucking bag of cash. If they don't take us up on our offer, and also not put a bullet in our head right there, are we just going to spend the rest of our lives on the run?"

Jude removed one hand from the steering wheel, directing the chariot with the other over a frozen beat-up highway, and combed his jet-black mustache with his forefinger, pressing it hard against his upper lip. Then he spoke. "As you fucking said, this is a sick world we live in now. Maybe it's always been that way, I don't know, but it sure seems harder of late to do more good than evil. I've spent my whole life trying to do right, not for some higher Goddamn purpose, but so I can sleep at night and not look over my shoulder every Goddamn day. Until these rat fuck *culeros* decided to stick their nose where it don't belong, I was mostly successful in that endeavor and planned to live a peaceful life with our family."

Jude then paused as his lower jaw extended over gritted teeth and his eyes became small.

Billy seen this look before on his brother's face and it usually meant someone was going to need a doctor in the not-so-distant future.

Seeing this now, forced Billy to turn away, not because he feared Jude would turn this aggression on him. Rather because it would force Jude to bury those feelings inside, in a futile and shameful attempt to shield Billy, still protecting his little brother. It was a ridiculous and exhausting concept that Jude always had to be the big brother, the *hombre* with the plan, more collected and less affected. His entire life, Billy had witnessed the effect repression had on Jude. Eruption. Destruction. Fleeting but severe bouts of anarchy. In some sense then, Jude's sense of needing to be the calm and composed brother was correct. In another sense, when that switch of chaos flipped in Jude's head, there was no controlling it, no going back, and it was one of only two things on the earth that truly frightened Billy even to this day.

"You remember our Uncle Graham?" Jude asked. "Pop's brother, our *tio*, who came to visit us when Ma first got sick?"

"I remember he had a really red face and wore a kind of aftershave I had never smelled. And he talked like Pop but with much more of an Irish brogue."

"Until Pop got drunk, then he sounded like a Goddamn leprechaun."

"*Simon*," said Billy.

Both brothers chuckled.

"You remember, he came all the way from Ireland when he got word about Ma?" Jude asked. "And he stayed for that year helping out before he had to go back and take care of his farm?"

"That's some of the last good memories I got," Billy said, his eyes full, staring into the past. "He was great. Kept Pop reasonably sober. Kept Ma reasonably sane. Kept us fed and healthy. I always felt bad I didn't stay in touch with him with the letters like you did."

"I've always kept in touch with him. They still got the farm. He's got kids our age and grandkids. When this horseshit first started going down, I got word to him. I had to go all the way to fucking Albuquerque every time I wanted to get him a single message, and there would be one of those Pinkterton bastards following me all the way down and all the way back up. After a while, I started fucking with them just for shits and giggles. Driving around in circles, taking them into the *barrios* hoping some *vato* would do me the grandest of favors. Anyway, I have a friend in a secret FBI field office down there, and he helped send a message to Uncle Graham."

"You telling me your Plan B is for us to be Goddamn Irish potato farmers?"

"You're damn right. Even the Pinkertons don't know about Uncle Graham in Ireland. If we can get there. Get Luisa and the kids there. It will be a quiet life, but it will be a safe one. No more looking over our shoulder."

Billy shook his head and palmed his face again. "*Erin go bragh.*"

CHAPTER
TWENTY-SEVEN

"**Y**ou think the train is our best bet?" Billy asked, swiftly walking while lugging the heavy bag of guns as gently as possible to avoid any suspicious clanging , regardless of them all wrapped in cloth. The damp early morning chill nettled his tight knuckles, and he saw a small vapor in the frozen air every time he exhaled, a little reminder of the life still flowing from him. Billy squinted up at the sky. The High Rockies' western sun was at war and losing badly with the heavy thick Midwest clouds, doing it damnedest to fight through that dark fucking fog. *Buena suerte*, he thought.

"I haven't known what was *best* since this circus started," Jude said, ducking and dodging through the scampering ants, straining themselves with overstuffed suitcases and dragging boxy trunks against the gravel. "It's a fucking bet. That's it."

The train station, like the sky, was a physical manifestation of Denver, where the wild unruly mountains of the west clashed and fell to the Midwest plains. The train station was more bustling than anything you would see in New Mexico, with Chicano and *gavacho* cowboys alike, stuffy businessmen, hobos and farmers of the grasslands north and east.

BOOM.

Some type of engine backfired, and suddenly, Jude found his hand on the grip of his pistol.

The train next to them started chugging along and Jude relaxed his grip. He kept his head low, but his eyes wide and shifty, under the brim of his hat.

"If I was a novice lawman, I'd probably be south looking for us," Jude said. "Most people B-line it right to Mexico. They think, once they get over to the other side, they're scot-free. They don't realize we can lock down the border tighter than a pork knuckle. They can get creative and try to get through the desert, but you go that route you're as good as dead between the heat, dehydration, starvation and the *coyotes* that will tear you to pieces."

"You ain't talking about the animals," Billy said, keeping his eyes down and all around.

"They're animals all right."

"The Pinkertons ain't novice."

"No, they ain't."

"So, if you know this, chances are the Pinkertons know this."

"That's right," said Jude. "Reckon they got people looking south for us, but if I were hunting me, I'd be looking north. Have roadblocks on the highways. APBs. That's why we wanna get the fuck out here as quickly as possible. We can disappear in big cities like Chicago, but not here."

"Hey, look," Billy said, nodding to a stack of freshly printed newspapers still bound with chicken wire, the bottom issues already wet and muddy from the gravel and snowmelt.

Jude glanced down to the headline that read: *FOUR POLICE OFFICERS IN NEW MEXICO SLAUGHTERED AFTER HARROWING JAILBREAK.*

Jude almost stopped for a moment. "*Puta de madres,*" he muttered.

"Landry and the other cop are dead," Billy gasped, reading just enough before moving again.

"Yea," Jude said, defeated and following.

"Those brown-eyes killed them and pinned it on us."

"Yea."

"Why?"

"What's worse than two *cabrons* on a jailbreak?"

Billy shot him a puzzled look as they marched along.

"Two *cabrons* that killed four cops."

"You still want to make a deal with them?" Billy asked.

"No. I wanna kill every last one of them."

"*Carnal*, we're finally on the same page."

Jude looked down at the train ticket in his hand then through the crowd, moving his head right then left, and then right again, searching for their platform number.

Every fucking person seemed to get right in his line of sight.

No one seemed conscious of the fact that another human being happened to be walking on the same fucking planet at the same fucking time trying to find his own fucking train.

Businessmen bumped into one another, their heads buried in a newspaper, without apologizing or acknowledging the other.

Vendors dragged their carts through the horde, indifferent of the hefty wheels breaking one's foot or toes, by simply rolling his cart over you.

It was a zoo of chaos, everyone out for *numero uno* only.

Jude was sure someone would steal his last fucking breath if they could.

Billy laid the bag down gently, his arm strained and needing brief respite from tugging the four shotguns, two rifles and six pistols, plus ammunition.

Up yonder, Billy finally caught a glimpse of *Platform 24* and the sign above that read: *Denver-Chicago.* "Hey, that's our train."

"Yea," said Jude.

Billy pulled his head down and gripped the bag for the final lug.

Through the jungle of beasts and brutes, Jude's eyes caught something that made the blood freeze in his veins. His heart stopped like ramming a crowbar into a turbine while soul crawled out of his throat.

He almost didn't believe his eyes until he blinked again.

Through the swaying anarchy of the bustling train station, not 50 yards away, stood Leslie Dahl glaring back at him. His icy stare as dark as his ink black thin fucking mustache.

Dahl did not move. He also did not seem alarmed or affected at the sight of Jude, aside from his pulling hand gently gliding over his holster under his long purple overcoat.

Jude scanned his surroundings. Dahl seemed to be alone, at least for the moment.

Only when Billy trudged along past Jude, did Jude blink again.

"Billy, hold up," Jude mumbled.

Billy must not have heard, as he moved forward.

"Billy," Jude said again, this time prompting Billy to stop and turn.

"*Que pajo?*"

Jude moved his gaze to his brother. "Dahl is here."

"What?" Billy almost whispered.

"Over your right shoulder." Jude's eyes turned to Billy as Billy craned his head over his shoulder.

"Where?" Billy asked.

"Right there," said Jude, except Dahl wasn't there. He was gone, like an apparition in the night.

"I don't see him," Billy said, moving his head more frantically.

"Fuck. He's gone. Just fucking gone."

Billy's head shifted back and forth from Jude to where Jude was looking. "But you're sure you saw him?" Billy asked.

"Sure as sin. He was standing right in front of the platform of our train."

"Well did he get on it?"

"I don't know."

"You see him with anyone else?"

"No. I don't know."

"How'd he know? And how did he get here so fast?"

"He's good. That's how."

"What was he doing?"

"He wasn't doing anything. Just staring at me with those beady fucking eyes. Wasn't even really staring. Just watching."

Billy rummaged in all directions looking for Dahl. "Jude, I don't see him."

"He was there all right. These motherfuckers are probably scattered everywhere around us now like hungry wolves."

"What do we do?"

"I don't know but we ain't getting on the train. Not that one anyway. I think he's hoping we get on our intended train or scatter back to a car and then he'll flush us out. Probably roadblocks, maybe not around downtown, that would cause too much of a commotion but on the highways for sure."

So far, it had been Jude's rodeo and the gut-shot padre's, but now it was Billy's turn.

Jude was always good with the planning.

Billy was always good with scraping shit off the heel. His eyes combed the station.

The hot steam from engines tangled with the frigid sunup air, creating a hazy mist.

Ice dripped into puddles from winter battling spring.

The wealthy wayfarers attempted to step around or over the slushy sooty puddles, usually in futility, plunging into the next or bumping into another *cabron* trying to do the same.

The peasants, peons and boors simply moved as one with the earth, honest and cool with the elements.

In war, it was clear who the enemy was. Now, Billy saw no one suspicious so everyone was suspicious.

"Sitting here like two fucking hogs waiting to be slaughtered," Billy eventually uttered.

In the gap between the two passenger carts, he noticed a freight train on the next track over, puffing and panting. "Tell you what, I'm done playing defense here," Billy said, eyes sharpening on the freight car. "You see that train, behind ours, the one readying to leave?"

Jude looked slowly to the train, careful to not give away any plan Billy had. "Yea, I see it."

"You ever hopped trains before?"

Jude couldn't help but shoot his gaze to Billy. "No."

"Well no better time than the present, *carnal.* I jumped a few down to Juarez just for kicks."

"I remember. Kept waiting for the call that a railroad bull split your head."

"We ain't gotta worry about them today. Jumping those sons of bitches is no different than climbing a big fucking tree or a horse, and sure know how to both. *Mira,* you see how them rail wheels are already turning real slow?"

"Yea."

"That means we got less than five minutes before that locomotive rolls out. You got your sidearm on you?"

"Yea."

"Good. I got mine too. That's all we can roll with it. Have to make do. In less than five minutes there's gonna be a grand fucking ruckus. When it happens, you'll know. People are gonna scatter like shooing crows on a road. I trust you know how to make yourself invisible and hop on that third cart. The train is gonna be pulling out when it happens so there ain't gonna be time for hesitation."

"Hesitation ain't never been a riddle for me."

"That's why this is gonna work."

Jude hit his brother with a long look. They were waist deep in dire straits, but in some way, Jude felt a credence staring into his brother's eyes. *He had this shit.*

Billy must have sensed it too, nodding slightly. "Like I said…tired of playing defense. When it happens, you make yourself fast and invisible."

Before Jude could say a word, Billy was off.

Billy strolled up to a Chicano vendor's cart, peddling steaming burritos wrapped in tinfoil, the daily print, and the hourly tobacco fix.

"*Que dice hombre?*" Billy asked the cordial man of forty, his hands stuffed in his pocket and shuffling off the cold.

"*Que tal, senor?*" said the man, smiling.

"*Manana fria, si?*"

"*Siiiii*" said the man emphatically agreeing.

"*Por favor, necesito un favor.*"

"*Si, señor.*"

"*¿Verás mi bolsa mientras uso el baño?*" Billy asked, placing the bag of guns at the vendor's feet.

"*Si señor.*"

"*Bueno,*" said Billy, pulling his cash roll from his back pocket.

"*Eso no es necesario,*" said the man placing his hand on Billy's roll.

"*Gracias,*" said Billy, saluting his *paisano* before walking around the back of the cart, parading through the horde and into the crowded train station.

He scooted into the bathroom and his eyes caught exactly what he was looking for-windows above the stalls.

He slid into a cell, removed his jacket and button-down and then his undershirt.

He ripped the white cotton into three separate pieces of three varying lengths.

He dressed again and shoved the pieces into his pants pocket.

He jumped onto the toilet, prying the knob first from the latch before pushing the thick musty window out from the grimy steel frame.

Then hopped up and out and hit the ground outside as graceful as a cat.

The backside of the station was a barren tundra of frozen mud before the large parking area.

He swiftly moved to the lot, peering over his shoulder, catching no followers.

He ducked behind a car, and quickly removed a gas cap from the tank. He tucked the longest piece of shirt into the tank and lit the cloth on fire with his Zippo.

Staying low behind the parked cars, he raced to another car, closer to the railyard. He pulled out a shorter piece of cloth and did the same.

Finally, he darted to the last car on the lot and removed the shortest piece of cloth from his pocket.

As he squatted behind the car, he could feel his shoulders drumming up and down, his chest moving in and out from breathing hard, but his breath made not a sound, and the air did not signal in his lungs. He held the shortest piece of cloth steady in one hand, the lit Zippo in the other, crouched like a tiger ready to pounce.

BOOM!

Suddenly there was the familiar sound he was waiting for.

Metal crashed on metal.

Glass shattered.

Humans screamed and Billy lit the last piece of cloth before bolting back to the train.

The delirious mass scrambled inanely in all directions, running into and over each other.

Billy careened through, doing his best to hide amongst the roaches while covering as much ground as possible.

In one quick glance, he caught his breath again and felt air in his lungs and it was that moment he saw Leslie Dahl and three other men rifling through the bag of guns as they pressed the poor confused vendor. If the Good Lord allowed Billy on the train, on hind legs sucking air for another day, he'd make amends somehow, he swore, but, so far, the plan was working.

Some type of siren blared, only rousing the rabble.

The train, unhindered by the chaos, was getting the fuck out of the station and Billy caught sight of Jude peeking his head out of that third cart.

Maybe The Almighty was rooting for the *dos hermanos, los coyotes*, after all.

Billy took one long deep breath and shifted into fifth gear, running as hard as he could now. A cold gust rushed across his face. He wasn't sure if it was a winter wind, or if he was really running that fast to join his brother. He was bolting straight ahead, straining with all his might to keep up with the train, following it parallel. He feared the moment he turned his body, he would lose ground and the train, and his brother would be gone forever.

Abruptly, Jude leaned his entire body out of the cart, his one hand desperately gripping the frame, the only part of his body not flailing in the wind. He threw himself down to Billy, and the desperation in his eyes screamed *Hermanito, it's now or never.*

Billy turned and lunged his entire being.

If Jude couldn't grab him, he would surely flail to his death under the crushing wheels of the train.

But if he didn't make the leap, the alternative was more dire not because he feared a slower more painful death and he was not going to give those *culeros* the satisfaction of taking him out. Since the war and Marion's death, Billy did not hold a great appreciation for his life, but he did hold a great disdain for letting those cowardice swine have any other victory over him. And there was no way in hell, he was gonna let Jude go at those bastards alone.

Before that thought was even finished, Billy felt his brother's hand grab his forearm. He looked up and suddenly saw Jude's face, the smattering of green he remembered in his brother's brown eyes. The red in his otherwise dark mustache, like their father, and that pleading gaze that Jude used to give when Billy was acting out and against his own best interest that said, *Please little brother, if not for you then for me.*

Billy could feel the strain in Jude's arm, in his entire body.

The train was firing along now, faster with each second, and Billy felt his legs being dragged from underneath him. Those big ole steel wheels calling his name and then he realized *Jude wasn't going to be able to do this alone.*

Suddenly, Billy was pulling himself up to the cart.

Hoisting himself as the cold wind blew in his face

Icicles of tears piercing his eyes.

The sound of the rolling wheels whistling his demise.

Needles stinging his lungs as he heaved and his muscles twinging from strain.

Then, there was silence.

Icicles turned to tears.

He took a long deep breath.

The air entering and exiting through his lungs seamlessly and his body relaxed.

He then realized he was lying on his back, in the cart on the train, staring up at the metal canopy of the ceiling.

He turned his head and saw his brother lying there next to him, staring at the same shroud of shelter and momentary refuge, panting like a whipped dog, then aware of his own hard breathing.

"Any idea…" Jude managed between breaths, "Where this train is headed?"

"Yea…" Billy said between huffing and puffing, "The fuck out of here…"

CHAPTER
TWENTY-EIGHT

The two boys leaned against opposing walls of the cart, facing one another. Both sat with their knees pointed up and their forearms resting over them. Their eyes did not depart the other.. As if one of them blinked, maybe the other would be gone.

The train gently rocked back and forth, almost soothingly. Maybe it was simply the sense of escape they were feeling. The train sped fast and the sound of a large machine flying across space and time provided almost a cloak of silence.

Finally, Jude spoke. "You still thinking about that Mexican vendor?"

Billy looked away first, to the space between his knees. The dirty floorboard of the cart with old hay, wood shavings and even oil. "Yea."

"Well, I can tell you not to. Dahl is scum be he's smart and he won't waste his own time. It took him less than five minutes to realize the poor Mexican was just a distraction and let him be."

"Probably," said Billy.

"Yea, probably," said Jude, resigned, looking off for a minute. "You're sure they didn't see us?"

"I'm sure he didn't see me scamper past him when he was fucking with the Mexican. I ain't sure he missed my *huevos* dangling from the train."

Jude mashed his mustache with his forefinger. "Well, I guess there ain't shit we can do now until we know where we're going and we ain't gonna know that until we stop. Out of our control. Just two helpless *pendejos* bumbling across the mesa like a Goddamn tumbleweed."

"Jude, as long as I can remember, you've futility attempted to have some type of semblance of control over everything. Starting with a drunk father and looney mother. It's why you're a sheriff and a Goddamn lawyer. But from the moment our mamma thrusted us into this world to the moment the Good Lord takes us back, we got no control. We don't get to choose where we're born to what blood, how we die or anything in between. You can bullshit yourself into believing otherwise but you'll only be bullshiting yourself."

Jude pressed his lips together as hard as his forefinger mashed his mustache. He hadn't always had a mustache but he'd always pressed his finger to his lip when he was pouting.

He was pouting real good now, Billy thought. He almost wanted to laugh but that'd really piss Jude off.

"When the fuck did you get so weird?" Jude eventually asked, instead.

Billy smiled. He had the old boy riled without even trying. "Shit, I was born in Taos to a *brujeria* mother and a leprechaun father. Been weird all my life."

Jude relented, smiling

"It's weird that you ain't weird," Billy continued.

Both men fashioned a grin produced by truth.

The day seemed to drag long.

Granted, dawn started early for the two boys, or, last night never ended, but every time the train seemed to slow, they would gander their heads out of the cart expecting to see some big city, small town or any indication of where they were on the planet. Instead, they would only find the train dawdling in preparation for a bend or seamlessly nothing at all.

They should have been tired.

The train was not uncomfortable.

But both men had found sleep in more distressing and awkward conditions.

Billy in the trenches with gunfire, explosions, and rotting flesh.

Jude in the cramped cold quarters of a pickup cab on a stakeout.

Both understood, for the moment, they were safe.

Safe to close their eyes.

Let their minds and bodies rest.

Their foreseeable future was as uncertain as the direction of a crow but their immediate was absolute and definitive, sitting in a moving box until the box decided to stop. The scenario provided the perfect environment for sleep, but there the boys sat, wide-eyed and stolid, simply watching the day pass.

The horizon that pictured outside of the cart began to sour into a purple and then gray as the train ran full-bore into dusk. The kind and soothing sunbeams no longer wrung through between the girders of the cart providing warmth, and the temperature dropped quickly.

The boys stiffened, grasping themselves tighter to find warmth from within.

Brakes squealed and the train lunged forward shaking them loose from their own grip.

Billy glanced his head out the cart.

By now, it was dark, and the land looked no different than the obscure black ocean of nothingness, he would stare out abroad. Through the murkiness, he saw a smattering of lights in the distance, as if dancing upon the crest of waves.

"I see lights. We're approaching somewhere." Billy said.

Jude stood and peeked out. "My guess is Kansas City. Those cornfields tell us we didn't go north, we didn't get west and we sure as shit didn't go south."

"That's as good a guess as any. If you're right about Kansas, are we still on with the plan?"

"Slip past the railroad bull. Steal a car, swap the plates, and keep moving. Yes sir," said Jude.

"At some point we're going to have to sleep and eat."

"At some point we will."

The cart rocked and shook.

The screeching of the brakes grew louder, and the train slowed.

Momentary pictures of a city flashed by the boys' eyes like looking at a film reel.

Suddenly, there were brick buildings with windows and lights on inside.

Restaurants with patrons sitting across from one another eating.

Pedestrians on sidewalks, bundled up, trotting along, and cars puttering around the quiet streets.

Perhaps it was the sight of diners serving hot food and hotels with heat and soft beds that provided a sense of comfort to the boys. Or perhaps, being surrounded by civilization again did not make them feel so desolate and alone. The train rolled through the city and into a train yard, barren of the pleasantries that passed their eyes.

Billy pointed his head out of the cart. "Looks dark and empty. The moment the train stops, we hop off and we don't stop moving. We don't wanna run though. That attracts attention and there's no telling what you're bound to run into the dark. Fucking rebar that will slice you three ways from Sunday. Holes you can fall into and break your leg. It's a mine-field."

"Sounds about right," said Jude.

The train clunked along, almost completely stopping a half dozen times before making its final check.

The boys sailed off the train, and before their feet hit the ground, they were moving parallel back towards town.

The dirt crunched under their boots, the only hint of their trespass.

Billy contemplated walking less swiftly and more quietly but decided against it. He remembered weighing that same option moving through the forest as they surrounded the unsuspecting Nazi camp. It was the first time he *removed* an enemy post, sending a legion of souls to their Maker in less than an instant, but certainly not his last. He recalled each moment moving closer to the enemy barracks, seemed as if it was one second closer to his own last breath, not some stranger. He smelled the damp fusty bark of the trees and mud. He felt the wide flat leaves of the plants heavy with dew swipe across his legs and he took in every moment, every blink of the eye, as if his executioner were hot on his trail and not contrariwise.

Now, Billy was not surrounded by the canopy of a living breathing alpine rainforest, but inanimate, torpid, and rusted railcars, caustic cinder block structures and the smell of exhaust. Yet, the march seemed similar. Perhaps because, this time, there was an executioner in pursuit. Or perhaps, Billy realized each breath could be his last regardless of any circumstance.

Billy and Jude moved swiftly down the track, ducked under another stopped train and plodded closer to town.

They were almost out of the train yard when they heard that familiar sound – hard breathing, vulgarity and knuckle meeting flesh.

They peered down the track and saw a shadowy ruckus.

At first, it was hard to make out how many there were through the dark and rabid motions, but it was very clear there was one on the ground getting the ever-living shit kicked out of him. If the assailants continued at this rate, there'd be nothing ever-living about the poor soul soon enough.

As the boys closed in, they could make out the finer details.

The horde was only twenty yards away now and there were at least four of them.

They hadn't noticed the two boys, focusing their attention on the beat down instead.

Reading Billy's mind, and pushing back against his own, Jude gritted his teeth and then whispered, "It ain't our problem. C'mon." He tugged his brother's jacket while ducking under the train, but Billy stood defiantly. "Billy" Jude pleaded again in hush.

"They're gonna kill him, Jude," Billy said matter-of-factly.

"Yea, whoever *he* is."

"You're just gonna allow that?" Billy finally moved, turning to Jude peering under the cart.

"I'm gonna allow us to get the fuck out of here and worry about our own problems. We already got enough of them." Jude held his eyes on his brother. "Billy, *por favor.*"

Billy finally nodded and both men ducked under the cart until one of the assailants yelled, "Hold up. Keep him alive until we string him up."

Both men halted, hunched underneath the confines of the metal train above them.

"Well that about settles it, don't it?" Jude whispered.

He didn't wait for a response. He was already scooting out and back towards the horde.

And Billy was in front.

Both men calmly walked toward the group as they removed their guns from their waistband and cocked them.

"You steering this ride?" Billy asked as they neared.

Jude nodded.

"Okay, then, Sheriff."

"Excuse me," Jude announced to the men, startling them.

They all ceased and gave the boys their undivided attention.

By now, Billy and Jude were not ten yards away.

They could smell the torrid whiskey on their breath and the stink of sweat.

The four men were all white, with beards of varying length and all around fifty years old. Three of them were in working men's clothes. The fourth looked like a politician.

The politician looking man stepped forward from the group. "Mister, this don't concern you. Move along."

The man spoke with some kind of southern accent or maybe all white people outside of Northern New Mexico just sounded like that to Jude.

"You're wrong there. I'm a sheriff," said Jude.

"You may be a sheriff but you ain't *the* sheriff," the politician said, "So I'm only gonna tell you one more time to keep moving. This is a world of pain you want no part of."

Jude motioned his pulling hand on his pistol. "You're gonna step away from that man right now or you'll see how fast my jurisdiction is."

Through dark thick night Jude could see the politician's eyes narrow.

He was pondering.

Deliberating.

Then he spoke. "You was hopping trains. You ain't no sheriff and I doubt you want any attention from real police or the railroad bull. Even if you could, you ain't gonna pull that sidearm."

"That would normally be a logical assertion, but logic departed my way weeks ago and I don't suspect it will be back anytime soon," Jude said.

"Welcome to hell, son," said the politician as the four men circled together and closed in on Billy and Jude.

The man on the ground mumbled something, moaned, and rolled to his side.

"Not one more inch, or you'll be there soon enough," said Jude.

The men were now in striking distance, as one swinging dick suddenly pulled a knife from his side, lunging at Jude.

He didn't take one step before Jude pulled, firing two rounds into his chest.

The gunshots echoed off the train cars shattering the silence of the night.

The man dropped, dust fleeting into the air from the impact, or maybe his soul departing.

Another man reached for his gun, but Billy pointed first and fired twice.

The man dropped and suddenly the two standing before them looked afraid.

"Stop right there!!! Missouri Pacific Police!!!" someone yelled behind the two men.

A pool of lanterns suddenly fluttered in the distance.

"We're over…"

BAM!

Before the third man could finish his sentence, Jude blasted him in the knee. Before the man could even squeal in pain, Jude hissed. "Make another sound and your brains will be in that dirt, next."

True to form, the politician-looking man was indeed the cowardice of the group and the last one standing.

"Pick him up!" Billy demanded to the politician, nodding to the beaten man on the ground. "Pick him up and bring him to me!"

The voices of the group down yonder grew louder, their lights larger.

The politician, frozen with fear and anger, did not move, only leering at Billy.

"Pick him up or so help me God," seethed Jude.

The politician turned back to the man on the ground, while keeping his eyes on the boys. He halfheartedly tried to pry the man up.

"That don't suffice," said Billy. "You bring him to me."

"Come on," said the politician, contempt, or annoyance in his voice, dragging the other up.

The beaten man stood and stumbled forward. Billy braced the man's weight, ducking his head and then shoulder under the man's arm while Jude kept his aim on the politician.

"Can you walk?" Billy asked.

The man, his face matted with blood and dirt, nodded.

A train horn suddenly blared.

Jude and Billy turned to see the train on the next track moving slowly, departing.

The politician saw it too. "I'll find you. And I'll kill you."

"Pull a ticket and get in line," said Jude before firing a round into the man's knee cap.

He dropped, and before the two boys could even savor one moment to hear him yelp, they, along with the battered stranger, were off, chasing another chance at survival.

CHAPTER
TWENTY-NINE

Once again, the two boys were soaring across land, hapless and helpless, their destiny resting solely in the confines of the speeding metal box. This time, they were not alone in their journey, however.

Billy and Jude sat next to each other watching their new and unexpected companion on their wild ride. He looked to be in his 30s with bushy red hair and a matching beard, now stained with blood, dirt, and oil. Billy nor Jude realized how big the man was until everything settled and it was just the three of them in the box together. He was at least 6 '4 and broad. He looked like his family was probably Vikings at some point and now farmers.

Probably took all four chicken-shit sons of bitches to bring him down, Jude thought.

"You didn't have to do that," mumbled the man, his sharp blue eyes piercing through the black night separating him from Billy and Jude.

"You harm some woman or molest some child?" Jude asked.

"What?" grumbled the man.

"The reason they were gonna kill you? You harm some woman or child?"

"No."

"You steal from them?"

"No."

"Then I reckon, we did have to do it."

"You gonna live?" asked Billy.

"I got some broken ribs, but I'll live," said the man, looking off, cradling his sternum, as if embarrassed. "Survived worse."

The wind howled scraping past the train, and the cold bit the men everywhere they already hurt.

The city was gone, and only black space surrounded the train again.

"Are you actually a sheriff?" the man asked, after a long silence.

"Not anymore," Jude said.

The man nodded again, and blinked hard, probably from the pain, maybe from thinking.

He stared sideways, as if he could not look straight at his two newly minted guardian angels.

When his gaze finally returned to the two men, they rested on Billy. "You was in the war," he said.

"What makes you say that?"

The man looked away again. His mouth made some sound like he was fishing around with his tongue to measure how many loose teeth he had.

Billy studied the man closer. "You were in the war too."

The man turned back to Billy and nodded.

"Germany?" asked Billy.

"Mostly. And France," said the man.

"Me too. 37th Infantry Division."

"4th Armored Division," said the man.

"Shit, you were in the thick of it."

"So were you."

Jude studied both men curiously. Aside from Sid, he had not seen Billy associate with another soldier since he had been home. Their lack of words spoke of a bond louder than any shared parlance.

"Sheriffs tend to be curious," said the man, turning his attention to Jude after a long silence. "You gonna ask me anymore about those men?"

"I told you I wasn't a sheriff anymore."

The man sat quiet again for a moment and then spoke. "Those men were the KKK. The Klan."

He gently brushed the dirt and rocks and grime and blood out of his beard with his hands and then spoke again. "If we survive until sunup, you're bound to see some mistakes on me. Scars from old Klad ink."

"All right," Jude said calmly.

"I don't associate myself with those people anymore," the man blurted out, as if Jude made an accusation.

"All right," Jude said again, this time more definitively.

"Is that why they were after you?" Billy asked.

"You could say that," said the man, looking off again.

The brothers' eyes bent to one another, straining to silently confer and converse their read on the fellow rider.

Then the man spoke again. "If I came off as ungrateful for your help, I apologize. Whatever pickle y'all are in certainly wasn't made easier helping me out."

"We've been making it harder on ourselves long before tonight," said Billy. "You just happened to be a bystander of it, I reckon."

"Not sure we did you any favors tonight, introducing you to our world, and the people chasing us," said Jude. "Up to you, but you'd probably be wise to shake loose of us, first chance you get."

"Well at this point, I'm obligated to help y'all anyway I can," said the man.

"You ain't obligated…"

"…That ain't your decision to make," said the man, suddenly terse, cutting Jude off. "That's not how I was raised."

"I understand," said Jude. He reached over to shake the man's hand. "Jude. This is my brother Billy."

"Christian," said the man gingerly, reaching over to acquaint himself properly. "Reckon we both have some stories to share."

Jude grinned. "Reckon we do. Billy's is a Goddamn fairy tale; it's so long and twisted."

"Well, we got all night. This train ain't stopping till dawn in St. Louis," said Christian.

"That's where we're headed?" asked Billy.

"For now, yea. I wouldn't be surprised if folks are waiting for us there if they saw us get on the train. You expect the people chasing you to be there too?"

"I doubt it, but it's hard to say. These Goddamn Pinkertons have been two steps ahead of us before we even knew we were in the race," said Jude.

Christian's blue saucers widened. "You're right. I would be wise to shake loose of you two."

"How's that?" Billy asked.

"I got irrational men with hate in their heart chasing me but you two fellas pissed off much worse."

"Who's that?" asked Jude.

"Rich sons of bitches," Christian said.

Both boys grinned.

"How the fuck did you boys manage to get the Pinkertons after you?" he asked half astonished, half impressed.

"Clearly you don't know Billy," Jude said. "He could find the wrong side of the pope."

"It's mostly about a woman," Billy said, suddenly sullen.

"It usually is," said Christian.

All three men grinned.

"Was a woman behind them Klan wanting to string you up?" Jude asked.

"I thought you said you wasn't curious anymore?" Christian blurted out. He blinked hard again and lowered his head in shame. "I'm sorry. I ain't had nothing but trouble in front of me for a while and I've forgotten my manners."

"It's all right," Jude said.

"I guess you could say it was about a woman in a sense. There was this black fella in our town who was just minding his own business. Working and living with his Ma and Pa. But he was seeing a white woman and they were in love, I reckon, because there was no stopping those two from seeing each other. Not their parents, not their separate pastors, nothing, not even the Klan."

The train whistle bellowed long and hard, and the box slowed, shaking the brothers' attention.

"It's all right," Christian said, noticing. "We're just going over a bridge."

The brothers nodded.

"You were saying," Billy said.

Christian inhaled deep and painfully, maybe from air moving past his broken ribs, maybe not, and he looked away again.

"You don't… It ain't our business," said Billy.

"I was in the Klan," Christian interjected. "Before the war. I was angry and confused and lost. I didn't know why I felt the way I did, but the Klan gave me a reason. I went all in with them boys. And then all of a sudden… Just like I didn't know why I was angry. And just like I didn't know why I was in the Klan … I was signing up for the war. I was probably just puckered, tuckered, and bored. I managed to still be a dumb hateful son of a bitch through basic but soon as I got over-seas…Bullets and shrapnel, bombs, that shit don't see no color but red. Some of the bravest men I ever met over there were black.

We'd sit in the foxhole at night talking and I realized I had more in common with these boys than my own *citizens* in the Klan. We all poor. Worked our whole lives. Nothing to show for it and nothing given to us. So many of my fellow Klansman were the same rich sons of bitches that owned banks that took away our farms. Owned oil fields that polluted our water and politicians who constantly had a hand in my pocket. I started thinking, shit, why do I hate the negro? He never did any of that. Then I realized, maybe them Klan sons of bitches, the smart ones at the top, not the pawns, didn't hold hate in their heart but greed."

"Greed?" Jude asked.

"Yes sir. You see, all them rich swine at the top can rob and steal and pillage from us as long as we believe we have an enemy far worse than them. The poor negro. The German. The Indian. Whoever. I started to understand part of the reason I was so angry was I'd been kicked a dog every day of my life and I didn't even realize who was doing the kicking. Didn't have no intention of coming home and starting some kind of revolution but I sure as shit didn't want to be no pawn no longer either. But when I got home they didn't see it that way and didn't make it easy for me. I managed to keep my head down for a while until I heard they were gonna string up that poor negro boy for being with the white girl. So I got word to him. Somehow that got back to the Klan and here I am."

A deep hush fell over the three men in the box.

The metals wheels of the train scraped and chafed against the track.

The sodden chill nipped fiercely at their bodies as they stirred, hopelessly trying to keep warm.

Then Jude spoke. "Well shit, Christian, you're on the run because of some righteous resolve. We're on the run because Billy had enough lashings from his girlfriend's old man. Lost his temper and stabbed the son of a bitch."

It had come out fast and quick and was probably just brotherly barbs, but it was the first time Jude threw some shade at Billy for the pickle they were in.

"No, we're on the run because my brother thought he was as smart as Winston Churchill with his genius plan," Billy countered. "And when that didn't work out, he summoned his inner Pacho Villa and decided a midnight jail break would be a good idea."

Maybe the lack of sleep and food and all around amenities had removed the guardrails between the two brothers. With no insulation between them, all that was left was fisticuffs and Jude didn't want that, so he decided to pivot the best way poor people and family knew how.

Humor.

"It was closer to 11," Jude said."

Both men looked at Jude puzzled.

"When I broke you out of jail, it was closer to 11."

Billy half chuckled and then Jude right on cue.

Christian remained still, only his eyes moving between Billy and Jude, studying them, and then he spoke. "You boys are crazy. I don't think the Pinkertons have any idea what they're up against."

"Oh, I think they do," said Billy. "Jude made his intentions clear when he swore blood right to their face."

As if some radio journalist with a microphone, Christian's eyes carried back to Jude for a response.

"You saying you don't want to kill every one of those sons of bitches now?" Jude asked.

"I didn't say that. Just making it clear who's responsible for the pickling here."

"I may be speaking out of turn here, but I have a feeling this ain't something new with you two," said Christian.

"What's that supposed to mean?" asked Jude.

"He ain't wrong," said Billy.

"I managed a pretty fucking quiet and pickle-free life with Luisa and the kids up until a few weeks ago," Jude said, holding the pointed edge.

"Would have stayed that way if you minded your own Goddamn business," Bill said.

"Jesus Christ!" Christian yelled. "I'm a little too banged up at the moment to separate you two swinging dicks so will you both calm the fuck down?" His otherwise soft voice until this point was suddenly ringing louder than the roaring engine or wheel turning over the steel rail.

The boys quieted and looked ashamed, as if they were ten years old in Father Alonzo's rectory.

When they finally simmered, Christian exhaled long and hard. "All right. Thank you," he said, still frazzled but also relieved. "You boys must be brothers."

"What makes you say that?" Bill asked.

Even in the blurry pitched black night Billy could see Christian shooting him a look that said, *Hey numbnuts, why do you think?*

"Your wife and kids safe?" Christian asked Jude, soberly.

"For now, yes," said Jude in the same tone.

"I take it y'all got some plan?" asked Christian.

"Yes sir, we do," said Jude.

Christian sucked in air and swallowed dryly before speaking. "Since I've been back, back from the war, I've been asking the Good Lord to show me my calling. His will. Seems to me he's answered my prayers."

"How's that?" asked Jude.

"Make sure your family gets to see their daddy again." Christian's eyes moved back and forth between the two brothers. "And ensure you two don't kill each other first."

PART

FOUR

HEY, IT'S STILL CHICAGO

CHAPTER

THIRTY

"How did you know where I'd be?" Billy asked.

"True detective work," said Christian.

The men sat at a small table in between deep booths lined with plush satin walls. In the booths were women wearing almost nothing or nothing at all draped over men, some with cocktails in their hands, and hookahs they puffed from. The den sat below ground in the basement of a large building, with little windows showing a bit of street above. The single chandelier and low the outside beams winnowing a halo of light like heaven above the lost.

The low hanging gray opium smoke seemingly below Christian's long pointed head reminded Billy of the early morning clouds lingering below Taos Mountain and above the flatlands of the Pueblo. By noon, it was like they never existed. Burned away right before your eyes.

Billy squinted, his face pale and clammy, hugging himself tight with his hands buried in the front pockets of his leather jacket, bent in the corner of the booth. He had misplaced who was speaking last, and then he wondered if it was his head in the clouds, not Christians.

"I asked the lady running the brothel where I would go to score," Christian continued.

Christian talking helped Billy remember where he was in the conversation.

"Funny, I asked her the same thing."

"Hence the true detective work," Christian said dryly.

Billy half smiled. He'd left the hotel to get away from everyone there and all the heaviness in between but he was already glad to see Christian.

"You get triggered?" Christian asked.

Billy's gaze widened and slowly rolled around the fog. His blood shot eyes, watery and red, moved up to the light bending in. "What?" he finally asked, coming to.

"What triggered you?" Christian asked kindly.

Billy seemed to focus in on the little table between the two men. "Being back in the city," he said and then fell silent.

Christian held quiet, studying his new comrade in a way that would not offend him. If there was anything Christian despised since returning home, it was the worried and sympathetic eyes others would hang on him. Eyes said that said, *Yea, we put you through the meat grinder and made you an animal, but if you bite now, we're gonna have to put you down. Don't make us put you down.*

Christian finally had a chance to look around the room. He was no quaker but he'd never been in a place like this, not even when he was using. Quite the opposite, when he got high, he got high alone.

He'd never been around so many people in his life until he went overseas. All the *forts* and *camps* and *barracks* filled to the brim with red, white and blue Americans from all stripes of the country. At the same time, Christian never felt so alone, in a good way.

Maybe that's why he became a sniper.

Maybe that's how he survived.

It was like Christian had created this layer of ice all around him during the war, wherever he was fighting or stationed. Like a mushroom cloud of nothing, and he was protected in the vacuum. And when he realized he was actually coming home, alive, he knew he had to escape that cloud because he didn't need it anymore and it would only cause destruction now instead of granting safety. So as the war winded down and he readied himself to come home, he thawed himself out, only to come back to find his wife reeling from polio and *home* now seeming as strange and distant as Germany itself. And suddenly, he needed that cloud again but there was no military regiment to slip into. No mass of soldiers to slide between. No sniper rifle to hide behind in his hidden outpost.

There was only alcohol and opium.

Christian saw Billy was back in his dream, and he quite honestly didn't know how long he'd been lost in his own thought. "Back in the city?" Christian asked. "You mean just having it around?"

Billy faintly snapped back to reality. "Nah. If you're really hard up, you can find it anywhere."

"I know." Christian lowered his head, his eyes meeting Billy's head-on.

Billy nodded.

Both men understood.

"Being back in the city. I met my Marion in a city. Paris. Paris and Chicago are nothing alike, but we met on a windy damp day surrounded by buildings. Big fucking buildings towering over us in a concrete jungle. When I walked out today, the same wind rushed down the alleys of the buildings. The same cold shadows hung off the corners…and I swear I felt Marion looking over me, in every direction off every building." Billy's eyes widened again, went somewhere else, and filled with tears. "I hadn't used since her funeral."

Christian nodded, squinted his eyes, and they traveled somewhere else also.

He folded his arms over his chest and looked up at the daylight bleeding through from above.

The smoke or dust in the air sparkled when combined with the light. It was almost beautiful.

"Fuck…" said Billy, shaking his head slowly, his eyes widening almost with tears. "I was able to last seven days here before…"

"That's seven days," said Christian. "That's something. And the good news is you'll have another chance to start over tomorrow."

"I ain't gotta tell you not to mention this to Jude, do I?" Billy asked.

"Mention what?"

Billy nodded. "I'll be ready for tomorrow."

"I ain't worried about that."

"You ain't worried about tomorrow?"

"I didn't say that. I ain't foolin 'myself. I got concerns…" Christian looked Billy over. "I just ain't worried about you, being ready and all," Christian said.

Billy nodded, exhaled deeply, and sat up a bit. "You worried about anyone getting hurt?"

"You mean us?"

"No."

"Yes sir. That's what concerns me most."

"Me too."

"Not sure it's preventable."

"Not sure either…"

Both men held quiet for a minute then Billy spoke again. "You don't gotta worry about Jude."

"I wasn't."

"He's a hot head…but not in these kinds of situations..."

"You boys been robbing a lot of banks together in *these kinds of situations?* Sheriff, bank robber and war hero. That's a first."

Billy grinned and so did Christian.

"No, I mean…," said Billy.

"…I know…," said Christian.

"Shit. After tomorrow, if we're lucky, it may be a first," said Billy.

"Maybe. If we're lucky."

"Jude's always had a plan for everything."

"He seems like the planning type."

"He just can't seem to understand that ain't how life works."

"No sir," Christian said.

"You think this is the best plan?" Billy asked.

"Robbing banks?"

"Yea. I guess."

"I've never figured out how to earn an honest nickel in my life without losing a dime. I don't think there's an honest way of procuring…"

"…Two hundred and fifty thousand."

"Two hundred and fifty thousand."

Christian wrassled with his beard, combing his thick fingers through the dense forest of red and then he spoke. "Can I ask you something?"

"Shoot," said Billy.

Both men shot each other an uneasy look.

"Maybe not the best choice of words considering…" said Billy.

"Maybe not," said Christian.

Both men smirked.

"My question is why two-hundred and fifty thousand?"

"You mean why not more?" asked Billy.

Christian stiffened up in his chair and turned his head down sorely. "I didn't say that."

"You want a bigger cut."

"I don't want *a* cut."

"Well, you're getting one."

Christian eyes steered into Billy and broadened. "No, I'm not, God-damnit. That's not why I am doing this."

Billy leaned back in the booth, gulped down his entire drink and then laid the heavy glass on the table. "Me neither. Or Jude, so you just answered your own question."

"In case you haven't noticed, I'm an inbred hillbilly that can't follow much, so you're gonna have to lay it out for me real nice and slow."

"Why you do that?

"Do what?"

"Disparage yourself. We both know you're one smart son of bitch. Stubborn and quiet but smart."

"Why do you?" Christian asked.

Billy squinted, looked away and then returned. "As long as I can remember, people were always calling me dumb and wild. I guess I just started obliging," Billy said.

Christian pursed his lips and raised an open palm in agreement.

"Fair enough," said Billy. "Darcy Simon paid the Pinkertons a hundred thousand dollars to hang a noose around my neck. We figured if we offer them double, the suckling swine might take it and leave us alone. The rest is just to make sure we have a little something for whatever comes after if we get that lucky."

Christian nodded.

"We ain't doing this to get rich and comfortable," said Billy. "We ain't fucking criminals. Not like that."

Christian nodded.

"You think it's wise trying to reason with these people?" Billy asked.

"I don't know these people."

"You know *these* people."

Christian breathed in deep and exhaled uncomfortably.

He sat up in his seat and uncrossed his arms.

Right on cue, the barmaid approached knowing what the sign of a man that needed a drink looked like.

"Can I get you something, sugar?" she asked, her eyes fluttering lightly, laying her arm around Christian's shoulder, in her short frilly dress and black stockings.

"Bourbon. Double. Neat. Please."

"Is that it?"

"That's it," he said matter-of-factly but polite.

Her eyes turned to Billy.

'Same. Just the same," said Billy.

She smiled cordially and pranced off.

"You haven't answered my question," said Billy.

Christian grappled with his beard again, making a scratchy noise. He looked away, his eyes narrowed and the rassling of facial hair with his hand continued until the barmaid returned with the drinks.

She quietly placed two coasters and the cocktails down before the gentlemen and walked away, probably sensing the heaviness like only someone who intervenes in conversations often can.

Christian took a long slug of his drink and then spoke. "This is y'all's rodeo. I'm just along for the ride."

Billy had already taken a swallow of his drink. The spirits burned strong and soothing in his chest that had felt vacant and cold from the opium. He went there to feel vacant and cold but now his brain tingled, and he felt alive again.

"That don't fly with me," Billy said. "Not with this." He looked Christian hard in the eye.

"I hear ya," said Christian. "You ain't twisting my arm. I'm making my decision under free-will if that's what you're asking."

Billy's eyes relented and he sat back again in the booth holding the wide bottom of the cocktail glass in the palm of his hand.

Christian continued to the question. "I think as a husband and a father, Jude has to try all reasonable means to get back home to his wife and children. Wherever home now is for y'all. I don't blame Jude for trying to reason with these people then. I'm making a decision to help."

Both men sat quiet, sipping their whiskey, and maybe thinking about tomorrow.

"If it was me? Just me?" Christian asked.

Billy nodded.

"I'd go in guns blazing and kill as many sons of bitches as possible before they can fill me with lead. Make one hell of a mess," said Christian.

"I would of done the same if not for Jude and planning. Now, I ain't got no choice but to worry about people other than myself."

"Reminds you of the war," Christian said.

Billy's glassy blues sparkled as they blinked fast at Christian. It was the only thing moving on the man and then Billy spoke. "Yeah. Didn't realize that's what was bothering me." Billy nodded to himself again and then spoke. "You ain't?... No wife or kids?"

"Had a wife.... Polio." Christian blinked and then spoke again. "She had it when I got back. Ended up dying in our bed while I was on a fix."

"I'm sorry," Billy said.

"Me too," said Christian.

"You blame yourself for that?"

"Yes, sir."

"Won't help one bit if I tell you it ain't your fault."

"No sir."

"You found forgiveness for yourself?"

"Fuck no." Christian paused for a moment and then spoke. "Marion? She was your wife in France?"

"Yea... Overdose... I was with her. Right there in bed but didn't know."

"Nodded off?"

"Yeah."

"That's rough. You blame yourself for that?"

"Yes, sir," Billy said, and looked away."

"You found forgiveness for yourself yet?" Christian asked.

"Fuck no," said Billy.

Christian grappled with his beard then he hit his medicine. He looked at Billy who was still looking away.

"It's funny," Christian eventually said, "I've had a lot things not go my way but I've never blamed anybody for any of it. Not my family, God, nobody."

"And yet, you blame yourself for what happened with your wife…" Billy said.

"Hardest person to forgive is oneself," Christian said.

Billy only nodded.

The room around the two men buzzed with jovial laughter and spritely conversation, between them, silence.

"And this other woman?" Christian finally asked and then stopped himself. His words trailed off as his head lowered. "Didn't mean it to sound like that and it ain't my business."

"No. It's all right. She was the woman I was going to marry before…"

"Before you went away?"

"…Yeah."

Christian nodded. "It was her old man that came after you?"

"Yeah."

"And her brother that Jude went after?"

"Yeah."

"Jude was right."

"How's that?"

"It is a Goddamn fairy tale. And now I'm wrapped up in it. If I walk into that bank tomorrow and there's some fucking dragons, I'm done with this shit."

Billy laughed.

"Only one creature on this earth I ever seen breathe fire," said Billy, "And that's Luisa."

"Jude's wife?"

"Yeah."

"I'd imagine she'd have to be."

"You should have seen him in the old days."

"Honestly, I'm pretty fucking grateful I didn't see either of you two *in the old days.*"

"Something tells me, I'm lucky I didn't come across you in your prime either."

Christian brushed off his chest. "Who said I'm out of my prime?" he asked, almost merrily.

Both men laughed.

"We'll see tomorrow," Billy said, suddenly sober.

"Yeah…We'll see tomorrow."

CHAPTER
THIRTY-ONE

In the eight days the boys were in Chicago, it was the first truly pleasant morning.

When Jude stepped out of the drab hotel, soft friendly sunshine splashed on his face. He closed his eyes for a moment and turned his head up, soaking it up all over. He opened his eyes to Billy and Christian seemingly unaffected by God's grace, marching down the street, focused and severe, like two soldiers ought to be. Jude's eyes shut once more, devouring the warm air scented with April flowers from somewhere else, and the sea-like lake that surrounded them. The briefcase in his hand, brushed against his pant leg, snapping him back to the cold reality.

Jude glanced over at Billy and Christian again, both looking sharp and awkward in their suits. He realized the effect a suit can have on a man the first day he slid his arms through the silky sleeves and felt the knot of the tie nuzzling against his neck, dressing for his first trial. It made him feel proud, confident, bold, brazen even. Then he remembered feeling embarrassed that the suit made him feel that way. He was raised to hate men in suits.

True grit came from a working man's hands and a tool belt not linen and a money roll.

Jude single-handedly chased depraved killers and vile rapists through dark alleys, taking down some of the most uncanny and unimaginable monsters that somehow crept out of God's creation. If anything, saving the greater society from those folks should have given him a sense of pride and valor not some twisted thread only procured by spending money and a Goddamn law degree.

Maybe Luisa had been right along. Maybe Jude was meant to earn a living with his educated mind, in a suit and tie and polished wingtips, not with his gut and holster and ass-kicking boots. Maybe that's why Jude enjoyed the sentiment the suit provided. And maybe there were two kinds of men on the planet, those who feel well-heeled in a suit and those who don't.

Christian and Billy were clearly the latter.

But today, the suit was a sham. Worn to defend against unwanted attention and bring about the proper. Donned to get him past the gatekeeper peon bank-tellers and to the president himself. The only one who held the real keys to anything significant – the vault – then the cash. The suit would be used to fraudulently hide his intentions until his true self was revealed, and then, it would be too late, like a spider with a fly.

Maybe Jude felt comfort in the suit as a lawyer because it also hid the fraudulent fact that he had no business being one. Poor orphan half breeds, *coyotes*, were destined only to be poor, never mind a sheriff and definitely not a lawyer. In his role as the sheriff, it didn't take long for Jude to earn respect – or fear – and sometimes those were one in the same. Something about a shiny tin star and pistols on your hips instinctively allotted you respect. And most importantly, those two accessories provided the wearer self-respect. It allowed a glow of confidence that radiated out to others.

Maybe that was the power of the suit too, it fooled everyone including Jude into thinking he wasn't a sham, choosing to be a barrister instead of a scum-bag buster. Then Jude realized, maybe that's the whole purpose of the suit for everyone that ever hung two shoulders through the sleeves and two legs through the trousers- to hide one's true intentions and true persona. Perhaps that's why all the most perfidious and deceitful devils on the planet all wore suits.

Politicians.

Bankers.

Salesmen.

And yes, lawyers.

Jude was about to sit across the desk from someone he never met, who from his limited experience following, seemed like a God-fearing good Christian man, a devoted father and loving husband, and threaten that man's very existence and the existence of his wife and children. Understanding that, in this moment, Jude did not feel guilty and disgraced about that fact. Instead, he felt shame and dishonor, guilt by association- like a German soldier in a Nazi uniform- for wearing a suit the last few years, and for relishing it.

Perhaps this sickening he felt now indicated maybe he was no different than the likes of Billy and Christian and was just fooling himself otherwise for a while. Or maybe, this internal strife meant just that Jude was complex, part good ol' boy part prevaricator. Then he realized he was going to have to be both, if their plan, *his* plan, was going to work.

Billy must have noticed Jude lost in reflection. "You okay?" he asked, as they marched down the street.

"I'm minutes from threatening to put a bullet in the head of a man I never met, with no due cause or provocation and then threaten to do the same to his wife and young children, so, no, I'm not okay."

Billy halted.

Christian was up ahead but noticed and turned back.

All three huddled on the sidewalk and Billy leaned his head to Jude. "Listen, *carnal*, we ain't done nothing yet. It ain't too late if this ain't what you want to do."

"*Want* ain't an appropriate word for our current circumstance."

Billy nodded, studying his brother intently then spoke. "This was your plan, *carnal*. This is how you wanted the picture to roll but we can stop it. No shame in you changing your mind."

Jude could sense that Christian was trying to keep his prying eyes out of the conversation, but he felt them regardless, then Jude spoke. "If there's any bloodshed in this whole ordeal, it's on me. Way I figure, I don't like what I'm about to do, but in the end, it may mean less people getting hurt."

"I can't speak for the latter statement, but the former is fucking hog-wash," Billy said. "If there's any bloodshed, and I ain't praying to the Almighty but if I did, I'd pray for none. But if there's any blood spilt today, it ain't on just you. This *ordeal*, we all signed up."

"That's right," said Christian, his sharp eyes directly at Jude.

"It's my plan. It is on me," said Jude.

"There's two things' you boys can't help but stumble over every God-damn day," said Christian. "Trouble and your bullshit sense of virtue. I don't know if it's a Catholic thing, an asshole thing or what."

Billy puckered his lips and nodded affirmatively. "It's mostly an asshole thing."

Jude grinned. "I'd say it's mostly a Catholic thing."

"Well then, you two Catholic assholes listen up. Sounds to me like this little journey started with Billy and his pecker. Then Jude had to swing his dick around and get involved. And then, when y'all saved my ass from being hung upside down from a tree, I threw my hat in the ring. Way I see it, we all free, white and eighteen here. We made this decision with our own free-will, every bit of it, we in together. I ain't no ra ra fucking general, I'm just saying we in the thick of it together, and we might as well concen-trate on getting to the thin of it together."

Jude pursed his lips this time and thought for a moment. Christian had possibly said more in the last thirty seconds than in the last eight days of them knowing each other. "All right," Jude finally said.

Billy looked at the two men and nodded.

"All right then," said Christian, both surprised and relieved.

Christian and Billy started up ahead again.

Jude held back for a moment observing the two men.

Christian lumbering down the street like a stiff giant, trying not to bump into people. His trousers a bit too high, one of his socks falling down his leg and crinkling around his loafer. His unruly thick hair now greased behind his ears with Billy's pomade. He looked like a fish out of water, or a hillbilly out of Kansas, Jude observed.

A fine-looking woman passed Billy, maybe giving him the eyes, forcing him to turn and look twice at her shape, almost running into a streetlight pole. Billy buried a wife, was on the run because of a girlfriend and about to rob a bank, and he was still checking out women.

Jude could only laugh to himself. There weren't two men on the planet, he'd rather march into battle with.

CHAPTER
THIRTY-TWO

"So, Mr...."

"Whitmore, Tim Whitmore," Jude said.

"Mr. Whitmore, yes. It's my understanding you're interested in opening up an account here," Henry Lout said. He was a paltry man in both height and weight, early forties with brown hair just starting to thin, probably the last physical attribute he had going for him, and small eyes behind wire framed glasses.

Jude wished the man exhibited some kind of smug or arrogant behavior. It'd make it easier to threaten his life in a few minutes, but so far, he came off humble and polite.

"You could say that, yes," said Jude.

"Very good, sir. Are you new to Chicago?" Henry asked, sounding sincere.

"I am actually."

"How do you like it?"

"Well, people told me it'd be windy, and so far, they ain't lying. It's a fine city, though. You from here?" Jude asked. As he held his salesman smile, his eyes probed the room. It was the first time they did so from this side of the track. Instead of reading the room for armed assailants or shifty snitches, he was surveying for undercover security and wily vigilantes. He didn't think the average joe average carried a side piece in Chicago like they did in Taos but that didn't stop him from patting down each customer with his eyes in search of any suspicious bulges.

And then his eyes made their way to Billy. *I got this*, they were saying. *Put attention back on ole Hank.*

When returned his focus where it belonged, Billy scanned the crowd again as he fictionally fiddled with a deposit slip. He could only look at the damn piece of paper for so long and eventually his eyes dragged back to the grandiose architecture of the bank. Appearing more like the cathedrals he saw overseas, with high ceilings, marble floors, and ancient debris sparkling in above, like angel's dust. Maybe all the historians had got it wrong. Maybe all the old churches scattered around Europe were not places of worship back in the day, but banks. Or maybe there was no difference.

"Third generation Chicagoan," Henry was boasting proudly but not rude. "And so is my wife."

"Wow, two native Chicagoans," Jude beamed, the only one in the conversation full of total bullshit. "Is this her here?" he asked, leaning over the desk at the picture.

"Yes," said Henry. "And my two children, Dorothy and Hank Jr."

"Dorothy and Hank Jr," the salesman's smile growing grotesquely wider as Jude pretended to gaze at the picture. In reality, this was his cue.

He cleared his throat for what was about to come next and scanned the room one more time.

Checking the security guard by the door, half asleep standing up.

Scoping the bank tellers, big toothy smiles with red lipstick as bright as their eyes – seemingly lambs not wolves – talking to unassuming patrons, the remaining clientele daydreaming in line.

Then veering to Billy one last time, as if saying, *Here goes…*

When their gaze converged, they collectively steered to Christian, sitting in a black leather chair, innocently not reading the Chicago Tribune.

The coast seemed clear, so Jude moved to lay it on thick now. "What darlings," he said, returning the picture.

Henry brimmed, his eyes now on the picture of his family and Jude knew this was his moment.

Jude's gut tightened.

His Catholic soul squeezed his insides.

He felt his face become flush and hot, like the burning embers of hell were closing in on him and he knew that if he didn't do it now, he'd never do it at all.

Jude swallowed hard and then spoke. "Which is what brings me in here."

"A family savings account?" Henry asked. "For your wife and children."

"No," said Jude, now dead serious and calm. "A family savings on your account."

Henry frowned as his head twisted slightly. "I'm sorry, I don't understand."

"Your wife is named Rebecca. I already knew Hank Jr and Dorothy's name before I walked in here today. I also know you live at 235 Maplewood Drive. This morning, you left the house at 7:25 on the dot. You have red roses growing under your kitchen window. The window that has trim painted baby blue. I know these things..."

Jude leaned forward in his chair.

He watched Henry's face grow from not-believing what he heard to confusion to now fear in a matter of seconds, but Jude did not want Henry to be fearful.

Fear alone would make Henry do something erratic and dangerous.

Jude wanted Henry to move from fear to hope but not yet.

"Now this is the important part Henry, so please pay attention. I know these details because I have been watching you. We have been watching you and your family and we know everything. We also have someone in a car right now in front of your house."

All color departed Henry's face.

His eyes teared up, not from sadness but fear and rage.

Erratic fear and rage that steamed through his tiny glasses.

Jude pulled up the sleeve of his suit jacket and looked at his watch. "I misspoke, Henry. This is actually the most important part. It is now 9:48

AM. At exactly 10:05 AM I need to make a telephone call to the phone booth on the corner of Elmore and Broadway. Do you know that telephone booth, Henry?"

Henry held still in shock.

"Henry" said Jude, snapping his fingers lightly just once. "Henry, you need to stay with me. Do you know that telephone booth?"

Henry blinked and cleared his throat. "Yes…" he whimpered. "That's the telephone booth at the end of my block."

"That's correct, Henry. Good. I need to walk out of here, with $250,00 in this briefcase and then I need to make a phone call by 10:05 AM. Can you surmise who I need to make that phone call to?"

Henry was shaken again by another question.

His lips quivered and his hand trembled. "Um… I'm guessing one of your men in that booth."

"That's correct Henry. And if my man does not get that phone call, he and two other men are going into your home. When they leave, the next living souls to walk in or out of your home will be the police and the coroner.

Do you understand what I am saying?"

Henry's head shuddered. Maybe he was nodding.

"Henry, I need you to say you understand."

Before Henry could assuage Jude's jittery nerves, the seat next to him scooted out. Jude's palm was already gripping the 6 shooter's handle, thumb on the hammer and forefinger on the trigger. He would have blasted a hole clear through the canary colored upholstery of the armchair and kept firing until he saw that yellow turn red if Billy hadn't preemptively grabbed his arm, reading his brother's mind.

"Y'all mind if I have a seat?" Billy asked, already settling in.

Like a Goddamn cartoon character, Jude's eyes craned in two different directions at once. One eye steered on Billy now sitting next to him, the other on Henry looking jumpier than a spooked horse. Maybe's Jude's eyes were literally twisting out of his skull because when Henry gazed back at Jude, Henry's lips started quivering and his hand on the desk started shaking.

"Hank, you don't mind if I call you Hank, do you?" Billy asked.

Henry's head only shivered as if his bare feet had just stepped in ankle deep snow.

"All right, Hank, that left hand of yours, the one I can't see, the one in your desk drawer holding a pistol, I'm gonna need to see that hand, real nice and slow, and most importantly, when I do see it, I don't want to see it holding that pistol."

Jude's face darted to Henry's, as if he was the horse now spooked and betrayed, only startling Henry more. Even Henry's small buttony eyes, behind those thin spectacles were quaking, and Jude swore, Henry was now pleading with him.

Please.

I haven't done anything.

I was going to give you the money.

And then Jude realized his own hand was still cradling his pistol, still aiming next to him, even though he now knew it was Billy that was the source of the commotion. That forced the reflex, but the reflex had subsided and yet some instinct in Jude kept that gun on his brother. That instinct that had never betrayed, never led him astray. What was it telling him now?

"I'm guessing y'all were just discussing the red roses and blue window trim in the front yard before I so rudely interrupted you two," Billy continued. "You ever want to get out of your car, gaze across your perfectly manicured lawn to your beautiful house and see those impeccably pruned rose bushes and blue baby blue window sills again, you're gonna show me that other hand, Hank. Then you're gonna show us the money, and then the front door and then…"

Billy suddenly snapped his fingers…

Henry winced and jumped back like he'd been shot.

Jude's whole body cringed, and for a moment, he actually thought he'd pulled the trigger himself or fired the next one. Jude was that fast in a duel, rarely even remembering pulling that first shot, and on the rare occasion when he wasn't the fastest, he was saved by being the most accurate.

Jude felt his breath sigh from his lungs, his shoulders slacken and his finger ease, when he saw Billy still sitting next to him whole.

"…And then you'll never see us again," Billy was saying. "Do you understand, Hank?"

Henry trembled a nod.

"Good, now I can see them hands of yours shaking, and that's completely natural considering the circumstance, so when you pull that other hand out from underneath, why don't you do yourself a favor and clasp both hands together right there on top of your desk. Do you pray, Hank?"

Henry cleared his throat as he spoke at the same time. "P…p…pardon me?"

"Do you pray?"

"Y…yes."

"Alrighty, well then just clasped them hands together, casual but tight as if you were praying. Now here we go…"

Henry's twitchy eyes moved from Billy to Jude.

"It's okay, Henry," Jude said. "It's okay," he said again, as if Ole Hank wasn't the only one needing convincing.

Henry's right arm remained across the desk, and soon enough, his left arm reappeared from under the dark red mahogany, joining the right. His hands clasping together so tight, Jude thought Henry's fingernails would draw blood to the back of his hands.

"You're doing fine, Hank, mighty fine in fact. Just one more thing, smile," Billy said. "Smile."

"What?" Henry muttered.

"*Smile*, Hank, so people don't think you're being held up."

CHAPTER
THIRTY-THREE

Jude collapsed to his knees.

The heavy suitcase full of money pulled him down like an anchor.

His face steamed, his eyes watered and before he knew it, he was vomiting into a sewer drain.

The sunbeams that felt warm and comforting earlier now singed the back of his neck.

His suit seemed glued to his skin and he couldn't breathe.

And then there was more vomit.

Christian calmly stepped to Jude's side and picked up the suitcase, securing it and inspecting their full surroundings.

Downtown Chicago mid-day was bustling.

Cars sped by only to slam on their brakes in traffic.

People of all colors and walks of life, swiveled by one another, while seemingly acting like every other person on the planet was invisible.

It was impossible for Christian to get a beat on anything suspicious because everything seemed so foreign to him.

Billy bent down next to Jude. "*Estas bien?*" he asked.

Jude turned his head up to Billy.

His eyes were bloodshot, he was sweating, and a vein pulsed in his forehead.

He opened his mouth to speak but only vomit found its way out again.

When he finished, he wiped the saliva and residue that trickled from the corners of his mouth with the back of his hand. He felt weak and fragile and could barely hold himself up on all fours.

"Just give me a minute," Jude said.

He watched water rush through the sewer below.

The rank odor punched him in the senses.

An ant toddled by, stopping at the fleshy part of his hand that met the concrete, attempting to wrap its mandibles around Jude's hand to sting his flesh.

A loud car horn suddenly blared near Jude's ear, startling him and he realized it was time to go.

He wiped his mouth one more time and then braced himself to stand.

Billy slung his hand under Jude's arm, helping him up.

"We're good," Billy said to Christian, relieving him from his watch post as the three men began walking down the street. "*Todo bien que no?*" Billy whispered to Jude.

"Good ain't on the table anymore. *Que no?*

The hotel room door hadn't closed, and Jude's fist was already bunched tight into Billy's shirt collar driving him across the room.

"What the fuck was that?" Jude seethed, slamming Billy's back into the wall, Billy's neck snapping with whiplash from the mere force.

"That was me saving our ass," Billy said. "He was *making a move.*"

"Bullshit!" Jude yelled into Billy's face, causing Billy to wince from the piercing spittle.

"He was making a move, and you were to blind to see it," Billy said, flattening his arms against the wall while holding his hands above his head, as if he truly was being interrogated by a cop, relenting.

Since the boys were old enough to bite, hit or swing, system dynamics had dictated their relationship, keeping them whole and alive from each other. If one fell into a violent fit, the other typically ascended to a pillar of peace and armistice, avoiding a nuclear holocaust.

It was Jude's finger on the red button now and Billy waiving the white flag.

"From where you were sitting, you probably couldn't see," Billy said. "But I was watching Hank's hand move across his desk, when y'all were talking. And when it slipped into that drawer, I darted over."

Jude released his grip on Billy and backed away, his breath slowing as his internal temperature dropped.

Billy slowly lowered his hands unbuttoning his knotted up shirt.

Jude looked to Christian who only shook his head.

"I wasn't in a position to see anything," Christian said from Switzerland.

Jude heaved in another weighted sigh, collapsing into a small wooden chair.

Billy studied Jude, letting him simmer before asking, "What was that about outside the bank?"

"That," Jude said, "Was a physical manifestation of guilt," he tented back in his chair, limbs dangling, appearing exhausted.

"We got the money. We ain't dead or bleeding and, most importantly, we didn't have to hurt anyone," Billy said. "I'd almost say that's cause for celebration, not a heavy conscience."

Christian sat on the bed next to Jude. His wild red curls now sticking straight up, like electricity was running through his scalp. His suit jacket was rumpled next to him, his shirt now unbuttoned. A 20-gauge shotgun cocked and loaded laid across his tree trunk legs and his eyes were steady somewhere between Jude on the chair and Billy at the window. Once in a while, they blinked. His only movement.

Jude leered up at Billy from his chair.

Billy must have felt his eyes.

He turned around, studied the condition of his brother and sympathy washed over his face. "It don't get any easier."

"What's that?" Jude asked.

"Doing shit that don't feel right."

Christian turned his head, as if he could not look at either man.

His eyes narrowed and he kind of just stared into the long thin mirror mounted on the closet door at the far end of the room.

"Do we need to count the money?" Billy asked.

"No. Old Hank counted every dollar out loud when he was putting it in the briefcase. It's separated into clips of a thousand," Jude said.

Billy nodded, still studying his brother. "Maybe we should take a few days off before moving forward with the Pinkertons."

"Maybe I just need some Goddamn peace and quiet for a minute," Jude said.

Christian's attention returned to Jude.

His baby blues shining out from under his bushy red eyebrows.

Jude turned to Christian, shooting him the *What the fuck are you looking at?* glare.

Christian stood up and walked to the corner between the window and the wall and stared out, the shotgun resting under his arm.

Billy slightly nodded again and returned his heed to cautioning out the window.

Quite enveloped the room until Jude finally spoke first.

"It's why you didn't come home sooner…" said Jude, more tender. "Part of the reason, at least."

Billy turned back to Jude confused.

"The guilt," Jude continued.

Billy nodded.

"I couldn't come home for a while after…" Christian blurted out, still standing awkwardly in the corner. His giant frame wedged between the wall and window, the massive gun between his legs, the butt resting on the ground. "That's when my wife died of polio. Not when I was dodging bullets and shrapnel or hunkered down in a fox hole. When I was lying in some gutter on a six-month drunk with a needle in my arm."

Billy's back remained facing the two men, but Jude could see the reflection of his eyes in the window. They were wide and heavy. The same as Christian's and maybe his own.

"That's the one," Christian continued.

"The one?" Jude asked.

"The one that keeps him at night," said Billy, still finding solitude facing the window.

"That's right," said Christian. His eyes centered on Jude. "I feel for you, Jude, I do. But if we get through this, and holding that man up today, is your one, the one sin you can't find forgiveness for in yourself. The one that kicks you in the nuts at 2 AM and gives you nightmares in broad day-light. Consider yourself lucky. Consider yourself divine."

Christian turned back to the window.

Jude caught Billy peeking over his shoulder for a moment at his older brother, then he checked the clip of the gun hehe held in his hand, ensuring it was still loaded.

"The Klan boys?" asked Billy.

"What about them?" asked Jude.

"Those hooded sons of bitches you shot and the one still living you knee-capped don't bother you? But threatening this Hank fella simply with words does?"

Jude's eyes became as wide and pale as a full moon. "I almost forgot those Klan boys."

"That'll happen too," said Christian.

"What will?" asked Jude.

"Losing track," said Billy. "How many people you hurt and kill."

"I'd like to walk away from this and be able to count on one hand, how many people I've killed. But even two hands is looking foolishly optimistic," said Jude.

"You'd like to walk away," said Christian. "That's it. It's a zero sum"

Jude slightly nodded and blinked the full moons away.

"Zero sum. Those are complex words for a hillbilly," Jude said with half a smirk.

Christian held up two fingers and said, "Them words only got three syllables."

All three men chuckled. Laughter the only true medicine for guilt.

CHAPTER
THIRTY-FOUR

"I've got it," said Billy, almost galloping through the door.

Jude and Christian peered up from the cards in their hands and the game on the little wooden table between them.

The room was dreary and stale, the shades dulling the late spring sun, and the closed windows winnowing the fresh florid air.

"Got what?" Jude asked.

The stakeout, or time away from his family, was clearly taking its toll on Jude. He hadn't shaved in a week, and when he wasn't in public, he relegated to wearing nothing but an A-shirt, Levi's, hat and boots, his current attire.

Christian and Billy seemed more at ease with the process of the mission. Perhaps they had less to lose, nothing left to fill a vacant heart, or perhaps they were simply used to the long slow process of hunting humans.

"Sons of bitches are remodeling," said Billy. "The whole Pinkerton office. That's our in."

For two weeks, the three men hunkered down, setting their sights on how to have a word with the Pinkertons, while also having a bullet ready, if necessary. The men knew Allen Pinkerton III would never agree to meet them somewhere other than the safe confines of his office, his fortress. Yes, it was located downtown, with fancy trim, a kind and cordial receptionist and a delightful sign that read "Pinkerton Agency." But a closer look revealed it was a Goddamn garrison, with armed guards hiding machine guns under expensive suits, thick concrete walls essentially bullet-proof, and tortuous dungeons where dirty secrets bled out.

The men also knew to even get face time with the Pinkerton heir and Chief Executor, rather, Chief Executive Officer, they would need to speak his language. That's where the stolen money came in.

There was no misconception as to the true nature of the Pinkertons. They were hired thugs, albeit high-priced hired thugs, no more no less. Walking into any *meeting* even in a downtown office in broad day light while being escorted by a friendly woman that would remind you of your grandmother, without a gun, was sheer suicide. The men also knew they'd be frisked by the dapper machine gun-toting junkyard dog of a *doorman* before they had two feet in the door.

"Go on," said Jude.

Christian's eyes blinked from across the table, faster than usual, probably indicating the same.

"We get in on the crew doing the construction work," said Billy. "Once we set up a meeting with the *Culero Numero Uno*, we'll stash our guns and explosives the day before. Obviously, it can't be you or I strapping on the tool belt."

Billy and Jude's eyes made their way to Christian.

"Only time I've ever felt at ease in my life was with a tool in my hand." Christian looked down at the pistol on his lap. "This one or otherwise."

"How we gonna get him on the crew?" Jude asked.

"I scoped out the construction company doing the work," said Billy. "They're Goddamn Union. All we need is grease," nodding to the briefcase full of cash.

"You're telling me the biggest union busting-assholes in this country hired union workers?" asked Jude.

"Hey, it's still Chicago," said Billy. "Who's the one group more feared than the Pinkertons?"

"Organized labor," blurted Christian.

"*Simon*," said Billy.

"Those Union whores will take money from their murdering thieving mortal enemies," said Jude. "Maybe there is hope for the American Dream yet."

"We just gotta figure out how to grease Christian in with the union while not raising any red flags," said Billy.

"That's right," said Jude. "Any little eruption is bound to put the Pinkertons on notice and make it that much more difficult for us. We've been laying low hunting them, and don't think they ain't been doing the same. It's been quiet but they've been circling."

"I don't disagree but I ain't seen Dahl once," said Billy.

"Pretty sure I'd know the snake in the grass if I'd see him and I ain't seen him," said Christian.

"He's around," said Jude. "I can feel it in my bones."

"All right, well how we gonna get Cinderella into the ball?" asked Billy.

Christian looked down at the Klan tattoos scarred on the top of his hands that constantly stared up at him, taunting and sneering, reminding him of his old self. His past that he'd never truly escape.

"It's time I finally take these ugly hateful self-inflicted wounds and do some good with them," said Christian.

CHAPTER
THIRTY-FIVE

"You ain't some trouble-making rabble rouser are you?" Salvatore asked, leering up at him.

"No sir, Mr. Salvatore," said Christian, standing at attention, arms behind his back.

The short Italian man lunged himself out of the chair that squeezed him like a balloon. He shuffled around the gray steel desk. His suspenders around his belly barely clung onto the pants that hung below his waistline. Only his hair, a few greasy strands combed over on top, and his mustache, were thin on the man. He stared up at Christian, his brown eyes squeezing through his round perspiring cheeks.

"I don't know, you look like a troublemaker to me," Salvatore said.

Christian's unblemished blues eyes remained fixed over the man's shiny head. "No sir. I'm no troublemaker."

Salvatore moved in, scrutinizing Christian closer.

Christian swore he could smell cured meat and red wine on the guy's steamy breath.

Salvatore did not waver.

Finally, Christian cleared his throat and spoke again. "Aside from, you know, being in the Klan. I ain't no troublemaker."

Salvatore must have been somewhat appeased by the answer. He backed down and wobbled around his desk. The chair shrieked and floorboards moaned when Mr. Salvatore set back down. "Yea, that's what I don't like. I ain't never dealt with you boys."

"Well, sir, you wouldn't be dealing with other boys. Just me and them presidents," said Christian nodding to the stack of cash on the desk between them.

Salvatore couldn't help but look down at the whispering loot and then back up the lingering caveman.

"Have a seat."

Christian sat down.

Salvatore's eyes narrowed on him. "I don't have a problem per se with your group… is that what you all call yourself? 'A group?'"

"Um… A clan, sir," said Christian trying to sound as humble as possible.

"Of course," said Salvatore, shrugging with his palms spread wide like an open-faced salami sandwich.

Every guap I ever met is the same, Christian thought. *They all talk with either their hands or their pecker.*

"Like I said, I ain't got nothing against your clan, the Klan. We've just never associated with them in Chicago. I know we have union brothers in the South who are in the Klan and they are all fine people. It's just a little different up here. Of course, we don't let *mulignans* into the Union."

"Of course," said Christian. *You see those three strands of black hair on your greasy head? And those high cheekbones under your fat face?* Christian wanted to say. *That didn't come from your grandparents fucking Vikings.*

"Of course," Salvatore mimicked again with hands. "That being said, there's a lot of black folk in Chicago. In many parts they out-number us here. They ain't got no money so they ain't worth the trouble, you hear me?"

"Yes sir."

"Do you know the greatest foe to the Union, Christian is it?"

"Yes sir."

"Well, do you?"

Christian brushed his wild red beard with the palm of his hand and then spoke. "Robber baron sons of bitches sir?"

Salvatore chuckled heartily and sat up in his chair. "Robber baron sons of bitches. That's good. Close but no. Factions," he said, dropping his elbows on the desk while pointing this thick finger at Christian.

"Factions sir?"

"Factions," he pointed again.

Salvatore relapsed back in his chair seemingly waiting for Christian to request elaboration.

Christian nodded and blinked and went back to grooming his beard. He was an uneducated hillbilly whose parents were cousins somewhere pretty-close in the family tree, but he was born with that rare combination of common sense and intellect. The only graces God bestowed on him. He followed the line of thinking Salvatore was on before Salvatore even knew he was on it, but just like in the Klan and military, he understood his part and played it like Charlie fucking Chaplain. Christian fidgeted and pretended to be thinking *real hard*.

Salvatore shook his head at the seeming Neanderthal in front of him. "I don't think I gotta worry about that with you."

"No sir."

"Uh huh," said Salvatore, his eyes narrowed now in condescension instead of suspicion. "I take it none of your Klan members higher up gave you any indication as to their intentions for you here?"

"No sir."

"And you never heard about any plans about a mass migration North? There ain't gonna be two hundred of you hooded-sons of bitches riding into town on horses and carrying crosses on fire are there?"

"I don't think so," Christian said, doe eyed.

"Then why are you here?"

"Well, my cousin lives near-by," Christian said, his southern accent suddenly more pronounced with each word. "On Michigan and Belmont. He ain't in the Klan or nothing."

"Still not making sense to me, boy," said Salvatore, losing his patience with the realization he was speaking with the village idiot. Even a village idiot showing up with five grand in cash.

Christian fidgeted again and stared at the ground, recalling how the farm pups would look after they ate a chick they damn-well knew they weren't supposed to.

Salvatore leaned forward again. "I asked you a question, Goddamnit."

Christian knew he had him. "Well, I got in some trouble at home."

"What kind of trouble?"

"I was just doing what I was told then they told me some Federal boys were looking for me and I had to come North for a while."

"You hang some nigger on a tree?" asked Salvatore.

Even hearing the word made Christian cringe. He felt this strange push and pull of never wanting to hurt another living soul again while also strangling this racist pig for the vile speech that spilled from his tongue. "Something like that," Christian said.

Salvatore reclined back in his chair again. "I don't know why I am asking you this. You probably can't even tell me one plus fucking one. But you have the most important quality in a Union man. Do you know what that is?"

"No sir."

"You do as you're told, and you don't ask questions."

"Yes sir."

"Welcome to the Local 710, hillbilly," Salvatore said, reaching his hand over the face of the presidents on the table, smiling up at them.

CHAPTER
THIRTY-SIX

"I guess it's as good a day as any," Jude said, surveying the stack of cash on the bed next to the open briefcase. The curtains on the windows had been pulled back and the cheerful morning sun provided the only vivid light in the room.

"We Union boys, for as much ass as we pick, are gonna be done by the end of the week," Christian said, adjusting the scope on his sniper rifle that stood nose-up between his legs where he sat.

His newly shaved face was glossy and smooth and almost pallid from his lush red beard shading his flesh for so long. His radical kinky red hair was now flat-top and uniform, standing at attention like a good soldier.

Billy was still shaking his head and chuckling at Christian's new effigy.

"What?" Christian asked, sounding almost hurt.

Billy continued to shake his head. "Every one of you are the same."

"Hillbillies?" Christian asked.

"No, snipers," said Billy. "Y'all are more superstitious than an *abuelita bruja.*"

"More than some childish superstition," Christian said, still pouting. "When the only thing between a bullet in your skull and walking away to fight another day, is my eye, my senses, and my trigger finger, you're gonna want me as focused as possible. That means no beard rustling up against my rifle or Goddamn pantywaist hair getting in my eyes."

Billy pursed his lips and nodded, looking Christian directly in the eye.

"It's mostly superstition," said Christian.

Billy grinned, gazing at the pasty skull once more. "Well, that *guap* barber did a fine job."

Christian stopped tinkering with his gun long enough to throw Billy the bird.

"Y'all are definitely the most sensitive too," said Billy.

"We'll see how you feel about my delicate sensibilities when you're ten stories below and thirty yards away knowing between your left shoulder and your right shoulder is my cross hairs."

"Jesus Christ, you two!" Jude shouted. "It's a wonder we managed to defeat the enemy at all with y'all so busy slanging shit at each!"

Both men understood Jude wasn't actually giving them a tongue lashing just as Jude understood the healthy banter that calmed men's nerves when facing mortality. He didn't fight in any wars, but he had been in plenty of battles where loss of life was imminent. Whether it be said or not, Christian wasn't the only superstitious fella in the room either. There was a reason Jude was wearing the dark blue Levi's he most preferred, button-down western shirt and cowhide jacket. True it was the only clothes he still owned from back home, but it was more than that. Somewhere in Chicago he probably could have found some half-ass western shop that sold similar clothes but the threads that hung from his shoulders and hugged his legs were what he felt most comfortable in, most at peace with, going into war.

It's also why Billy wore his same white V-Neck T-shirt, faded black denim jeans, matching boots and leather jacket. Granted, it was all Jude brought for him that harrowing night, but Jude brought it for a reason, knowing full-well it was Billy's armor. Armor from the outside world and for the stories of inadequacy in Billy's own mind. It was Billy's uniform that allowed him to truly feel comfortable with Billy.

Today, would allow no distractions.

If Christian could wear his military uniform, he would have, but that was not an option. Instead, he elected for a light blue pearl snap shirt, baggy enough to not hinder him, and jeans.

"That rifle gonna do?" Jude asked, watching Christian disassemble and reassemble it for the umpteenth time.

"The best money can buy," said Christian before his eyes ventured to the briefcase of stolen loot it was purchased with. "No, uh, pun intended," he muttered bashfully.

Jude shook his head slightly and laughed.

"So, hillbilly, you know what a pun is but you got an issue with numbers?" Billy said, placing a small card in Christian's breast pocket.

"What's that?" Jude asked.

Christian cleared his throat and fidgeted.

"Nothing," said Billy, picking up his pistol, inspecting it one last time.

Christian noticed the queered look that remained on Jude's face. Today the boys needed no more surprises. "Numbers for whatever reason, don't stick in my head. That card reminds me what floor I need to be on. It's in code though, that we used in the war, so if I get jammed up, it won't reveal nothin."

Jude nodded, seeming satisfied.

Billy pulled the slide of his 9mm, cocking the pistol, and tucking it into his waistband under his jacket.

Jude snapped open the chamber of his Winchester revolver, ensuring all his friends were in attendance, and then did the same.

Christian stood, lightly placing the sniper rifle on the bed. He pulled his dog tags out from underneath his shirt, kissed them and then returned them to his chest. He noticed Billy's eyes. "For all the fallen," Christian said.

"Yea," said Billy.

Christian cleared his throat and fidgeted.

"What is it?" Billy asked.

Christian cleared his throat again. "I saw a lot my brothers fall while my eye was staring through a scope on them, while them boys counted on me to have their back. His eyes inflated and he stared off past the worn brown carpet of the dingy hotel room.

Billy walked over and placed his hand on Christian's shoulder.

Christian blinked and looked Billy square in the face and then Jude. "I got y'alls back today."

"I know," said Billy. "I don't believe in fate, but I believe we ran into you for a reason."

"And it ain't because of your fanciful eloquence, ability with numbers or personal hygiene," Jude said grinning.

Christian glowered, and gave his arm pits a sniff. "What's wrong with my hygiene?"

CHAPTER THIRTY-SEVEN

Jude pointed the top of his head straight ahead, using his hat's wide brim to shade his eyes as he marched down the street. For the last week, every conversation he overheard in the city, whether businessmen over martinis or newspaper and cigarette vendors, involved the unusually warm weather. *Warm?* he thought. *Feels like a fucking Louisiana swamp.*

The temperature wasn't hot. It was mild and sunny and that alone would be bearable, enjoyable even. But the humidity, sticky and thick, was down-right oppressive.

Jude sweated more in these 70 degree April days in Chicago than he ever did on those rare days it hit 80 in Taos, before the monsoons rolled in chasing away any real heat for the remainder of the summer.

Jude was no cow town ninny. He understood Taos had its flaws - poverty and violence to say the least- but in that moment, he thought about how perfect Taos was in every conceivable way, including the weather, and he yearned for home.

Then a sadness more heavy and viscous than the midwest humidity fell over Jude, realizing he may never see Taos again. Even if he survived this preposterous nonsensical ordeal, he might never again experience the thin dry air filled with rich pinon burning and chile roasting.

He might never see the blood orange sun crest over the lavender-colored rocky mountain as the snow on the horizon glimmered below almost in unison with the stars above.

Never again here the coyote howl out, worshiping the moon, or the rumbling thunder echo off the canyon walls of the trickling Rio Grande as lightning sizzled the sky.

An even deeper sorrow descended upon Jude, slicing through his flesh, past his heart and into his soul. It was the recognition that his children would never be able to experience the wondrous magic of the *Sangre de Cristos*.

Never hang freely from the branches of the pinon trees.

Run boundlessly through the hills, swimming fluently in the rivers, one with the earth, as he did in his childhood memories.

Someone tried to kill Jude's brother.

Someone tried to kill Jude.

Someone upended and dismantled Jude's family, but in that moment, what suddenly enraged him most was that someone robbed his children, innocent children, that had done nothing wrong, of their birthright. The sacred inheritance of growing up in Northern New Mexico.

Billy looked both ways waiting to cross the eight-lane *street* of downtown Chicago. He caught a glimpse of Jude, and a cold shiver ran up his spine. "*Esperate*, Jude!" Billy yelled, seeing his brother about to step out into traffic.

Jude paid no heed, marching dead on into the sea of cars. Even his walk said he was on fire.

"Jude, hold up!" Billy said again, resigned to diving in after his brother.

Jude turned his head from under the brim of his hat, fury in his eyes and grit in his teeth, as he stood aimlessly in the middle of the Goddamned street. "What?" Jude seethed.

"What do you mean…" Billy paused, car horns blaring, tire screeching, as the city slickers careened around the two cowpokes out of their element. "Let's step back for a minute," he said as gently as a man can shout while standing in the middle of traffic.

Jude raised his head in indignation.

"*Por favor*," said Billy.

Jude palmed the side of his face down to his jaw and stepped back onto the sidewalk almost running into a woman hurrying by, shooting Jude a vexing eye. Normally, Jude would have tipped his hat and apologized with a simple *ma'am*. Instead, he almost growled at her, and Billy knew for sure he was in deep *that way. Jude's way.*

"*Que es?*" Jude asked looking everywhere but at Billy in front of him.

"You tell me," Billy said, kindly to his brother.

Jude took a deep breath.

A good sign, Billy thought.

"I just got to thinking..." Jude said.

"That's never good," Billy cracked a half smile.

Jude only rolled his eyes to Billy.

At least the son of bitch is looking at me now, Billy thought.

Jude cleared his scratchy sounding throat and then spoke. "Out of nowhere, Patrick and Wyatt popped into my mind just now and I started thinking about how maybe I've robbed them..."

Jude's eyes went back to the cracked sidewalk.

He palmed his mug again and scratched his eyebrow.

"Robbed them?" Billy asked, when he saw Jude wasn't going any further.

"Just uh...you know, robbed them of what we had."

"What? A drunk father and a loon mother?"

"No. Growing up in Northern New Mexico. Running free. Falling in dirt. Climbing from trees. Fishing. Slicing open our hands on rocks and cactus."

"General hell-raising," Billy said, almost nostalgic.

Jude grinned slightly and looked up at his brother. "General hell-raising."

"Jude, if them two boys are unlucky enough to get any of your blood and any of my blood, they don't need the Goddamn *Sangre de Cristo Mountains* or the Land of Enchantment to raise hell. They gonna find a way to raise plenty all on their own whether it be Ireland or Timbuktu."

Jude smiled again. A little wider.

Billy stepped back giving his brother another once over. "But that's not what's going on here."

"What do you mean?"

"I mean you're in that way, where hell or high-water you're gonna bring hell."

A little of Jude's snarl returned.

"I don't like when people tell me how I'm feeling," Billy continued. "Like they know what's in my Goddamn head, so I ain't saying I know what you're feeling or what you're thinking. I sure as shit don't and that's kind of what concerns me right now. But I can tell you're in that way that starts with anger and ends badly for everyone. Just trying to understand what brought you there."

Jude looked away again and gritted his teeth. "That *culero*, Dahl."

"Yea, I think we established he's a *culero*."

"No. I started thinking about him and how Wyatt and Patrick didn't do nothing wrong to nobody and that deviant corrupt son of bitch upended my sons' lives."

"So, it's Dahl who robbed your boys?"

"Yea…" Clarity flooded Jude's eyes and he looked up at Billy. "Yea…" he said definitively.

"Dahl is a murdering thieving brown eye son of a bitch, he is, but the worst thing he can rob them two boys of he hasn't. Not yet."

"What's that?" Jude asked.

"Their father." Billy held his eyes on Jude until Jude's met his and then spoke. "Shit is fucked up right now. But we're moving. So far so good. Our plan is working and today that plan requires you to be motherfucking cool. The time to set it all on fire is upon us soon, *carnal*, but it ain't today. We walk into this today with you holding that match of fire and gasoline, your temper, and Dahl *will* rob Wyatt and Patrick of their daddy. Now if you want to get it on today, let's go get machine guns, and dynamite and we can take half the city with us. Your boys will hear that you went out in a blaze of glory, probably hear other stories about you too, and at least they'll have that…"

Jude's shoulders loosened.

He removed his hat, wiped the ire from his forehead and looked up at the sky. He saw a seagull seamlessly sailing, its wings spread wide, floating high between skyscrapers, like bald eagles he would see soaring through the rocky Gorge of the Rio Grande.

Jude put his hat back on, this time the brim a little higher on his head. "*Gracias, hermanito.*" Jude looked Billy straight in the eye. "*Hermano.*"

"Like mamma used to say. Don't thank me for showing you the moon exists."

Jude chuckled. "What the fuck does that even mean?"

Billy smiled and shook his head. "I still don't have a clue."

"Where do you suppose that sayin' even came from?"

"Taos. That's got fucking Taos written all over it."

"Sure does," said Jude smiling off somewhere else. "I'm gonna teach Patty and Wyatt that one."

"You damn right," said Billy, stepping off the curb.

CHAPTER THIRTY-EIGHT

"**W**ell, it's only gonna be three o clock for another thirty seconds," Jude said watching the second-hand tick by on his wristwatch.

Billy's eyes were tight and small, not squinting from the rare blooming Midwest sun but from concentration. Even as a child, tasked with coloring within the lines, tying his shoe, or steering his bike on the loose dirt, when Billy got quiet and squint-eyed, Jude knew he was *putting attention.*

Billy turned his head slightly, perhaps trying to avoid all the fleas and gnats in business suits and pecuniary garb that just had to step right into his line of sight every other fucking second. He couldn't concentrate for a minute on the *pendejo* across the street posing as the doorman of the Pinkerton Agency without some hasty *cabron* aimlessly skipping in front of him.

Never mind he was in downtown Chicago on a Tuesday afternoon trying to look across Michigan Avenue unimpeded.

Never mind, Billy and Jude specifically chose this day, time and location because it would be obnoxiously crowded with people.

But was it too much to ask for everyone on Earth…?

…Fuck Earth, everyone in Chicago?

…Fuck that too, everyone on Michigan Avenue in this exact moment to simply step behind me instead of in front of me for one Goddamn minute so I can get a beat on this motherfucker? Billy wondered.

After the U.S. Military turned Billy into a soldier and the war was over, he'd tried booze, heroin, marriage and returning home to turn it off. None of it worked one bit. So, soldiering wasn't gonna be a problem. But Billy never had to try and do it in the middle of a Goddamn city with so many innocent civilians and a different set of rules. Jude devised plans and set rules, and Billy always put a jack hammer to both. But in the war, there were rules of engagement that allowed Billy to focus on the engagement. Here it was different, and he just couldn't concentrate. Get his mind sharp and pointed where it needed to be. For them to live and kill.

"Billy," Jude said again, studying Billy the same way Billy was trying to study the son of a bitch. "You ready?"

"Yea, I'm ready," Billy said half disgruntled. "God forbid we keep the sons of bitches waiting."

Jude brushed his right arm with his holster under his jacket, just to make sure his gun was still there, and then picked up the weighty briefcase stuffed with money.

"I can feel him," said Billy.

"Who? Christian?" Jude asked.

"Yea. We're good. He's set too."

Jude's eyes scanned the sky as if he could see Christian or God watching over him. "Okay then," he said, taking a deep breath before his boot stepped off the sidewalk.

"Whoa. *Con cuidado* !" Billy said, putting his arm in front of Jude.

Jude turned quickly. "What's up? What do you see?"

"I see it's a green fucking light and you almost just stepped into eight lanes of traffic *again*."

Jude shot a look to the traffic lights and the half dozen lanes of American made automobiles barreling by.

"Wait for the light, *carnal*. We ain't crossing the Taos Plaza here."

Jude seemingly snapped out of it, or back into it. "Whew. Wow," Jude said.

"You're still fired up."

"Yea, I guess I am."

"And I'm pissed off in my own way but we gotta get our heads on straight here. I think the both of us are already thinking about tomorrow but we still got today in front of us. Remember what Ma said about the moon or whatever? That you're gonna teach your sons.?"

"Maybe that's what she meant."

Jude's eyes bent to Billy. "*Simon.*"

"Okay then."

Jude and Billy stood idly on the corner with their dicks in their hands like the rest of the schmucks.

An elderly man with wrinkles and freckles on his bald head who barely reached Jude and Billy's shoulders squeezed in between them, wearing a gray suit, thick eyeglasses and newspaper under his arm. A few strands of gray hair wandered in the breeze. He turned up to Billy with his jam-jar size glasses and asked, "You hear the Cubbies game last night?"

Billy turned down to the *viejito* squinting up at him.

Then Billy looked over the man's head to Jude for an answer.

Jude smirked. His face clearly said, *What are you looking at me for pendejo? The man asked YOU a question.*

Billy's attention drew back down to the old-timer, still squaring up at him waiting for a response. "The Cubs game? No, *senor*. Didn't catch it."

The old-timer shook his head dismissively and grimaced. "Typical Cubbies."

"Oh yeah?"

"Epic collapse," said the man, still shaking his head.

"Is it a sign of things to come?" Billy asked.

The old-timer turned back up to him. "For the season?"

"For the world."

The old-timer blankly stared off across the street.

Billy wasn't sure if the old-timer was deaf, offended, or lost on the question.

Eventually the old timer nodded and turned back up to Billy. "Probably for the world, yeah, the way things are going." His glance moved to Jude on his right and then back to Billy on his left. "I feel sorry for you boys. I ain't gonna be around to see it but you…" The old timer shook his head as his voice trailed off, maybe into sadness.

"I think it's already happening, *senor*," said Billy.

The old timer's head craned upward studying Billy, his magnified eyes looking like an owl's when he blinked. He turned his attention back to the street, nodded and then spoke. "I think you're right."

The light turned red, and everyone stepped off the sidewalk shuffling across the street.

The old man seemingly nodded to himself again. "Maybe there's hope for the Cubs yet," he said, before scooting between the two men, swiftly wobbling across the street.

Jude and Billy's eyes met, and both men smiled, forgetting for a moment what they were about to walk into.

CHAPTER
THIRTY-NINE

The closer Jude got to the doorman, the more he looked like a guerilla, or a caveman in a suit, with his pronounced forehead, jutting under-bite, and thick una-brow. The doorman was as tall as he was wide, but he was not fat. He'd be tough to handle one on one. The machine gun peeking out from underneath his trench coat would be tough to handle one on one too, Jude surmised.

"I don't think the *culeros* have this baboon out front for his good looks," Billy said as they neared the doorman.

"I don't think they have him out front for his door opening abilities either," said Jude nodding to the machine gun.

When they approached, Jude tipped his hat cordially. "Afternoon," he said, stepping in front of the doorman's purview.

Only the man's eyes, under his thick brown eyebrows, moved down to Jude. "Afternoon," he grumbled.

"We're here to see Mr. Pinkerton or Mr. Dahl," Jude said.

"If you step inside, Ms. Hadley will gladly assist you," said the doorman, sounding rehearsed.

"We won't be stepping inside. Hence our request to you."

Jude had the doorman's attention now.

"You heard what I said," grunted the doorman, now in his natural state.

Jude looked around and stepped closer to the man. He opened the briefcase, showcasing the neatly buddle stacks of cash inside. "I did, but we both know this conversation just progressed past your pay-grade."

The doorman's eyes moved to the contents, but he did not seem impressed, then to Jude's holster. "You keep that right there," he said.

"That's where it will stay. Just like us right here."

The doorman's eyes moved to Billy for reassurance.

Billy didn't flinch.

His cold stare returned to Jude.

Jude didn't flinch either.

The doorman opened the door and a bell jingled, as if he was entering a toy store, not an assassin's den. The man backed his way inside the door, then disappeared behind it.

"So far so good," said Billy when he was gone.

"So far," said Jude.

Neither sounded too sure.

Billy bent his head up to the red brick building in front of them. It appeared meager compared to the rest of the block, only five stories high.

A small circular reflection flittered off the window of the door for a moment before disappearing.

"Christian?" asked Jude at the sight of it.

"Yea," said Billy. "Just letting us know he's got our back."

"Glad someone does."

"Big brother has to threaten one innocent bystander and all of a sudden he's an atheist abandoned by God."

"Fucker was a banker," Jude muttered. "He wasn't innocent."

"Glad you finally see that."

The bell jingled again, and Dahl floated out, suddenly in front of the two men, looking as polished as ever.

The doorman followed behind him.

"Whhhhhhh," Dahl whistled, looking back and forth at the two men, but not seeming otherwise impressed. "You boys are just full of surprises, aren't you?" he said in his buttery southern accent.

"Show him the briefcase," uttered the doorman.

Jude did not take his eyes off Dahl as he opened the briefcase.

Dahl did not blink.

Didn't even look down at the contents.

"And here we have another," Dahl said.

Billy was squared up to Dahl.

Dahl had Billy's full attention, but Billy was loose.

He was almost having fun now.

Billy's eyes darted to Jude for a moment and could see his brother was the exact opposite.

Wound tighter than a bull rope just about to explode like one.

Jude and Billy were the perfect duo.

One unbridled like a twister on the mesa.

The other coiled like a rattlesnake.

Both destructive and deadly.

"Is that money meant to impress me?" Dahl asked.

"No. To make a deal," Jude said coldly and even.

"A deal? For your life?"

"For yours," Billy said.

Dahl's eyes narrowed. "Let the adults talk, boy."

Billy's eyes returned, small and red.

"Darcy paid y'all $100,000 to string Billy up. We got over two hundred here." Jude said.

"Tsssssk. Tsssssk. Tssssk. So that was you." Dahl said. "The president of that bank himself was in here last week. You boys just walked right out the front door with all that money, didn't ya?"

"You know," said Billy, "I'm not sure if it's Mr. Dahl's almost regal southern accent or fancy colored clothes, but this is the first time it don't sound like he's chiding us. It almost sounds like he's…"

"Impressed?" Jude asked.

"Impressed," echoed Billy.

Two brothers, one thought.

They were always at their best sharing a common enemy.

Alcoholism.

Insanity.

Poverty.

Racism and oppression.

Dahl sounded almost impressed now.

"The two-hundred is for a sit down with Mr. Pinkteron," Jude said, back to the point, back to being the big brother.

"A sit down?" Dahl asked, rebuffing the fat, sticking with the bone. "I am sorry but you boys came a long way for nothing. Darcy is a ninny, but he is our client. We're not simply some hired thugs pimping ourselves out to the highest bidder. We hold integrity."

"I'm going to *hold* my tongue for the sake of our future business dealings," Jude said. "Billy wasn't speaking solely as an adolescent just now. We understand your contractual obligations with Darcy Simon and your… integrity and all. We also understand Mr. Pinkerton is a businessman and we are presenting an opportunity that you will take to him. But the deal is two-fold. There is the money, sure. But there is also your life at stake here and the life of Mr. Pinkerton."

Jude took off his hat and suddenly that little flicker was back, glimmering directly in Dahl's eyes.

Dahl squinted away from the blinding light, as if shooing a fly.

"Now that there is to impress you," said Billy.

Billy now had Dahl's undivided attention. His menacing glare evident of it.

"We have four snipers with you and only you in their crosshairs right now," Jude said, noting Dahl's dis-ease, enjoying himself a little. "I don't expect you to make any kind of real deal under duress. You being a man of integrity and all."

The doorman became shifty, and his hand moved a little closer to his undercoat where the machine gun hung.

"You know, Jude," said Billy, "If we're gonna be entering into future business dealings with these fellow respectable businessmen, we better shoot them straight. No pun intended. Two of them four snipers are not on Mr. Dahl here, they're on you, big boy." Billy leered up at the doorman. "You move your hand any closer to that gun, and it will be the last inch you ever move."

The doorman's eyes widened, his mammoth furry hand shook.

He stood slightly behind Dahl's line of sight, but Dahl must have sensed his apprehension. "Calm yourself Leroy. If you know what's good for you," Dahl said.

The doorman moved his hand away from the gun and straightened up.

Dahl studied Jude as if two players across a poker table.

The street was bustling and loud.

The smell of hot dogs wafted in the air, mixed with exhaust and tobacco.

Somehow the masses of innocent bystanders simply trying to move from Point A to Point B were keen to the fated showdown, none darting between the two gunslingers.

The sun remained high, beating down on the men, not yet crossing the concrete canyons of the city creating shade.

Dahl paused and counted his odds.

Jude didn't have to. He knew what he held.

"You got one sniper," said Dahl. "That's it."

"It only takes one to put a bullet in your head," said Jude.

Billy turned his head slightly, staring Dahl down.

"One way to find out, cocksucker," Billy said.

Dahl sneered at Billy. "You show your true colors, *boy*, with language like that. And as I show mine, I find that word particularly offensive."

"Say what?" Billy asked.

"If you want to insult me personally, fall back on your primitive nature with vulgarity, that is fine. But to insult homosexuals generally because of me specifically, that is what I find offensive."

Jude and Billy shot each other a curious look. Both had imagined this duel a hundred sleepless minutes in the night but this conversation now was never conceived.

"What? Billy asked, turning back to Dahl.

"You heard me," said Dahl.

"I did." Billy fidgeted some and then took a harder look at Dahl. "That ain't something man lies about," Billy said.

"I don't speak for man, I speak for this man," said Dahl.

Billy fidgeted some more.

There was not a single human being on the planet he held more hatred and aversion for than Dahl. He had to dig down to his soul and place the faces of Luisa, Wyatt and Patrick squarely in his mind so as not to commit the glorious masturbatory act of killing the snide motherfucker this instant, however, he held nothing against Dahl due to his sexual orientation. He had witnessed the difficulties a homosexual man experienced in a fearful and cowardly macho environment, like the U.S. Military and Northern New Mexico.

"I ain't scared of you, so I'll say whatever I Goddamn please," Billy said, "But I'll leave your sexual orientation out of this. I meant no disrespect in that regard. I never equated that word to its true meaning to be honest."

"It's common misspeak but I do appreciate it," Dahl said, nodding.

Jude cleared his throat. "That goes for me too if I ever called you that. I meant no disrespect in that way."

"Obliged," Dahl said.

"Can I still call him a cocksucker?" Billy asked, pointing to the man named Leroy.

Dahl turned back to Leroy, giving him the twice over.

Leroy was still and pale as a sheep in a den of wolves and looked as lost as a baby lamb.

"I guess that depends," said Dahl. "Leroy, do you enjoy the company of men?"

Leroy only answered with a confused frown.

"I'll ask a simpler way," Dahl continued. "Leroy, are you a homosexual?

Leroy revolted slightly. "No, sir, Mr. Dahl."

"Then, yes, you can call him…that word if you please, Mr. James," Dahl said. "It's entirely your business if you want to sound like a fatuous simpleton."

Billy turned his mouth sideways speaking with a put-on hick accent. "I understood half of one of them words. How about you, big brother?"

Jude grinned mildly. "And here for a moment, we were almost civilized. Cordial even."

"For a moment, we almost were," said Dahl.

"We request a meeting with Mr. Pinkerton," Jude said. "What we have in this briefcase demonstrates our intentions."

Jude took off his hat again and the flagrant glare of the sniper scope flashed in Dahl's eyes until Jude returned his hat to its proper place. "What we have from that window demonstrates our intentions if Mr. Pinkerton decides he does not want to consider our offer. Now, if you believe there is no room to negotiate, or if we're just beating a dead horse, to speak my... what was it...fatuous simpleton language, then that's fine, you can let me know right now. We won't bother you any further with our futile attempts to engage civilly nor will we toy with shiny objects in your eyes. We'll put a bullet in your head, and then as Mr. Pinkerton currently sits in his maroon leather chair in the 5th floor southwest corner office, we'll put a bullet in his head. That may or may not seal Billy and I's fate as well, but at least we'll be done wasting y'all's time and our own."

Dahl stood even and cold. "How's nine o'clock tomorrow?" he finally asked.

"Nine o'clock will be just fine," said Jude with that salesman's smile again.

CHAPTER
FORTY

It got sticky quick.

Those four nice Chicago days were perhaps an enigma after all.

Christian remembered how Kansas weather shifted from bone-chilling cold to swamp-like steamy in a matter of days. He didn't realize it would be the same in Chicago or maybe he just never gave it much thought. He'd only been three places really in his life. Kansas, Western Europe and now Illinois. That was two more places than most where he came from. He didn't recall Germany and France being so muggy then again, his attention was usually occupied elsewhere than with the mere happenings of the daily weather.

Billy, Jude, and he had been in that small hotel room for almost three weeks, and it never seemed cramped and stuffy until tonight.

At first, Christian thought it was due to the suddenly muggy and sodden weather. The rain and humidity that started last night had yet to cease for seemingly one Goddamn minute.

That was the reason Christian tucked a pistol behind his waistband, excused himself, and wandered out of the hotel and down the street.

He desperately needed a little room to breathe and some fresh air.

He roamed from awning to awning of storefronts closed for the night, watching the pelting downpour gush off the veils of the buildings.

The city suddenly seemed desolate.

Cars passed by, sure, but the sidewalks were agreeably vacant, occupied instead by whisking water from car tires and deluges from gutters.

Christian had no plan or destination. The end goal was simply anywhere but the hotel room prison.

As he crossed a street, a buoy of yellow and red light caught his eye. The yellow emitting from the window of a bar and the red from a sign above that read *Kelly's Saloon*.

Christian recognized he needed his wits about him tomorrow but that couldn't happen if he didn't get his mind right tonight. He had also grown tired of the pissing rain drenching him and sure as shit he wasn't ready to go back to the hotel room either.

Considering all of that, *Kelly's Saloon* was really the only answer.

Christian swung the heavy door open and stumbled inside. He felt like an awkward mule immediately, soaked, squinting, and puddling up the floor. The bruising eyes from the tipplers hunkered over their medicine at the long dimly lit bar didn't help either.

Christian rambled past a few rummies and anchored down on one of the red spinning stools.

A woman bartender with more wrinkles and tattoos than teeth wearing not nearly enough clothes slid over in front of him.

"Wetter than a whore's cut out there, huh?" she asked in a heavy Chicago accent.

Christian processed each word separately before putting them together in a full sentence. "Yea," he managed.

"What are ya having?"

Christian looked down the bar. "Pabst. Please."

The bartender waddled down toward the draft.

Christian's eyes fell on the ripened bar in front of him as seemingly endless water droplets dripped from his clean-shaven face and newly minted prim hairdo. He wished for his thick red beard to soak up the water and hide his boorish ungainly mug. He also yearned for a shirt less soused to his body.

"Running from the storm?" the bartender asked suddenly in front of him again.

"Running from *a* storm," said Christian.

The bartender peered out the window, watching the heavens fall. "That's what these places are for. Refuge from what's out there," she said, nodding to the window.

Christian plopped his clean-shaven lips on the head of the beer, sipping it off. "Yes, ma'am," he said, before taking another long sip.

The bartender stared off past the window for another moment before shuffling down the bar again to the other patrons.

Christian's shirt clung to him, and he felt like he could barely move, much less breathe.

He rolled up his sleeves and continued his perch. The cold beer was a welcoming first step, only enough to remind him of the power of alcohol. "Excuse, ma'am?" he asked. "I'll take a double bourbon back with this here barley pop please."

"I know you will," she hollered back, pulling a bottle from the shelf in front of her.

This time, his head and eyes remained low when she placed the drink in front of him.

"Where ya from?" asked a man four stools down, with a scraggly brown beard and a stained once green John Deer hat.

"Not here," Christian said dryly, not looking at the man.

"No shit," said a second man, sitting one stool past the first, leaning his torso over the bar to get a better look at Christian.

Both men were smaller than Christian but the second shot him that look that said he thought he was bigger still.

"Didn't mean no disrespect," Christian said, acknowledging the men. "Down South."

"Uh-huh" said the second man, older and bigger with a worn face, maybe the first man's father.

Christian remembered his sleeves were rolled up past his elbows, his disgraceful past shining for all to see. His eyes veered straight ahead into the dusty mirror in front of him. He wondered why there were always mirrors on the other side of bars? People went there to escape that son of bitch staring back at them, or at least forget about him for a little while. But them mirrors were just another reminder, another re-introduction. He slowly rolled down his sleeves and snapped the bottom on his wrist so as not to inadvertently roll them up again.

He prayed not to God, but to someone, that his scars went unnoticed and then spoke. "Kansas."

"What brings you up here?" asked the first.

"Work. Just work," Christian said hastily, trying not to be rude, but clearly yearning for some peace and fucking quiet. He didn't care if other's yapped, he just wanted silence in his own mind. He then realized he may have come off as coarse and that wouldn't lead to peace either. "Y'all have a fine city," he said, raising his glass to the two men.

"Uh-huh," said the second man again, still staring at Christian.

Christian took a healthy dose of bourbon. The warm serum cooled his fiery nerves and lubricated the gears in his mind. There was something more he sensed in that hotel room that caused him to leave. Maybe it was the simple jitters that came the night before battle. He'd seen men vomit, cry, shit themselves, not shit at all, and even pull out their own hair the night before D-Day. Jude and Billy exhibited none of that behavior but there was still an anxiety lingering that Christian couldn't put his finger on.

Maybe Jude was thinking about his wife and kids.

Maybe Billy was using.

Maybe Christian was the one losing it. All the uneasiness he thought he felt in the room maybe was only in his own head.

Whatever the distress and wherever it lay, it better be gone by morning, or they didn't stand a chance, he thought.

Christian finished his bourbon and sipped down half his beer.

The bartender had moored her elbows between the two men at the bar, chatting and fawning with them.

Christian pined in the woman's direction hoping that alone would get her attention. When it did not, he called out,"Ma'am,"making a circular motion with his hand indicating another of both.

"Sure, sweetie," she said.

Christian noticed the pisser down the bar past the two men through the dark narrow hallway.

He hopped off his stool, strolling past them and entered.

He finished taking a leak and washed his hands in the rusty sink. He was grateful there was no mirror in front of him there. His mug was ugly enough never mind seeing it up close with razor burn. He grabbed a few paper towels, pressing them to his shirt and face, drying himself off as best he could. He was still wiping his hands with one when he walked out of the bathroom, not noticing the second man standing on the other side and bumping into him.

"Excuse me," said Christian trying to slide by on his right. "Wasn't watching where I was going."

"Yea, but I've been watching you, boy," said the second man, stepping in front of Christian.

Christian attempted to move left, ignoring the man, but to no avail.

The man fronted Christian, sticking his face so close to him, he could see the veiny capillaries in his fat fucking nose and his foul heavy breath was like a wall.

"You some kind of race traitor boy?" asked the man.

Christian looked past the man's shoulder and realized the bar was empty.

"I don't even know what that means," said Christian, his voice void of any more amends.

"Sure you do," said the man.

An alley door behind Christian burst open.

A coarse rope suddenly zipped around his neck.

The fibers piercing his flesh.

Someone's knee plunged into the center of his back and as was he bent over and dragged outside.

Christian aimlessly swung behind him until the second man drilled him in the gut with his fist.

He keeled over while still being yanked back by the rope around his neck.

The man bashed his fists into Christian's stomach two more times, knocking his breath clear out.

Christian desperately bent backwards, willing air into his lungs that could not be found as the rope choked his windpipes and the throbbing pain clenched his lungs and gut.

He grasped for the twine, but it was dug too deep into his flesh and then the man slugged him in the gut again.

The first man jerked the rope back like Christian was a steer.

Raindrops pelted the top of Christian's face.

He heard himself wheezing and the men were talking.

"You see them scars on his arms Jimmy?" asked the second man before landing another fist to his gut.

"Sure did, Al," said presumably the first man in the bar.

"I guess this boy had some second thoughts and reservations about his obligations and responsibilities as a free white man," said Al before ripping open the buttons on Christian's shirt to reveal a burned out scar of a KKK cross on his chest over his heart.

"I guess so," said Jimmy.

"You know the only thing worse than a nigger?" Al asked, shoving his baboon ass looking face into Christian's once more. "Is a nigger lover. I don't blame niggers for being niggers, it's how they were born. But white nigger lovers are a Goddamn disgrace to us all."

Jimmy cinched the rope tighter around Christian's neck.

Stars blinked everywhere before Christian's eyes and his brain felt tingly.

He knew it was getting close.

"I'm gonna do you one favor, boy," Al said, his face now as intimate as possible to Christian's. "I'm gonna allow a white man's face to be the last thing you see. And when you at the pearly gates and you see God is white and Jesus is white and St. Peter is white, you'll know the error of your ways."

The twinkling stars faded.

The brain tingling dulled, and his legs felt heavy.

He wilted, the first man holding him up entirely now.

His eyes made their way up to the gray and purple sky and the orange lights from the city. He was not gonna allow that vile son of a bitch to be the last thing he saw. Then it became insurmountable to keep his eyes open and he knew. Life itself had turned so insurmountable so why should death be any different? he thought, letting everything go.

Suddenly, he heard a *CRACK.*

The rope loosened and Jimmy wailed.

Christian dropped to the ground in the same moment he saw Jude drill Al right in the chops.

Al sailed back against the wall.

He recovered just as Jude clocked in the face with his revolver butt.

Blood exploded from Al's nose, and he collapsed.

Jimmy was still on all fours reeling from his ear being battered with that same butt.

Jude took two big steps before punting Jimmy's face with his heavy cowboy boot.

Jimmy's whole body flipped in the air before landing on his back.

Al got to all fours just in time for Jude to do the same. Turning Al over like a barrel.

Both men languished and whined on their backs, the rain doing all the battering now.

Christian tried to stand but stumbled into the wall, his brain not yet having the requisite oxygen to perform its normal operating functions.

He leaned against the wall, sucking in all the air that he ever imagined existed, then coughing violently, his lungs working on overdrive. The force of the hacking then bent him over on his knees.

Jude placed his hand on Christian's back, startling him.

"It's alright. It's alright. It's just me. You gonna live?" Jude asked.

Christian could only nod.

"Okay," said Jude. "Take your time."

Christian leaned his shoulders against the wall, calming his breath, slowing everything once the blood and oxygen started flowing again. He blinked hard and saw the two men laying on the ground. He realized once more everything was soaking wet except Jude's dry mug staring back at him from under his wide brim cowboy hat.

Christian's eyes traveled down to Jude's hands screwing a silencer on the muzzle of his revolver.

His eyes made their way back up to Jude's face, stale and flat, staring back at him.

Christian found himself shaking his head, *no*.

Jude shot Christian a questioning look that said, *You sure?*

Christian stared down at the two men sprawled out in the alley like garbage from a blown over can.

"Pieces of shit ain't worth the blood on our hands," Christian said between heavy heaves of fresh breath.

Jude looked at his knuckles, already swelling and his boots speckled with blood, and nodded, holstering his weapon.

CHAPTER FORTY-ONE

"Y ou cocksucker," Christian muttered, his voice still hoarse from near strangulation.

"What?" Jude asked, turning his head sideways while they trudged through the heavy rain. The streetlamps above casting halos on the two men before passing into darkness once more.

"You heard me," Christian grumbled.

"I thought we weren't gonna use that word anymore," said Jude.

"What?"

"Oh wait. Never mind. You weren't there but we ain't using that word anymore."

Christian shot Jude a confused look.

"Anyway," Jude continued. "Hell of a thing to say to the guy who just saved your life."

"You were following me… After all we been through."

"I'm sorry."

"Should have known better."

"How so?"

"You're a fucking cop."

"It wasn't the cop in me that didn't trust you. It was probably the lawyer."

"Oh yeah, I forgot you were one of those sons of bitches too."

"Truth be told, it wasn't either," Jude said, burying his hands deeper in his tight soaked Levi's, almost making it hard to walk, never mind race down the street while trying to not look suspicious.

"What was it then?"

"Hard to say. With all due respect, I was trusting you just fine for weeks now until your leaving tonight. Didn't sit right. I didn't think you were a Pinkerton but something with leaving was just not okay. Maybe my cop senses, my lawyer or just being a *coyote* always looking over both shoulders."

A long silence stooped between the two men.

Water whisked off the tires of cars.

A horn beeped now and again.

Somewhere the L rumbled overhead.

And then Christian spoke. "I hear you. That's why I left tonight."

"How's that?"

"Something in the room was not okay. Suddenly I felt like there just wasn't enough air or space in it. Felt like I couldn't breathe."

"When did that start for you?" Jude asked.

"Reckon when you came back up in the room. No disrespect to you."

"I was talking to my wife on the phone."

"I know. I wasn't accusing you of anything else."

"I know. Maybe I brought that energy back up into the room with me."

"How's that?"

"Us talking tonight…" Jude slowed and then remembered his circumstance and peered over his shoulder. Nothing behind him but obscure darkness. He marched forward again and continued. "Just felt like it was going to be the last time I ever talked to her. Last time I was gonna hear Luisa's voice. I never felt that before heading out on a man hunt or even that night I sprang Billy. But tonight…" Jude shook his head and his eyes traveled off far past the spewing rain, or concrete towers. "…Maybe that's what you felt."

"Maybe," said Christian softly. "Or maybe it was three men not used to being scared, even in dire straits, suddenly scared and not knowing how to handle it."

"Maybe," said Jude. "You scared?"

"Maybe" said Christian smirking at Jude.

Jude smiled back under his wide brim. "Maybe we have a right to be. Hundred ways this goes wrong tomorrow, only one way it goes right."

Silence draped the two men again for half a block and then Jude spoke. "Billy was adamant there was nothing to worry about with you. Insisted we could trust you and I didn't need to follow or nothing."

Christian took several long steps before speaking. "Well, I'm glad you did."

"Why them boys want to throttle you? You mouth off to them?"

"Have I ever demonstrated being the mouthing-off kind?"

"Nope."

Christian palmed his face wishing the rain was magic and allowed his beard to grow back in full already. "Them boys were idiots."

Jude held off. Either Christian was going to elaborate on his own volition or not.

Christian finally obliged. "Just came in for a beer. I didn't know the place and I was wet and sticky, so I rolled up my sleeves." Christian grew quiet again then spoke softer. "They got a look at my scars and took exception to me burning that garbage off my own body, scorching my own flesh."

"They were Klan?"

"Probably wannabees. There's a lot of dumb fucks out there that wannabe dumber fucks."

"You know…," said Jude. "I ain't the keeping score kind but that's twice now that I've saved your ass."

Christian leered down at Jude, the top of his cowboy hat barely meeting Christian's shoulder.

The men's eyes locked.

"Guess that means, I better save your ass three times tomorrow," Christian said.

"If were to walk out of that shit storm alive, it's gonna require at least three."

Both men smiled and then sobered realizing the truth of that statement.

CHAPTER
FORTY-TWO

"Hot damn, he ain't here!" Jude's head thrashed around the empty hotel room, all the lights still on.

"Nothing looks out of the ordinary other than him not being here."

"Nope," Christian said.

"You think someone grabbed him?" Jude asked, shuffling through the closet, surveying the bathroom.

"Nope," Christian said again, oddly composed.

Jude peeked his head out of the bathroom. "Well, he didn't follow me."

"No."

"Maybe he went out for a bite to eat by himself?"

"No," Christian said, standing steadily in the narrow and dim doorway, his blue eyes a sharp beacon in the hotel room's obnoxious cheap yellow light.

Jude paced back to Christian. "Well, you're a lot of Goddamn help. Five minutes ago, you were ass-chapped that I didn't trust you and now you couldn't give a good Goddamn."

"About what?"

"What do you mean about what? About Billy."

"I give a damn. I just ain't getting all stirred up like you."

"I'm stirred up because I care."

"And I'm cool because I know where he is."

"I hope you're wrong," Jude buzzed, walking down the bleak alley. The rain finally stopped but a hazy mist hung low.

"Hope so too," said Christian.

Jude halted at the front door of the opium den. "Let me ask you something."

Christian could only stand there, like in the war when the sergeant would hand him a rifle and tell him to go see what lay on the other side of that blind hill.

"When I was sitting with the president of that bank, before Billy came over, was he about to make a move?" Jude asked. "Did you see it too?"

Christian scratched his face uncomfortably, seeing what was on the other side of that hill. "Old Hank wasn't my post. I had the crowd and the door."

"You didn't see any movements from the guy that suggested he was about to…"

Since the bank, Christian sensed an edgy current, this low voltage charge buzzing at Christian's nerves. Like when he used to work as an electrician, and he wasn't sure he had just been shocked by the single phase until he wedged his needle-nose further into the voltage terminal, and sure as shit, he was being electrocuted.

Christian now realized this uneasy arc is what pulled him out of the dry safe hotel room onto the rainy street and then the bar that almost killed his ass.

"Billy and I are brothers…" Jude was saying, "But at this point you may know him, or understand him better than I do. Since the night he got back – from the first minute I looked in my little brother's eyes, and it wasn't exactly him that I saw – he just ain't been the same."

"He ain't the same," Christian interjected, even surprising himself. "The boy that left ain't the man that came home."

Jude nodded, like he had to hear it from someone besides his own thoughts to make it true. "I don't even pretend to know what y'all went through but I know it can fuck with your perception on things."

"You get real tight when you realize everything is the enemy. Only way you even got a chance at surviving. Hard to unwind that, even when you're back home safe…"

"Billy did get stuck with Edwin's knife, I mean I saw Billy bleed all over my floor, but who's to know if… And Hank's hand did disappear under the desk but I just didn't read the son of a bitch as making a move but… Is it possible that Billy is making these things up in his own head?"

"Jesus, Jude, I got a *JR* at the end of my name not an *MD*, but let me ask you something now? Does it matter? Does any of this change the blood running through your veins? Blood you share with Billy?"

Christian could only read the top of the man's dimpled cowboy hat. Jude's face hanging low and to the toe of his boot that was rubbing on the wet on the sidewalk.

"Sure don't," Jude eventually said, grabbing for the door.

"All right then," Christian said. "And Jude…"

Jude leered up at Christian, their eyes connecting. Christian's eyes bloodshot and molten from popping out of his head while being strangled. Jude's wide and weary with bags all around.

"…Be easy on him," Christian continued. "This ain't the time for a boot in the ass. Maybe a bending ear and that's it."

Jude's eyes widened, he looked off for a moment, and then maybe nodded. "You sure you ain't got an *MD* at the end of your name?" he then asked Christian.

Christian pretended to be adjusting a necktie. "Maybe I've found my second calling. Used to kill 'em. Now, I save 'em."

Jude grinned and pulled open the door. "After you, Doc."

CHAPTER FORTY-THREE

The two men stepped down the few stairs into the duskily barroom. Wealthy men, many still in business suits from the daily grind, sat in the plush booths puffing opium out of hookahs with scantily robed women draped over them. Some men and women sat in corners alone following the dragon on their own journey. A few patrons chatted at the L-shaped bar in the corner while the barmaids pranced in silk as black as the substance they were selling.

Christian's eyes immediately crisscrossed the room to the far table where he and Billy had sat, but it lay empty. In his experience, addicts were habitual in more than just their addictions. Same beer. Same stool. Same opium den. Same chair to lounge and smoke the dream stick. It appeared Christian was wrong so far.

One of the barmaids with curly red hair and spacious blue eyes scaped with dark eyeshadow fluttered up to Jude. "Evening, handsome. Table for two?"

"No…" Jude stopped himself for a moment. "Actually, we're meeting a friend of ours who I believe is already here."

The barmaid looked around slightly sarcastic. "Do you see him?"

Jude realized it was time to sound less like a cop or concerned older brother and more like a degenerate sleaze. "What's your name, sweetie?"

"Molly."

Jude turned to Christian, talking out of his mouth with a silly grin. "Holy holly Ms. Molly."

Christian forced a smirk keeping his eyes on the aforementioned.

"Never heard that one before, mister," she said. "What's your friend look like?"

"About my height, blonde hair, handsome, not as handsome as me, but then again, who is?"

"You are real firecracker aren't ya?" she said.

"Well, ain't that what we're here for? A little fire?" Jude said, with that salesman grin.

"Uh-huh?" Molly said, looking him sideways, not so convinced.

Jude realized he could talk all night but there was only one thing that truly spoke Molly's language. "Do you know who else is handsome, Ulysses S. Grant," he said, flipping a fifty-dollar bill from his roll of cash, placing it on her cocktail tray.

"That friend, yeah," she said, plucking the bill. "You know, I thought you were a cop for a minute."

"What would make you think that?"

"You got that holier than thou cop face. Handsome, but a cop face," she said, lightly slapping Jude on the cheek. "He's in the exclusive lounge." Molly turned, sashaying down a dark hallway with a deep purple glow, and low-lit green lanterns on the soft concrete walls.

Jude and Christian's eyes met for a moment before following.

The hallway got smaller and more amethystine, the deeper they followed, like Alice in the rabbit hole. Jude and Christian ducked their heads and twisted their bodies to fit as they trailed. The burrow eventually ended at a red door. Molly opened the door, skipped through and then cordially held it open for the two men.

Jude and Christian ducked through and entered the cavernous lair.

A dazzling woman with blonde hair similarly curled and the same dark eyeshadow greeted the men. "Welcome gentlemen."

Jude smiled, trying to hide the quizzical Alice in Wonderland look on his face while desperately trying to get a read on where he found himself. The prism-like room seemed more of a waiting or greeting area, whatever on the other side of the small doors, the main attraction. In a dark corner stood two Chinese men, tall and stout with long thin mustaches, wearing black Changsha robes. Their eyes were directed at Jude, but they did not blink or move, statuesque, as if they were there strictly for the ambience but Jude knew better.

"This is Genevieve," said Molly. "She'll take great care of you. These gentlemen are joining the party in Room Six," Molly said to her cohort.

"Yes, of course," said Genevieve. "Right this way."

"Enjoy the ride," said Molly, coquettishly.

Jude and Christian watched her glide back through the portal before remembering to now follow the other Emerald City sprite.

Genevieve led the men to a door with a frosted glass window, only allowing a dim flicker to be seen from the other side. "You should be all set, but if you need anything else, just ring the little bell."

Jude nodded long and slowly then waited for Genevieve to depart before opening the door.

Inside, Billy lay in a booth, the thick cushions, almost couch like, his forearm over his eyes, his boots kicked off and his dirty white socks up on the cushions. The same divan lined the other side of the corridor with a small table in between. Shadows danced on the walls and ceiling from the one candle lantern perched on the center of the wall.

"Billy, what the fuck?" Jude asked.

Billy slowly removed his arm from his eyes, barely prying them open. "Jude?" he asked faintly.

"Yea, fucking, *Jude.*"

Christian placed his hand on Jude's shoulder, a subtle reminder.

Jude exhaled and his shoulders drooped slightly. "Can we sit down?"

Billy closed his eyes again and rubbed his face with his hands.

"Billy, hey, can we sit down?" asked Jude, this time more benign.

"Yeah, yeah, of course," Billy said, sitting up and scooting in. His body melted into the corner like dripping candle wax and his head fell against the wall.

Jude and Christian sat down on the other side, in between them on the table, a bag of heroin, and Billy's tools - a needle, a spoon and a thin rubber hose.

Billy molted with the corner, able to lift his heavy eyelids again. "Oh, hey Christian," he said, a blissful smile spreading across his pale clammy face.

"Hey, Billy," said Christian.

As if Billy fell out of his tar-infused dream, his head popped up and his blood shot eyes, and eight-ball pupils gaped wildly at Jude and Christian. He straightened up, rubbed his hands on his arms and cleared his throat. "Shit, what are y'all doing here?"

"About to ask you the same thing, *hermanito*."

Billy's eyes clinched. They no longer seemed like they were drifting, quite the opposite. He got straight in the booth, opened them again and looked at Christian. "You bring him here?" he asked, ire peeking from his voice.

"I did," said Christian stolidly. "He was concerned about you. Reckon, I was too."

Billy curled forward, not able to sit straight up. "Nothing to be concerned about."

"Yeah, I can see that," said Jude.

"Ain't my first dance with the dragon," said Billy.

"You being able to *dance* with that shit ain't exactly what concerns me," Jude said.

"There it is," said Billy, his neck snapping forward and head nodding affirmatively with his eyes half closed.

"*There it is?*" Jude asked.

"There it is," said Billy. "You ain't here because you actually care about me, you're here because…because…because…"

Jude leaned forward, his torso hanging over the scag on the table. "'Because' what Billy? Because what we got planned tomorrow?"

"Yeah," said Billy, his head nodding to himself again. "Exactly. Make sure everything goes according to the good sheriff's plan."

"I'm in this mess solely because I care about you. Because I cared enough to squeeze my balls into this Goddamn vice you put yourself in."

"Yeah and nobody asked you to!" Billy shrieked, his voice rocking like his head.

"Nobody had to, I'm your Goddamn brother."

"You should have asked me!" Billy said, slapping his hand into his chest. "You should have asked me. It wasn't your decision to make."

"There was no decision to make…"

"…I'd made peace with it Goddamn it! I wasn't ready to go but I made peace with it and then you come in guns blazing. You sacrificed your life, your family, everything for, for me! But did you give any thought to how that would affect me?"

"Geez, I guess not. I was too busy thinking about how the noose around your neck was going to affect you."

"Do you understand how heavy this is on me? Whatever happens, for the rest of my life I gotta live with what you had to sacrifice because of my fuck up. I made peace with dying. I didn't like it, but I made peace with it because at least I was out of the fucking shadow. My ass hanging from a tree but at least I'd be in the sunshine, out of that fucking shadow."

"What shadow?"

"The Jude James shadow."

"I don't…"

"…All my life, I've just been this fuck up that you've had to follow around and clean up after! Make sure I stay in line, don't go crazy, fall down the well of insanity like Ma. My fucking shadow. Do you understand the profound effect that had me? Never feeling like I could do anything good myself? Behave on my own? You understand that only made me more fucking crazy? Made me think I wasn't good enough even for myself."

"I was just looking out for you…" Jude muttered, eyes low.

"You know, when I left? I wasn't running from Taos. I wasn't trying to prove the size of my *cojones* to Addy or that Goddamn Edwin. I was running from you, Jude. Away from that condescending, worried burdensome look you always had on your face, that I could see deep in your eyes, every time you looked at me. I was running away from never having to see those eyes again. When I hit boot camp, I realized I was good at something. I was good at being a soldier and I could stand on my own two feet. I was a fucking man. They used that. They used that and I did some terrible things, but it was me standing on my own. Without that shadow. My two feet on this earth. That's why I never wanted to come back. What happened in the war wasn't shit. I handled it, even getting blown up. But when Marion died, I thought my world had ended but I came out of that still on my own two feet and I thought if I could handle that, I could handle anything, even seeing your sad patronizing eyes. But I was wrong. Even that first night back at the Alley, I was wrong. Immediately, I was right back to that fucked up cowardice little boy in the shadow of his big brother who couldn't do anything right. And that night I killed Edwin, I think I did it just to wipe that same fucking look off his face. I don't know…"

Jude leaned back in the deep booth. He studied Billy long and hard and then spoke. "I don't know what to say, Billy, other than I'm sorry."

Billy's head drifted down like a leaf slowly falling from the sky and his body continued to sulk into the corner of the booth. "No, I'm sorry. You had a good life before I showed up again. You found your way, had a family and now all of that is gone…"

"No, it ain't. Not yet it ain't…."

"… Yes, it is. Even if we somehow get through all of this. Your life and the life of your family will never be the same. Never." Billy sat up now, canted over the table to his brother, his face clenched, and his eyes drained with tears. "And how am I supposed to live with that? How am I supposed to live with that?"

Jude jumped over the table, wrapping his arms around Billy, enveloping his brother in a bear hug.

Billy buried his head into Jude's shoulder and wailed.

Jude held Billy's head, like he did with Patrick and Wyatt as babies.

Jude's eyes met Christian's through Billy's muffled sobs and then Jude closed his eyes, sharing his brother's anguish.

Finally, Billy cleared his throat, sniffled, and coughed. Jude relaxed his grasp as his brother pulled away and sat back down. Billy wiped the tears away with the palm of his hands. He looked over at Jude and Christian, his eyes puffy and even more blood-shot from the crying.

Suddenly Billy's head startled at the sight of Christian's face. "What the fuck happened to you?" he asked, finally noticing the bruises and blood.

Christian stirred for a moment, not ready to suddenly be engaged in the conversation. "Ahhh, ran into some aspirant dumb fucks."

"Looks like they ran into you," Billy said.

"Is there a difference?" Christian asked.

"No, I reckon not," Billy said, seemingly shaking himself sober by running his hands over his face repeatedly. "You okay?"

"Ain't the worst beating I was on the wrong side of. Would have been a lot worse if your brother didn't show up."

Billy's eyes locked with Jude, who sat completely still, not even appearing to breathe. "Yea, he's got a knack for showing up when your tits in the ringer," said Billy.

Jude did not relent.

"What?" Billy finally asked after a long uninterrupted silence.

Jude shook his head. "Nothing. You want us to get out of here. Leave you be?"

Billy looked away, his eyes yawning awake. "No, no I'm done. Besides, we all need to get some shut eye for tomorrow."

Jude guffawed. "Are you fucking serious?"

"What?" Billy asked.

"Tomorrow? You think we're still on for tomorrow with you in your state?"

"I'll be fine."

"The fuck you'll be fine! You know, I'm done babysitting you but I also ain't walking into war tomorrow with a dope fiend nodding off who is supposed to have my back. It ain't about judgment, it's about survival. Plus, after the beating he took tonight, he won't be able to see out of one eye tomorrow with the swelling."

Christian looked suddenly embarrassed. He scraped the soft cold concrete floor with the nose of his boot. "I'll be ready. One eye or no eye."

"Fuck no," said Jude. "I want us to be prime and ready for this and we ain't neither. We did the planning and now I ain't going until I'm sure we can perfectly execute that plan."

"Life don't work that way, *carnal*. Man makes plan and God laughs," Billy said.

"Man makes plan and man's brother shoots up on heroin fucking the whole plan up."

"We ain't got no choice," said Billy. "All the explosives are set, and the guns and ammo placed. If they even decide to rearrange the furniture and find our stash, we're just fish in a barrel."

"He's right," said Christian. "We can't afford even risking one day of them finding any of our guns, ammunition, explosives. We know right now, when I walked out of there at 5pm today, they found nothing. When we walk in tomorrow morning, we are walking in with our best chance of survival. Every hour that passes, the chance of them finding any of our equipment increases and decreases our odds of survival."

"Plus," said Billy, "If we don't show up tomorrow, that's gonna tip our hand."

"Fuck!" yelled Jude, chucking his hat in Billy's direction.

Billy picked up the crunched-up hat, dusted it off and straightened it out. "Life don't come in a tidy little box with a pretty bow on top. You gotta take what it gives you and everything else is a fight."

"That was always your problem, Billy," Jude said scowling but resigned. "You'd rather fight with life than simply live in it."

"Make no mistake, *carnal*, we fighting just to live now. And tomorrow, it's gonna be the fight of our life."

CHAPTER
FORTY-FOUR

Allan J. Pinkerton III sat proudly in his throne-like leather chair, his back straight and arms neatly placed on the broad arm rests, as if he believed he was king. He sat high above the matching cherry oak desk, and to his back, shined his kingdom, the city of Chicago.

He was younger than Jude imagined. Maybe forty. Thin but good looking. Thick black-hair parted neatly and a preserved complexion. The only sun he probably saw was on a beach sitting with a cocktail, but he held a savant stare. He didn't look like the railroad bull his grandfather made his stripes as. Nor did he appear a foaled dunce who simply sucked off daddy's tit. A living gunfighter never underestimated his adversary, even if he looked soft and rich.

The room was lined with bookshelves of the same cherry color, and on the wall, hung Pinkerton's law school diploma from Yale and undergrad from Harvard.

Jude sat across from Pinkerton, in a chair less ornate and lower to the throne, an obvious intention of his foe.

Dahl stood in the doorway of the office, as if guarding the exit, leaning on the door jamb, his hands idly in his trouser pockets. His eyes did not leave Billy who ambled around the room scanning the books neatly wedged together on the shelf.

"You went to Yale Law School?" Billy asked when he made his way to the hanging degree on the wall.

"Yes," said Pinkerton politely, not caring to move.

"What's a matter? Couldn't get into *Haavad Law*?" Billy asked with a put-on Boston accent.

Pinkerton turned to Billy a little less polite but not giving him the dignity of being perturbed. "My wife's family has a rich history at Yale. We wanted to continue that."

"*Rich* history huh?" Billy said, continuing his promenade around the office.

Dahl's eyes continued to follow Billy like a conniving cat.

"I understand you hold a J.D. as well, Mr. James," Pinkerton said.

"I do," Jude said, smiling genteelly, as if to compensate for Billy's misbehavior. "Not from anywhere as prestigious as Yale, however. UNM."

"U-N-M," Pinkerton said following suit. "University of New Mexico."

"That's right."

"And you practice there?"

"I did," Jude said, more sober.

"Yes, of course," said Pinkerton, now a little awkward, picking up on Jude's well-earned yet well healed spite. "And your profession Mr. James?" he asked Billy.

"Who me?"

Pinkerton nodded.

Billy pulled up the chair next to Jude and sat down squarely in front of Pinkerton. "I've spent the better part of four years killing people on the order of other people. I guess you could say we're colleagues then."

"Boy," Dahl hissed in his southern drawl. "We're nothing alike."

"You know, those might be the first honest words out of your mouth." Billy's head twisted as if he just had a momentary epiphany, sitting on the top floor of the Pinkerton agency, negotiating he and his brother's life across from non-assassins with a suitcase of cash they robbed from a bank. With his eyes closed, his head continued to nod while his knuckles rapped on Pinkerton's desk, as if he heard a song in his head for the first time. Like he was playing an invisible piano only he heard.

The noise and the odd gesture clearly confounding everyone, perhaps his own brother most.

"Yep, you're right," Billy continued. "We got nothing. Not even killing. Maybe you've actually killed some poor sap, with your actual hands, not like the horseshit you tried to pull on me. But you ain't a killer." Billy's cold eyes centered on Dahl while also going somewhere else. "I know…a killer…"

"Billy, for fuck sake.." Jude attempted.

"Maybe a whore…" Billy continued, undeterred. "Maybe that's what you are. You ain't a killer. Maybe you're a whore."

Pinkerton's eyes moved to Dahl.

Dahl ceased his lean and removed his hands from his pockets.

Billy's fingers continued to rap on the desk. "Nope, not a *whore* either," Billy muttered, shaking his head. "That don't really fit the description of Mr. Dahl either. A whore works for her money. Hard earned on her back every day." Billy turned around, putting Dahl on full display. "Mr. Dahl don't know that kind of work. More so, he looks down on it. As if real manual labor is something to be ashamed of."

As Billy spoke, Dahl circled around the young orator, standing by Pinkerton's side. Two men on one side, two on the other.

From across the desk, Billy could see Dahl's clenched hands. His neck clinching so tight around his jaw, it looked like a mountain, and a strain in his eyes. He was trying *hard* not to react.

And Billy was just getting started.

"After my wife died of a heroin overdose in my arms while I was nodded off, I spent a lot of time in a lot of fucked up places fucked up myself and I think…. Yeah, it was in Amsterdam, that's in Holland, by the way, where I saw the most grotesque thing of all. Which is why it reminds me of Mr. Dahl…

So we were in this whore house and heroin den and we're getting into what you get into there. Women and men carrying on with each other and so forth, and I'm just sitting there spun out of my mind when one of the ladies opens up this tiny door that I never noticed until that moment. And out of this little, tiny door comes this … *thing.* It's wearing all this crazy leather. Even around his face, it's all leather, except where his mouth is, it's got this zipper that almost looks like teeth," Billy said, his forefinger and thumb zipping across his own mouth. "I'd never think there was even a human under there except I can see it's fucking eyes blinking, looking at me. Sizing me up even. And then, one of the ladies grabs this chain that looks like it belongs around the neck of an animal, and she collars this thing and when it gets down on all fours and turns around, I can clearly see there's one other place it ain't got leather…"

Billy paused for dramatic purposes and perhaps read the room.

Pinkerton's throat was already into his chest, as if he was trying to hold down his breakfast.

Dahl's eyes were wide and did not blink, as if he didn't dare take his eyes off this sick fuck for one twinkle of a second.

Jude had simply turned away, head low into the floor, probably wondering who the fuck this degenerate pervert was sitting next to him?

At the sight of the three men, Billy knew he had all of them, so he continued.

"So someone else unzips that mouth and everyone starts going to town on this thing from all sides. And when my mind actually processes what I'm seeing, I figure I gotta get myself a gun, shoot all these fucking heathens and either save this pour thing or use my last bullet to put it out of its misery.

But son of a gun, wouldn't you know it? In the middle of it all, this thing starts rocking back and forth. Men, women going at him and he's just grunting and rocking and taking it, until everyone, and I mean everyone, is done with him. And he gets up, and he's tall when it actually stands. And for some sick fucking reason, I look into his face, and I swear from even under that mask, that I can see in its eyes that he's proud. That it took some kind of special pride in letting people do what they just did. And then the thing gets back on his hands and knees and crawls into his little hole."

The three men's faces were as white as the walls, but Billy wasn't finished.

"Now someone told me later they got a word for this thing. They call it a *gimp*. Now see – and stay with me, because this is where the train turns down the relevant track – the gimp ain't a whore. It ain't hard working for hard money and believe me they *worked it* hard. It ain't a john, paying to do this. And it ain't some lazy fuck collecting the money like a pimp. No, this gimp does what it does because it thinks it's important. The gimp thinks there's some glory in its service to all these other fucking animals. But it wasn't important, or significant or noteworthy. The moment it went back into its little cave, rode hard and put up wet, so to speak, these other people cleaned up and laughed and forgot about their little pet. See this gimp was nothing but a fuck toy.

And I buried that memory in a deep hole of bad memories but when I met you, Mr. Dahl, something just kept scratching back to the surface and I couldn't put my finger on it until just now when I realized your place in all of this. You think you are important. You think there's some honor in your service but you're just being used and abused too. You ain't nothing but a fuck toy. Nothing but a gimp."

Dahl suddenly erupted, lunging over the table with clenched fingers as if he was going to claw Billy's eyes out of his skull or the words off his tongue.

Pinkerton jumped up, yanking Dahl back.

Jude hopped in front of Billy, pushing him. Holding both arms between the dueling rattlesnakes like a crossing guard.

"Jesus Christ, Leslie, control yourself!" Pinkerton yelled, holding Dahl against the wall until he simmered.

Dahl shook off his boss, then looked him in the eye, nodded slowly, remembering his place perhaps. "You'll have to excuse me, Mr. Pinkerton, my apologies," he said, straightening his vest, and combing back his ink-black hair with his hands.

"All right then," Pinkerton said, as much to calm himself down, as Dahl. Then Pinkerton's

eyes returned to Billy. "It's unfortunate to find your crass reputation precedes you, Mr. James."

"In a long list of unfortunate events of late," Billy said, "I'd go so far as to say my smart-ass is pretty low on that list."

"Isn't your 'smart-ass' the very reason said list exists?" Pinkerton asked.

"No, I'd say it was a crotchety old fool pulling a knife on me."

"Those facts are irrelevant to me. I am neither a judge nor jury," said Pinkerton.

"Ain't you though?" Billy asked. "Or you just the executioner?"

"That's enough, Billy," Jude finally said, loud and exasperated. "Mr. Pinkerton is a businessman. That's why we are here today."

"That I am, Mr. James, so let's get down to brass tacks. What can I do for you?" Pinkerton asked, pointing back to the chairs in front of his throne.

"Mr. Simon. Mr. Darcy Simon and you have an arrangement with him. A deal," Jude said, taking his seat while directing Billy to do the same.

"Yes."

"We would in essence like to submit a counter-offer."

"I'm sorry but we are not auctioning off cattle or negotiating a used automobile here," Pinkerton said.

"No, you're auctioning off people's lives," said Billy, garnishing feisty eyes.

Pinkerton returned a blatant glare.

"All right," Jude said, "There is no possibility for a counteroffer of sorts."

"I'm afraid not," said Pinkerton, chivalry returning.

"Then perhaps we can contract your services?" asked Jude.

"Dare I ask what for?"

"Dare you may but there is nothing daring about our proposition. You're a businessman. Mr. Simon paid you $100,000 for your services. We are offering you $200,000 for your services that include much less labor, and cost."

"And they are?"

"To let us walk away," Jude said, all the cards on the table now. "To let us just walk out of your life and Mr. Simon's life forever. You can tell him whatever the hell you want. Tell him we're at the bottom of Lake Michigan or the Rio Grande for all I care because for all intents and purposes, we are. You'll never see us again."

"You must be aware that others in your…position have made similar propositions in the past?" Pinkerton asked.

"I imagine I am."

"Then you are aware our agency would not exist today if we even considered one of those propositions regardless of the monetary offer or otherwise. What we hang our hat on, our reputation, is that we fulfill our services. We get the job done."

"I fully appreciate your position, I do. The 'otherwise' you mentioned is what I believe of most interest to you," Jude said finding his jurist swagger.

"How so?"

"At my feet is a briefcase with over two-hundred thousand dollars."

"Two hundred thousand stolen dollars," Pinkerton interjected.

Billy leaned forward in his chair seething. "Who you kidding? That there is the only money that ever walked in here that don't have blood on it."

"As I was saying…" Jude said. "At my feet is a briefcase with over two hundred thousand dollars. Not a small sum. I am sure in relation to your full estate it pales in comparison, but a substantial amount considering what's involved to procure it, however, that is not the aforementioned 'otherwise.'"

"And what is the aforementioned 'otherwise' Mr. James?" Dahl asked, slithering up to Pinkterton's side. "Please do tell."

"Mr. Dahl has no interest in the otherwise," Jude said, "Or should I say only holds interest in the otherwise. Mr. Dahl is a cowboy. A gunslinger. A hunter and a killer. I know because when I was a Marshall, I held many of those same qualities. But you, Mr. Pinkerton, have a diploma from Harvard School of Business and Yale University School of Law hanging on your wall and you have it there for a reason. Mr. Dahl is an astute and sharp chap, one of the best hunters I've come across, but I'd venture to say he doesn't have any diplomas hanging on the wall in his office. I'd venture to say, Mr. Dahl may not even have an office. Mr. Dahl also does not have a wife and two young children."

Pinkerton's chair squeaked as he squirmed slightly. "Are you threatening me, Mr. James?"

"You damn right," said Billy.

Pinkerton scowled at Billy long enough to make sure Billy felt it in his gut and then moved his eyes back to Jude.

"Quite frankly, I'm disappointed in you Mr. James." Pinkerton said to Jude.

"How so?" Jude asked.

"Surely you're also aware others in your position have come in making similar threats?"

"Surely, I am, but I am not here to make threats. I am here to offer peace and peace of mind. One father to another. You take this money today, you have two hundred thousand dollars to add to the future of your family. That two-hundred thousand also buys you and me, and most importantly, our families, the peace and peace of mind of never having to look over our shoulder again. Now I don't expect Mr. Dahl to consider this offer. It took some serious arm twisting to even get Billy to agree."

"It's true, it did," Billy interjected.

"But Billy here is more of a hired gun, like Mr. Dahl," Jude continued, ignoring his brother. "With all due respect to them both, you and I got them diplomas on the wall because we are reasonable men with foresight to plan for the future. Your granddaddy did not hold a fourth-grade education and instead made his way as the roughest railroad bull north of the Mason Dixon Line. His venture was his iron first. Your daddy, on the other hand, held a college education and turned the small family business into a continental enterprise, however, he still roamed the yards dirtying his hands because he liked the hunt and enjoyed cracking open a skull now and again. I met your daddy, did you know that?"

Pinkerton clasped his hands together in front of his face, perhaps to hide his heed and stir. "I did not."

"Oh, Mr. James," said Dahl. "Exactly like the others after all."

"How's that?" asked Jude.

"Say anything to avoid the noose."

For the first time in the conversation, bluster dripped off Jude's face. "I don't see no Goddamn noose yet," Jude seethed. He turned back to Pinkerton, more affable. "Tulsa, Oklahoma, eight or so years ago, y'all were busting up some boys trying to organize. Railroad hands."

Pinkerton blinked and held his hands clasped. Probably meant he believed Jude or knew Jude was in fact telling the truth.

Dahl didn't say another word.

"I was chasing a fella, and we happened to be sitting at the same watering hole one night," Jude continued. "He saw my Marshal's badge, bought me a drink. We ended up sharing a bottle and sharing some war stories."

"Maybe you met my father. Maybe you two even shared a drink. Lord knows the man loved whiskey and tales. What's your point?" Pinkerton asked, a certain ire now in his voice.

"My point is this," Jude said. "Upward mobility."

"Upward mobility?"

"The American Dream. Your granddaddy was a thug. Your pop was well to do and worked hard to ensure his children never had to get their hands dirty like he did, even though he enjoyed it. You got two diplomas on your wall and married into money because you don't want to get your hands dirty and you never want your children to really know the family's 'rich history.' The two hundred thousand and the 'otherwise' allows you to keep all that. That's what I am offering."

Pinkerton looked hollowly at Jude and then asked, "Do you know what a *fugazi* is Mr. James?"

"You shouldn't use that word in front of Mr. Dahl," Billy said. "His sexual orientation is his business."

Pinkerton ignored Billy, his eyes not departing from Jude, waiting for an answer.

"I do," said Jude, stiffly.

"Your closing arguments, counselor, are like a *fugazi*. Shiny and bright at first blush, but ultimately fake and unpersuasive. These last few minutes were entertaining, I'll give you that. And you almost make a distinct argument but alas, you see, Mr. James," Pinkerton said, spreading his hands as if powerless or unimpressed, "Lions will always be lions and lambs will always be lambs. You speak of 'upward mobility' but mostly what you are at birth is also what you are at death. If you're born a negro, an Indian, or even a poor Mexican, chances are, you will die as one. That's just the God's honest-truth. From what I hear, you and your brother overcame some adversity growing up to become the proud men you are today. Sometimes, it can seem, one may almost escape his birthright whether to be better or worse off, until the nature of things, the natural order if you will, becomes diligent again. It was admirable how far you two boys came before Billy's unfortunate circumstance put you back in line where you belong, and therefore in essence, it was not so much unfortunate as unavoidable. You see, Mr. James, I may have the diplomas on the wall, but I am still a lion. You may have the diplomas on the wall, two hundred thousand dollars at your feet and a novel proposition but you are still a lamb and shall be eaten. It is the nature of the beasts. The natural order."

Jude exhaled deeply and sat back in his chair. He stared off pondering, possibly posturing, mashing his mustache with his forefinger, as he often did. "Well, I guess that's it then huh?" he finally asked.

Pinkerton once again motioned with his hands, as if they were tied.

Jude nodded in agreement, leaned forward in his chair, and then spoke. "You know, what you said there was almost poetic, Mr. Pinkerton." Jude tilted even further forward, raising his index finger. "There is just one distinct difference…"

"And that is?.."

ZIP!

Dahl dropped to the ground.

Billy flipped the chair over, ripping his Glock from the fabric bottom it was taped to.

Jude did the same, raising his Winchester.

Billy bolted to Dahl pointing the silenced muzzle over him. "Not a word," he whispered.

Jude hopped across the desk, pistol whipping Pinkerton, sending Pinkerton out of his chair sideways.

"…I'm a lamb with a fucking hillbilly sniper," Jude said. "That's the difference."

Dahl squirmed on the ground, a .338 sniper round clear through his shoulder, looking up at Billy.

"Ssshhhh," Billy said to Dahl, putting his finger over his mouth with his free hand.

Jude, dashed to the office door.

The long plush hallway was quiet and vacant.

He closed the door, ensuring not to slam it, locking it just as quietly.

He heard a desk drawer just as Pinkerton disappeared behind it.

Before Jude could react, Pinkerton popped up brandishing his own pistol.

POP! POP! POP! Pinkerton fired off three rounds.

Jude sailed back against the door, hit by one.

Then drew up his revolver. *BANG! BANG! BANG!*

Pinkerton flailed back and dropped behind the desk.

The door shook and the knob rattled.

"Mr. Pinkerton? Mr. Dahl?" a voice yelled from the other side.

"We're in here!" Dahl squealed from the ground.

Billy cocked the pistol.

"Billy! No! We need him alive!" Jude yelled, sensing his brother's next move.

Jude ran back across the room and hopped over the desk.

Pinkerton lay on the ground, his pressed white collared shirt now with raspberry puddles. Rouge-colored jam bubble from his neck. His eyes still present with light, widened, seeing Jude.

"You dumb son of a bitch," Jude said, shaking his head. "All of this could have been avoided."

"You don't know the world, do you, Mr. James?" Pinkerton muttered, his voice wet with blood, before trying to pull his gun up at Jude.

Jude was faster, firing one bullet square into Pinkerton's forehead. "Unfortunately, I do," Jude said, watching the blood pond behind Pinkerton's vacant face.

"Pinkerton's dead!" Dahl hollered. "Kill the sons of bitches!"

"Shut the fuck up," Billy said, kicking Dahl first in the gut then in the chops.

Billy felt something snap in Dahl's jaw from his boot and it made him smile on the inside.

Suddenly the office door was shredded with machine gun fire.

Jude ducked behind the desk.

Billy yanked Dahl out of the path of gunfire, holed up against the bookcase as the bullets whizzed by.

Billy fired off three rounds into the door, simply as deterrence. "Any minute now would be just fine, hillbilly," he said.

Jude pulled the pistol from Pinkerton's dead hand, pointed his arm above the desk and fired off three rounds into what was left of the door.

"You think they got Christian?" Jude yelled to Billy.

"They didn't get him!" yelled Billy, firing two more rounds into the door. "They didn't get him," he prayed to himself.

CHAPTER FORTY-FIVE

The homemade explosives worked fine, just like Billy promised.

The building shook.

The windows shattered.

And in the same moment, Christian was slammed in the face with a scorching wave of heat, almost knocking him off his feet, as he bolted across the street.

Along with the rich familiar scent of gunpowder and war, he smelled his own burnt hair. The smart-ass thought Christian only shaved his beard out of some silly sniper lore. Yes, some of his reason was based in puerile tradition, but Christian also saw the amount of gunpowder and dynamite and materials that go BOOM and set things on fire and he figured the less burnable particles on his face, such as hair, the better.

As they assumed, the moment Jude and Lee stepped through the front door of the Pinkerton Agency, the guerilla and his two cohorts closed off the whole block out front. No suspicious strollers or looky-loos to mind, also ensuring no innocent bystanders would fall victim to the initial blast.

Thick gray smoke billowed from the building as the frenzied mass stampeded like white-tail deer through the fog, and for a moment, Christian thought he was dashing through the cobblestone streets of Germany, not Chicago's blacktop.

Over the terrified shrieking and mass hysteria, Christian heard gunshots rattling off in the building. That meant the boys were still alive and fighting.

The shotgun strapped to his shoulder jingled, bouncing up and down, dodging the spooked herd while running full steam.

He made his way across the street and through the mist of strife, and he saw what remained of three henchmen, charred, and unfurled on the sidewalk.

As Christian approached what was left of the door, an agent burst out, in a coughing fit with his forearm over his face. He never saw Christian raise his Glock. Maybe there was an instant when he heard the two rounds before there was only black, then God.

The agent dropped halfway in the door.

Without breaking stride, Christian hopped over him, firing one more in his head for good measure.

Muzzle poised straight ahead he scampered through the debris, pieces of shattered glass cracking beneath his boots. Shifting through the gray haze, he felt his eyes burn, his ears ring and his senses sharpen, and Christian's mind dislocated, swearing he was back in Germany again.

Ash sifted around him like falling snow, and there were no shadows because there was no light.

Outside was bright, inside was lightless.

As Christian passed an overturned desk, an agent popped up from behind still lost to what happened.

Both men startled the other.

Christian regained composure first and swung the butt of this Glock into the man's nose.

The agent toppled over the desk and Christian fired hot pieces of lead into him.

Through the ringing in his ears, Christian heard footsteps near. He turned toward the sound, light glowing down the stairwell as if a portal from God. He knew it was not St. Michael barreling down those stairs.

He raised his gun, readying his aim about to send some poor soul back where he came from.

Finally an agent appeared, breathing hard, fear and anger beating from his face, a large machine gun in hand, clumsily rumbling down the stairs.

As he got to the bottom, he noticed Christian. "Shit!" he yelled, losing his footing in panic.

Christian fired three rounds, all too high.

The agent winced as bullets exploded in the wood stairs around him. Still on his back, he pulled up his machine gun, rattling off rounds.

Christian dived behind the desk, landing on the previous fallen soldier. He stuffed the corpse between him and the desk as machine gun bullets shredded through the table and the flesh of the human shield. He coiled behind both, reloading his Glock, tightening up his entire body, trying to get as small as possible, waiting out the assault.

The blizzard ceased, hearing the magazine click empty.

Christian bolted up, firing.

The agent frantically fumbled with a new clip before a bullet sailed into his leg. "Shit! Shit!" he shrieked again.

Giving up on the clip, the agent turned and scampered back up the stairs out of Christian's line of sight.

Christian gave chase, making his way to the stairwell, catching the agent in his sights, scurrying halfway up the steps with his wounded leg.

Perhaps sensing Christian behind him, the agent turned, and the two men's sights collided. The agent's eyes widened like spilt paint recognizing Christian's face was the last thing he would ever see. His jaw almost slackened like he was giving up, almost leaving Christian too much time to fire two shots into the man's chest and one in the head.

Instantly, the agent dropped, sprawled out like a snow angel, the machine gun resting on his lap, his face already blank.

Christian dropped the Glock and unsheathed the shotgun.

The long barrel slowly towed him up the stairs toward the sound of mayhem. A machine gun rattled off, and in between, sounds of a pistol. Maybe Jude's.

When he reached the top of the stairs, he quickly shot his head around the corner.

In one brief glance, he could see two men held up down the hall, flanked on each corner of a four-way intersection, firing off into Pinkerton's office. The men wouldn't be spilling their rounds at Pinkerton or Dahl meaning at least one of the boys was still on hind legs sucking air.

Fighting.

Christian leaned his back against the wall, stilling his breathing, then he heard the sweetest sound to pass by his ears since his wife had last whispered in them – Jude's Winchester revolver firing.

Even in the hellacious chaos, a little grin reared at the corners of Christian's mouth.

Jude was one obstinate son of a bitch.

"I'll take a gun that fires six bullets every time rather than one that fires ninety-nine out of one hundred," he said, as the three men discussed what tools to use for the job.

"I'm pretty sure you ain't fired anything else in your life but that six-shooter," said Billy.

"And I'm pretty sure it's kept me good and whole so far," said Jude.

Christian shot his head around the corner again, one more attempt to take in his next move.

The wrath of the explosion had not swelled to the second floor which remained shiny and bright. A menacing contrast to the snowy apocalypse below. The plush crimson carpet and cherry oak walls of the royal hallway were still intact. At least a chandelier had perished, the shattered glass sparkling off the remaining lights, awkwardly languishing in the hallway like a fallen tree on a mountain trail. And some, but not all, of the paintings of entitled men had fallen and were tilted sideways on the ground. Their crooked portraits now seeming awkward and surreal.

The two agents continued their machine gun assault on Pinkerton's office, then ducking back in the hallway when a few bullets whizzed by.

Christian wrapped his left hand around the fore-stock of his shotgun while bending his right index finger around the trigger.

He bent his neck, straining to hear over the gun fire waiting for that sound of no sound.

When the machine gun fire ceased and he heard the empty metal clip hit the ground, Christian flung around the corner. Soaring and steady up the long hallway, like a knight returning, he aimed the huge cannon in his grasp.

BOOM!

He cocked the shotgun again.

BOOM!

Two slugs exploded into the first agent, toppling him back, his blood painting the wall behind him before slouching to the ground.

The second agent swiveled to Christian.

Christian felt the trigger tighten for a moment before the agent's insides exploded out of him and he fell.

TAT TAT TAT!

Christian heard behind him in the same moment he felt a sharp hot singe in his back, as if a burning coal erupted inside him.

He closed his eyes tight, twisted around as he cocked and fired the last two slugs in the gun.

There was a grisly scream and Christian knew he hit the son of a bitch somewhere.

He opened his eyes noticing there was a hallway behind him where he came up the stairs.

He never thought to inspect his six. That was sloppy and he hoped it was not his last mistake.

He felt something deep and warm like candle wax run down his leg.

His head dropped to his torso where he saw ponds of blood bubbling from his stomach.

He realized he was shot, and he became irate that he allowed himself to be wounded.

His head turned back up to the agent fumbling his own shotgun, attempting to load the slug with his own gaping wound in his side and half his hand now shredded.

The agent was tall, lanky, and pale, maybe even before being shot. His long frame leaned against the wall like a weeping willow.

The two men's eyes locked.

Christian reached in his back pocket for more slugs. He fumbled with the bullets, his hands not communicating with his brain and the gun suddenly slipped from his grasp.

The agent was finally able to slide the bright yellow slug into the slide. Hope washed across his face as his hand grasped tight to cock the gun.

Christian dropped the bullets while reaching around his waistband. The leather handle of his M3 Fighting Knife provided an instant sense of comfort and connected the phone lines between his brain and his hands. He yanked the knife from where it was nestled between the small of his back and the belt line of his Levi's.

Christian bolted toward the agent while coiling the knife behind him, loading it like a slingshot.

The agent cocked the shotgun and aimed it directly at the rushing bull.

His finger found the trigger and he was about to release the torpedo point-blank into Christian's skull.

He was so close now that he could not miss Christian if he tried.

Suddenly, Christian grabbed the muzzle of the shotgun with his free hand, raising it above the agent.

The agent panicked and fired as Christian released his fastened arm, sending the serrated double edge stiletto seamlessly into the agent's chest.

SWOSH. SWOSH. SWOSH.

The blade slid in and out smooth like hot butter.

Only when his body fell over the knife, his weight falling into Christian, did Christian exert any real effort.

He yanked the knife from the agent's cavity as the listless carcass thudded to the ground.

Christian felt something scatter on his head and he looked up.

Plaster from the buckshot to the ceiling sprinkled down like a snow flurry. For some reason, in the middle of the chaos, Christian raised his head to the falling debris and closed his eyes. A smile slid over his face thinking back to when he and his brother would dash outside every year as children to the first Kansas snowfall, raising their heads to the sky, closing their eyes to the ample flakes capering on their eyelids and the wet crystals melting on their tongues.

Christian's nostalgia was then interrupted with the sound of footsteps behind.

He turned just in time to see Dahl dash from the room and down the hallway towards the dead agents.

Without breaking stride, Dahl scooped up one of the machine guns and disappeared around the corner.

Christian pried the shotgun from the hands of the severed agent and gathered the unspent shells at his feet.

He then raised, loading the shotgun, following the aimed barrel down the hallway corner where he saw Dahl escape behind.

Suddenly, Jude's head peeked out of Pinkerton's office, almost prompting friendly fire from Christian like a hunted bird scattering from a tree. Christian turned the barrel away, breathing a quick sigh of relief.

Jude appeared whole, his six-shooter drifting languidly by his side. Both men shared a quick nod, as if to say *Fuck. We're still in it.* Christian saw no sign of Billy but something on Jude's face told him the smart ass was still of this world.

Interrupting the moment, Dahl suddenly shot out in front of Christian, the muzzle of his machine gun peeking from the corner of the hallway, pointed directly at Jude.

Christian's eyes widened, then fired a round at Dahl who had not seen the gun-toting giant until the drywall exploded around him.

Dahl shirked back around the mangled corner of the wall while still firing at Jude.

Bullets littered the swiss cheese door that had been reduced to saw dust, but no sign of Jude, who seemling ducked back into the office, safe.

"You boys are just full of surprises!" Dahl bellowed from around the corner. "I take it this here is the sniper," his voice loud enough to hear but not rattled.

Undettered, Christian ambled down the hallway toward the voice.

Before another word was uttered, Dahl sprang from the corner, this time pointing the machine gun squarely at Christian.

Before Dahl could light it up, Christian fired another round. More drywall exploded, dust scattered, and Dahl disappeared around the corner again.

Christian heard footsteps behind him.

He turned to see an agent appear at the top of the stairwell. He fired a shot, hitting the agent somewhere, sending him fleeing back down the stairs, at least momentarily.

Christian knew he had one slug left.

He also recognized Jude and Billy, if Billy was still alive, would be cornered by Dahl and that Goddamn machine gun, whether they had bullets left for rebuttal or not.

Christian suddenly understood the moment before him.

He felt a clarity wash over his eyes.

He felt a peace in his heart he had never felt.

His soul inhaled deeply.

He no longer sensed the hot slugs burning in his gut or the sticky blood coalescing on his flesh.

He closed his eyes, his soul exhaled and…

Christian dashed to the corner.

He swung the cannon around and for one instant caught Dahl square, standing there with his battleax pointed at Christian.

Dahl let his machine gun rip, spraying every part of Christian.

Blazing pebbles stung like fire-ants in Christian's flesh.

His head became heavy.

His neck no longer able to hold his head straight.

His face was flush with the roof, his eyes wide-open staring at the powdery ceiling.

And then he remembered the shotgun in his hand, and he pulled the trigger.

He heard a scream and his head dropped in front of him to see the blast hit Dahl.

Dahl flailed back through a large window behind him.

His torso flipped over the window frame first, and his legs were the last thing Christian saw before he disappeared into the air.

Christian released his grip on the gun and tried to blink. His eyelids seemingly sticky now from sweat or blood or he didn't know what.

Then he realized was staring up at the ceiling.

There were needles in his lungs that prickled and suddenly he could not breathe enough air. Like oxygen had departed around him.

Jude was suddenly lording over Christian, sweat pouring from his face and his eyes puffy. His lips were moving at Christian, but he heard no voice.

Jude was shaking Christian now, and then, as if the volume on a record player was turned up, Christian could tune it Jude's words.

"You're gonna be alright. Just stick with me," Jude was saying.

Jude wrapped his arm under Christian's back and scooted him against the wall allowing his head and upper torso to rest in an "L" shape.

Jude knelt in front of Christian, the two men's faces parallel.

"You're gonna be alright," Jude said again.

Christian felt his body seep into a crevice between the wall and floor, his arms withering into his lap.

His head became loose from his neck, like a tied balloon that becomes untethered and floats away into the ether.

"Just stay with me. You're gonna be alright," Jude repeated.

Christian blinked and smiled kindly at Jude. "You know how I know I ain't?" Christian found himself asking.

"How's that? Jude asked, his eyes heavy with tears now.

"Because you look scared as shit. More scared than I ever seen you."

Jude's face tightened, causing more tears to escape.

Christian's eyes drifted to his shredded shirt. "Well that don't look good."

"Christian you're gonna…."

"…It's all right. Jude, it's all right. I ain't scared to die now."

"Christian…" Jude pleaded, squeezing Christian's hand tight.

"No, listen, I ain't never done anything worth a damn in my life. If I was able to help get you back to your wife and kids, well that's something."

"You loved your wife right?"

"Yessir."

"That's something too."

Christian's eyes remained vibrant and blue even as the rest of this body faded away and then nodded in agreement with Jude. They blinked hard under his unruly red eyebrows, like they always did when he was thinking. "Reckon, I can add that to the ledger," Christian finally said. Then he grew silent, staring off past Jude and with each breath, his chest elevated and lowered a little less.

Jude knelt next to him, one arm under his back. He realized his other hand was holding Christian's. It felt dry and stale unlike the rest of his sopping body.

Christian's head turned up to Jude. "Billy? Where's Billy?"

"He's fine. He's wrapping a knife wound he got in the leg."

"What?"

"Dahl stabbed him in the leg with some knife we didn't see. That's how the cocksucker got away from us."

"I thought we weren't using that word anymore"

Jude smiled long and wide.

Christian's head bobbed again, and his eyes slowly lowered, like the curtains from an old theater.

Jude felt Christian's hand start to go limp then Christian's eyes popped back open again. "Oh shit," Christian said. "I still owe you one."

Jude laughed again through the rue on his face.

"I got some bad news," said Christian.

"Yea, what's that?"

"I might be ducking out early before settling my tab with you."

"You blasted Dahl from here to hell, saving my ass and Billy's in the process. Consider our tab square."

"Fair enough," Christian said. His eyes blinked hard and raced from side to side and then he looked up at Jude again. "You love them boys every day. Shower them with so much love, there'll be no room for hate in their hearts. You hear me?"

"I hear you," said Jude, smiling and crying simultaneously.

Christian nodded slightly. "All right then, I'll be seeing you."

Jude watched Christian's head droop into his chest again, his body melt into the ground and his hand went soft in Jude's.

Only Christian's vivid blue eyes remained, now glassy and vacant like a marble.

"No, man, no," Billy said, wrapping his hands behind his head and turning away as he stood behind Jude now.

Jude looked up at Billy. "Saved our life," he muttered through the tears. "He was at peace when he went. His last act was blasting Dahl right out of that window," he said, nodding to the shattered glass that a rainy breeze now blew in from.

Billy shook his head in disbelief or wonder. "Christian, *mi hermano*, the hardest person to forgive is oneself. In that last sliver of light, I hope that's what you found there."

Both men remained fixed and muted on their fallen friend, perhaps a silent wake occurring in each of their heads and hearts.

An incoming siren blared out the window, coming closer and closer, interrupting the wake.

"Jude," said Billy, placing his hand on his brother's shoulder.

Jude came to. "Yea," he said standing. "Can you walk?"

Billy looked down at his ankle wrapped in shreds of his white T-Shirt now stained ruby red "Fucker went for my tendon, but I caught him in time. I don't think he got anything important. I can walk to Ireland if I have to."

"Let's just focus on walking our asses out of here first," said Jude.

CHAPTER
FORTY-SIX

Billy and Jude squinted as they exited the building, shielding their eyes from the ash, soot and debris that still fluttered in the air, leaving a gray haze over an already foggy drizzled day.

The blaring sound of sirens seemed to surround them. Perhaps the noise ricocheting off the buildings, or conceivably, the block was filled with the entire Chicago police department.

Jude looked up the street to find spinning cherries on top of the boxy police cars heading his way. He turned to his right, only to find more of the same. He pulled a hard breath, sizing up his next move when he noticed a sliver of an alley behind what was left of the Pinkerton Agency, "This way," Jude said, grabbing Billy, turning down the corridor.

They hobbled down the alley, trying to appear as innocuous as possible, one with a gunshot wound to the shoulder, the other with a knife wound to the leg.

Billy craned his head up toward the building as he limped down the street. "Ain't that window that Christian shot Dahl out of?"

Only Jude's eyes turned up, not breaking stride. "Yea."

Billy's eyes shifted to the ground. "Then shouldn't Dahl's body be right there?"

Jude stopped dead in his tracks.

Below the window was a heaping pile of rubbish surrounding a rusted dumpster.

Jude and Billy shared a curious and foreboding look in the same moment, Jude pulled his Winchester from his waistband, slinging open the chamber. "Fuck," he said at the empty cylinder.

Billy raised his arms in the air, his empty palms wide indicating *I ain't got shit.*

Jude warily approached the heap, both men keeping four eyes on the soggy mountain of garbage.

As Jude neared, his eyes widened. "Well I'll be damned."

Jude motioned with his head toward the pile and Billy staggered over.

"Goddamn," said Billy, equally astonished.

As if simply lounging on a bundle of cushions, Dahl lay unfurled on his back, heaving, bleeding, squirming, and still alive. He pressed his hand around the maroon puddle on his shirt, blooding gurgling out between his fingers. His face was white but his eyes sharpened when he saw Billy and Jude. "You know," Dahl said, "Every day I would implore those heathens not to simply throw their rubbish out the Goddamn window but walk it down to the dumpster like civilized men in a civilized city." Dahl's eyes glanced around the parachutes of waste around him. "Luckily for me, they did not heed my repeated requests."

"There ain't no God if this son of a bitch is still alive," said Jude.

"I love you think that much of me," Dahl said with a flirty grin. "That my mere existence has some divine consequence."

Jude gritted his teeth fuming. "Our friend is dead."

"I imagine so. Now, that would be a miracle if he were still alive. I put at least a dozen bullets into that fellow."

"That 'fellow' was our dear friend, and his name was Christian," said Billy.

"Well in my defense, your dear friend, Christian, did shoot me with that canon of a shotgun sending me two stories to what should have been my death." Dahl's eyes shifted to the pistol Jude still held in his hand. "From the moment we laid eyes on each other, we both knew that we shared that singular and extraordinary bond."

"What bond is that?" Jude asked.

"The bond that one of us would fall at the hand of the other. To be honest, I thought the roles would be reversed, however."

Jude squinted, his face perplexed, and he looked to Billy for clarity.

Billy's eyes met Jude's with the same vexing stare.

"Go on then," Dahl said, nodding to the pistol. "No use prolonging the inevitable any longer."

Jude stared down at the pistol resting in his hand. "It's empty."

"Ah," said Dahl. "Surely a fellow killer such as yourself can find another instrument to use in your close vicinity. Perhaps your bare hands even. The same hands you've undoubtedly held Wyatt and Patrick in."

Jude flinched at the mere words flowing from Dahl's lips, like they were punching him in the face and he bolted to Dahl, raising the thick heel of his boot to Dahl's defenseless skull.

Billy hugged his brother from behind, desperately dragging him backwards. "No Jude, not like this," Billy pleaded as he pulled. "He ain't long for this world. Ain't no use in soiling your own heel anymore."

"Perhaps it's Wyatt, Patrick and Luisa not long for this world," Dahl teased.

"I'll stomp the light out of you!" Jude yelled, breaking through Billy's clutches.

Billy twisted in front of Jude, then pushing him back, as if he were breaking up a dog fight. "There ain't no light in him. Not now not ever," he said, jabbing Jude away from Dahl.

"I might be dying but you're the one talking nonsense, boy," Dahl said to Billy. "Billy is just a caveman thug, Jude, but you and I are one in the same. Finish it," Dahl called out to Jude.

Sirens blared louder, closer.

Voices scattered down the street as police officers dashed past the alley in both directions, closing in.

It was only a matter of seconds now, both boys knew it.

"Jude, come on," whispered Billy, still desperately clinging to his brother.

Jude's eyes remained fixed on Dahl, even as he lowered his boot and began retreating. "I ain't like you," Jude hissed.

"If you believe that, then in some sense you are correct then. Only one of us is self-delusional," said Dahl.

"I ain't delusional about shit," Billy said, suddenly letting go of Jude, landing his own boot twice into Dahl's stomach with a running start.

Dahl curled into himself, grasping where Billy booted him, and the gunshot wound, leering up. "You are God's pestilence," Dahl wheezed.

"Maybe a pestilence, but not God's," Billy said. "I used to believe for One to exist there had to be the other, but I've learned now there is no God, and yet, I know the devil so well. Our creator, your creator is coming for you, crawling up inch by fucking inch to drag you back to where you belong. Christian sent the homecoming flare right to your gut and now He's on his way to reclaim what's his. I ain't got no delusions, I'm on the list too," Billy wound back and drove his boot one more time into Dahl's bleeding soul, "But you're up first, you son of a bitch."

CHAPTER
FORTY-SEVEN

True to form, Aneta knew a doctor who pulled the .38 slug out of Jude's shoulder, cleaned the wound, and plugged the hole. The doctor also sewed up the gash in Billy's leg as methodical and seamless as a seamstress. He never asked any questions, perhaps because he spoke no English. The occasional shake of the head and the glare of the glasses that hung over his nose said it all. Only when he was finished with Billy after Jude, did he sit upright on his stool, placing his hands on his knees, did he utter one word in a heavy Polish accent, "Okay."

Jude handed the good doctor a stack of cash and the man smiled and patted Jude on the shoulder, as if saying *Good luck*. The doctor most likely understood all too well, being on the run, a Polish Jew fleeing the Nazis when the first tanks rolled into Krakow. The doctor killed a man who threatened his escape and he feared that act would lead to his ultimate fate if he ever returned. As such, the three men were all refugees in Chicago bound by a similar plight, the only difference now, was two of the men were heading the opposite direction back over the Atlantic.

Aneta and her parents did not share that bond with the James boys. It was never discussed why the Nowaks not only looked the other way in harboring fugitives but aided and abetted the boys. Sure, Jude paid her family much more than what they owed for lodging and food. Considering the neighborhood of the hotel, it was almost an occupational requisite to not ask questions. But there was solidarity and kindness in Aneta's eyes that went deeper than the doting late teenage lust for Jude. Even Mrs. Nowak's frigid and hardened visage seemed to melt slightly at their farewell. Lord knows, no smile crossed that crinkled spiteful face that served as an open history book of struggle and discord, but she nodded slightly, looking the two boys in the eye, out of the scarf that always wrapped her head.

Perhaps what Jude and Billy saw in the women's eyes was indeed that understanding of strife, the constant scraping and clawing to stay alive and hold on to what's yours. They were all simply fighting to get by. The women surely knew the boys were involved somehow in the explosion and gun fight that rattled a city even as colossal and violent as Chicago, but the women also knew someone, probably more rich and powerful than Billy and Jude, were trying to wrap their dirty fucking hands around the boys' throats, and the boys had enough.

Aneta followed the two boys out of the hotel to the running Packard in the alley they had purchased with cash. The gesture was more than a friendly host seeing paying guests out.

Jude opened the car, slung one leg inside, and tipped his cowboy hat to the adoring young woman. She smiled, and it reminded Jude that there were still some decent folk on this earth. He returned a smile and closed the car door.

"You thinking about Christian?" Jude asked, shattering the silence, as he steered the 42' Packard.

It was the first time in three weeks the two men were not surrounded by lights and sounds, and there was a peace in the black silence that enclosed them. Spring had not yet reached North Central Michigan, or perhaps their spring felt like a Northern New Mexico winter. The heater of the old boat hummed, and ice cornered around the windshield outside, a little reminder of how close and efficacious the circling elements were.

Every so often, Billy would roll down the window, allowing the frigid gust to sweep through the cabin. The air somehow felt free and pure and allowed Billy to feel the same. Jude never bitched or complained so Billy figured it must have bestowed a similar calm on Jude. Or perhaps, after all that had happened, Jude finally ceased sweating the small shit.

"Ain't you?" Billy asked, his gaze fixed outside.

"Yea, I guess so. Figure eventually we'll have to find a way to get word to his people in Kansas. Give them some clarity as to his last days. We owe him that."

Billy nodded, his blue eyes still pointing out the black of the passenger side window.

Jude rested his hand on top of the large helm, exhaled and then spoke. "Truth be told no, no bullshit?"

Billy turned to Jude. "Yea."

Jude rubbed his mustache with his forefinger, looked away and then back. "When I just asked if you were thinking about Christian…"

"Yea."

"I wasn't thinking about Christian."

"No?"

"No. I was thinking about Mrs. Nowak's pierogis."

Billy snickered.

"Fucked up right?" Jude asked.

Billy snickered again and shook his head.

"Really fucked up?" Jude emphasized gauging Billy's reaction.

"No, *carnal*, quite the opposite."

"I said, 'no bullshit.'"

"No bullshit. Remember when you were about to stomp in Dahl's head and I told you if you did, you'd never be the same?"

"Yea, I recall."

"If you did that, you'd never be able to think of that old woman's veal and spinach pierogies again. How the potato and grease would melt in your mouth like butter."

"That's what they did," Jude said, saucer-eyed as if a steaming plate of them were under his nose right now.

"Right. And now you're also feeling guilty, that Goddamn Catholic guilt, because you're thinking about food or how good that first hit of a bottle beer tastes with a little bit of salt, when you should be thinking about Christian, or Luisa and the kids or repentance or I don't know what."

"Well I wasn't thinking about a bottle of Pabst until right now either, but yea. Yea, you know, what the fuck? Of course, I'm mourning over Christian and wishing and praying Luisa and the kids are okay. I got ten thousand things to concern me so what does it mean that I'm thinking about Goddamn pierogies and beer?"

"It means you're the opposite of fucked up, it means you're still human. If you crushed that son of a bitches' head in with your boot, felt his skull cave in, see his brains bleed from his ears, it would have felt good for all of two seconds, and that would have been the last time you'd feel anything at all. You'd never think about the little things that make life not only bearable but beautiful ever again. And when you realized you were now hallow and callous, you'd try anything in the world to feel again, for just one minute to feel *something* in this life."

Billy hushed as if not aware he was still speaking. He breathed in deeply then tried to steady his own breath turning his gaze to the passenger side window again.

Jude pondered for a long moment and then spoke. "That night before we met Pinkerton? When I found you…"

Jude now stopped himself. He didn't really know what he was asking and there had never been anything that he and Billy could not talk about until maybe this.

"Yea… I was uh…" Billy muttered. He palmed his face that remained glued away from Jude and then continued. "Again, I'm sorry about that."

"No, that's not what I'm saying."

"I know."

There was another long pause and then Jude spoke. "I was so fucking pissed that night. Even walking back after. Even after Christian calmed me down, I was still pissed. I hid it but I was pissed."

"Jude, once your fuse is lit, there ain't no putting it out and there ain't no hiding it. I was stoned out of my mind on heroin, and I could still see that you were livid."

"It ain't right. That night was the first time I thought I would never be able to forgive you. Of all the shit we've been through, that's what I thought might break us. And now I realize, I had no fucking right. What you do with your life, your body ain't my business. Who the fuck am I?"

"You're a hot-headed self-righteous, at times, arrogant son of a bitch and you're my brother," Billy said with a grin.

"Well I don't wanna be any of those things except your brother."

"Well, if we're being honest, you're also an asshole."

Jude returned the grin now. "Fuck you, you're the most self-centered, inconsiderate selfish asshole I ever met."

"No argument here," Billy said. "And ain't self-centered and selfish the same fucking thing, counselor?"

Jude chuckled and shook his head. He grew silent again and then spoke. "I didn't understand why… I didn't realize how much pain you were in or lack of…"

"Feeling anything."

"Feeling anything."

"That night… I uh… If things didn't go right that next day at Pinkerton's. I just wanted one more night to feel something. To just feel. When you shoot dope, at least you can feel a warmth inside you." Billy peered over his right shoulder, as if there was someone creeping up behind him. "At least you feel something."

Jude found no words.

None crossed his always calculating and wily mind or poured from his usually fervent and stirring heart.

The only sound in the car was Jude's heart breaking from the realization of how broken and hurt his little brother truly was and how blind Jude had been to it.

It was always on Jude to fix *it*. Whatever *it* was. But just like his Daddy, with all the love and patience and then alcohol that couldn't fix his Mamma, Jude didn't know if he held the tools to fix Billy and that frightened him more than a jailbreak, bank robbery or gangster shootout.

"You were good to not kill Dahl that way," Billy eventually said.

Jude came to and inhaled deeply at the thought of Dahl. "Maybe not that way."

"You think he's dead? That we've seen the last of him?" Billy asked.

"We're taking a boat over a lake the size of a country to get to another country to cross a frozen tundra by train to then voyage over one of the biggest oceans in the world. But somehow, I feel in my bones he's still alive, and he will find us. So no, I don't think we've seen the last of him."

Billy palmed his face, gritted his jaw sideways and looked down at the Glock on his lap. "Me neither."

PART
FIVE

THIS ENDS. WITH BLOOD

CHAPTER FORTY-EIGHT

"Where you going?" Billy asked, looking up from the soft oily rag in his hand he cleaned the gun with. He sat on the bed in his A-Shirt which meant he was relaxing but the boys didn't even unbuckle one loop on their belt or take off their boots unless they were hitting the sack, even as they loitered or hid in the confines of their hotel room. Neither mentioned the practice but the motive was clear – at any moment the wolves could be at the door – and they needed to remain puckered.

Billy had noticed the puffy bags growing under Jude's eyes, pockets of sleeplessness that resulted from a man who was used to sleeping being denied the opportunity. Billy first experienced the same in boot camp, how a man's face would grow long and saggy until the body got used to no sleep, then it seemed, the nerves tightened up, the brain made a fist and after that, you were never really tired again. You were never alive and awake though either.

Jude had not reached that point yet, and Billy hoped he never would. They had four days until the train and a week before they sailed off on the boat. There was going to be idle time in between but no peace. Maybe when they finally reached the rolling green hills of Ireland, Jude could heal and rejuvenate, healing all the wounds inside and out, curing the acts committed, remitted into the slumbered ether.

The hotel room looked the same as all the others. Dim yellow light from a small lamp on a little stand between the two beds. The room was larger than the Nowaks in Chicago, almost too spacious for peace of mind, and it seemed vacant without a muted red-headed oaf lumbering around taking up space. Much to the boys' dismay, it also had a large window that looked out to the dotted lights of Detroit harbor before being washed into the vast obscure Lake Eerie. The window with the view would have been a nice touch if they were tourists not fugitives.

"I'm uh, gonna see if I can find a phone. Try and reach Luisa," Jude said mutedly, holding at the door.

Billy nodded. "I forgot to ask. How did she take the news about what happened in Chicago?"

Jude's eyes fell to the green carpet at his feet.

Billy recognized the Catholic guilt oozing from Jude's face. "What?"

Jude scraped the carpet with the nose of his boot.

"You haven't talked to her since Chicago?" Billy accused.

"And when would I have done that?" Jude erupted. "Between fleeing a war zone and getting a bullet dug out of my flesh?"

"She don't even know you're alive?" Billy asked, a strange sensitivity in his voice.

"Well, Goddamn. You think you're in a position to be giving me relationship advice?"

"It ain't relationship advice, it's how to not be an asshole advice."

"Fuck!..." Jude yelled making a fist as if he were about to put it through the thin drywall then stopped.

He simmered down, exhaled, and mashed his mustache with his forefinger.

"What is it?" Billy asked, his tone shifting accordingly.

"I just…" Jude's face looked pale and exposed. "…Nothing," he finally said, placing his hat on low, hiding his sallow mug. "I don't anticipate being long. Three knocks on the door."

"Three knocks," Billy said, trying to steal one more clue from his brother's face as Jude departed.

"Hello?"said a voice on the other line, sounding distant and plastic like. It wasn't the tone so much as the actual sound, like it started out whole and then sifted through multiple filters or traveled underwater. Perhaps it was the result of a long-distance phone call from 1,000 miles away. But Jude never remembered it sounding that way in Chicago or when he would call from the road when *he* was the one chasing bad guys. Maybe the issue was on the receiving end of this phone, or worse on the caller himself.

It was Luisa's voice. And she had never answered the phone at the *hotel* before. It was always the *Madame* or *one of the girls.*

"Luisa?" Jude asked, one shoulder leaning into the corner of the telephone booth, the rest of his body hunched over the payphone. Jude made sure he only used phones that were surrounded in glass to avoid any surprises from behind. He might be more exposed in a box of windows but at least he'd see the coyotes circling.

The red booth oddly stood by itself on the boat dock, between barges that pointed out to the windy and uninviting lake. Teardrops of water shimmied and frolicked against the panes, picked up from the spreading wind over the lake, splattering against the glass of the booth. When the wind really howled, the water would quiver, rattle, and separate only to mellow again when the air calmed.

"Jude," Luisa said, sounding relieved and delighted.

Luisa was not the type of woman to greet her man upon his return from work each day by leaping into his arms and smoldering him with kisses. Luisa loved Jude dearly and she expressed it but she was cool and even keeled. She was not stiff or unaffectionate; she simply held a confident peace of mind that most did not. It was one Jude's favorite attributes, a serene Ying to his fiery Yang. Tonight, however, in that one word, Jude perhaps heard something more.

"It's me," Jude managed.

"Are you okay?" The relief seemed to evolve into concern.

"I'm okay," he said slowly.

"And Billy?"

"He's…okay…too."

Jude heard a deep breath on the other line and then it sounded like Luisa pulled the receiver away from her face. Suddenly, the thousand-mile distance felt like ten-thousand miles. Jude held still, his eyes wide, straining to hear any clue. "How are you?" he finally asked.

A muffled sobbing was the only answer.

A kind of crying he never heard from Luisa before.

Not when Billy was convicted to hang and not that last night when they said their goodbyes.

"Luisa, are you okay?"

He heard shaky deep breaths and sniffles, as if she were willing herself not to cry any further.

He clasped the center of the phone tight, desperately searching for assuaging and soothing words.

But found none.

He lacked all capacity to do anything but clutch the hard cold plastic tighter and tighter.

"I'm sorry…" Luisa finally said, still sniffling, "I just needed a minute," her voice evening out more with each word. "When I heard your voice… We're okay. I'm okay. The children are okay."

Jude exhaled.

It was his turn to drop the receiver from his head, closing his eyes, perhaps in prayer, leaning his head against the glass, crinkling his cowboy hat that he usually never let anything touch aside from his own hand.

Jude returned the receiver to his ear.

"Oh…" Luisa's voice trailed off again as she took another deep breath. "It's just…"

"I know," said Jude, for the first time feeling like he was not miles away, but intimately close with his arms around her, his chest in hers, their hearts beating together as one.

Perhaps she felt the same, as they both simply listened to the sound of the other's breath.

"You uh, you answered the phone," he finally said.

"Yeah," a laugh still littered with tears. "Helen has put me to work at the front desk. Earning our keep, I reckon."

"The front desk of the brothel?" he asked.

"Yeah," she said, sounding half amused, half amazed herself. "It's about the only duty I'm comfortable helping out with in the whole enterprise and…"

Luisa trailed off.

"…What?" Jude asked when he realized she was not going to finish.

"…It helps with the time…" she said, sounding reluctant. "Especially lately when I hadn't…"

She trailed off again.

"…When I hadn't called you?.." he asked, ashamed.

"I don't mean to…"

"…No, you're not…"

"I just can't sit around and not do anything. Not how I'm wired."

"Not how *we* are wired."

"Ain't that the truth," she said with a laugh almost ribboned in tears again. Truth.

Jude lightly snickered back, tying a bow on that box of vulnerability. Marriage.

"How are the boys?" he then asked.

"They are fine. They are fine," almost like she was convincing herself.

"Good. Good."

A sludging silence seeped in between the two until she spoke again. "Are you where you were before?" she asked carefully not to hint at any whereabouts. They had discussed all of that the last night. No exact location in case they were being wire-tapped. They devised a code. Point-C was Chicago. Point-D was Detroit. Point-Q was Quebec. Point-X was someplace in between points they had not discussed. Treasure Island, their final-destination, was Ireland named because Jude had been reading it to the boys before the insanity. Luisa had expressed concern they were too young to which Jude responded, "No boys are ever too young to hear about pirates."

"No, we are in Point-D."

Jude suddenly hated how official and detached the conversation was again.

"So that means…Did you have your meeting?" she asked.

"Yeah, yeah we did. It uh…"

He removed the receiver from his face again.

He feared Luisa would hear the sallowness in his breath.

He inhaled deeply, summoning the courage to continue. "It didn't go as we would have hoped," he finally said.

"But you and Billy are okay?"

"Billy and I are okay. We're uh…Gonna keep moving. We have that train in four days to Point Q," he said blankly and methodical, reverting to the mannequin state he had become accustomed to.

"I see."

"So when we get to Point Q, I'll reach out and that's when you and the boys will start moving."

"Okay," she said placidly.

"Okay."

A stocky silence fell between the two again. So much had happened since they last spoke, the day before the Pinkerton meeting. He could not give details in case *they* were listening, that ever present *they* who was always looming around the corner, but he could share how he was feeling, there was no harm in that even if *they* were spying.

Jude was born in a tough town with no figure to guide him through emotional maturation, but he learned how to be intimate with Luisa. She had demanded it when they first got together. She was unwavering and intrepid even in her insistence that love was not possible without intimacy and honesty. This even meant Jude revealing he had been scared entering a dark alley or heartbroken at the sight of a dead child when she asked him how work was after the children were put to bed or when he called from a payphone each night on the road. Being on the run now was different. He was the one now being chased. He was the bad guy, and until tonight, that had not prevented him from being able to confide in Luisa.

Tonight, however, he just stood there.

Receiver in hand.

Head down against the window.

Eyes straining in every direction guarding his periphery.

"Oh, I forgot. How is your friend? Is he still coming with us?" she asked, breaking the daunting silence.

"My friend?" Jude asked, his mind still not in the present.

"Yes, the one you met on the… the one you and Billy met."

"Oh...." he said, closing his eyes tight at the thought of Christian. "Um no. He's not... he ain't coming with us now..."

"I see," she said.

"He's uh...He..."

Suddenly the locked floodgates of emotion sprang a leak in the dam, knocking Jude's legs out from underneath him, like being washed away in the tide. He collapsed, crunching his body tight into the corner of the booth underneath the base of the phone, like a small child hiding, still holding the receiver in his hand. He buried his head in his arms pulling in deep shaky breaths. "We lost him at the meeting," he muttered.

"Oh Jude, I'm so sorry. I didn't...I didn't know it went that bad."

"Yeah...it did," his voice quivering

"I know you said it didn't go as you had hoped but I didn't know..."

"It got bad, Luisa, it real got bad."

The dam completely gone now, a flash food of misery.

Christian was dead.

Billy was broken.

Jude was lost and sacrificed his wife and children to...what exactly?

"Oh Jude," she said, hearing his sob. "I'm so sorry," her voice drenched in compassion but not crying herself, perhaps understanding she needed to be the strong one. A role she knew well. Jude was often the hammer to the nail of life, but Luisa was the hand that held that hammer, steered it. Directed it.

"It was so violent and bad." Jude's words buried in his sobbing, his head buried between his arms and legs, no longer watching his front and back side at the same time. No longer peering over his shoulder every other second at every other turn. His eyes were closed hard, even as tears squeezed out, running down his face.

"I'm here, Jude, I'm here," she said gently and brave. "I'm here."

"It's been bad. It's just so constantly fucking bad. And it ain't even over yet. Not yet. And I'm so tired and lost. So tired and lost, Luisa. I didn't think I could ever feel this weak. And I couldn't call because..."

He continued to wail.

She continued to let him, without saying a word, probably understanding the importance of allowing the fulmination and mourning to happen uninterrupted.

He finally calmed the stormy sea of anguish, gathering himself, sniffling and clearing his throat before speaking. "And I know, I shouldn't even…I know it's not easy for you and the children either and I'm so sorry to put y'all through this."

Now it was time for Luisa to speak. "Jude, me and the children are okay," she said, firm but kind. "Of course, we want to be with you, but we are okay. And YOU didn't put us through anything. We are a family and we are in this together. I made a choice to marry the most wonderful and loving man I ever met and have that man be the father of our children. As far as I'm concerned, that was the last choice I've ever made in that regard. There are no more choices. We are simply one. The four of us and Billy."

Jude began weeping again but not from sorrow.

Tears of appreciation and love and adoration streamed down his face now and relief expelled from his lungs. It poured out into the air around him and he found himself sliding upright in the booth.

He was now standing.

"Luisa, we're gonna be okay," he said with a lulling breath, wiping away the snot with his shirt sleeve. "We're gonna be okay."

"Yes, my love. We are going to be okay."

CHAPTER
FORTY-NINE

For those four days in Detroit, the boys did nothing. They didn't even buy their train tickets ahead of time for fear of being seen or tipping someone off. Instead, they hunkered down in the room churning out the hours, waiting. Billy cramped into one of the small uncomfortable wooden chairs with his feet up on the other, gazing out the window to the gray musky docks, usually cleaning a gun. Jude mostly laid on the bed, his boots hanging off the bottom end and his hat over his face.

"You okay?" Jude would ask every once-in-a-while, inquiring as to whether Billy needed guard relief.

"Yeah," Billy would say the same every time.

They would meander out of the hotel in the morning for grub, never hitting the same diner twice, and the same for dinner but nothing more.

They were essentially in purgatory.

"Fuck," Billy said one morning, his mouth so full he could barely choke out the words.

The boys were not raised in a barn, and although poor, they had manners. Elbows on the table or talking with your full would elicit a guaranteed smack everytime, even when Pop was drunk or Ma was babbling herself.

Not only was Billy now talking with his mouth full but he had both elbows on the table, one hand holding a fork, the other a steak knife, and in between, a steaming heap of Jude didn't what. There was some kind of breaded meat covered in a white chunky gravy that literally reminded him of dog vomit. He thought he saw some potatoes and onions somewhere in the piping mess. But whatever *it* was, Jude was glad Billy was chowing down on *it*. He couldn't recall the last time either of them really ate. Instead, usually just pushing the food around the plate until one of them said, "Ready?"

Neither boy was heavy, and the James clan weren't necessarily known for their voracious appetites, but Jude never had a problem choking down mere sustenance until these last few days so he was grateful Billy at least found a way.

"Hot damn," Billy said again.

"What?" Jude asked, only a tan mug of coffee in front of him in the booth.

"This chicken fried steak is really fucking good."

Jude looked at him curious, the mug over his lips. *Chicken - fried - steak?* Jude thought, trying to put all those words together then re-studying the plate.

"I never had it before," Billy continued. "Guys in my unit talked about it. We'd be in a foxhole at night fucking starving with nothing for days but hard biscuits that tasted like rocks and we'd start dreaming out loud about if we could eat anything..."

Billy plunged his fork into a mound of gravy, while the knife carved away a piece of chicken, the only part of the whole ordeal that somewhat looked like food to Jude. Jude then watched Billy mop that piece of chicken up in the gravy, as if it were a sopapilla sponging up chile.

"Of course, I'd go off about *Dona* Maria's *Carne Advovada* and her tamales at Christmas," Billy continued, grease and gravy running down his cheek. "With *posole* naturally."

"Naturally," said Jude.

"And all these guys, mostly from the South, would just howl about their Goddamn chicken fried steak. They would describe it in detail to me and it sounded like some back-woods hillbilly garbage but…"

Billy's words were interrupted by stuffing his face with another bite.

"…But…" said Jude nodding to the plate with biting eyes.

"But this is *chingon!*"

"Is that why you ordered it?" Jude asked. He regretted the question immediately, but it was too late.

Billy was already looking at him lost on the question, so he had to finish.

"Because the guys in your unit."

"Oh," Billy said, chewing slowly for the first time, gazing out the foggy diner window. "Yea. Maybe."

Jude saw his opportunity to lighten the mood again. "Or maybe you're a backwoods hillbilly and you just don't know it. You are a *guedo.*"

Billy nodded, as if considering the possibility, his cheeks bloated from another gorging forkful. "You know, I never heard the word *hillbilly* until I got to boot camp. And then when I did hear it, I thought it referred to some racist bigoted imbecile who married his sister. I'd hear the officers, mostly Yankees from up north, calling guys that. Guess that's where my original assumption came from. And then I started meeting these so-called hillbillies and I realized they were just hard-working God-fearing men who happened to be born at the bottom of the totem-pole is all." Billy's eyes moved up to Jude's. "Just like you and I really," he continued. "Only difference is we're *coyotes* and don't belong to either tribe. Not the poor white. Not the poor brown. I looked at them differently after that, and I didn't try to hang out with no more officers always looking down their noses from the top they only earned from being born."

Billy chewed for a moment as the gears grinded and then continued.

"I think I'm gonna add that word to the list."

"List?" Jude asked.

"The list of words I ain't gonna use anymore. That's their word for us and fuck them."

"Reckon, I'll add it to the list as well," Jude said and then sipped his coffee.

It was Jude's turn to look out the window.

He folded his arms around his chest, exhaled and then spoke. "Everyone, including you probably, just assumed I went to law school on account of Luisa' unwavering persistence…or scorn."

Billy nodded and grinned in agreement.

"Or maybe because we now had a child on the way, and I was responsible for more than just me and the bad guy I was chasing." Jude's eyes narrowed as he gazed out the window. "That's probably what I even told myself. But truth be told, it was just some bullshit I fabricated to move up that so-called totem pole. I guess I moved up but the higher I got, the less I liked myself, and sure as shit, the less I liked the people I found there. Reckon, perhaps I understand partly why you went off to war."

"Reckon, perhaps you do."

Billy didn't look up.

Maybe he was afraid what he would see.

Maybe he knew his brother needed a minute, but he wouldn't be impolite enough to excuse himself, so he buried his attention in the chicken fried steak.

He waited until Jude's eyes were back in front of him before speaking again. "You want a bite? I'm telling you, *carnal*."

Jude surveyed the unidentifiable mass smothered in the sultry white substance that smelled both salty and rank, almost making his eyes water and his nose run. "No, thank you."

"Suit yourself."

"But I'm glad you're enjoying it."

For a moment, he was mocking Billy. Since the boys were old enough to speak, almost every word to the other was some form of jovial shit-talking. There were no boundaries or subjects deemed inappropriate. Occasionally, a jest went too far evoking some form of physical response from the other. Often the party affected by the shit-talking would then receive further *mierda* for being exposed and *butt-hurt* about it, often eliciting more violence until there was blood or their father had enough.

But now, as Jude watched his brother stuff his face in total gluttonous glee, he was immensely grateful that Billy was in fact *enjoying it*. He was grateful to witness his brother experience joy even if it came from a foul torrid pile of what looked like a physical manifestation of illness. Perhaps the vile and corrupt, soul consuming world had not defeated them yet.

"You think they got chicken fried steak in Ireland?" Billy asked, not looking up from his plate as the shoveling continued.

Jude smiled, nodded, and took another hit from his coffee. "I don't know but for your sake, I sure hope so."

The boys walked out of the diner, Billy with a full-belly of lard and excess, Jude's head half-filled with a strange sentiment, *hope*. Everyday so far seemed gray and dreary in Michigan, the bleary clouds hanging so low, it was hard to see where they ended and the ashen lake began. And it never felt cold exactly, but there was a wet chill that constantly nipped. Jude thought about how beautiful April could be in Northern New Mexico, the snow melting to reveal the thick mud that then dried allowing the first hint of spring to unearth with a sprinkling of flowers. He never realized how weather could have such an effect on him. Perhaps one didn't recognize or appreciate a pleasant climate until they were constantly berated with a bad one.

Perhaps that's how one comes to appreciate anything.

Don't know how good you got it until the good goes south, Jude thought. *Or north in this case...*

Usually the boys would head directly back to the hotel after eating, their core mission of sustenance complete. But today, maybe with a flicker of hope still in Jude's heart, the thought of imprisoning himself in that stuffy box seemed merciless and unnecessary. He stuffed his hands in his pockets and peered down the pier, mostly lined with docks and fisheries and longshoremen.

A few vendors had hot dog and sausage stands set up and carts with cigarettes, newspapers, and candy bars.

Billy had already started the other direction toward the hotel when Jude asked, "Hey, you want to take a walk down the docks for a minute?"

Billy turned back looking confused. "Take a walk?"

"Yea."

Billy's eyes shifted, surveying his surroundings. "What's going on?"

"Nothing is going on," Jude said, "I just feel like some fresh air."

Billy looked up the smokestacks and the silty soot puffing out, smelting as one with the hazy clouds. "Fresh air?"

"Yeah, move the legs. Do us some good."

"All right," Billy said, still suspicious and confused.

Jude wrapped his arm around Billy's back, slapping him on the shoulder yanking him in close as they began their stroll. Jude used to do the same to Billy as a kid on the playground, always prompting embarrassment from Billy, even at an age when bravados affection from a big brother usually incited pride and haughtiness from the younger.

While teenagers, Jude did it sardonically because of the effect it had on Billy.

Now, Billy wasn't sure why the fuck he was doing it.

Maybe the son of a bitch was just happy for a minute and who was Billy to ruin that?

Jude finally released his grasp and the two meandered.

There were boats, large and small, and foul brutal reeks of fish hit them in the face as they passed certain boats.

They heard small waves crash against the stalwart bows and the creaky wooden docks stir and budge with the lake tide.

Trucks' engines roared, ignited, and stalled.

Something heavy dropped and clamored somewhere.

Men worked diligently hauling nets and cargo across the docks with ropes, and nets and pulleys. Their faces flush with manual labor. For a moment, Jude was worried that one of these men would somehow recognize them until he noticed how their eyes never left their work, their attention strictly on using every ounce of energy to work as quickly and efficiently as possible. A circus elephant could walk down the docks without the men noticing, Jude realized.

Jude then observed these men wore the same leather gloves, thermals, flannels and Carhartt jackets as the ranchers and farmers in New Mexico.

The universal working man's uniform.

"Did you ever think this is what Detroit, Michigan would look like?" Billy asked, observing all the same.

"The question of what Detroit, Michigan looked like never crossed my mind," Jude said, his entire head following a forklift whizzing by with longshoremen hanging off each side.

"Sure is busy."

"Sure is."

"I hope Ireland is quieter."

"I hope so too."

"Strange thing is, I'm kind of looking forward to it," Billy said, squinting, maybe scrutinizing the curious arena more closely.

"To what? Ireland?"

"Yeah, I guess. Or maybe I just want to be done with all of this and can start to see the light at the end of the tunnel. I don't know."

"Reckon, I know how you feel," Jude said, almost to himself.

Neither brother looked at the other, instead both musing over the landscape of the docks or something else.

Two men's voices were yelling in the distance in what sounded like Polish or Greek.

"Feels…good don't it? That light?" Jude said after some silence between the two.

Billy nodded, his eyes still small. "Yea, but *cuidado*. That light will getcha killed. Too busy looking at it, getting all excited and that's when you let your guard down and get dead. I lost more men that way than…"

Jude chewed the side of his mouth for a long minute and then spoke. "A little hope don't hurt though either. Remind you it ain't all darkness."

Both men remained silent, staring off.

The beeping of a truck reversing echoed somewhere in the distance.

Jude finally turned noting a vendor stand. "I'm gonna grab a newspaper for the room. You want anything?"

"Nah. Thanks," Billy said, his eyes still somewhere else or. He didn't know how long he had zoned out until Jude was next to him with a newspaper in hand.

"You ready to go back?" Jude asked.

Billy nodded and started walking.

Jude took one step, looked down at the paper and froze. "Fuck me," he whispered.

Billy turned around. "What?"

Jude stood both panicked and spooked stiff, almost too rattled to breathe. Similar to a soldier realizing he'd stepped on a landmine, as Billy recalled. Jude's eyes too fearful to even depart the newsprint, like that soldier staring at his own boot that suddenly bared the weight of his destiny.

Billy slowly retreated to Jude, craning his head to see the paper Jude held.

Chicago Authorities Say Local Teamster Union Responsible For Pinkerton Agency Massacre.

"Ain't that something," Billy said, still staring down at it.

"It's more than something," said Jude. "It's Dahl."

"How do you mean?"

"There is no way the cops could be that wrong unless…"

"…Someone purposely fed them the wrong information."

"And who would do that?"

"Dahl."

"That's right."

"Reckon he lived."

"Reckon so."

"But why would he tell the police it was the Union and not us?" Billy asked.

"Because he wants us for himself."

"Well I guess I'd rather have that brown-eye looking for us than the police."

"Dahl knows something," Jude said, his face still pale and spooked. The landmine now rearing his ugly little explosive head.

"Bullshit."

"If he didn't, he wouldn't be trying to throw the police off our trail, he'd be using the police to sniff us out."

"*Carnal*," Billy pleaded, like trying to wake his brother from a bad dream. "Dahl is a wiry fucker, he is, but you're being paranoid."

"Remember what you said just now about that light?" Jude asked, stuffing the newspaper under his arm. "We ain't there yet. Not even close."

CHAPTER
FIFTY

The boys didn't take any more strolls down the promenade after reading the headlines and for the first time since the trial, Billy started smoking cigarettes again. Jude started to doubt whether he should have voiced his alarm to Billy. Those thirty or so minutes in the diner and the ramble after, was the only time Billy almost seemed like his old pre-war self and now Jude had robbed him of that. Maybe Jude should have let Billy revel in that warm glowing light while Jude encumbered that burden of anxiety, watching Billy's *six*, after all, ain't that what big brothers for? Since their mother went mad and their father drowned in the bottle, Jude was shouldering that load. Why didn't he just shut up and do it here?

Laying in the dark oblivion of their hotel room at night, these thoughts rolled around in his Jude's head like a boulder rumbling down a hill, getting bigger with a greater head of steam.

And while most children were afraid of the dark, even from a very young age, Billy seemed to find sanctum in it. When their mother fell into one of her fits, shrieking babble at the top of her lungs, Jude would find

Billy hiding in the dark closet. When their father was in a booze infused tear, knocking over tables, punching out windows, lamenting over the destruction of his family by physically destroying their home, Jude would find Billy under the bed hiding in the darkness.

Earlier in the night, Billy had taken the scratchy elastic comforter off the bed and hung it up over the hotel windows, at twenty-seven years old, once again creating his sanctuary. "That Goddamn streetlight been keeping me up every night," he muttered.

Jude didn't say a word. Why would he?

Now with the shoddy hotel blanket shielding Billy from the monsters outside, and all light, there was only sheer blackness and Jude's thoughts swirled around in his head as he laid on his back, not even able to stare up at the ceiling, his preferred procedure when thinking hard. He closed his eyes and then opened them, only to see the same. Had he not heard Billy breathing in the bed next to him, Jude was almost sure he was dead laying in a dark coffin in the ground somewhere.

Jude continued to lay buried in a claustrophobic anxiety until Billy shattered the casket with his voice.

"Jude, you awake?"

"Yea. You?" Jude asked before realizing the absurdity of his question.

There was a long silence and then Billy spoke again.

"You really think Dahl is on to us?"

It was as if the Good Lord was answering Jude's prayer, providing him penance for the sin he was just suffering over, giving Jude a second chance to perhaps provide Billy with ignorant bliss. Direct Billy back to that glimmer of hope, that shining light at the end of the tunnel.

"Unfortunately, I do," Jude found himself saying.

He realized there was another sin he could not force himself to commit, lying to his brother. Jude had shouldered the burden of being a parent while still being a child himself. Buffered their father's drunken attacks and their mother's insane acts but he never lied to Billy in doing so. Never sugar-coated any dire fact or blew smoke up Billy's ass in some fruitless attempt to protect him. Maybe that's why Billy came to Jude that night after sticking old man Simon. Jude always trusted Billy with the truth, so in turn, Billy trusted Jude just the same. Not doing so now would be a graver sin than maybe even murder. It would be a violation of the sacred trust between brothers.

"Maybe I'm just being paranoid but…" Jude continued.

"…No. If you say he's after us then he's after us," Billy interjected. "You've only been right about the son of a bitch so far."

The two boys spiraled in the long dark silence and then Billy spoke again. "It's like you two are opposite sides of the same coin."

"Who me and Dahl?"

"Yeah."

"What makes you say that?"

"I don't know. Just the way you two carry yourself. The way he talks, I can tell is the same way you think."

"You calling me queer?" Jude asked.

Both men laughed, splintering the somber oblivion burying over them.

"Shit, you're both lawyers," Billy said, after the laughter subsided.

"What do you mean?" Jude asked.

"You're both attorneys."

"What in God's name are you talking about?"

"You didn't know that?" Billy asked sincerely, but also enjoying the rubbing. "Yea, Stanley dug that up on him during the trial. I thought he told you."

"You're fucking me with."

Even in the dark, Billy could see Jude mind's exploding. "I promise you, I'm not. Went to Cambridge or some shit," said Billy. "That day in Pinkerton's office when you were pontificating, I should have realized then, you didn't know. At that point, I didn't want to make you look stupid, though. You were doing a fine enough job of that on your own."

Both men laughed again until silence wedged its way back in, and Billy could almost hear Jude trying to piece his mind back together, like Humpty Dumpty.

"Well, I'll be damned," Jude eventually said, as if realizing the pieces no longer fit.

Silence again until Billy spoke this time, more pained and less jovial. "That's why I say, if you think he's still coming for us then he's still coming for us."

Billy heard Jude take a long deep breath and then exude hoarsely and anxious. That said it all for Billy.

Another speed bump of silence until Billy spoke. "You remember when we used to play *Scramble and Hide* with Pop when we were kids?

"You mean *Samble and Hi* as you called it?" Jude asked fondly.

Billy chuckled. "Yea, for some reason I just couldn't say·those two words together."

"And after a while, that's what it became, *Samble and Hi*. Even Pop called it that."

"Probably just sounded like that's what he was saying in his *borracho* slur," said Billy.

"Nah, that was before he was drinking," Jude corrected. "He'd do the dishes after dinner and then take us out to the barn. Give Ma some reprieve from our antics."

"I remember we'd come back in after, out-breath and wore out and she'd be knitting, rocking calmly back and forth in her rocking chair, always greeting us with that same smile as we tottered through the door."

"That was the most at peace I ever saw her."

"Yeah," said Billy trailing off.

Ponderous quiet spread between the two and then Billy spoke again.

"Pop would hold that lantern in his hand and have that big silly smile on his face."

"He'd look like Mickey Mouse with his eyes all wide and hilarious before yelling *Samble and Hi!* blowing out the light," said Jude.

In the sheer darkness, both men's recollecting words seemed to be smiling.

"The lights would go out, and we'd hit the deck scrambling around on all fours," Billy said "Why the fuck did we feel the need to duck down? It was already pitch dark?"

"Because we were kids," said Jude.

"Reckon so. We'd be crawling around on all fours, knocking shit over, bumping our heads into each other and random blunt objects in the barn."

"But we'd always manage to find a place to hide before the old man turned the light back on," said Jude.

"Yeah," said Billy. "You think the old man did it on purpose?"

"What?"

"Not hit the light until he knew we found our hiding spot."

"Yeah, probably," said Jude. "He was good like that, in the early years."

"I guess I tend to not remember all that. The good shit."

"It's what we tend to forget for some reason," said Jude.

"Yeah, I reckon so…"

Another hush fell over the two until Billy spoke.

"In a sense, been kind of thinking of *Samble and Hi* a lot lately though. Really even since I was in the war."

"How's that?" Jude asked, both curious and cheery, his mind still enjoying the pleasurable ride down memory lane.

"When there were air raids" Billy said, his voice already turning down the street of a very different conversation. "Either us or them, the sky would light up and people would freeze and then there would just be this explosion…"

Jude could hear Billy's breath get clammy and distressed.

"And all of a sudden, what was just next to you wasn't there anymore. Like suddenly you're on this distant planet with nothing but mayhem and destruction. Almost like waking up *in* a bad dream."

Jude held deathly still, straining to hear every morose-filled word from his brother's lips, every avowal his heart allowed to pour out. As if, if Jude heard it, it would alleviate Billy's pain, like a priest in confession.

"So…" Billy continued. "I trained myself, when I saw that light it was like *Samble and Hi*. I'd drop to all fours, scamper, get small and hide. Just hide…"

Perhaps the opacity between the two boys also served like a confessional box, hiding Billy's countenance which in turn allowed him to speak freely. Jude was immediately grateful his brother was sharing but he wished he could see his face, look him in the eye just to say, *I hear ya. I'm here*, without having to say it. Saying it somehow seemed naïve and less honest, so Jude simply sat quietly in the black hole of the hotel room and let his brother continue.

"And then I would be lying in bed with Marion, asleep, someplace quiet, someplace peaceful and I'd swear someone hit that light. My eyes would go white, and I'd drop off the bed, hit the floor, run and hide. This would go on for at least a minute until poor Marion would wake up. She'd find me under the bed or in the corner curled up. She literally called them my *Samble and Hi Fits*."

"You told her about our game huh?" Jude asked but didn't really ask. More just pleasantly surprised.

"Yeah, I did. She thought we were playing some form of Cowboys and Indians, maybe because we were from New Mexico, or she thought all American boys ran around playing it. But that wasn't what we were playing."

"No, it wasn't," Jude said warmly.

"Anyway, she'd talk me out of my fit, calm me down. And eventually they started happening less and less…. Even when she wasn't there anymore… They'd still happen though once-in-a-while. And now the funny thing, ever since that night of the Simon's party, they haven't happened. First time since the war, they don't happen."

"Why do you think that is?" Jude found himself asking.

"I know why," Billy said, almost defiantly, but not towards Jude. More mutinous toward the source or reason. "Because ever since that night, I've actually been scrambling and hiding. Running and ducking. Cowering and retreating. That's all our life has been, that's all my nerves know when I'm awake. *Samble and Hi*."

Jude was never short on a retort. Never voiceless or mute in consoling and comforting others, whether it be a victim of a crime or a dear friend, but his lips and heart were vacant with any assuaging lyrics or comments.

"*Carnal*, Billy continued. "We get on this train, then we get on this boat. We sail off to a far-away place and then I'm done with the *Samble and Hi*. I can't take it anymore. I'll wake up every night in a cold sweat in one of them wretched fits but I ain't gonna have no more *Samble and Hi*."

Jude wanted to tell Billy it was going to be alright.

Assuage Billy New Mexico to Ireland was a long fucking distance.

Far enough away that no ghosts from the past or bad guys from the present would find them.

Jude wanted to tell himself that too, but Jude was never good at lying, to himself or others.

Jude then came to wish, laying in that bed, feeling Billy's nerves like waves of electricity fizzling in the black air, that he had killed Dahl in that alley.

Jude had won.

He had him dead to rights and could have finished it all.

True, there were still the various police agencies, and the Pinkertons searching for them, but they didn't daunt or unnerve Jude and Billy the way Dahl did.

For some reason, Dahl held a menacing dedication to destroying Jude and Billy. One that would transcend any ocean or continent. Perhaps, Billy was right. Perhaps, Jude and Dahl were two sides of the same coin, but Jude still could not get a read on Dahl. Not a beat. He could forecast Dahl's tactics because they shared a predatory acumen of hunting down men. In a sense, Jude was able to chase Dahl chasing him. Two pursuers constantly closing in on the other.

And yet, Jude had no understanding whatsoever of what drove Dahl. Jude was good at chasing down bad guys. Half the reason was his ability to get in their head. To understand them. Jude was also good at getting them to confess afterwards, or in the rare occasion, sniff out a poor sap who was actually innocent by also getting a read on them. Seeing a glimmer of truth in their eyes, a quivering tell in their voice, or a twitch in the body. Sometimes there was no clue at all, only Jude's gut bestowing the truth. Call it intuition, extra-sensory perception or even *brujeria* that he inherited from his mother. But he had nothing on Dahl. No rhyme or reason why the bastard was dead-set on being the one to end Billy and Jude.

There was, of course, the reward money, the bounty Darcy Simon had issued but Dahl didn't seem motivated by money despite his polished and refined fashion sense. Jude was utterly lost as to what he and Billy had done to deeply offend this man, that he would stalk them to the far-ends of the earth. Sure, the two boys casted some rude and disparaging insults at the assassin, and sure the two silver-tongued devils were known to provoke even a halcyon monk with their shit-talking ability, but Dahl didn't seem like the type to be bothered by mere words.

What was it then?

Jude did not fear the depraved and deliberate motive of Dahl or even his fabled and notorious quick draw. Jude feared Dahl's motive because he did not know Dahl's motive. Perhaps that was the root of Billy's anxiety. Jude could see his little brother was traumatized from the war, but the panic and trepidation towards Dahl was something more. Perhaps the *bru-*

jeria blood the brothers shared, running through veins, inherited from their lunatic mother, presaged warnings about Dahl and their existence.

If only that brujeria blood in Jude told him to stomp the lights out of the fuck that day in the alley.

After they walked away, and Jude's hot temper cooled, he was grateful Billy had talked him down from sending Dahl to his maker. At the time, Billy had been right. If Jude killed Dahl in essentially cold blood, his Catholic guilt-ridden soul would be haunted for the rest of Jude's natural life and probably the next. But now, realizing this man was never going to stop until they or he witnessed the other's last breath, Jude regretted not ending Dahl's life, even if it meant strangling it out of him with his bare hands.

If he did, Jude would be forced to live with the fact that he killed a defenseless and wounded enemy but at least he would be *living* with that fact. He would have not only eliminated the existential threat of Dahl, he would have eliminated the maddening fear that Dahl evoked, causing so much misery and anguish to Jude's little brother.

Perhaps, in Jude saving his soul and conscience from an unpardonable act, he had also been unforgivably selfish. He was put on this planet to protect his little brother at all costs, and so far, he'd failed him. As Jude lay in that impenetrable and cabalistic dark silence, he vowed he would not make that mistake again.

CHAPTER
FIFTY-ONE

Jude was Goddamned grateful. As grateful as he could remember feeling in a long fucking time.

More than when he strolled out of the bank with that big bag of money under his arms and no blood on his hands.

Or when he and Billy stumbled out of the hazy gunpowder ridden alley in Chicago right past the boys in blue rushing by, not noticing Billy's limp or Jude's bleeding shoulder.

No, Jude was most grateful to get out of that Goddamn hotel room that was choking the air out of his spirit and grating what little of Billy's sanity remained.

In those last two days, the walls seemed to close in more and more every time Jude blinked. As if, in the one second he took his eyes off them, they inched closer to swallowing him and Billy whole.

Jude realized four days on a train, holed up in a bunk room not much bigger than an automobile, and smaller than a jail cell, was more physically confining. Even the thought should have induced more anxiety and stress about being boxed in somewhere, but it didn't.

In the hotel room, Jude felt like a sitting duck. A hog tied to the butcher block waiting for the hammer. It was Jude's plan that required the two boys to grind out those six grievous days in Detroit waiting for the train. Perhaps, Jude miscalculated the toll that kind of idle time, or worse, idle movement would take on the two boys, but the way he saw, a four-day train from Detroit, Michigan to Quebec City, Canada was the most infallible route to throw off any remaining scent in the wind. Plus, they would be moving. There was some comfort in that. Even if they were confined, they were moving.

The train also allowed Billy and Jude the least direct contact with possible witnesses or good Samaritans. Jude tracked down at least a dozen bad guys from the simple eyeball of a gas station attendant or diner waitress. Each person a man on the run comes in contact with, no matter how brief or immaterial the interaction, is another possible eyewitness, another hand leading to the guillotine. The outside world was made up of every-day bored citizens who wanted to be heroes and have something to discuss at dinner or the church steps come Sunday. And death row was filled with prisoners, who's only mistake in getting caught was stopping for gas or smokes. Jude understood there would surely be others on the train, but doing the math, the train allowed them to travel a greater distance with less human contact than any automobile. Plus, who knew a train even existed that ran from Detroit to Quebec City?

Jude glanced over at Billy as they waited their turn to board the train. He did not seem to share Jude's peace with the idea. Jude had seen that look on other men's faces but never Billy's. It was the same look when a novice rider's legs first perch on a bucking bull, or a young boy comes across a rattler in the field.

Dread and trepidation.

A thick vagrant fog loitered low, the long train disappearing in the mist on both ends.

Billy's eyes narrowed and he took a long hit on his cigarette.

Jude watched Billy inspect the train from one direction and the other and then back again.

"You okay?" Jude finally asked.

Billy nodded, taking another long drag. "Just don't like trains is all," he said, the smoke billowing out with his words.

"Since when? You loved them as a kid."

"Since the Goddamn Nazis decided to fill them with poor unwitting Jews. No food or water or shelter from the cold. We'd find carts stuffed with starved skeletons frozen together." Billy leered up at the train. "Even women and children."

It was Jude who's head twisted in agony. He'd never seen those images but just thought of them seemed to choke the air out of his throat. "Jesus, Billy, is there any act 'man' - 'kind' ain't capable of?"

"You asking me?" Billy said, the long cigarette hanging from his lips, looking his brother dead-on.

"No… I reckon I aint…" Jude paused, his face flush, and chest tight. "I'm sorry." The words, the sweat festering on his face, his thumping heart, these were all the things that happened to Jude right before he was gonna let a woman know she was now a widow, or a boy an orphan. These were the reactions within Jude when he contemplated the dead, but his brother was alive standing right in front of him. What did that make Billy then? The undead? Jude shook off the thought. "I didn't know…"

"How would you?" Billy asked, sneering up at the train as if Hitler himself stood in front of them.

"It's not too late. We can take a car or…"

"You say this train gives us the best chance to get to the boat?" Billy asked, turning back to Jude.

Jude's sallow eyes met Billy's before nodding slow and regretfully.

"Then it's settled," Billy said, taking one last hit on his butt before flicking it. "Looks like we're up."

It was now Jude held frozen watching Billy pick up his bag and step up to the train stairs.

Then it was as if Billy could feel Jude's eyes, his head craned back, looking over his shoulder, catching Jude's stare. Jude exhaled, cleared his throat, and stepped forward joining his brother.

Billy's out-of-nowhere disclosure about his experience with trains jolted Jude. The content of his revelation evoked horrid images in Jude's head but that's not what startled him most. Jude had never lied to his brother, and as far as Jude knew, Billy had never lied either. There were certainly

Irish embellishments sprinkled into a good story or the occasional white lie about how many beers one consumed before falling off the horse, but there was never dishonesty. That's not to say, however, Billy was always forthcoming with what bothered him.

No, Billy usually liked to stew in his grievances. To hold his cards of conflict or discord close to his chest, even when the strife was only with himself. *Especially* if it was something Billy was battling within himself. As if Billy was ashamed to let anyone know his thoughts of apprehension or anxiety. Jude used to think it was an act of machismo, Billy not revealing any vulnerability or weakness.

Then Jude realized it was something more.

Perhaps it was a result of Jude always wearing his emotions on his sleeve… or his knuckles and boots. Billy rarely expounded how others should live their life, but he would give Jude *mierda* for his peppery temper, often fanning the flames.

When their mother's endless stumble into insanity commenced, their father tumbled joining her, in sheer weakness and grief. At first, Jude felt there was a romantic honor in their father's deep-seeded lament and pain over their mother. But the boys soon came to realize they still needed a father, a strong father, to go to work, put food on the table, put the boys to bed at night and nurse their ailing mother through her terrifying illness that filled her head with monsters. Sadly, their father held no such strength.

Perhaps this is why Billy never showed weakness, Jude thought. It was only through Luisa's unflinching love and condition of intimacy that Jude came to understand there is also strength in being vulnerable. Jude had never seen such understanding in Billy until his almost-unprompted revelation about the train. Perhaps, Billy found a similar understanding in the arms of Marion, or worse, perhaps the train was so ghastly hair-raising to Billy, that he was unable to shroud his malaise.

Five minutes after the train started churning along, Billy placed his bag in their bunk cart and disappeared out the sliding door, leaving Jude alone with his thoughts in their cramped little cage. Jude wanted to tell Billy the prudent act would be to lay low and hole up in their room as much as possible the next four days. He wanted to tell Billy the whole point of the train was not to be seen by people, and Billy roaming it now was in direct contradiction to that strategy. But Jude understood Billy's restlessness, because he felt it too. And since the day Billy was born, he was restless. Never able to sit still at the dinner table when they still had dinner. Helpless to fidgeting in church even when it resulted in lashes from the unsympathetic priests and nuns. Even when Jude would bring him to the pictures, he would fiddle and fuss and often leave before the show was over. It was for all these reasons Jude said nothing when Billy meandered out of their quaint quarters, not even communicating where he was going and why.

The door suddenly slid open, and Jude peeked his head out from the bottom bunk he had cornered into. Billy was standing in the doorway, peering off to his left down the hallway. His eyes slimmed, and he palmed his cheeks down to his jawbone.

Jude waited for Billy to enter but he continued to stare off just the same until Jude spoke. "Everything okay?"

Billy continued his vast gaze with no words.

Jude felt almost impotent not being able to see what Billy was looking at and Billy not clueing him in.

"Billy," Jude said again, more affirmative. "*Todo bien?*"

"What?" Billy asked, turning to Jude momentarily. "Yeah, um, I don't know."

Jude reached under his pillow for his pistol and then cocked it.

"No, it's okay," Billy said at the sight of Jude puckered. "It's probably nothing." He stared down the corridor for a long moment, then stepped in, closing the door behind him.

The two men awkwardly stood in the negligible space.

"What was it?" Jude asked.

Billy chewed on his fingernails and said, "Just a guy."

"Just a guy? Did you recognize him from somewhere?"

"No, it wasn't like that."

"Then how was it?" Jude asked, holding back his frustration with the few crumbs of information Billy was divulging.

Billy turned his gaze back to the door, now closed, staring at it in similar fashion, as if the bothersome issue was still in front of him. "I don't know, he was just looking at me kind of funny."

"This *guy*?"

"Yeah."

"Like he was trying to make you or something?"

"No, more the opposite. Like he was trying *not* to make me."

"I don't understand."

"Like he was trying to avoid looking at me. Like I was there but he was trying not to see me."

Jude sat back on the bed, uncocking the gun, returning it behind the pillow.

"Just seemed odd," Billy continued.

"It seemed odd that some fella wouldn't look at you?" Jude asked, trying to hide his cynicism.

"Yeah," Billy said, seemingly unaware how ludicrous his frame of mind appeared to Jude.

Jude held his eyes on his brother who continued to hold his eyes at the door, like a perched dog.

A prayer began to plead in Jude's heart.

Not to God.

Maybe a plea to his dead parents if they could hear him and cared, that his brother, their son, could make it through the next four days. That whatever demons were parading around in his head, that Billy had the strength to keep them at bay until they could get on that Goddamn ship.

CHAPTER FIFTY-TWO

Jude watched the beer bubbles fizzle to the top through sparkling salt that fell like falling snow until they settled at the bottom of the pint glass. He didn't always pour salt in his beer but when he intended to sip and savor instead of *drink*, he did. He took the first hit, feeling the foam tickle his mustache and the salty lager treacle his tongue. He remembered seeing his father speckle his beer with salt when Jude was a child, but he didn't think he learned the habit from him. In fact, most of Jude's adult life centered around him making the exact opposite choices or habits of his father. On the rare occasions he tore into a drunk and salting his beer, perhaps the few exceptions.

Jude had instructed Billy to lay low but after only five hours in their cramped quarters, Jude felt his brain was going to cave in if he stayed in there a minute longer. He was relieved to at least hear Billy snoring below him, finding some rest and hopefully some peace, so he decided to medicate and celebrate with a beer in the lounge cart.

If the Good Lord is sadistic enough to have me snagged or whacked while enjoying a beer, then so be it, Jude thought. Maybe the run-away felon Jude caught literally with his pants down in an alley behind a hooker, or the junkie bandit who nodded off with a needle in his arm on a park bench, had the same thought. One time, Jude nabbed a guy who couldn't resist the urge to come home just to have his mother's *posole.* He remembered the greasy red chile shining around the guy's mug as he lay on his traitorous belly while Jude strapped the bracelets on him. That was Jude's secret to tracking down so many bad guys. He would find their weakness and then wait. *Holy fuck* Jude then thought. That's exactly what Dahl did to Billy. The day in the courtroom when Billy savaged the son of a bitch who disrespected the uniform. Maybe Billy was right. Maybe Jude and Dahl were comparable after all.

Billy slid into the booth across from Jude, interrupting Jude's self-assessment. Billy's face looked puffy from grogginess, and he still had sleep in his eyes. Billy rubbed them with the bottom of his hands and yawned like a house cat aroused from a nap. He squinted out the window of the train car, the April sun finally shining somewhere north, as a seemingly endless palisade of evergreen trees whizzed by, all one large green mass blurred together like a melted green crayon.

Jude watched Billy, relieved at the semblance of serenity and humanism in his brother.

Billy yawned again, his eyes widened and adjusted and then he noticed the beer in front of Jude.

"You want one?" Jude asked, detecting Billy's attention on the frothy pint half gone. "Never had a Canadian beer before. It's pretty good."

"What happened to laying low?"

"What happened to living?"

"You always were a hypocrite," Billy said, taking note of the big, beautiful world outside the window. "Probably the Catholic in you. Or the cop."

"Fuck you."

"Fuck you," Billy said, looking at his brother.

Both men smiled and looked away.

"How long was I out?" Billy asked.

Jude looked at his watch. "Probably two hours. Must have needed it."

"Must have."

"I always envied that about you," said Jude.

"What's that?"

"How you could always shut it down when you were tired, didn't matter what was going on."

"I heard that in the war too."

"Pop would be throwing shit. Ma would be babbling, and you'd be sound asleep, snoring even."

"Yeah, guys told me they would hear me snoring in the fox hole when I wasn't on watch."

"And I've never been able to sleep. What's the secret?" Jude asked warmly.

"I don't know," said Billy, gazing out the window. "I think it's always just been a necessity. It's like my motor is always running in high gear so when I get tired I need to sleep, or my brain gets all wobbly. It's always been that way for as long as I can remember."

"Was your brain feeling *wobbly* earlier?" Jude asked, trying not to pry.

Billy nodded. "Didn't get much sleep those last few days in that God-damn hotel room."

"Me neither.".

"I know where you're going with this," Billy said, his tone suddenly shifty and his eyes almost leering.

"What do you mean?"

"You know what I mean. And to answer your question, I don't know. I swear that guy was looking at me."

"You said he wasn't looking at you."

"I meant he was looking at me, pretending to not look at me. It was just for a brief second, but it was so… on point that it was suspicious."

"Okay," Jude said.

"I don't know," said Billy, squinting out the window again. "I just don't know."

The train rocked on the track, shifting north or east.

A stifling stillness descended upon the two brothers until a slender bird-like waiter approached. "Something to drink, sir?" he asked Billy.

Billy squinted up at the waiter and then moved his eyes to Jude.

Jude made eye contact with Billy and took a big gulp of his beer almost enticingly.

"What he's drinking," Billy said, nodding to Jude's glass.

"Very good, sir," said the waiter before sliding away.

"There, you happy?" Billy asked.

Jude faultlessly turned his head, as if he had no idea what his brother was talking about.

"Beer is different over there…in Europe," Billy said. "And they have a lot more wine."

Jude nodded slightly, some gear turning in his head and then he asked, "Is it good? The beer?"

"*Aye, más y menos.*"

Jude displayed his *thinking* nod again and then asked, "*Tiene whiskey?*"

"*Tiene whiskey.* It's good."

"*Bueno,*" Jude said, before taking another sip.

The waiter re-appeared with him a bottle of beer and a frosty glass that he placed in front of Billy.

"Much obliged," Billy said.

The waiter turned to Jude and his half full beer.

"I'll let him catch up first," said Jude.

The waiter nodded and departed.

Billy took a hit of his beer straight from the bottle, winced slightly and then examined the label. "This is what you call *good?*"

"It's what I call here and now."

"Fair enough."

Billy took another swig and then nodded slightly, the beer more persuasive with each hit. He settled into the booth, his shoulders slinking as if some weight had just fallen from them dazing out the window. The sun outside penetrated the glass warming Billy's face gently and even, closing his eyes, then, basking in the warmth. He didn't know how long they were closed but when he opened them, he saw a man behind Jude's shoulder, two booths in front of Billy on the adjacent side of the cart, studying him, pretending to read a newspaper.

Billy's eyes widened as the delicious sunbeams departed.

Careful to give nothing away, Billy shifted his attention to his brother, as if to say, *Are you seeing this?*

But Jude seemed oblivious, sipping his beer, staring out the window, clueless to the danger lurking over his shoulder all along.

"Jude," Billy murmured.

Jude's eyes drifted to Billy, looking confused by the sudden shift in his brother's demeanor.

"Stand up casually, turn around and get the waiter's attention for another beer," Billy continued, his voice hushed and hasty.

"You want another beer?" Jude asked. "You ain't drank the one in front of you."

"It ain't about the beer. It's about the fella over your shoulder. That's the fucking *guy.*"

Jude frowned.

Perhaps from the sudden awkwardness in Billy's behavior, perhaps from something more.

He uncomfortably stood up in the booth and twisted around.

He signaled another round to the waiter, while momentarily reading the poor hapless reading the Detroit Sports Section.

Jude sat back down and looked at Billy.

"Well?" Billy asked.

"Well what?" asked Jude.

"What do you think? About the guy behind you?"

"Billy, what do you want me to say? I think he's just some guy enjoying the company of the sports page and his beer."

Billy leaned forward over the table between them, ensuring he had Jude's full attention. The uneasiness now sparking from Billy's eyes. "Was he sitting there before you sat down?"

Jude exhaled exasperated, understanding here they were again, in the dark alley of Billy's paranoia and possible insanity."I don't know, Billy," he said, not able to hide the vex in his voice.

"Think!" Billy hissed, startling Jude.

Jude put attention, if for nothing else, in hope of quelling Billy's alarm. He looked off in his own recollection, blinking every so often as the motion picture of his own memory flashed by his eyes and then he finally spoke. "I think he was there before I sat down."

"You *think* or you *know?*"

"Goddamn it, Billy," Jude sizzled back. "I don't know. I'm pretty sure that son of a bitch was already sitting there minding his own Goddamn business before I showed up. Now I ain't got eyes in the back of my head, but I don't think he passed by me while I was sitting."

"I mean, what are the odds?" Billy asked. "The whole fucking train, and he's sitting right there?"

"Are you actually asking my opinion, because if so, I'd say the odds are probably pretty fucking good. This is the only cart that serves beer. People like drinking beer while reading the sports page so..."

"... So I'm crazy then? Crazy because of the war. Crazy because of Ma. Which one is it? All of the above?"

Jude lost the air in his lungs and his gut felt like it just got drilled by Jack Dempsey. It took every ounce of strength in his body to stay upright. From the moment that peckerwood sailed into this world and became Jude's little brother, he was Billy's unyielding and unquestionable defender and guardian. It didn't matter how old Billy was or what he did, Jude was in his corner when the bell rang.

And that unwavering loyalty was both reciprocal and necessary. Billy was the wild and uncontrollable partner in the relationship until Jude lost his temper, and then, as if the coin were flipped to the other side, Billy would step in to curb and sanction Jude's fury. It was a requisite dynamic for the brothers' survival. An unspoken awareness that they were all they had, and a tacit pact was therefore bonded in blood.

Billy's nonsensical paranoia was now threatening that sacred covenant for the first time in the men's existence and if there was ever a time the boys needed each other, it was now. And if Jude told Billy what he was truly feeling, he feared that bond would be severed for good. As much as Jude wished sanity and sense to return to his brother's heavy head, what he truly yearned for was unyielding trust in Billy. Jude's skepticism was a betrayal that went deeper than even the sin of murder. It was that sin that gouged him in the stomach ripping air from his lungs.

"All right, Billy," Jude found himself saying. "If you think that fella might have some ill intentions with us, I believe you. I'll keep both eyes on the son of a bitch."

Jude didn't think there was a sin greater than betraying that brotherly bond until he lied to his brother's face for the first time in their existence.

CHAPTER
FIFTY-THREE

Billy paced through the train for what seemed like hours, rambling over every inch of it. Each time he strolled back to his cabin door, light bled out from underneath, indicating Jude was probably in there awake, worrying and waiting like an old maid. Billy's head was as tired and wobbly as his legs, and he pined for the sanctum of that hard lumpy mattress where he could curl up in the shadowy cave of his bottom bunk and at least pretend he was asleep to avoid any more talking.

Billy didn't want to hear one more Goddamn lie out of his brother's mouth. But now, with the light on once more, and Jude in the cabin, Billy was sure Jude would attempt small talk or worse and Billy just could not stand that thought. He'd make a hundred laps on the fucking train before he would subject himself to Jude's patronizing eyes and hollow words.

He considered booking his own cabin. They weren't short on cash after failing to buy their way out of the shit storm of Billy's making. If he did, though, he'd tip his hand about the rift he felt between the two. Allowing Jude to know that Billy felt betrayed and abandoned seemed as sinful to Billy as Jude's iniquitous act.

Billy also understood Jude would view such a bizarre decision on Billy's part as more proof of Billy's poor mental health or judgment and Billy did not care to give his brother any more ammunition.

And finally, in all of Billy's twisted thoughts, he realized that if he was right and this fella was after them, then the two brothers needed to stick together, even if only one of them was aware of the danger.

Especially if only one of them was aware of the imminent threat.

Jude needed Billy now more than ever, Billy realized, even if Jude was acting like a lying horse's ass.

So Billy moseyed on past the door once more, continuing his endless journey.

As nightfall spread its heavy shade, the entire locomotive was swallowed up whole by the sheer black, the train descending into nothingness. Each cart was eerily quiet, the buzzing hum emitting from the yellow incandescent lights overhead, the only sound.

On occasion, Billy would come across another wearied-eyed passenger, a fellow wandering ghost held up in their own sleep-less purgatory. They would pass, usually not making eye contact, their heads low, deep in their own anguish or insomnia.

The long train carts were hitched together, sometimes requiring Billy to exit one cart, temporarily passing outside on a walkway, before entering another. As Billy slid the door open, he was once again swept into a tunnel of wind. It danced across his face, tickling his nose. He could feel his heavy greased hair frolic freely like it was surging with electricity and the lingering chill lightly prick his skin all over. As he inhaled, he came to smell lush night misting over the rich abundant forest as the howling gusts whispered secrets into his ears. He raised his arms, as if he were floating in the ether, and he felt as if he was hurling backwards through space and time. He closed his eyes, enjoying the fluttering of his senses, and the peace that suddenly draped over him with the wind.

As if the last five years were all a bad dream.

As if, when he opened them, he would be back in Taos, his legs dangling off the back of his pickup bed. Adeline sitting next to him, her hand clasped in his, as they watched the sun slowly fade behind the purple horizon sharing a cold Budweiser. When the sun had set, and the shadows from the gorge of the Rio Grande swept over the brown and green mesa, they would finish their beer and then gaze into the light that still existed in each other's eyes.

They would quietly and serenely ramble down the rugged dirt *road*, the truck tipping and rocking into hard ruts here and soft arroyos there, as the orange prismatic dust surrounded them.

Billy and Adeline would arrive at the James residence just as Jude returned home from work, sheriff's badge shining proudly on his cowhide jacket. Luisa greeting them at the door, they would all enter the home together, the scent of roasted green chile in the oven welcoming them in along with Luisa's harmonious smile.

Jude and Luisa would sit, he sipping on a glass of bourbon, her a beer, as Billy and Adeline set the table, the four catching up on the day's events.

After dinner, Jude would wash the dishes as Billy dried, while the women gabbed on the front porch. Jude would tell Billy he was drying incorrectly, and Billy would point out the soap still on a plate. Light obscenities would be shared, perhaps a jab here and there, before the men would join their ladies for a quiet commencement of the evening.

Billy didn't know how long he stood outside between the carts, floating in the wind and reflection, but when he opened his eyes he realized he had been smiling. His chest that had felt tight and constrained now felt empty and clear and he could breathe again. His shoulders no longer felt heavy and his spirit no longer exhausted.

A momentary sadness then eased into Billy, knowing that memory would never happen again, and maybe never existed to begin with. If it was ever real, it was all gone now, only his brother remained, right now, at least.

And then that sadness and something deeper lifted from Billy and fluttered away in the train's howling wind. He realized he no longer felt any ire towards Jude. He now welcomed the thought of being with his brother once more, even in the cramped quarters of the bunk room.

Billy was almost back to the room when he glanced up and noticed a reflection in the window to his right. There was an obscure image idling behind him. Billy squinted to make out the image clearer through the reflection and yellow light. As he did, his chest suddenly locked up once more. The enormous weight once again rained down on his shoulders and his fists clenched tight.

In the same moment, Billy recognized the figure was a person.

Not just any person, it was the *guy*, the *fella*.

The son of bitch who had been tracking and following him like a wounded buck since the train ride began.

The untroubled Billy was once again whisked away, like a grain of sand in a tornado, and in its place stood a soldier.

Billy continued his pace as he evaluated his options. He had no gun on him. Jude insisted that if anyone saw them carrying on the train, it would cause unwanted attention. Billy had disagreed with Jude's approach but ultimately acquiesced, and now he regretted it deeply.

He still held his knife, tucked safely away in his left boot. That was something he would not part with even at the behest of the Good Lord himself. If he pulled it however, he would tip the fella off, and lose the element of surprise. He also didn't know how long the ferreter had been on his scent and feared that any small response now would tip him off.

Billy realized because the man was behind him, at least Billy's eyes could not betray him. He began scanning his surroundings looking for an out, or better, a weapon.

As if waking from a dream, Billy recognized the dinner cart was still in front of him. There would be silverware for sure on the table and the man was far enough back that Billy could swipe a knife off the fine linen without being seen.

Billy continued his pace until he reached the dinner cart. He slid the door open to find the cart empty aside from a mopey-eyed waiter re-setting the tables, sharing a nod when Billy passed, but really browsing for a weapon.

As he scanned the tables, his insides twisted, and his gut knotted. The waiter had yet to set the knives on the tables. He almost stopped, not believing his own eyes or bad luck. He slanted his neck to see only the settings *behind him*, where he had passed, had knives, placidly laying on the white tablecloth shiny and sharp and mocking him.

Billy glanced further over his shoulder to find his newfound devotee lingering on the other side of the cart peering through the glass of the door. For a moment, their eyes locked and any doubt Billy held of the man's intentions were swept away like a seashell in the incoming tide. The eyes of two killers collided, no different than when Billy captured those damn German soldiers. They held their hands high in defeat, on their knees in surrender in the boggy cold mud but their piercing eyes still said *kill* even with Billy's rifle barrel and bayonet pointed straight at their flesh.

If Billy the killer made the man, then the man as a fellow killer made Billy making him. There was no turning back now and he would have to make do with what the Good Lord or Devil provided. Billy turned back in front of him and scanned the table once more. He swiped a fork, sliding the long end of the handle down his sleeve, the neck resting tightly at his wrist and the prongs hugging the palm of his hand.

He slid open the dining cart door with his free hand and his face was once again met with the dashing wind. This time, no sweet-smelling dew or lavish flowery scents rushed through his nostrils nor was the air crisp and rejuvenating because all Billy felt was the cold steel weapon that kissed his hand.

He entered the last wagon, the most crowded and cramped of the sleeper cabins. The corridor of the sleeper cart was tight and constricting, allowing barely enough room for one person to pass. The prison cell seemed to be swallowing him up whole, *squeezing* the life out of him like an anaconda. With each slow deliberate step, Billy pressed his hand on the door handle, hoping just one would open, he could slip into.

None obliged.

The levers all holding perpendicular.

Not moving.

Locked.

With each failed attempt, he veered one step closer to the end.

The end of options.

The end of the charade.

The conclusion of the fantasy that he was going to remain alive.

In reality, he was already dead.

Or should have been.

Slain at the hands of piercing German bullets or vaporized by shrapnel and gunpowder.

Drowned in the black tar, slowly fading away in his lover's arms in Paris.

Strangled by the coarse gritty twine clasping tighter and tighter around his neck with each swing of the noose and dangle of his legs.

Billy had spent his entire life defying rules, norms, and expectations. Perhaps he had even found a way to defy death until now. For the first time in his life, he should simply and quietly acquiesce. Cease braving the inevitable. Halt his headlong journey into the storm.

The end of the train with no escape was an indication he should put down the fork, face his faceless executioner and simply say, "I am ready. Do your worst."

Suddenly a door rattled to his right in front of him. An older black man with cotton white hair stepped out, a toothbrush still hanging from his mouth. Both men startled the other, like two lone wolves coming across one another in a forest.

The man smiled politely to Billy, backing himself up against the wall, allowing Billy room to scoot by.

In the same moment, Billy recognized the man had come from the lavatory. Billy stepped aside and motioned for the man to pass.

"Please sir," said the man.

"No, it's all right. I insist," Billy said.

The man hesitated, shooting Billy timid eyes until Billy bowed his head, almost absurdly. The man locked eyes with Billy once more and nodded before he passed.

Immediately, Billy slithered into the lavatory. The chamber barely fit a cold steel sink with a pump pedal and a drop chute with a lid.

Billy grasped the fork tight, holding stiff and still, not even breathing. His ears whetted and the hair on the back of his neck stood up like a dog raising its hackles. Only his thumping heart made any movement and sound. He didn't know how long he held utterly motionless, ready to strike but the door never opened. He never heard footsteps or breathing or any other sign of a lurking assassin on the other side.

Finally, Billy took a long deep breath. Suddenly aware of the rancid stench of the latrine, that burned through his nose before entering his lungs, causing him to both cough and gag and water his eyes instantly.

He flung the sliding door open, stumbling out, panting for unsullied air...

... and running clear into the fella.

Both men toppled over the other in clumsiness, velocity, and surprise.

Billy gathered himself first realizing who he had inadvertently thrust himself into.

"Pardon me," the man said.

"Who sent you?" Billy asked.

The man did not answer.

Instead, his eyes bulged in terror.

No words spilled from his tongue.

But the fork jutted from his throat.

All four prongs rutted so deep into the man's neck, only the handle Billy gripped tight, remained outside his flesh.

The man seemed to have frozen, only his eyes, not shaking, but flickered, like a flame fighting to stay lit in the wind.

Only when Billy slid the sharp tines from the man's gullet, did blood spurt out like an unkinked hose, spraying all over Billy's face but he did not turn away. Predator drenched in his prey.

The man's eyes stretched in rage and fear at the sight of his own mortality spilling from him.

Adrenaline and the wit of survival must have suddenly shot through the man's brain.

His burly hands clutched around Billy's jaw.

His thick fingers dug into Billy's lips and face.

The tighter the man gripped Billy's skin, the larger his eyes gaped with a crazed fury.

And suddenly the teeth of the fork were deep into the man's flesh once more.

Billy could feel the sharp prongs scrape against the hard slab that must have been the man's jawbone.

A pain shot through Billy's arm.

For a moment, he thought it was a strike from his enemy.

Then he felt his arm, and the hand that held the fork, quiver. The brute force of driving the utensil through man's jaw, was like electrocution through his appendage to the man's throat, the fork the conductor.

The man squealed like a slaughtering lamb until Billy pressed his free hand up to the man's mouth, suffocating his plea.

The man begged for mercy without words.

Only his eyes now begging.

Then, Billy watched the black in those eyes grow like spilt ink.

Billy no longer had to force the pikes of the utensil into the man. There was no struggle.

Instead, the man's head drooped over Billy's fist like a melting ice cream cone.

His body went limp and became heavy in the same moment.

His weight was too great to bear, and Billy was done fighting.

He slid the fork from the man's meaty pulp.

His carcass fell helplessly into Billy's arms like a swooning lover, the listless remains of the man melting into Billy's embrace.

CHAPTER
FIFTY-FOUR

The cart door slid open so fast and hard that Jude thought it would roll right into the next room. Before he could even sit up to investigate the ruckus or pull the pistol from under his pillow, he heard the door slam shut just as violent and frantic. He craned his head, peering down from the top bunk and then felt that gut punch again, knocking the air clear out of him.

Billy's eyes were as wide and face as white as a pale full moon. His breath short and anxious, and when he almost collapsed into the door, Jude thought his brother was actually having a heart-attack.

And then Jude saw the raspberry splatter on the forearm of Billy's leather jacket. Even the most seasoned killers always missed the blood on the front side, out of sight to the killer, while a spotlight to the living world. In that one quick moment, Jude realized the realization that he considered Billy a *murderer*.

Jude hopped off the bed, standing within inches of his brother, the killer.

Jude became aware that he was holding his pistol in his hand, it was cocked, and Jude's finger coiled on the trigger.

When did that happen?

Jude was so close to Billy, he could feel his shaky breath. "Billy, what the fuck?" he found himself asking.

As if answering the question, Billy pulled the fork from his pants pocket. The points were bent and stained with the same rouge as Billy's sleeve.

Jude's eyes were glued to the utensil. "What did you do?"

Billy palmed his clammy dire-filled face, seemingly as spooked with himself, as Jude was.

"Billy," Jude said again, putting his hand on Billy's shoulder and then recoiling back, aware of that fork and the stranger holding it.

"You know that fella?" Billy finally said, as if, in a trance watching the entire memory play out before his very eyes.

"Yes," Jude uttered slowly, petrified of Billy's response.

"He was following me, Jude. He was following me."

The fist somehow expelled from Jude's gut. He took a long deep breath, steadying his nerves, and

then spoke. "Okay, Billy, break it down for me."

"Ain't nothing to break down, Jude," Billy said, still gazed. "I was just walking and then I caught sight of him in the reflection of the train window lingering behind."

"Lingering?"

"That's what I said." Billy pronounced, suddenly defensive.

"Okay. Okay."

Billy looked hard at Jude, ensuring there would be no more bullshit questions from the peanut gallery. "So, I walked to the end of the cart, Jude. I mean the Goddamn caboose just to be sure and then I ducked into the bathroom…"

"Okay," said Jude, holding onto every word, desperate for a single clue that Billy wasn't a monster. "Did he come in after you?"

"No, not exactly."

"Billy, did he come or didn't he?"

The interrogatory tone naturally bled from Jude's lips despite his best efforts otherwise.

It didn't go unnoticed by Billy either. "He didn't come in, okay, God-damnit!"

Jude retreated back, his palms wide in the air. "Okay, Billy. Okay."

Billy looked sideways at Jude, long and hard and then continued.

"I ducked into the commode. And I waited there and waited there but he never came in. I didn't hear nothing on the other side of the door like there was someone there waiting. So I eventually came out, and that's when I ran right into the son of a bitch. Or the son of a bitch ran into me…or… I don't know."

Instead of Billy obliging his brother with the slightest hint of his innocence and lucidity, every word from Billy's mouth was another act of contrition.

"He said something like 'pardon me' but I knew better. I saw the truth in his eyes and that's when I…"

"That's when you what?"

Billy's eyes reddened with anger and glossed over. "That's when I stuck him. Stuck him with the fork." Billy's eyes drifted to the fork nestled in his hand. "I don't even remember the first time. Just acted quick. I saw that look in his eye and had the fork ready and I stuck the son of a bitch, right in the throat. He was a rabid dog after that, and we tussled and I then stuck him again in his fat neck, and I just kept digging into him with that fork until he didn't tussle no more."

"Why did you have a fork?" Jude gasped, unable to hide the terror in his voice.

"I told you. Because he was following me. Pulled it off a diner table when I knew for certain he was behind me."

Jude laid his gun on the bottom bunk, ensuring it was out of reach from Billy.

He combed his thick black greasy hair with all ten fingers and then wrapped his hands around the back of his neck.

He paced a tight circle in the room and then suddenly stopped. "What did you do with the body?"

"Threw it off the back of the train," Billy said, matter-of-factly. His indifference, ghastlier to Jude somehow than the act itself.

Jude sucked in another long hard breath, eyeing Billy down, trying to read his brother.

Read his mind.

Read his heart.

Read his soul.

"I'm telling you, Jude," Billy said, now the mind-reader.

Jude blinked and then resumed his circled-pace.

Billy idly stood, watching the gears grind in his brother's swamped head.

It was now Jude who appeared to be replaying the act in his mind. His eyes racing back and forth. "Did anyone see you?"

Billy drew a raspy grating breath, bit his lip and cocked his head. "That's the worst part."

Jude stepped back preparing himself. "Billy," he said, drained and weary, "What could be any worse?"

"I think Dahl saw me."

"You saw Dahl?" Jude asked, inching closer to Billy.

"I don't know," his head low, his face sheepish and vulnerable.

"What do you mean you don't know?"

"When that fella was finally done, he got heavy like a ton of bricks. I was fighting for a while to open the caboose door and get him off the back of the train.

"Okay..." Jude said, still waiting for the guillotine of bad news.

"Well, when I finally flung him out and turned around, I saw another fella at the other end of the cart, going the other way." Billy braced himself now. "I think it was Dahl."

"You saw him?"

"Not exactly."

"What exactly did you see?"

"I saw the back of his head. I saw the back of his head walking away."

"You the saw the back of a head walking away? Was he wearing one of his fancy suits or carrying a gun?"

"No, he just looked like a fella walking away."

"Billy, I'm trying…I'm trying…"

The eloquent and loquacious barrister suddenly could not find a single word to roll off his tongue.

Jude was *trying* what?

Trying to control an uncontrollable situation?

Trying to figure out how Dahl tracked them down?

Trying to believe his brother was not a mentally ill murderer who just slain an innocent man with a fork and was now on the hunt for some other poor sap who just happened to be walking away after Billy tossed the first poor sap out the back of the train like a bale of hay?

Jude plopped down on the bunk.

He buried his head between his legs and clasped his hands tight as if he was praying.

But there were no prayers.

He was simply trying to grasp his own sanity.

There were only three things Jude knew to be undeniable in the world.

Death.

Taxes.

And the unconditional love he held for his family.

There seemed to be a condition placed on that love now.

And instead of feeling acrimony towards Billy, Jude felt guilt against himself.

Shame that he sensed he was giving up on Billy.

Abandoning or forsaking his own kin. Just like his father had quit on them when the shit got thick.

Retreating into a black hole of cowardice self-pity instead of galloping headlong, fighting for the existence of the James family that remained.

The Bible taught forgiveness. Luisa was a shining example of mercy and compassion and Jude believed greatly in both, but his father committed a sin against he and Billy that Jude would never forgive.

Was Jude now committing that very same sin against his only brother, the only kin he had left?

Leaving Billy the victim to such a hideous act twice now?

Jude didn't know how long these questions engorged through his head when Billy finally broke the silence.

"Oh…No, I get it," Billy labored softly and slow.

Jude peered up at Billy. His blood-shot eyes, woeful and filled with tears.

"I wouldn't uh… I wouldn't believe me either. A Goddamn shell shock junkie. A murderer."

Jude stood. "Billy you're not…"

"It's okay, Jude. I've suddenly come to accept who I am. For the first time in my life, I ain't running from me. I'm staring that son of a bitch right in the face and he's no good. I ain't never been good. All this… just a Goddamn exercise in futility. Just like mamma. Spinning them tractor wheels in the Goddamn mud. And I've dragged you right in with me. You and your whole family. If that ain't the worst sin in this vial wicked world, I don't know what is. But I'm putting an end to it right here and now."

"Billy…"

"Goddamn it, Jude! Not this time! This has gone on long enough, big brother, our whole fucking life. You ain't convincing me otherwise this time…."

"NO!.." Jude suddenly interrupted. "Ain't gonna happen you son of a bitch!"

Billy's eyes were suddenly shaky and full.

His face shocked and stunned.

Maybe because of Jude's foreman against his throat, man-handling Billy against the door.

Perhaps from the hot-tempered flare burning off Jude's face, his clenched fist hovering over Billy's mug.

"You don't get to do that," Jude hissed. "You don't get to just give up. I ain't giving up on you and I sure as shit ain't letting you give up on you."

Billy hurled himself into Jude, driving his brother so hard against the window, it should have shattered.

Billy's face fumed red and that same James storminess erupted from his eyes. "Do you understand that I don't even believe me? I stabbed an old man *three* times with his own knife until he bled out right in front of me. I just bludgeoned a man with a Goddamn fork and threw him out the back of a train for no given reason whatsoever. I didn't have that poor soul's blood off my hands for five seconds when I saw the back of another man's head thirty yards away and convinced myself it was Dahl. Lord knows what I'm capable of if I see that poor son of a bitch again or any other sap my sick twisted head convinces me is against us. Just ask the fucking the Germans what I'm capable of! I'm not so unhinged to know how this sounds. I don't even believe me. You understand that? I don't believe me."

It was Billy who had a clenched fist in Jude's face now. It was as wobbly as the last words off his tongue. His face was still flush, but tears now flowed from his swollen eyes.

Jude let go of Billy's shirt collar, he didn't know he had grabbed. He stepped back and put his hands in the air. "You don't gotta believe you," said Jude "That's what I do. I'm your Goddamn brother."

CHAPTER
FIFTY-FIVE

If Jude had to eat, it might as well be a fine steak to force feed himself, he reckoned. He held no appetite but after he calmed Billy down, and after he calmed his own self down, he realized he couldn't take care of Billy unless he also took care of Jude. If Dahl was in fact lurking in the shadows, somehow on this train, then Jude needed to be at full strength. That meant eating something. It also meant no longer following the rule of no weapons while out of the cabin, hence the pistol that lay on his lap, under the table and cocked.

He took a deep breath and looked down at his plate. Nearly a quarter of his steak was gone that he flat-ass couldn't recall eating. If he sucked his teeth, he'd surely find beef in them, he couldn't remember tasting. Jude had those incremental blackouts his whole life, however, when he usually came to, his knuckles were bloody, and someone's face was ground beef.

Jude never hurt a woman or child while benumbed in one of his fits, but he was capable of almost anything else when succumbed to his temper. Luisa had given him two ultimatums when he got down on one knee.

Unconditional honesty and no more rage. It wasn't exactly a fairy tale response, but Jude smiled and agreed.

He had learned to control his intractable fury by sensing when it was coming. Once triggered, he was done, gone into the abyss of violence until it released him. But if he could sense the plunge coming, he could step away from the cliff. And with diligence, and the unparalleled love of a good woman, Jude's blackouts diminished.

One foot dangled from that precipice earlier when he had his hand around Billy's throat.

When did that happen? Jude thought.

He was thankful the spell was brief and relatively non-violent. In many of his spells, he wasn't angry at the victim of his rage, he was angry at himself. This he eventually learned after thorough self-examination and arm-twisting into *talking about it* with Luisa.. His interaction with Billy was no different, and he was deeply grateful he didn't commit any further regretful acts.

Also, if the two brothers ever came to serious blows, Jude wasn't even sure he could handle Billy one-on-one anymore, even in one of them insurmountable fits. If Dahl was in fact on the train, the boys would do him a favor and likely destroy each other first. Jude was sure of that. Another reason he was grateful cooler heads prevailed.

Jude took a deep breath, trying to center himself. *No more blackouts* he thought, *even while eating a fucking steak.*

He watched a young mother help feed her son in a booth across from him, one arm around the boy, the other guiding a fork of vegetables into his small mouth. Jude suddenly missed Patrick and Wyatt immensely. If he ever wanted to see his sons again, there could be no more blackouts.

He picked up his fork and knife. The filet carving from the blade like hot butter, the beef then melting in his mouth just the same, rich and savory with some pepper. He laid the silverware down, and closed his eyes as he chewed slowly, *willing* himself to enjoy.

The food was good.

Really good.

Before he'd even finished swallowing, he felt around the table for his fork and knife for the next bite.

"Food is better than expected, no?"

Jude didn't have to see to know who the voice belonged to. His eyes fled open.

And, before Jude could respond or even look up, Dahl slid into the booth across from him.

Jude's vision tunneled fully on the man now sitting across from him.

The rest of him froze.

He couldn't even choke down the food that remained in his mouth.

"First Canadian train I've had the pleasure of traveling on, and I must say, I'm thoroughly impressed," Dahl continued. "Our American counterparts have some competition on their hands."

Jude swallowed hard finally. The tender steak no longer delicious sustenance instead feeling like gritty coarse lumps of coal. His eyes made their way down to the broad steak knife that lay across the top of his plate on the table, shiny and reflective. The serrated teeth and sharp point almost mocking him.

"Please don't even consider it," Dahl said, noticing. "I've already lost one man to cutlery at the hands of a James. I won't lose another, present company included."

Jude now blinked, but nothing more.

Both eyes straight ahead on Dahl.

Jude was centered and attentive now, no fucking doubt about it.

Dahl looked pallid, sickly even, his flesh barren of color making the crimson in his left eye from a busted blood vessel more prevalent.

"So that fella was with you?" Jude squeezed out.

"You mean the gentleman that your brother bludgeoned with a fork and then tossed off the train? Yes, of course he was." Dahl's vacant crow-like eyes draped over Jude, studying every square inch. "Who else would he be?"

Jude mildly gritted his teeth.

"Oh, I see," Dahl exhaled, settling into the booth. Then he oddly turned his head as if an invisible ghost had just whispered something into his ear. "I see, indeed," he said, as if responding to the ghost.

"See what?" Jude hissed, confused and apprehensive.

"You didn't believe your brother. You thought he killed an innocent man."

Jude inhaled and raised his chin, like a rooster sizing up another cock that entered the roost.

"Your brother may be the murderer of innocent men, but rest assured, the man he gored was not one of them. A seasoned killer, and yet, still did not stand a chance against William. What do you suppose that says about your brother?"

"It says my brother hasn't killed anyone that didn't have it coming to him, Edwin Simon included."

"You don't really believe that and nor do I. At any rate, that question is of no concern to me."

"Really?" Jude asked.

"Really," said Dahl.

"So, it's just about money with you?"

"What is?"

"All of this. From the very start. Hell bent on putting a noose around Billy's neck. Coming after us."

"Oh, I see," Dahl said again. "No, Mr. James. What the Pinkertons pay for my services is nominal compared to what I could be procuring in other ventures."

"It's about the hunt then? Just a sociopath who's found a legal avenue to quench some sick vice or violent thirst?"

Dahl bit his lip and sucked in air, like he was trying to clean his teeth with his own tongue, a hissing noise that sent shivers down Jude's spine. "You constantly disappoint me, Mr. James, and now, even somewhat offend me."

"How's that?"

"No, Mr. James. I'm not in it for the money. Or the glory or the blood. I'm in it to maintain the natural order of things. Like a rancher or shepherd."

"No wonder I couldn't get read on you."

Dahl blinked almost boastfully. "How's that?"

"Because you're utterly insane."

Dahl stiffened up, looking perturbed. His eyes wandered to the sling around Jude's left shoulder. "How's the shoulder?" The care in his voice unholy.

"Feels like I got shot," Jude said. "But I'll survive. How's the…" Jude eyes pranced around Dahl, only now noticing how delicate he sat. "…Everything?"

"I'm stitched together like a rag doll," Dahl said, surveying his own torso. "I wouldn't be here if not for the best doctors money can buy."

Dahl almost sounded proud by that last sentence, Jude thought, while his trigger finger literally scratched at that bullet-hole scar on his other hand.

"Your friend did quite a number on me," Dahl continued, sounding impressed for a different reason now.

"My friend had a name," said Jude, trying to steady the fury in his voice and yearning retribution he felt sizzling out of his hands like un-grounded electricity.

"I'm sure he did. If you're still reeling from his departure, you may find solace in knowing it was he that betrayed you. Or I'm guessing some inability to remember numbers."

"The code on his card. That's how you tracked us," said Jude.

Dahl nodded, almost modestly, really throwing Jude off.

"You may also find solace knowing that man sent more hot lead into me than anyone else on this planet. Lord knows others have tried but not with the success of your friend. If not for the best doctors money can buy, well, I wouldn't be sitting across from you having our little chat here today." Dahl looked away, narrowing his eyes. "That was quite a feat you three accomplished," he then said, turning back to Jude. "Brazenly strutting into the den of the enemy, out-gunned, out-numbered and still causing so much destruction." As Dahl spoke, his chest puffed out and his shoulders danced, as if it were he that accomplished the great feat. "So much chaos and mayhem, which in essence answers your question."

"Which question is that?"

"What I'm *in it* for. Why I do this."

"You already answered that. You're a fucking lunatic shepherd, or rancher or zoo keeper…"

"Don't be crass, Mr. James, you're better than that and it does not suit you."

Jude inhaled and leaned forward over the table. "I'm gonna shoot you straight…in more ways than one…I ain't being crass, or rude or intentionally offensive. I just have no fucking idea what you are talking about. Maybe you think you're being cute. Maybe you think you're being sly or coy. I don't really give a good Goddamn and I no longer care to know why you do anything because when there's a bullet in your head, and your brains are dripping out of the back of your skull like jelly, none of that will matter. And for your sake, maybe St. Peter will be smarter than me and understand what the fuck you are talking about."

"Interesting that you bring up St. Peter, Mr. James. He and I have a lot in common. He guards the pearly gates of heaven, keeping order...." Dahl, delicately laid his arms out on the table, clasping his hands. "... And I guard the pearly gates of earth. You see, Mr. James, to get back to your original question, I do this work to maintain the natural order of things. Without it, we are no better than the animals. We are nothing but animals."

"What's that got to do with Billy and I?"

"You and your brother have defiantly snubbed your nose at the natural order since the day you two entered this world. Your mother was a poor Mexican witch. Your father a poor Irish potato farmer. How he found his way to New Mexico is still beyond me, which only furthers my point. Your mother was mentally ill, and I say that with no disrespect. That assessment comes only from a clinical perspective. And your father, true to his natural order, was a drunk. All those facts dictate that you and your brother were to live a life of pestilence and scourge and manual labor. That was your destiny, the order, and you, and your brother to some degree, defied it. As previously mentioned, I am quite deliberate in the cases I choose to take. When your brother's file came across my desk initially, it only moderately interested me. A poor half breed in bum fuck New Mexico stabbing a magnate at his own party. However, when I reviewed your family's history and then read your brother's military file, the awards, and medals he received, my interest evolved. Not piqued but evolved until I got a hold of your brother's sealed military file..."

Dahl's eyes fluttered as he paused.

"What?" Jude dared to ask.

"He didn't tell you that either?" Dahl said, seeping in smugness. "You two are vastly humble, if nothing else. Your brother is a war hero, Mr. James. He saved twelve of his own men's lives while capturing an entire enemy troop alive. They were later mowed down by other American grunts, after great protest and refusal from your brother. Even disobeying direct orders. Hero one minute. Coward and traitor the next." Dahl's eyes narrowed. "You think that's what bothers him so?"

"I reckon it's more about a rat bastard son of bitch trying to hang a noose around his neck."

Dahl's eyes somehow tightened further sending sharp daggers into Jude's chest.

Jude almost wished for the vainglorious demeanor again that grinded his gears moments earlier.

"Make no mistake, there will be no noose," Dahl whispered. And then, as if Jekyll and Hyde, Dahl leaned back in the booth, his eyes glowed and a smile draped across his face, bestowing that eerie reverence towards Jude again. "And when I read your file. Sheriff at twenty two. Part-time marshal at twenty five. Lawyer by thirty despite no undergraduate education… Well… Color me intrigued."

"Let me get this straight. You want to kill us because Billy's a war hero and I bullshitted my way through passing the New Mexico Bar Exam?"

"Perhaps I am not being clear. What do the Bolsheviks in Russia, the Franco Army in Spain and even the now defeated Nazis all have in common?"

Jude did not answer.

He was clearly unamused and unimpressed.

When Dahl realized Jude was not going to engage, he continued. "They all revolted against the natural order. And we now see the danger of such acts and the necessity of maintaining it. Each of those disastrous and devastating infernos of upheaval started with a single match. A single person bucking the natural order. You and William's relative success as adults despite your familiar history and upbringing is one match, though not a worrisome one.

However, him disobeying the direct order of a commanding officer to execute the prisoners he had captured only to have every other soldier in his troop rally around him is another match.

You bucking the entire higher education system of our nation yet another.

None of these strikes so far warranted my concern but when your brother killed Edwin Simon, an affluent Lion at the top of the food chain, and then through your undue influence as a district attorney, it was possible he would go unpunished, well, the Bolshevik match was lit, the Franco kerosene poured, and the Nazi flame singed.

Your brother's crime was not that he murdered an innocent man. Your brother's crime was that he was a poor peasant who had the impetus to strike back against a nobleman. Your brother's crime was that he did not know his place in the military or to Mr. Simon.

You have no business being an attorney, I don't care how naturally gifted you are. You do not know your place either so I am here to put you in your place. I see the social ladder you are so desperately trying to climb, and I stand on the rung above to crush your fingers that grasp on. To crush any hope and delusion you have of upward mobility.

I hope you don't think I take pleasure in any of this. I assure you, I take none. As much as it is a burden for you and William to be born into your downtrodden class and struggle to not only survive but thrive, it is equally burdensome for me.

Just like you, this burden is a birthright. My great granddaddy was one of the first settlers in Alabama, his family's wealth allowing him the luxury of exploration. My granddaddy in turn built one of the largest plantations and cotton mills on that land until some bleeding-heart Yankees marched in on their high horses abolishing the natural order."

"You mean abolishing slavery."

"I mean all the animals in God's kingdom knew their natural place and lived in harmony.

Now I may no longer have control of the soft and weak government that allowed the monkeys to run free in the jungle, but rest assured, their freedom is only an illusion, just like your upward mobility, only a peasant's dream.

You and others like you have fought against history, Mr. James, not only the history of this country but the history of humanity. There have been valiant efforts but ultimately we have always succeeded, and we always will."

Jude blinked.

He sat back in the booth, mashed his ink-black mustache with his finger, scratching his upper lip every now and again, peering out the vastness of the train's window. Trees whizzed by as blurred images, like his children's finger paintings. The hills behind, appearing like one long wall. Leaves on the trees like bricks, and the branches and trunks, the mortar.

Jude mashed his mustache one last time and then spoke. "I reckon I'm relieved."

"Relieved?" Dahl could not resist asking.

"Yea. Relieved." Jude picked up his fork and knife, carving off a generous piece of red juicy meat from the larger share, taking a bite while his eyes remained out the window. The sun was setting somewhere in the distance and the images seemed to gray more with each second. It seemed like only a minute ago everything was draped in forenoon and now dusk. Maybe the whole word was just turning incrementally dark.

Jude took another bite of the meat. His cheeks incurved into his cheek bones as he savored the fine cut. "Mmm. That is a fine steak," he said, before pointing the fork and knife in Dahl's direction, "Would you like to try a piece?"

Dahl simply shook his head.

"That's right. Your kind ain't too keen on sharing, which, to borrow your phrase, answers your question."

Jude sliced off another piece of meat, avoiding the untouched mound of mashed potatoes and enjoyed another bite. He noticed Dahl surveying his eating habits. "Don't much care for potatoes," Jude said. "Never have, despite being a thick-headed mick and the son of a potato farmer. Guess that's me..." Jude postured for a moment, "...*bucking the natural order again.*"

Jude swallowed the remainder of his food. He cleared his throat, wiped his face neatly with his napkin and then continued. "No, I'm relieved I'm not sitting across the table from a sociopath, as I originally thought. I'm most likely not sitting across the table from a maniac with a thirst for violence either. No, I'm relieved to know that I'm only sitting across the table from a conceited racist asshole. Them folk are easy to handle and all the same. Been dealing with *y'all* my entire life. Usually kicking your ass for one thing or another."

Jude stared out the window. He fished a bothersome sliver of meat from between his teeth with his tongue, his mouth shut, so as not to offend Dahl.

When the bothersome scrap was cleared, Jude turned back to Dahl again and spoke. "I reckon Billy and I should be relieved and flattered."

"Flattered? Dahl asked, once again sucked into the good barrister's web.

"Flattered that we're part of your holy crusade of simply putting the *chingas* to the working class. You know, it's funny, for as much emphasis as *y'all* put on being high and mighty and better than the rest of us peons and yokels, you sure do like to concern yourself with our business, usually to your detriment. Maybe because *y'all* have so much idle time on your hands, you got nothing better to do than launch into these silly campaigns and conflicts, as if we're the ones conspiring against you."

Jude paused.

He sliced off another piece of meat and slowly chewed.

He swallowed.

Wiped his face again, and then continued. "In reality, us simple folk got more important matters, *real* matters like…" Jude pointed his fork and knife at his plate, "...putting food on the table, to concern ourselves with. We much prefer to just go about our own business, working hard, enjoying our family and what little fruits of our labor we have. We tend to mind ourselves. Follow the rules. Not step out of line until one of you whoreson pricks start grabbing for what don't belong to you. We'll take it for a little while, not reacting, and continue to mind our business. You think we're so dumb that we don't see it or we're weak and crippled. We're neither. And what you filthy fucking pigs never seem to realize, is we'll only take it for so long before we snap and fight back. That's evidenced in the history books too. Rome. Greece. Shit, even those Egyptian slaves that broke their backs and died building the ridiculous pyramids eventually had enough too. They too had a breaking point. Even in this country, this country…"

The table suddenly rattled, and the silverware chimed. Jude almost thought there was a train wreck until he realized it was his slamming fist on the table that shook it, unaware how fervent he had become.

Dahl stared down at Jude's fist too, as if a foreign object fell from the sky between the two.

Jude unclenched his fist, and he removed his arm from the table. He gathered himself and settled.

"…Less than two hundred years ago we did the same. Same God-damn story. The king kept squeezing and squeezing until we had enough, and we ran his ass out. Why do we study history, Mr. Dahl? Aside from the sentimental value of it."

"To learn from it," Dahl said, begrudgingly.

"That's right. To learn from it. *Y'all* are the educated class. You surely learned this history in school, so it perplexes me as to why *y'all* make the same mistake again and again throughout history. If you simply just left us alone, we'd do the same. *Y'all* can sit in your high towers behind your great big wall drinking your fancy wine, and for the most part, we'd be happy to keep serving you as long as we got to go home to our family at night and have a day of rest every now and again. And there'd be peace and equilib-rium until *y'all* go and make the same mistake.

This curious phenomenon left me wondering why for years now.? What was so inherent in each and every one of you that caused *y'all* to make the same mistake again and again?

And then one day, I was sitting at the Alley Cantina, in my hometown, having a beer when I saw the man next to me get up and exit, leaving a quarter on the bar as tip for the tender. Before the barkeep saw it, out of the corner of my eye, I witnessed a local well-to-do, two stools down, slide his hand across the bar and steal that quarter. That also left me wondering, why in God's name, would that rich son of a bitch, who probably had a hundred dollars in his back pocket, feel the need to steal a quarter from the hard-working beer-man pouring drinks to put food on the table for his family, while that son of a bitch sat on his fat ass sipping a margarita. Then I realized the answer."

Jude paused.

The train rocked slightly back and forth curving into a bend.

The child across the aisle from Jude and Dahl tittered, perhaps from the movement of the train. His mother sniggered back, and the boy's eyes lit up.

It made Jude smile, observing it all, and then he turned back to Dahl. "You wanna know the answer?"

This time, Dahl was not going to oblige, only answering with a callous stare.

"It's simple," Jude continued. "You fat fucking pigs can't help yourself. You got this immeasurable and insatiable appetite for greed and thievery. You'll never have enough so you keep taking and taking and taking. You're smart enough to know it ain't sustainable. You're smart enough to know, eventually we're gonna fight back. But you're sick. You can't help being anything but a Goddamn parasite.

I don't know how long we've been on this planet, nor do I know how much time we have left, but I surmise, since the first day two cavemen started gathering berries, until the last day of reckoning, that pendulum is gonna swing back and forth between us and you avaricious swine."

Dahl held his icy glare, his eyes unwavering from Jude's.

From their first interaction, Jude had no ability to read Dahl's emotions or thinking. Couldn't see anything past those inky soul-less headlights in his cadaverous skull. Dahl was either cold-blooded, a pro, or both.

But now, Dahl almost looked hurt, or at least annoyed.

Jude felt some satisfaction in that until Dahl grinned.

"You know," Dahl said, still beaming. "The Greeks are known for their myths and tragedies. Of course, the English have Shakespeare, but I always found it's the Mexicans and the Irish that spin the most tantalizing tales. In their stories, they always explore their afflictions and yet, also maintain this glimmering light of hope, even when by all indications, it's illusory."

Dahl's attention turned to the child across from the two men.

The boy now had a red wooden fire truck that he was steering back and forth on the table while his mother read a book. A dabble of drool nestled on the corner of his lip below his plump rosy cheeks.

"Much like a child," Dahl continued.

The way he studied the boy scratched at Jude's nerves.

"They're old enough to experience pain. To understand in some sense, the painful gravity of the world, and yet they still believe everything will be okay," Dahl said.

Jude sat quiet pondering Dahl's words, or something else, and then realized, he too, was watching the child. He was flooded with uneasiness and that burning impetus in his gullet. Then he turned back to Dahl, that tunnel vision returning, square on his enemy. "No more discourse. No more intellectual circle jerk back and forth. This ends. With blood. With violence. With death," Jude said, his words as cold as the sound of his revolver being cocked under the table. His eyes pointed as straight at Dahl as the barrel of his gun.

Dahl calmy bowed, "Agreed."

Then Jude heard the hammer cock on Dahl's gun, undoubtedly pointed at Jude under the table.

"It appears we have reached that precipice," said Dahl.

He did not blink but he was not staring at Jude either.

He was simply holding, like a mountain lion in position to pounce on the unsuspecting deer.

But Jude was not a deer.

His world silenced.

His senses still.

For he too, was a lion.

The train no longer swayed and vibrated.

The aroma of the steak no longer steamed up into his nostrils.

He no longer tasted the stale heavy cigarette smoke stinging his breath that lingered in the train car.

He did not hear the coos and *vrooms* from the boy toying with his firetruck or the train engine puffing along.

All he sensed was his finger on the smooth trigger. It felt as tight as Jude ever remembered without that allaying, fitful almost orgasmic pull…

Suddenly, a raucous horde of swingers stumbled into the train car. Young men, gaily and loud with their arms around their girlfriends, spilled into the booths behind both Jude and Dahl, surrounding the two men in their swell of youthful pandemonium.

Jude could feel their spry commotion edging into his back through the cushion as they overflowed into the booth behind him.

Dahl's relentless stare was interrupted by a woman's elbow to the back of his head. His neck turned back to her, as if he expected an apology but she did not seem to notice or care.

Jude's finger eased from the trigger. "There ain't nothing I would like more than to end this right now," he said. "Whatever that result may be, I've made peace with it, but I ain't about sending anyone else to their maker in this ordeal besides you and me."

Dahl's body contorted forward, and for one instant, Jude thought Dahl had fired his gun, prompting him to almost do same.

Then he realized the lurch was due to one of the hooligans pounding into Dahl's back through the cushions.

"As tempting as it may be to teach these children some manners," Dahl seethed, "I agree. There is a discipline you and I follow, regardless of our shared yearning for conclusion."

Jude heard Dahl's hammer unclick.

"Our final song has commenced. The first motion of our last dance initiated, but our waltz continues, Mr. James."

It was now Jude who found himself nodding as he un-cocked his pistol.

CHAPTER
FIFTY-SIX

Billy heard the door slide open and then roll closed as he vacantly stared off at the top bunk mattress lingering above him. Each fuzzy fiber like a star in the sky. The spongy mattress squeezing through the braided metal, like seeping hot lava. How many nights in the barracks did he stare at those twined coiled wires? Making loops in his head, stoically following them with his eyes, his hands behind his head, thinking about everything and nothing all at once.

Billy came to, realizing Jude had not moved or said a word since he entered the cabin. He craned his neck out from the veil of the top bunk. Jude had his back to Billy, staring at the gray dull cabin door. He was motionless aside from his shoulders, seemingly with the weight of the world on them, lifting and lowering with Jude's slow breath.

"You all right?" Billy finally asked, after a long survey of his brother's hind side.

Jude turned his head slightly to Billy. "You want the good news or the bad news?"

Billy sat up in the bunk, anchored his legs on the ground and his elbows on his knees, bracing himself. "I've always preferred the bad news first, but seeing the whole world is upside down now, let's have the good."

"The good news is, you ain't crazy," Jude said, turning around, his jittery eyes meeting Billy's.

"I don't know about that, but all right And the bad?"

Jude hunkered down on the bunk next to Billy. His elbows fixed on his knees, the same as his brother's. It was now Jude that studied Billy.

Billy's eyes were wide and attentive, but he didn't look scared. The *fear* reservoir probably bone-dry. He seemed calm. Maybe Billy was right to ask for the good news first. Maybe, in Billy's mind, the idea that Billy was spiraling into insanity was the worst possible news, and anything else would pale in comparison. Maybe the assertion from his big brother that he wasn't going insane was the only news that truly mattered and everything else was trivial. Maybe, after all these years, Billy still secretly yearned for Jude's affirmation and now that he had it, he could handle anything.

Jude took one more long moment to gauge his brother's demeanor and capacity to wield what Jude was about to lay on him and then spoke. "The bad news is Dahl is on the train."

Billy took in a long wheezing breath and turned his head straight. His eyes seemingly not fixed on the confining and cramped wall in front of him, but there nonetheless.

"Good," Billy finally said.

"Good?" asked Jude.

"Yeah, good." Billy turned to Jude, the brothers' eyes locking. "It means we can finish this. Right?"

Jude nodded slowly, looking at his brother. "That it does," Jude said. "One way or the other, it will be finished."

Billy's head and shoulders cocked. He sniffled slightly, cleared his throat, and then spoke. "I don't believe in God, but my prayers have been answered."

CHAPTER
FIFTY-SEVEN

"W asn't exactly how I pictured our final liaison," Dahl howled, nervously peering off the side of the train into the black sea of quietus. His knees awkwardly bent and legs standing wide, futilely trying to balance himself through the curvy bends of the speeding train roof. His usual impeccably combed hair danced wildly in the air like it was on fire. His eyes squinted and watered. His entire face seemed to wince, and it was the first time Dahl appeared the least bit rattled to Jude in their ever-changing affair.

"It never is," said Jude, scooting his own feet a little wider apart to brace himself.

"How'd you know I'd come for you up here?" Dahl asked over the rattling wind.

"Because it's what I would have done. As soon as you said *tomorrow at noon* I knew you were coming tonight."

Dahl nodded, peering over the hurdling edge and then back at Jude. "I fear we missed out on an opportunity, Mr. James."

"How's that?"

"If you and I met in another life. On the same side of the coin… Well we could have been something."

"As flattering as that may be, you and me on the opposite side is about right. Keeps that pendulum swinging."

As the men swiveled back and forth, their bodies always reacting one second too late to the unpredictable twists and turns of the careening train, Jude could see he finally had Dahl out of his element. Drawing down while standing on the roof of a spurring locomotive, while also desperately trying not to fall to one's death, wasn't exactly in Jude's comfort zone, but at least the playing field had been leveled. From the beginning, it was Jude constantly backed in the corner, unsettled, riled. While Dahl was left comfortable and content, dictating the terms and turns of their ever – evolving engagement.

"I'm saddened, you didn't take me at my word, Mr. James," Dahl yelled, his voice scattering in the wind like shattered glass.

Before Jude could speak, he noticed Billy emerge behind Dahl, hoisting himself up on the top of the train. Closing in.

"I took you at your most basic and predictable nature," Jude shouted back.

As Billy neared, Jude didn't dare make eye contact with his brother, fearing even his eyes would betray his position to Dahl.

"Eloquent, clever and a fast trigger," Dahl hollered. "You could have been a Pinkerton."

Behind Billy, Jude noticed the train approaching a black tunnel, swallowing them up whole into darkness, at least for a split second, and Jude knew this is where all three men would collide with their fate.

Dahl was rattled, but Jude needed him furious. For whatever reason, Jude always found anger slowed you on the draw. The mind had to be a blank canvas when reaching for that cold steel.

"Don't have it in me…" Jude said inching to his hardware… "Ain't a gimp!"

Dahl's eyes widened with rage and his hand hurled toward his holster.

From behind, Billy saw it too. "Dahl!"

Dahl's hand hit his pistol in the same moment he twisted toward Billy.

Jude pulled and fired and all went black.

A deep echo roared, and Jude felt like he was hurdling through a black empty nothing.

As he fired again and again, there were little flashes, like lightning bugs flittering at night.

Jude thought maybe they were angels.

Maybe the howling that surrounded him was the devil sucking him into hell.

Jude could feel nothing but the cold hard trigger, so he pulled it again and again.

It was so black, he didn't know if his eyes were open or closed then his boys appeared in front of him.

Patrick's joyful and tender eyes spilled into Jude's.

Wyatt's chubby portioned fingers reached out to Jude nose, grazing, and tickling.

Luisa's face glittered before him. The small brown beauty mark under her tender emerald eyes and her smile warming his heart.

With the love Jude felt, and his family surrounding him, he knew he wasn't in hell.

But no sign of his brother.

Suddenly, the dark shattered, and light prevailed, the train exiting the tunnel.

Dahl stood in front of Jude once more.

Billy, behind him on his belly.

Dahl's eyes seemed perplexed. His entire being bewildered. His gun dangled loosely from his hand and then it dropped, vanishing off the train.

Jude watched red silky puddles spread across Dahl's body, as if the devil were swallowing him up, piece by piece ,while Dahl's lips moved, already bargaining.

Jude turned down to his own body, spreading out his arms from his torso like when he and Billy would inspect the other for ticks.

Dahl coughed and that same red silk spilled from his mouth. His eyes were no longer confused with the strange happenings, now looking at Jude with clarity. His mouth moved once more like he was trying to speak but no words spilled from it.

Only more blood.

Dahl remained standing but started twisting with the wind, like he was being pulled from two different directions.

And then he was gone. His body whisked from the train.

Jude felt the gun in his hand. He looked down and saw all six chambers empty and his body whole.

Billy slowly stood, a defiant grin wiped ear to ear. That fucking grin that shined on his face since the day he was born.

Jude shook his head and then collapsed.

His body melting over the brisk metal dome of the train like a tired sun at dusk over the Taos Mesa.

Billy bolted to Jude, fearing he was shot.

As he neared, he found Jude staring up at the heavens they had so far avoided but were graced by, nonetheless.

Billy scanned Jude's entire body. Jude was okay. As *okay* as anyone alive could be.

Billy's head suddenly rattled as if he were back in the foxhole.

His legs gave out, falling to his hands and knees.

Hot singeing bile bubbled up from his throat.

The faces of those twelve prisoners flashed before his eyes. Their tired begging faces, each one only staring into Billy, until each one fell like the last.

His nose burned as the vomit retched from it.

The image of Marion's stiff mouth lulled open, dried drool over her yellow lips, in front of him on the other side of darkness.

His eyes watered, as the sickness now seeped through his eye sockets and ran down his cheeks.

And there was Adeline, her lips pressed tight, desperately trying to hold back tears as Billy said both I'm sorry and goodbye at the same time.

His body convulsed and sputtered and then stiffened. His stomach muscles now aching and tight as it searched for anything else to dispel while Billy's mind went blank.

There was nothing left.

No pain from the inside.

And when he realized what had just happened, he muttered out loud, "I didn't murder Edwin Simon."

His insides turned over clean and now he was on his back next to his big brother, but Jude's gaze remained fixed on the sky and Billy wasn't sure if Jude heard what he said or if it even mattered to him.

Both men sprawled out on the top of the train.

Utterly exhausted.

Finally able to rest.

The brothers stared up at the chalky moon and the ring around it.

The dark sky turning a purple, the orange of a new day bleeding through the black night.

"You okay?" Jude asked.

"When uh… when Dahl turned around…And he looked at me and was about to pull… I realized I didn't want to die. I wanted to live and then I saw that gun coming my way…"

"He was fast," Jude said.

"You were faster. I knew you would be."

"Dahl was almost there, I could feel it."

The wind mewed.

The boys silent.

That moment everything.

Eventually, Jude spoke. "If you didn't want to die, then why didn't you follow our plan?"

"*Your* plan."

"Okay, *my* plan."

"Since when have I ever followed your plan, except that one time and look where that got me?"

"Fuck you *hermanito*," Jude chuckled.

"Fuck you, *carnal*," Billy rattled off.

"We got lucky," Jude said.

"Bullshit," said Billy. "Those sons of bitches underestimated us at every turn because they never understood we still had the one advantage they he could never account for."

"And what's that?"

"Two James boys."

"Reckon they know now," Jude said.

"Reckon so," said Billy

Like when they were boys laying in the dirt watching the stars, they stretched out watching the turning sky, elbowing and tussling while…

The wind whistled fits of laughter in their ears.

The sky brightened more with each newborn second.

And the train suddenly wheezed and howled, yawning and now awake.

Brothers in the night, full steam ahead into a new day.

The End

ACKNOWLEDGMENTS

CYLE BARNES AND THE WEEKS whose song planted the seed that grew into this son of bitch.

Alan Klein, maybe my first reader, and my most honest.

Suzuya Bobo, who is stronger and more fierce than even the submarine she was named after.

Shaz Khan, keep swinging, brother.

Kate Gale, my self-described literary champion.

Mr. R. and Ben who continue to move my paradigm.

Anyone else who has laid eyes on my pages.

&

My family who has always had my back in good times and hard.

ABOUT THE AUTHOR

MICHAEL MULCAHY HAS BEEN writing since his appendages allowed. Once a filmmaker, Michael now takes the motion pictures playing in his head and puts them to page, penning four novels to date. He lives in Taos, New Mexico in a home he proudly built with his father.

Turn the Page for An Excerpt of Michael Mulcahy's next novel, O. G. Diplomacy

After he survives a brutal shoot-out that culminates with his best friend, Lee, dying in his arms, Victor Cordova relegates himself to a peaceful existence serving tacos out of his food truck in Santa Fe's glitzy downtown. His monk-like existence is then threatened two-fold.

First, by the return of Lee's sister, Dani, who is seeking answers about her brother's death, and maybe something more.

Second, by the sudden disappearance of Victor's surrogate father, and streetwise sensei, Niko.

At the same time, two knucklehead thugs approach Victor with a proposition that threatens everything he has buried since Lee's death. Victor can't help but fear all of this is related, ghosts coming back to haunt him.

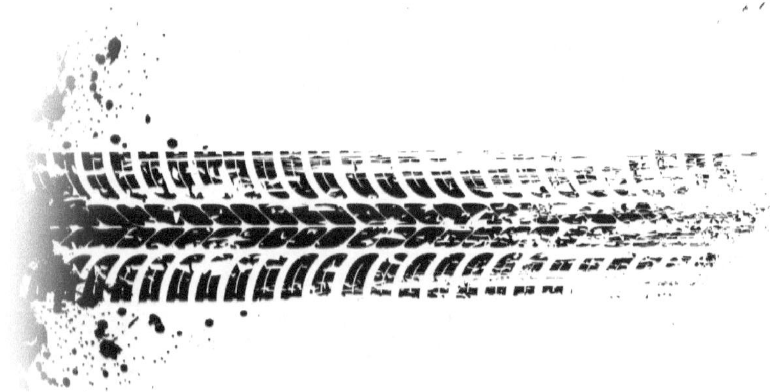

PROLOGUE

This thing of darkness, I acknowledge mine.
- William Shakespeare

"Don't you fucking die, Lee!" Victor screamed over the pelting rain and rattling blades frivolously swiping the hammering deluge from the windshield. "You too, Mia!" he howled. "You hear me? You hear me?"

Victor's blood-crusted hands gripped the worn curve of the steering wheel as if *he* was the one holding on for dear life. His gaze dogged and steady. Head pointed over the steering wheel like a bow over water.

When he flipped on the dome light of the old truck, a burst of light suddenly revealed the pallid face of his friend's empty eyes staring back at him. Blood bubbling from the stab wound in Lee's neck, the only part seemingly alive.

"Nah bro, it ain't gonna be like that, holmes." Victor's shaky voice pleaded at the mannequin-like figure leaning against the passenger-side window. "You don't get to die on me."

He then glimpsed down to Mia's lifeless head resting on his lap. Her sallow face and heavy eyes barely peeled open. Her body folded into Lee, like a wilted leaf.

"Mia, you ain't going nowhere either, *chica,* you hear me?" he whimpered, lightly slapping her cheek.

Victor's big brown eyes squinted over the steering wheel trying to discern the winding narrow road through the monsoon rain, foggy windshield, and tottering wipers. Blood, sweat and rain dripped down his face, gathering in his ink-black goatee. Constantly clearing away the mixture of blood and sweat from his eyes with the back of his hand, just so he could see. The salt stinging his eyes. Blood gathering in the bristles of his facial hair.

His attention constantly torn between the black misty windshield and the two carcasses in his truck. One bleeding out before his very eyes. The other lost in a deep heroin spin.

Surveying the state of his friends, battered, bloodied, and almost dead, Victor's face clenched so tight, he almost appeared smiling. "You ain't dying on me *hermano*! Not like this!" Bags swelled in his eyes before tears broke like a levee, streaming down his cheeks still smudged with blood and into his goatee now purplish and red. "You two can't die on me. *Familia holmes!*"

Fucking Lee.

Always had to be a Goddamn *cabasuro.*

Victor didn't even know what an ox was, but was sure an ox was as stubborn as Lee.

Rebel who's only cause was to stick it to you more. Whatever you were asking, he was gonna do the opposite.

Was Lee tenacious enough now to defy the knife wound in his neck? His body unrelenting enough to sustain the blood loss until Victor got his ass to the ER?

Somewhere on the thin bridge between life and death, could Lee hear his brother's plea? If so, did that send Lee towards the light, veering him to the pearly gates and not back to Victor? One last fuck you, dear friend.

Lee would do that.

Never did himself any favors.

Smart enough to recognize the right decision. Wayward enough to choose the other.

That was always their tug-of-war. Victor too simple and naïve. Lee too cunning for his own good.

Maybe that's what made them brothers. Not blood brothers but enough shared blood and history to have a bond deeper than chromosomes.

A lot changed after Lee left.

Some believe a man is not truly a man until he buries his father.

Victor never had a father. He had father-figures. Cormack and Niko.

But Lee was more like a big brother. Same age but always looking out for Victor with an eternal ribbing and sibling rivalry between the two. This kinship came in different forms over their twenty years together.

Lee's departure forced Victor to grow up. Led Victor to realize, when he wasn't thinking with his pecker or his knuckles, he was no dummy.

Earlier in the night, when Lee came to Victor with his plan, Victor felt in his bones, it was a bad fucking idea. He didn't need any of that newly discovered wisdom to gather otherwise.

Maybe it was Victor's duty as Lee's *hermano* to express those reservations.

Maybe it was also his brotherly duty to dive head-first into that deep-dark pool of a stupid with Lee, even when he knew this would most likely be the result.

That's what Victor decided and that's where they were now. Lee drowning in a pool of his own blood and bad decisions and Victor manning the lifeboat. That was his only duty now, keeping Lee alive and from the looks of it, he was failing miserably.

Lee's white T-shirt looked like raspberry jam now, the sticky deep red cotton clinging to his skin as the blood dried. It was hard to even see the ink that covered his arms. At least his slicked-back pomade dirty blond hair was still perfectly intact. Enduring the gory warfare and sousing rain. Lee would be grateful, aside from dying, that he still looked good.

Lee's head rested against the corner of the truck. His mouth lolled direly open like someone snoring. And for a moment, he looked merely asleep. Maybe they were just on some road trip again. Chasing Mexican tail and bounteous tequila in Juarez. Maybe it was actually Victor snoozing in the truck, his head nestled against the window as Lee steered his old man's ride south on Interstate-25.

Maybe this was all just a bad dream.

And maybe it wasn't Mia's heavy head pressed with heroin on Victor's lap. Maybe she passed out on Lee's. Maybe she snuck away from her mother's grasp to supervise the boys' adventure, ensuring Lee only crossed the border for the street tacos and cheap liquor and not the loose women and *chingasos* waiting around every corner with him and Victor.

In her heart, she knew Lee wasn't the wandering kind. He was almost loyal to a fault. Victor understood it wasn't Lee Mia did not trust. It was the sizzling dynamic between the two that simply pulled danger out of thin air. After all, the two boys found enough trouble in the quiet streets of Santa Fe, never mind the bustling circus of Juarez, Mexico.

Victor's eyes drifted from the bleary tenebrous road, the globed headlights of the old truck barely piercing through heavy rain, to Mia's sallow face. Wan from the opiates of past and present. Her cheeks no longer plump and peachy with color, now gangly and pale. Lips no longer full and red like a freshly picked apple, now thin and bleached. Her blue eyes that once sparkled like sunrays over a wave were now dark and vacant and like the sea at night. He remembered how her spritely curves used to titter with life. Now her entire body was skeletal and frail like she had been on the precipice of life and death long before tonight.

If not for the small Dave Mathews fire dancer tattoo on her arm, Victor could have confused her for a stranger.

That too changed after Lee left.

Mia.

Maybe that was also Victor's fault.

Maybe that was the real reason he agreed to the suicide mission tonight. He was responsible for her and it was on him to fix.

He sure had a funny way of fixing things.

The tires slid and the brakes screeched.

For a moment, they were almost flying.

The truck glided within inches of a parked ambulance in front of the emergency room corridor.

Victor gently lifted Mia from his lap. He jumped out of the truck while placing her slumped head on the seat. Clumsily skating around the front of the truck until he noticed the parked ambulance blocking him, then haplessly swiveling in the other direction. By the time he lugged open the passenger side door, he was already soaked again from the rain.

When he wrapped his arms around Lee's torso to tug him out of the truck, Lee's shirt, seeped with blood, oozed all over Victor like a squeezed soapy sponge.

As Victor fully yanked Lee from the cab, Lee's black Doc Marten boots made a thud as they hit the hard blacktop. Victor jerked himself back, desperately trying to grip and tug the anchoring weight of Lee. Instead, Victor lost his grasp, dropping Lee like a bag of concrete.

"Fuck!" Victor cried. "Somebody fucking help me, *ese!*"

He bent down, digging his long scrawny arms under Lee's shoulders, once again hoisting him up. "You always had to have those fucking beauty muscles, huh bro?" he muttered, straining to lift Lee's brawny torso. Pebbles and dirt gooped to Lee's cheek where he had slunk on the blacktop. Victor cringed, carefully wiping away the grime from his brother's face before proceeding again.

He dragged Lee up the long sidewalk until he felt the whoosh of the emergency room doors opening. White light from above suddenly blinded him and he smelled rubbing alcohol and Lysol.

"What happened?" a young white man in pink scrubs was asking him.

Victor turned around while laying Lee down on the tile floor. "You're the doctor, *ese.*"

The man shot Victor a hard look while surveying the marred body between them, Victor crouching on one side of Lee, the man on the other.

"He got stabbed in the neck," Victor answered.

The man's attention moved to the rest of Lee's battered remains.

"Some other shit went down too, but it's the neck, bro," Victor continued. The two men's eyes met over the frayed body as Victor's face scrunched up. "Please bro, help my friend. Please."

"We need a stretcher over here stat!" the man yelled over his shoulder, into the hospital lobby.

Suddenly, Victor was surrounded with other pink scrubs.

"Sir, please step back," he heard one of them say.

Then he heard the rattling of wheels.

He looked up and there was a stretcher above him and more pink scrubs.

He scooted back on his ass, the balls of his feet and the palms of his hands-not able to stand.

He watched the pink scrubs swarm Lee like bees, then lifting him in unison onto the stretcher. The pool of blood Lee left on the white floor made Victor woozy. He thought he might faint until he remembered Mia...

Victor swung his gaze through the emergency room doors to Cormack's puke green truck, still with the lights on.

"Oh shit," he said, running and trying to stand at the same time. His wet shoes slipping on the wet tile. Tripping into the wall before bracing himself and flailing back out the door like a drunk rodeo clown.

When he got to the truck, Mia's blonde hair hung out the door like wet spaghetti, and her blank face stared up at him.

Victor bent down, scooping her up and out of the truck. He was relieved he could carry her in his arms.

The door swooshed open again, and Victor was squinting at the same glaring white lights.

"I need some more help, please!" he yelled, carrying Mia through the lobby.

An older woman in scrubs dashed around the u-shaped desk, yelling down the hospital corridor. "We need another gurney!"

Victor helplessly stood with Mia draped in his arms like a willow tree.

The same man came running back out."What happened to this one?"he asked, inspecting Mia's slunk body.

Victor knew that tone. He was on the receiving end of that insinuating tenor his entire life. "Heroin," he said, meeting the man's eyes once more.

He swore the guy shook his head at the answer.

The gurney was suddenly in front of Victor, the weight of Mia suddenly lifted from his shoulders.

Scrubs prodded her.

Pried open her eyes, and shined a light in.

Checked her pulse with their fingers on her neck.

"Okay," one of them said, carting her away.

The man suddenly turned back to Victor as the other doctors and nurses continued down the long hallway. "Is there anyone else?" he asked.

Victor's eyes widened to the size of half-dollars watching them disappear through the doors with Mia.

Lee was already gone.

"Sir," the man said, snapping his fingers in Victor's face. "Is there anyone else?"

Victor did not blink as he re-focused. "Nah, *ese*, they all I got."